PRAISE FOR

TOO GREAT A LADY

"A thoughtful retelling of the life of a common-born beauty and her infamous love affair with Admiral Lord Nelson."
—Susan Holloway Scott, author of *Royal Harlot*

"An energetic portrait of a unique historical figure."
—*Publishers Weekly*

"[A] sweeping, emotionally intense portrait of . . . one of the most famous romantic couples from history. . . . Emma Hamilton is a historical novelist's dream subject, and her fictional voice is as entertaining as it is convincing. Elyot is a rising star in the realm of biographical fiction."
—*The Historical Novels Review*

"The author is seemingly a master at anything! *Too Great a Lady* is a truly an exceptional novel. Emma is bold, courageous, and yet her innocence is also well portrayed. The characters are sublime and the plot is delightful. Amanda Elyot turns out historicals that are unlike anything you have experienced—they're that good!"
—Round Table Reviews

"An interesting historical 'autobiography' of Lady Emma Hamilton . . . the most notorious kept woman of the era."
—The Best Reviews

PRAISE FOR THE OTHER NOVELS OF

AMANDA ELYOT

"Divinely conceived . . . white-hot passion . . . engrossing."
—*Publishers Weekly*

"Blending mythology with history . . . [an] unforgettable journey."
—*Booklist*

"Elyot keeps the action moving with lots of exciting drama . . . [a] fresh take on a legendary woman."
—*Library Journal*

"Teeming with period detail . . . a sly peek into Austen's England."
—Lauren Willig, author of *The Masque of the Black Tulip* and *The Secret History of the Pink Carnation*

"Richly textured . . . [a] fresh and wickedly clever tale."
—*New York Times* Bestselling Author Mary Jo Putney

FOR

THE SCANDALOUS LIFE AND TIMES OF
ROYAL MISTRESS MARY ROBINSON

AMANDA ELYOT

 NEW AMERICAN LIBRARY

New American Library
Published by New American Library, a division of
Penguin Group (USA) Inc., 375 Hudson Street,
New York, New York 10014, USA
Penguin Group (Canada), 90 Eglinton Avenue East, Suite 700, Toronto,
Ontario M4P 2Y3, Canada (a division of Pearson Penguin Canada Inc.)
Penguin Books Ltd., 80 Strand, London WC2R 0RL, England
Penguin Ireland, 25 St. Stephen's Green, Dublin 2,
Ireland (a division of Penguin Books Ltd.)
Penguin Group (Australia), 250 Camberwell Road, Camberwell, Victoria 3124,
Australia (a division of Pearson Australia Group Pty. Ltd.)
Penguin Books India Pvt. Ltd., 11 Community Centre, Panchsheel Park,
New Delhi - 110 017, India
Penguin Group (NZ), 67 Apollo Drive, Rosedale, North Shore 0632,
New Zealand (a division of Pearson New Zealand Ltd.)
Penguin Books (South Africa) (Pty.) Ltd., 24 Sturdee Avenue,
Rosebank, Johannesburg 2196, South Africa

Penguin Books Ltd., Registered Offices:
80 Strand, London WC2R 0RL, England

First published by New American Library,
a division of Penguin Group (USA) Inc.

First Printing, February 2008
10 9 8 7 6 5 4 3 2 1

N
A
L REGISTERED TRADEMARK—MARCA REGISTRADA

LIBRARY OF CONGRESS CATALOGING-IN-PUBLICATION DATA:

Elyot, Amanda.
    All for love: the scandalous life and times of royal mistress Mary Robinson/Amanda Elyot.
       p. cm.
    ISBN: 978-0-451-22297-8
    1. Robinson, Mary, 1758–1800—Fiction. 2. George IV, King of Great Britain, 1762–1830—
Relations with women—Fiction. 3. Actresses—Fiction. 4. Mistresses—Fiction. 5. Authors,
English—18th century—Fiction. I. Title.

    PS3603.A77458A79 2007
    813'.6—dc22   2007024752

Set in Adobe Garamond
Designed by Alissa Amell

Printed in the United States of America

*For my aunt, Gloria Goldsmith,
a redheaded writer who has allowed
neither adversity nor infirmity
to silence her pen*

There is not a woman in England so much talked of and so little known as Mrs. Robinson.
—*Morning Herald*, April 23, 1784

I have ever been disposed to speak my sentiments too freely. What I dislike, I condemn; what I love, I idolize . . . I write what my heart prompts. Perhaps imprudently; certainly unartificially.
—Mary Robinson
Letter to William Godwin, 1800

Act One

***

My Father Had a Daughter . . .

Prologue

*I*magine a meteor. Perhaps it will work better if you close your eyes. From the soft darkness that lies behind your shuttered lids you can picture it more clearly. You cannot hear its progress as it whooshes through the sky. The only aural proof of its passing is your own voice exclaiming "Aah!" in wonderment, if you can discern your expression of astonishment from the chorus of equally infatuated voices beside you. But you can *see* the meteor, can't you? Blazing through the night? Is it any wonder that we never think of meteors illuminating our days, daring to compete with the sun?

No, in our minds meteors are creatures of the night, which makes them even more alluring, even more a subject of fascination. Like actresses, and courtesans. Like me.

That's what they called me in my days of triumph. A meteor. A comet, too, on occasion. An atmospheric phenomenon observable by its incandescence as it streaks across the sky. From the Middle English *comete,* which derives from the Old English *cometa,* which springs from Latin, which comes from the Greek *kometes*—literally, long-haired. A long-haired celestial body with a highly eccentric orbit. Like a young girl from the rising middle class who becomes a wife and mother while still in the bloom of adolescence; then an actress and courtesan, a lover, a poetess, and a champion of the rights of women. Of course, there were other women of my age whose accomplishments won them the same journalistic epithet: other celebrated actresses; other royal mistresses and notorious courtesans—my greatest rival in that sphere, Dally the Tall, comes to mind—others made famous for their novels, plays, and poetry; and others—such as Mary Wollstonecraft—who brandished the banner of equality in their sisters' names. Yet I own it's worth a mention that not a single one of them, save myself, was *all* of those things. The press were wrong, you see. I was not merely a comet, or even a meteor. I was an entire shower of them.

One

More Sensibility Than Sense

One night in 1765 . . . my eighth year

"*D*ream well, my rosebud," my handsome father whispered. As Papa bent down to kiss me good night, his olive-tinted skin smelled comfortingly of bay rum and tobacco. I cherished the low rumble of his voice; when it was the very last sound I heard at bedtime, I knew the next day would be a lucky one. In the half-light, for then I feared to fall asleep in total darkness, I could still make out his striped waistcoat with its shiny brass buttons. Even as he tucked me into bed he looked like he was preparing to head off to the exchange.

But in the middle of that night I was shaken awake by the sound of raised voices. My parents rarely quarreled, so deep was the affection that ran between them. Mother saw Papa as I did: strong, kind, and generous.

"Their schooling, Nicholas. What do you expect me to do? Surely you do not expect proper English children to grow up like savages in the wilderness? Mary is the darling of the Miss Mores. And when Miss Hannah took her girls to see Mr. Powell in *King Lear* at the Theatre Royal,

Mary was in raptures for weeks, eager herself to tread the boards. Miss Hannah even wrote a special part for her in one of her dramatic parables."

"I merely thought, my dear, since you can scarcely bear to spend a moment apart from any of the children, that it would be more amenable to you to take them with us. If their education concerns you more than their companionship, perhaps it would be better to leave them here."

"And board them somewhere? With strangers? I don't even board Mary at the Miss Mores'."

"I am endeavoring to please you, Hester. It is only because of my esteem for you that I leave this decision in your hands, rather than ordering you to do your duty as my wife in whichever manner I see fit."

"And I thank you for that, my love. But each prospect seems so terrible to me. It is not just the health of their minds that I fear. Illness, dampness, droughts, disease. Before we even reach Greenland's shores—not halfway to our destination—we shall be compelled to endure weeks of being tossed to and fro in the middle of the sea like so many crates of tea, with no one to hear our cries should we become imperiled. My stomach turns at the merest thought of our accommodations."

My father grew testy. "Hester, I expect to be abroad for two years, perhaps longer. I should not ask you to join me on this venture were I not keenly aware of its dangers and equally certain of your safety and of the children's. You must think me a monster to believe that I would ever willingly put my family at such risk."

"How can it *not* be a risk?"

"Are you refusing to accompany me?"

The saddest and most plaintive moan escaped my

mother's anguished lips. "Nicholas . . . I dared not breathe a word of this to you, certain you would find it silly . . . I have such a horror of the ocean that it mortifies me to confess it. And I fear that even for your own dear sake, such dread is not to be borne, much less overcome."

Her words might as well have been made of iron, forming the nails for her coffin. Mother spoke her mind, revealing her darkest fears to the man she loved with every fiber of her being, and was to pay a horrible price for it.

In my early years growing up in Bristol, though I had three brothers, I was still my father's favorite. I was the one who'd replaced their little Elizabeth—the pink angel they lost to the pox before she reached the age of three. We were cosseted, petted, and spoil'd as rotten as week-old cabbage, given the finest of everything, as befitted the children of a successful—though often absent—British merchant and his doting wife.

I never was permitted to board at school, nor to pass a night of separation from the fondest of mothers. Mother adored her handsome husband and he delighted in her sweet and open nature. I recall caresses, even kisses, exchanged in front of my brothers and me, and gifts were bestowed in abundance. Mother's jewels were enviable, for my father possessed exquisite taste and the money to put it to good use.

I slept on crimson damask sheets in a bed fit for a princess. My dresses were ordered from London. We dined on the very best china and plate. And during the summer months we were sent to Clifton Hill for the advantages of a purer air. Mother was the kindest of women; if she had any faults, it was her too tender care that she lavish'd upon my brothers and me.

My father was a North American born of black Irish stock, a man of strong mind, high spirit, and personal intrepidity, and it was all three of those noble qualities that removed him from his family on more than one occasion. But from the moment of that midnight quarrel, my life's course took its first shattering turn, for Papa had devised an eccentric scheme as wild and romantic as it was perilous to hazard—and it would take him away from us forever.

In my romantic girlish mind my thoughts of him would fluctuate as if riding astride a pendulum. In one instant he was the American seafarer, off on another exotic venture to a faraway and savage land; but in the next moment Papa was the British merchant who would desert the family he adored when, surely, closer to hand there were equally prosperous projects to be explored. Caught between worshipping him and being cross with him for leaving all of us to fend as we might in his absence, I was as quick to defend him as I was to condemn. He broke my heart as often as he mended it.

After many dreams of success and many conflicts betwixt prudence and ambition, when I was but seven years old Papa departed for Labrador to establish a whale fishery amongst the Esquimaux Indians there, believing he could civilize them and teach them the necessary skills that would eventually make British America's whaling industry topple that of Greenland's, its greatest rival. It turned out to be a double farewell, for my elder brother, John, was sent off to Italy at the same time, apprenticed to a mercantile house in Leghorn.

My parents corresponded as frequently as practicable. At first, their letters were full of fondness, even ardor, for each other, as well as Mother's fears for Papa's health and safety, and his repeated tender assurances that all was well and that he missed his adoring family dreadfully. He would return to England even wealthier, as triumphant for himself as for the economy of king and country, and every day would be a holiday under the Darby roof. But gradually, the tone of his letters began to change. Warm affection was supplanted by a civil cordiality, as if he now wrote from duty rather than desire. My mother felt the change, and her affliction was infinite.

"Why did I not conquer my fears?" she lamented to me, as she pressed my auburn curls to her bosom. "Why did I let my own timidity divide me from the very man to whom I pledged myself, body and soul, and consigned my fortunes?"

At length, a total silence of several months awoke my mother's mind to the sorrows of neglect, the torture of compunction. "Has he forsaken us for my trepidation?" she would worry aloud.

And then, one horrible day, the penny dropped.

Two

The Mistress and the Mentor

1766 . . . age eight

"I have heard something from Lord Chatham," Mother wrote to my father, "which has been the cause of the greatest consternation; I beg of you to break the truth to me."

Lord Chatham, the elder Pitt, had been one of my father's sponsors, financing, along with others, a portion of Papa's commercial exploration in Labrador. His lordship would never have been indiscreet enough to speak of another's affairs, but one unguarded remark with regard to her husband's domestic arrangements put my mother into a dizzying panic.

At long last, a letter arrived from Labrador. There was a woman named Elenor, an attachment whose resisting nerves could brave the stormy ocean, and who had consented to remain two years with him in the frozen wilds of North America.

This intelligence nearly annihilated my mother. "When had she appeared?" Mother demanded to know. "How long have you been deceiving me that our home was a happy one, one to which you truly yearned to return? When did your letters first ring with falsehoods?"

Her sad and desperate remonstrances were met with no reply. Mother resigned herself to grief, and I felt powerless to comfort her. Though I was then at an age to feel her anguish and to participate in her sorrows, I lacked the skill to soothe her, try as I did. I often wept myself to see her weep. I was confused, my allegiances torn. My young brain was unequipped to comprehend how my brave and noble father, in whose eyes and face I so clearly saw myself, could commit so grievous a transgression against such a tender and loving creature as my mother. Not only did Papa appear to assign the blame for their too-sudden estrangement to my mother's dread of seafaring, but my mother accepted that burden as well, drowning herself in tearful mea culpas.

I have never owned the ability to sit idly by when I perceived an injustice. "He deceived you, Mama. How can you not hate him, if only for a while?" I asked her. I wanted her to stand her ground and fight for her rights to his love. If she resigned herself—however miserably—to his loss, then she also forfeited *my* marker, along with those of my younger brothers, William and George! Her maddening acquiescence to what she considered her own culpability in the alienation of Father's affections made me wish to turn warrior and take up the cudgels on her behalf! "Wouldn't it be splendid, then, if you could summon a champion to represent your true and just cause?" But Mother did not immerse herself in medieval romances and gothic fantasies as I did—stories where the fair damsel gains a defender and is never troubled for longer than it takes to increase the element of suspense.

Her mind was not made of the stuff that calls for revenge, nor did she harbor such notions in the recesses of her heart, for that organ was too true and too tender to admit any vengeance. It therefore was no consolation whatever to her that my father's financial scheme not only failed, but did so both miserably and brutally.

He wrote to mother:

> The Indians rose in a body, burning my settlements to a cinder. Many of my men were struck down in cold blood by their axes or bludgeoned before they could muster any defense. The fruits of our toil, brought about by arduous labor in an unforgiving climate, these were set adrift on the wide and merciless ocean. Compounding all, I hear from Chatham and the others of the committee that formed the chief cornerstone of my sponsorship that these once noble patrons have no intention of making good on their initial surety. For the time being, all, all is lost. It is with heavy heart that I thus enclose a copy of a bill of sale of my entire property, by whose authority you and the children will unfortunately be obliged to quit the house in Bristol.

My mother fainted on the spot.

It was a nasty surprise. I thought at that moment my life would end. I was just coming to grips with the death of our domestic felicity—but it had never entered my imagination that our situation would ever be anything but prosperous, my prospects anything but infinite, and my future assured as one of comfort and respectability. I was still a little girl. What would become of us now?

*   *   *

For days, Mother, who was never able to bear a burden with any degree of stoicism, would wander our rooms like a wraith, clutching Papa's letter, now stained with her copious tears, rivers of sadness sprung from double pools of fear and betrayal. "Retrench? But where?" she would cry, her disorganized mind incapable of focusing on making new arrangements for our habitation or the inventorying of our property. Every spoon she enumerated was the source of a fresh burst of tears.

That unerring touchstone—adversity—soon showed who were our real friends, and who revealed themselves as shams. Many, with affected commiseration, dropped a tear—or rather seemed to drop one—on the disappointments of our family.

"It must feel dreadful to see such lovely things command so little." Mrs. Linton, the wife of a well-to-do barrister of our acquaintance, shook her head with a little sigh as she handed my mother a draft for my beautiful bed, damasked linens and all. The bed was too costly for us to move, and in any event, too capacious for our new quarters. "What a shame that your beautiful home should be broken up for scrap, as 'twere."

"I should never have let Mr. *Mannering* embark upon such a risky venture." Mrs. Mannering, the wife of a prominent sugar merchant, had often dined in our home while her husband was at sea. Now the portly woman whose fleshy fingers bulged on either side of the corseted constraint of her garnets helped herself, at bargain prices, to my mother's port and sherry glasses. Her sister, equally as vulgar, fingered my beautiful Kirkman harpsichord, which she could, alas, purchase from us for a song, as the saying goes. Not only

would our retrenching deny me the proximity of the litur-
gical melodies I held so dear, but it was to deprive me of the
ability to make my *own*. I had been robbed by my father's
misfortunes of my much beloved instrument, as precious to
me as an artist's chisel and brush or a writer's quill.

Though Mrs. Abercrombie thought she was whisper-
ing to Mrs. Linton, her pronounced Scots burr did not
lend itself to the subtleties of gentle conference. "If Mr.
Darby hadna lavished sae much on his wife and bairns—
look at that fine candelabrum, will ye—and allowed her
to dress herself and the wee'uns in such elegant stuffs and
extended his hospitality to offering so many courses at his
dinners—I ask ye, who needs mutton *and* lamb, as well as
three different puddings—he wouldna found himself in
such narrow straits today. Prodigality is all very weel and
good, but frugality is the sign of a truly prudent man."

Through no fault of my own, it was clear that I was
no longer good enough to marry their sons. A merchant's
daughter would have been quite suitable to them if she
were sufficiently dowered, but now, said their pitying
looks, I should consider myself fortunate, with my background and schooling, to secure a position as a governess.

My mother suffered them all in modest quietude, but
our pecuniary losses were nothing compared to the emo-
tional casualties. At about this time, my brother William
was carried off by the measles at the tender age of six.
Though my mother had lost a child before, she did not
bear this all-too-common grief with equanimity, as did
many women of her acquaintance. The only mercy to be
obtained from this dreadful and most tragic event was that
Will's suffering was relatively brief. Dr. Samson bled him
thrice, but the fever persisted, the spots increasing rather

than abating, as the days wore on. Within a week, the bright blue eyes of my sweet brother, once so lively and animated, were closed for eternity, and his illness-ravaged body was laid in the cold and unforgiving ground along-side the church. I grew even more afraid to fall asleep at night, fearful that the Angel of Death might call for me as well. And I took to wearing nothing but white, so that I would be ready when he came.

Several days after Will's death, I encountered my mother sobbing over a box of dishes. I touched her sleeve. "Our wedding dishes," she wept. "As worthless now as . . ." The letter she'd been holding in her hand fell, crumpled, to the floor. I stooped to pick it up. Unfurling the paper, I read a love note, full of tenderness and passion, written when Papa was courting her. It made a grave impression on my young mind that my mother, as devoted to her children as the Madonna herself, and devastated by the death of her youngest son, was even more pained by the hurt she endured daily in the alienation of my father's affections.

Mother's one solace at the time was the genuine friend-ship extended to her by Lady Erskine, the widow of Sir Charles Erskine, and now the wife of a prominent medical man. Lady Erskine and her husband were willing to take us in after we were compelled to quit our home, and it was in this kindly woman's society that my mother gradually recovered her serenity of mind, or rather found it soften into a religious resignation. Her leather-bound prayer book, once kept in a drawer beside the conjugal bed, was now never far from her hand or the hidden pocket of her petticoat.

We remained under Lady Erskine's roof for close to a year, Mother getting word from time to time that her beloved husband was still residing in America with his mistress. And then, one day a letter from Papa was delivered to our temporary doorstep, summoning Mother to meet him in London.

"It is my particular request that the children might be the companions of your journey," he wrote coldly. It pained my heart that he had not even condoled with Mother over Will's too-early departure from this earth, for I know she had sent him more than one message to his American addresses.

Mother must have changed clothes a half dozen times before our departure, anguishing over the right gown, the most fetching bonnet. Would my father be repentant or contrite? Would he embrace her as she longed for him to do? She agonized over these questions every hour that we spent jouncing along the post roads from Bristol.

How different London was from the city of my birth! Bristol boasted a thriving port, rich in mercantile commerce, but the populace of the capital, even at first glance, was far more diverse. I was agog at the sights. So much color! In the people's skin, in their wardrobes and plumage, in the high-wigged dandies that minced through the streets and the painted ladies who would exchange their favors for a pint of cheap wine. I unloosed the drawstring of my purse and took out a little book of blank pages, in which I scrawled—for the coach was bouncing—my instant observations of the city: the sooty chimney boy with dingy face, the sleepy housemaid, knife grinders, coopers, squeaking cork cutters, the milk-pail rattles and the tinkling bell, the din of hackney coaches. It was a cornucopia for the senses.

Upon our arrival in the metropolis, we repaired to my father's lodgings in Spring Gardens, as well appointed as ours had been at Bristol. It was immediately evident to me from the spanking new Axminster carpets and damask draperies, the mahogany and crystal, that his commands to economize and retrench did not extend to his present household. I beat back the lump rising in my throat. I was angry—only to turn disconsolate moments later when he entered the drawing room. He looked upon me with the most quizzical expression. "Who . . . ?"

I opened my arms to him. "Papa, it is I!"

"Mary?" He scarcely recognized me and I felt my heart crack. "How . . . how long has it been, then?"

"Three years, Papa." I was barely twelve years old now, though so tall and formed in my person that I might have passed for fifteen or sixteen. Although I'd inherited Papa's olive complexion, my skin did not seem quite as swarthy as it had when I was younger and my hair had lightened a shade or two. Its auburn color now matched that of eight-year-old George.

"Hester." My father's voice was choked with emotion, his face bathed with tears. Was it the manner of a man consumed by love or racked with guilt? Mother stepped forward to greet him, and whilst he had welcomed George and me with sighs and tears, he held her with indifference. She did not know it at the time, but it was to be the last embrace she ever received from him. "I . . . I cannot," he said to Mother, and that was the extent of his capacity to be articulate for the remainder of the interview.

"The fair Elenor," as I termed his mistress with the tartest asperity my young mind could muster, was nowhere to be seen. After all, propriety must be observed at all costs; therefore the mistress and the wife were not to be introduced. I should not have been surprised to meet her there as she "accidentally" passed through, on the one hand curious to see what sort of creature had gained such a stranglehold upon Papa's affections, and on the other glad of the missed opportunity, for I might not have been able to answer for my conduct. Though I still loved my father with all my heart, I could not forgive him for so rashly treating my mother, the mildest and most unoffending of existing mortals.

Imagine, however, the astounding duo to whom we *were* presented shortly after our arrival. My father had brought back an Inuit woman and her young son. "Are they servants?" I whispered to Mother.

Her gaze focused upon the boy's smooth face, his complexion the color of white coffee, and his pale blue eyes. "I think not," she murmured, casting her eyes toward the floor.

I returned my gaze to the boy and then looked at George, wise enough to fathom the crux of my mother's reply. Had Papa betrayed his marriage vows with more than one woman, unfaithful even to Elenor? Or was this plump Esquimaux matron the mistress in question? I had always imagined Elenor as a dewy, yet intrepid, English rose. As Papa did not deign to introduce the Inuit by name, the mystery remained unsolved.

The following day, after passing an unhappy and sorrowful night, we were summoned to the salon.

"I have determined, Hester, that it is best for me to place the children in schools closer to London. As I propose to return to America very shortly, arrangements will need to be made with some degree of haste."

"And I?" Mother asked softly.

"I will readily subsidize your board with any private and respectable family."

She swallowed hard. "Then we are not to resume . . . as things once were."

Papa's expression was pained. He felt the impropriety of his conduct, but it was in vain that my mother tried to change his resolution. I was convinced that Papa was held by a fatal fascination, the slave of a young and artful woman who had availed herself of his American solitude to undermine the felicity of his family and his affections for his wife. I knew my father's better qualities: his mind was strongly organized, his sense of honor delicate even to fastidiousness—therefore, the only answer I could fathom was that he was the dupe of his passions, the victim of an unfortunate attachment. My girlish mind, and the conflicted loyalties of a devoted daughter, viewed Elenor as evil, my mother as blameless, and Papa as caught in a purgatory not entirely of his own making.

"My decision is . . . final," he said, his voice breaking.

Though in private I would rage against it, refusing to accept its finality, this information dealt the death blow to my parents' domestic hopes.

With no further expectation of future reconciliation, within a few days of our arrival in London, Mother made arrangements to board at a clergyman's home in Chelsea and plans were settled upon for the education of myself and little George.

I was placed at the nearby Lorrington Academy under the tutelage of a rare bird named Meribah Lorrington. All I ever learned I acquired from this extraordinary woman. Deprived of my chance to be father's little girl, his favored one, I threw myself headlong into the role of the diligent scholar, applying myself rigidly to study, and acquiring a taste for books, which has never from that time deserted me. Mrs. Lorrington herself had enjoyed the benefit of a masculine education, owing to the resolve of her father, who, once widowed, vowed to cultivate his daughter's superior mental powers in every respect.

Here was the opportunity for an education that would actually prove useful in the world beyond the confines of a middle-class drawing room. True, Mrs. Lorrington passed along to her charges the ability to paint on silk (she was in point of fact a great proficient in that most ladylike of pastimes), but at the eponymous academy girls were taught such "masculine" subjects as the proprietress herself had learnt. Even during that Age of Enlightenment, a female who was schooled in the sciences and mathematics was an anomaly. At most girls' boarding schools, an education was deemed sufficient if a pupil read authors whose works she did not comprehend, prattled a foreign jargon without knowing the meaning of the words she uttered, finished needlework which in half a century would only adorn the lumber room of her granddaughter, and learned by ear a few old lessons on the harpsichord—so little graced by science and so methodically dull that they would scarcely have served as an opiate to a country squire after the voluntary toil of a fox chase.

Mrs. Lorrington had but five or six students under her tutelage, and it was my lot to be her especial favorite, perhaps because I applied myself to my lessons with particular diligence. I even slept on a little cot in her bedchamber, and she made no scruple of conversing with me on domestic and confidential affairs, though I was still only twelve years old. "My little friend," she called me. Mrs. Lorrington would take it upon herself to read to me after school hours, and I to her. It was she who taught me to read aloud with dramatic inflection—she, herself, had a husky and melodic voice that reminded me of my father's, its warm tones caressing the words as though they were intimates—and it was under her tutelage that I first turned my hand to poetry.

Though Mrs. Lorrington was proficient enough in the classical and modern languages, astronomy, and arithmetic to impart them to her pupils, she suffered from a singular and unfortunate failing. The poor creature's frequent intoxication too often rendered her unable to withstand the task of her lessons. Though even the youngest student could detect, at least by virtue of her olfactory senses, that something was amiss, it was my special fate to learn the *root* of poor Mrs. Lorrington's misfortune. Taking me into her confidence one rainy evening, she knit her dark brows together—though they had not far to go, for they were nigh to greeting one another just above her nose—and confessed the immitigable regret of a widowed heart.

"Mr. Lorrington was a printer," she told me. "A fine man who worked long hours at his press, taking any job that came his way." She knelt down and began to search under her bed for something. "Broadsheets, ballads, newspapers, theatre programs . . . for he so loved the written word that he took delight in sharing it with others." With a triumphant "Ah!" she withdrew a large paper box, its surface covered with a quantity of dust.

The abundance of tiny motes tickled my nose; I sneezed into my sleeve and was immediately mortified by my own indelicacy.

"He would come home smelling of ink," Mrs. Lorrington murmured wistfully, her words slowed and slurred by the effects of the gin. "Pour me another; there's a girl." Fearing some sort of retribution if I did not comply with my tutor's request, I poured her half a tot.

"Don't be stingy, Mary. It's not a trait to be cultivated, particularly in one so young." Guiltily, I filled her cup to the rim. "I grew to love that odor."

"The ink, you mean?" I asked her, wondering if she was not referring to the spirits instead.

She nodded her head, eyes closed as if to conjure the scent through memory, transporting her back in time to happier days.

"What's in the box, ma'am?"

Mrs. Lorrington lifted the cover; the dust made me sneeze again. The box's contents were lovingly removed: a leather apron, which she laid across her lap, and a packet of letters, neatly tied with a length of black ribband. "He wrote many of these after he took sick," Mrs. Lorrington said, untying the ribband as if the letters themselves might disintegrate absent their silken binding. "Here." With trembling hands, she offered me one of her precious epistles. "Would you like to read it?"

Could I refuse? " 'My beloved wife,' " I read, feeling very much as though I was prying where I was not wanted. " 'I know not how many days are left to me, but I will account each one a blessing when I think of the woman whom God and Nature favored me as the consort of my journey through life. Daily—hourly—I feel the heavy obligation of apologizing to you, my fairest one, because it seems that journey will be so much shorter than either of us had ever planned. . . .' " I glanced up at Mrs. Lorrington; her eyes were once again closed, her cheeks stained with silent tears. "Do you wish me to read on, ma'am?"

Mrs. Lorrington's eyes flew open and she downed her tot of gin in a single draught. "No . . . perhaps better not. Thank you, Mary." She took the letter from my hands as though she were cradling a dying bird, and kissed the top of my head. "You're a good girl, my little friend. A dear girl."

With some compunction she declared to me, her voice softly rumbling with emotion, that she flew to intoxication as the only refuge from the pang of prevailing sorrow. Such a sad being she was that I clasped her about the waist, whilst she wept into her handkerchief, the occasional teardrop missing its net and tumbling instead into my auburn curls.

During the fourteen months I spent under Mrs. Lorrington's tutelage, she proved an inspiration, despite her unfortunate means of escaping her mental turmoil. Our reading sessions inspired me to indulge my fancy for writing verses, and my governess never failed to applaud the juvenile compositions I presented to her. Her own tales of woe—a personal tragedy fraught with despair, a swain snatched from her loving bosom by the claws of unpitying death, while her enduring love proved greater than any force of nature—all these formed in my young imagination the chief topics of my maiden efforts. Some of these, written between the ages of twelve and thirteen, I preserved and printed in a small volume shortly after my marriage, but as doomed love was the theme of my poetical fantasies, I never showed them to my too-sensible mother until I was about to publish them.

If nothing else, I proved consistent in my choice of subject, for not too long hence, when I would choose to dedicate myself to Erato, stanza upon stanza of gothic melancholy, of devoted lovers from each other's arms untimely ripp'd, would prove as valuable as a jailer's turnkey!

Three

A First Proposal and a Last Good-Bye

1770 . . . age twelve

It was my custom every Sunday to take tea with my mother at the vicar's home where she was boarding. She was always delighted to see me and the afternoons we spent in one another's company flew by all too swiftly. Mother would always begin by remarking on what a young lady I was becoming—"and could it be you've grown so much in a week"—and then she would inquire as to how my instruction was getting on and ask after Mrs. Lorrington. My answers were always the same; my governess was in tolerable good health. I would not betray my dear mentor's solitary weakness, even to my own mother.

One Sunday I found my mother in the parlor entertaining a gentleman near to her own age.

"Allow me to name you my daughter Mary, sir."

He rose and offered a polite bow. "Captain Fredericks, of His Majesty's Navy, miss."

"The captain is a friend of your father's," Mother added.

I dropped a curtsy. "A pleasure to make your acquaintance, sir."

"Oh, no," he insisted, "it is all mine, I assure you. We sailors scarcely have the opportunity to see a pretty face, let alone a lovely English rose such as yourself."

I thought he overflattered me, for we'd barely been introduced, but he was pleasant looking—good hair and teeth, a fine enough figure—so I smiled modestly and thanked him for his courtesies.

"Allow me," I said, and poured the tea for my mother and her guest, serving them with all the grace of a proper lady, rather than that of a coltish girl. Not a drop was spilt, nor a crumb of teacake lost. Neither dish nor spoon rattled or clattered.

Our conversation was polite. We discussed the weather, our opinions of the specimens in the Chelsea Physic Garden, and the hazards of shipboard life. Upon learning that he was fond of animals, I asked him if he had visited the menagerie at the Tower or seen the king's men exercising His Majesty's elephant on the grounds outside the Queen's House.

The following Sunday, Captain Fredericks was again at the vicarage when I called on my mother, and he was in attendance the next Sunday and the next again.

On the fourth Sunday after we'd first made one another's acquaintance, I encountered Captain Fredericks once more, but he didn't quite appear himself, his face coloring deeply when he bowed to me upon my arrival. Turning to my mother, he said, "I have something especial I should like to say to you, Mrs. Darby"—he self-consciously cleared his throat—"concerning Miss Darby."

As Mother could never have fathomed the import of the captain's business, she did not dismiss me from the room; nor did Captain Fredericks request me to absent myself, for it seemed that he wished to enjoy the favor of my company rather than miss it.

"I'm not a man of many words, as you know," he said, once more clearing his throat.

"Good sir, are you unwell this afternoon?" I asked.

"Heavens, no, Miss Darby. I've never felt more robust! I . . . I should not beat about the bush, for I'm bound to make a mess of it. . . . Mrs. Darby, I am quite taken with your daughter. Miss Darby's manners, her mien, her fine mind—not to mention her fair person—have quite struck my fancy. What . . . what . . . what I should like to say is that I would very much like to make her my wife."

My mother, taken quite by surprise, spluttered into her tea saucer and nearly dropped the thing into her lap. "Mary? Marry Mary?" It was some moments before she recovered her composure. It was all I could do not to laugh, and so I turned my head away and pretended to cough politely into my handkerchief.

"Captain Fredericks, how old do you think my daughter is?"

The poor man gave my mother a quizzical look. "Well, my mum always told me it was impolite to hazard a lady's age, but since you put my feet to the fire, I should guess from her height, and her looks, and from several afternoons conversing with her and observing her manners, that Miss Darby was sixteen years old."

"Sixteen! Oh, dear!" Mother clapped a hand to her heart. "Mary is not quite thirteen!"

Captain Fredericks looked dumbstruck.

"Not till November," I said.

He looked as if he doubted our veracity, but to have challenged it would have been the height of rudeness.

"Well, then . . . ," the officer said, coloring slightly and clearing his throat once more to cover his expression of dismay—or perhaps it was chagrin—"well, then, I take my leave of you." He rose and bowed to each of us. "I will be setting sail soon on a two-years' expedition to the Indies. In fact, that was why I purposed to break my disclosure to you this afternoon. May I be so selfish as to express the wish that upon my return, Miss Darby will still be disengaged."

Mother made no promises, and scrupled to say as much, for there was not a dishonest bone in her body. That afternoon was the last that she and I ever saw of the amiable and gallant Captain Fredericks.

Not too many months later, due to pecuniary derangements, Mrs. Lorrington gathered her students in the parlor of the academy. Her face was drawn and she appeared to be in a significant amount of pain.

"Circumstances compel me to close the academy," she told us. "I should be sorry indeed to see you go. But I will always carry an image of each of you within my heart."

It was a tearful dismissal. And no pupil felt the impending separation as keenly as I, the governess's favorite, her little confidante.

"I don't think I should ever be able to write another line of poetry," I snuffled. "No one else has encouraged me as you have done—and I daresay no one ever will!"

"Tush, child." Mrs. Lorrington stroked my head. "I am quite certain that the time will come when you feel you cannot abide it if you do not take up the quill again, and your future tutors will recognize merit when they see it."

"But what if there are no future tutors? My father has

been forced to economize, and when one is in his position, the daughter's tuition is the first casualty."

Mrs. Lorrington blinked back a tear. "I should hate to see that day come, Mary. But I have faith in you, my girl. You'll not give up an education without a fight." Pressing me to her bosom, she declared, "You'll turn out just splendidly, my little friend."

"But what about you, Mrs. Lorrington?" I feared for this poor woman's future more than for my own.

"Me?" She tried to smile. "I shall be . . ." Her voice broke and she glanced away, focusing her gaze on the dado rail. "Don't worry about me, my dear. I have my consolations."

After Mrs. Lorrington shut her doors, Mother removed me to a more traditional boarding school across the Thames in Battersea, run by the lively, sensible, and accomplished Mrs. Leigh. Mrs. Leigh's daughter Cynthia, a good-natured and lovely girl, was not much older than myself, so the transition from one academy to another was eased by the existence of an instant companion. Here I should have been quite happy, but then a few months elapsed during which my father repeatedly failed to send his remittance for my education. In a letter to Mother, Mrs. Leigh gently explained that she could not afford to extend her charity by keeping me on indefinitely with no guarantee of payment. Mother was beside herself. Deeply mortified, she was induced to remove me from Mrs. Leigh's, though my brother George remained under the tutelage of the Reverend Gore in Chelsea. My worst fears had come to fruition. I retreated to the solace of my room, angry and betrayed by the man I had so adored, feeling punished for being born a girl.

My father's impracticable arctic schemes had impoverished his fortune and deprived his children of the affluence that in their infancy they had been taught to hope for. I was now fourteen years old and my mother began to foresee the vicissitudes to which my youth might be exposed—unprotected, only tenderly educated, and without the advantages of fortune.

Mother now deemed her children fatherless, his payments having ceased entirely, just as his affections had done so many months previous. I bore her desolation in my own heart. Yet her indomitability in the face of adversity would not permit her to wallow in self-pitying despair. She retained a cheerful temper even as she struggled to find an honorable means to support her children, to that end hiring a convenient house at Little Chelsea and opening a ladies' boarding school of her own.

Assistants of every kind were engaged, and Mother surprised and honored me no end by deeming me worthy to superintend the English Language department! I resolved to be up to the task in every way, pleased to be able to be of consequence. I felt quite grown-up in my new station, the jump from being governed to being a governess such a small one, and achieved in the blink of an eye. I threw myself into the role of tutor with all the zeal I had shown in applying myself to the rigors demanded of the pupil. A new chapter had begun and I was surprised to find myself too exhausted by my responsibilities to dwell overmuch on events of the past.

Yet now I can recall as though it were yesterday the events of a stormy evening shortly after my mother had established herself in Chelsea. Midsummer thunder rolled through the heavens as though God and the angels were playing at ninepins. The streets had become muddy ruts in the matter of an hour. It was light enough to see the rain streaking down the windowpanes, and this had become for me a kind of meditative fancy. Ensconced in my window seat I hugged my knees to my chest and fixed my gaze upon the patterns made by the raindrops—God's tears—descending in a shimmering hush as they sought to humble themselves by kissing the ground beneath.

I thought I heard a deep sigh, but at first was convinced the sound had been my own, drawn from my melancholy reverie. I had been wishing Papa were home and we were all in Bristol, a happy family once again, with no Elenor and no Inuits to mar the brightness of my mother's days. But as I was wondering if the sigh had not emitted from my own lips, I heard it again, this time more a groan of anguish. A shiver of fear shuddered through me and I drew my knitted shawl more tightly about my shoulders.

Peering out the window, I spied a figure near the gate, evidently laboring under excessive affliction. As curious as I was anxious, I donned my shoes and threw the shawl over my head, descending into the street. The poor soul, drenched to the skin, was a lady, her thick dark hair—mostly hidden by an old bonnet—falling about her face. Her dress, torn and filthy, clung about her like rags upon a drowning woman. Underneath her scant attire she was nearly naked, her petticoats having been either lost or forgotten.

"Don't you remember me, child?"

When had I ever known such a disheveled being? The poor wretch's features were so obscured by the shape of the bonnet that I could not recognize them. My hand, as well as my heart, reached out to her as I offered her the coins from the pocket of my apron.

"My little friend. You are still the angel I ever knew you!" She raised her bonnet and her fine dark eyes—canopied by the thick arches of two nearly conjoining brows—met mine.

"Mrs. Lorrington!" How had my former governess fallen into such a state in so brief a space of time? It had been less than a year since we'd parted. "Come! You *must* come inside!" I led her up to my room, where Mademoiselle Millepied, the French instructor, and I sat the poor woman beside the fire and brought her a pot of tea to warm her innards. Mrs. Lorrington's figure, being of a similar stamp to the mademoiselle's, enabled us to fit her with enough dry garments to restore her modesty.

"I cannot expect to repay your kindness with another ensemble," Mrs. Lorrington murmured sadly.

"None is expected, madame," replied the mademoiselle.

"How came you to be in such a state?" I inquired, but Mrs. Lorrington dismissed my question with a heavy sigh. To press her would have been impolite, for even in her desolation I felt myself her inferior in every way.

Finishing her tea, my mentor rose from her seat by the fireside. "I must take my leave now. I thank both of you kind girls for your pains."

"But you cannot go back out into the night like this!" I ran to the window. "The streets are naught but mud and the rain is still coming down in torrents." Even in Mademoiselle Millepied's old boots, she would not long withstand the inclement weather. "Stay the night at least, I implore you, Mrs. Lorrington. You shall have my bed and I shall place the eiderdown on the floor for myself."

But my former governess would have none of it. I was powerless to persuade her to remain. I felt poorly at not being able to do more by her; had it not been for Mrs. Lorrington's long-standing love affair with spirits, my mother might have offered her a teaching position come daylight. "Then give me your address that I might know where to send to you."

Mrs. Lorrington shook her head. "But I will promise to call upon you in a few days' time, Mary. You have my word upon't."

My eyes brimmed over with tears. It has remained to my eternal regret that Mrs. Lorrington did not keep her promise to visit me again. I never did see her more. Some years later, I was informed that she had died in the workhouse in Chelsea, the martyr of a premature decay, brought on by the indulgence of her propensity to intoxication. I was not surprised, but I was disconsolate. How crack'd a noble heart, indeed. Yes, Mrs. Lorrington was felled by her fatal weakness—but as I saw it, her constant tippling was the tragic result of an everlasting love that formed the chief constituent of her widowed sorrows. It was a theme that would forever haunt me.

Four

Papa Returns

1772 . . . age fourteen

Within the space of a few months, my mother's pupils numbered a dozen. Though her heart remained heavy, weighed down by my father's betrayal of home and hearth, she was consoled by the knowledge of having risen from misfortune into an honorable independence.

The strike of three one afternoon heralded the arrival of an unexpected caller. "Hester!" My father's voice echoed through the narrow corridors. "I've had a deuced bloody time finding you!"

Assigning them a composition on the Greek myths, Mother dismissed her charges, sending them directly into the care of Mademoiselle Millepied for their French lesson. Raising me by the elbow from where I sat grading examinations, she promenaded me into the parlor, where we discovered Papa in a state of apoplexy, fairly wearing out the carpet with his angry pacing.

"What is the meaning of this, Hester?" he demanded. In an instant my mother's strength—so assiduously acquired over the recent season—evanesced, leaving her cowering in her shoes before her husband.

"You're one to talk of *means*," I retorted, the color rushing into my cheeks, "having deprived us of them these many months!"

"I was not aware that I was addressing you, Mary. Have you learnt your disrespect for your elders under your mother's tutelage?"

"Nicholas—" my mother pleaded.

"You have wounded me to the quick," he replied. "What is a man to think—how is he supposed to hold high his head among his countrymen—when his wife flagrantly reveals herself to be no better than . . . than—"

"Than an unprotected damsel?" Mother said softly.

"It is not to be borne, madam!" Father thundered. "I am offended even beyond the bounds of reason! My conjugal reputation is tarnished—"

"And you lay the blame for this at my feet?"

Ignoring her attempt to interject reason into the discussion, Papa continued to raise his voice in equal measure to Mother's increasing quietude. "You have tarnished my conjugal reputation by revealing to the world in a most public manner the landscape of our domestic relations. I am a target of derision at my club. My pride has been sorely tested, Hester."

"No more so than my heart. What would you have me do? If you do not, can not, will not send me the means to support our children, I am left to ameliorate the matter on my own. The academy is completely respectable in every way, I assure you, Nicholas."

"A respectable endeavor for widows and spinsters, perhaps, but not for a *wife*. *My* wife."

"In name only. In word but not in action."

She had finally scored a palpable hit. My proud father managed to appear both crestfallen and sheepish. "I confess, Hester, that my present . . . *ehrm* . . . *household* situation is now too strongly cemented by both time and obligations to ever be dissolved without my making ample provisions for the person in question."

"I have lost the thread of your meaning, Nicholas."

He slapped his gloves on the mantel. "It's this, damnit!" My mother bit her tongue; Papa never swore, and now he had done so twice within the space of five minutes. "There's been another reversal," he said, his voice strained and tight. "I have been accused by a British lieutenant of illegally employing Frenchmen and using French equipment for my ventures in Labrador. The authorities confiscated my sealskins—every last one of them—even the inferior pelts. Though I've brought a damages suit against the officer, I've come back to London with nothing. There," he said, taking the liberty of sinking into a chair. "That's the whole ugly business. Here's your bloody *thread*, Hester. I could not afford to provision Elenor even if I'd a mind to."

"In that case, it is fortuitous that I have found a respectable means of caring for our children."

"Respectable! Woman, you presume to use that word in connexion with your—this *establishment*!"

Whereupon poor Mother, who had more or less managed with astounding grace to maintain her equanimity in the face of such an assault upon her undertaking—and by extension, her character—lost those capabilities of restraining her temper. "You *dare* to speak to *me* of *respectability*!"

As witness to this appalling domestic spectacle, I was being indoctrinated with a lesson about the world that I should never have found in any text: If a woman is not permitted to assert a majesty of mind, why fatigue her faculties with the labors of any species of education? Why give her books if she is not to profit by the wisdom they inculcate?

My mother turned at the sound of alarmed footsteps belonging to small children and their governesses running down the narrow hall toward the parlor. With one deft movement she kicked aside the cast-iron doorstop, leaving the oaken portal to shut in their curious, though well-meaning, faces. Her foot would ache like the very devil come morning.

"You are still my wife, Hester, regardless of our . . . conjugal . . . circumstances." Papa gave me an uncomfortable glance. "And as your husband, I have the right to forbid you to do anything that discredits my name and reputation."

"Yet you're perfectly capable of doing it yourself," I said under my breath. Though I loved my father, I was torn between my duty and affection for him, my anger at his conduct, and my wish to protect my mother from the sting of his betrayal.

"At which seminary did you learn to cross your father? Hester, I warn you, Mary will never get a husband if she lets her tongue run away with her. I am exercising my rights—*as* a husband—to demand that you close this academy as soon as practicable. And if our daughter's sauciness is an illustration of what happens when you fill young ladies' heads with subjects and ideas suited only to the male mind, the sooner the better!"

What kind of civilized society protects the malefactor and punishes his victim? As a young girl I bore witness to this exercise of dominion in the bosom of my own family, and it festered within my soul.

How my heart broke for my mother; what consternation her fragile nature must have then endured, having valiantly struggled to make ends meet and still maintain all due propriety and decorum, while her philandering husband lectured *her* about respectability! Yet she was duty-bound to obey his wishes, for any business or property under a man's wife's control was *his* to do with as he saw fit. And so, at the expiration of eight months, my mother, by my father's positive command, broke up her establishment and moved us to modest lodgings in the neighborhood of Marylebone. Knowing that my father now publicly resided with his mistress (living in comfort off Grosvenor Square), Mother did not even hope for his returning affection.

Demoted from my brief status as a governess I became a student once more, enrolled at Oxford House, Marylebone. At this charming academy, picturesquely situated at the top of the Marylebone High Street bordering on the gardens, I was instructed in all the requisites deemed proper for a young lady's schooling.

Mother was compelled to increase her budget for tallow, as I was wont to stay awake halfway through the night writing verses. "Your complexion is sallowing, Mary," she insisted one night. "It's evident that you are not getting enough sleep." I began to protest, but she would have none of it. "And your scribbling during every hour of leisure has led to a want of fresh air and exercise, which will sap your beauty just as rapidly. There are two things a girl must have to secure her future, a fortune and her looks, and the former, alas, is of greater value than the latter. Thanks to the unfortunate outcome of your father's recent business ventures, your greatest asset, Mary, is your beauty, and I can't have you squandering your dowry."

"But, Mama, I am composing a tragedy!"

" 'Twill be a *tragedy* if you lose your eyesight before you turn fifteen." She sighed despairingly. "Who will marry a blind bluestocking?"

Not too many weeks later, my father paid us a call.

"I came to tell you that I have made plans to quit England," he told Mother.

"Another American venture?" With my ear to the keyhole, I could not tell from the timbre of her voice whether she had finally become indifferent to him or if she was masking tears.

"I shall miss the children greatly. You are sensible of the fact, Hester, that my heart cracks every time I am obliged to depart. It has not been easy . . . on me . . . I feel deeply the . . . *want* . . . of means. . . ." He was pacing the length of the carpet. I could hear the floorboards creak beneath his tread. "Damme!" He pounded his fist into his hand. "No man intends to fail!"

I inched the door open ever so slightly, hoping the hinges had been well oiled.

"Mary is nearly of marriageable age. If unchecked in her ways, and without a father's hand to guide her"—and here he stopped before the fire and raised his outstretched arm, leveling an accusatory finger at my mother—"Hester, take care that no dishonor falls upon my daughter. If she is not safe at my return, I will annihilate you!"

My mother heard the stern injunction and trembled while he repeated it. *"Annihilate!"*

I feared he might stride like mighty Jove through the parlor and catch me eavesdropping by the door, so I scurried behind the stairwell and hid myself in a broom closet until I heard the tromp of his boots upon the wooden floor of the vestibule and the sound of slamming doors.

Then I tiptoed back into the room. My mother's shoulders were heaving as though an invisible puppetmaster was shaking her up and down. She was sobbing into her handkerchief. I knelt at her embroidered slippers and placed my head into her lap. "I shan't disappoint you, I promise," I whispered into her apron. "Or him."

I rang for a cup of tea and remained with Mother until she had composed herself. Then I returned to school, heavyhearted. I felt that Papa had adjudged and condemned us, without our ever having given him cause to doubt my modesty or Mother's ability to raise me as a proper gentlewoman.

One afternoon I was summoned to the parlor of Mrs. Hervey, the governess at Oxford House. A rug was laid across her lap, the coals in the brazier providing an insubstantial defense against the frosty air seeping through the wainscoting. "Tea, Mary?" she inquired, motioning for me to sit across from her. She poured some for me and refilled her own dish. "I don't suppose you know why you are here," she continued, handing me the saucer.

I shook my head. "No, ma'am; I do not." I worried that I might once more be dismissed from school, turned out into the world like a half-baked cake.

"It has not escaped my notice."

"What hasn't, ma'am?"

"I should inform you that your performances in the student theatricals have been remarked upon by other instructors as well as by your classmates," said Mrs. Hervey, offering me a biscuit flavored with orange-flower water. "And a true talent is to be encouraged." She leaned toward me and favored me with one of her smiles, showing her immense front teeth. "Now, what do you say to that?"

My heart was beating in my chest, for she had singled me out as Hannah More and Mrs. Lorrington had done, for excelling in something I truly loved. To make believe that I was another person—even if that fictional young lady had her own perils—removed me, however briefly, from my tendency to melancholy and over-reflection and from my own fortune's state. These outlets for my precociously honed sensibilities were as exciting as taking a journey to a foreign land where one could reinvent oneself and begin anew.

At my request, a few days later, Mother was consulted on the matter. Mr. Hussey, our dancing master at Oxford House, was present as well, for he also held the position of ballet master at Covent Garden; Mrs. Hervey had told him that I possessed "an extraordinary genius for dramatic exhibitions." My head swelled from the compliment, and I could see that Mother, although she adored me beyond measure, was wondering whether my governess was of the sort who was prone to the use of superlatives.

"Is this truly what you want, Mary?" My mother's hands fluttered skyward in delicate despair. "Name me a single actress whose reputation has not suffered for going upon the stage," she lamented. "I read the newspapers! What of poor Mrs. Cibber—forced at gunpoint by her husband, so I heard, to sleep with a benefactor, in order to trump up an adultery charge and collect money for't! Or Peg Woffington—one of Mr. Garrick's former mistresses—who stabbed a rival!" Mother indeed presented a redoubtable argument. But together, Mr. Hussey and Mrs. Hervey assured her that there were in fact a number of young ladies who had led perfectly respectable lives, becoming stainless wives and spotless mothers while pursuing this admittedly dubious profession. Mrs. Pritchard, for one, who shared the stage with Garrick for two decades—without succumbing to any lustful advances—and whose Lady Macbeth was the nonpareil of tragic interpretation, was herself a woman of substance and tremendous personal dignity; however, this intelligence did not do as much to assuage my mother's misgivings as did another bit of news, this one much closer to home.

We had received word that my father's new Labradoran scheme was proving just as disastrous as his previous undertakings. His pecuniary embarrassments had once again brought us to the brink of ruin. I was now of an age where in short order I would be required to lighten the burden, either by making a good marriage or finding some means of employment by which I might procure enough for Mother, George, and me to live comfortably.

"Then at least permit her to try for the stage," my esteemed instructors insisted. After her resolve was worn down, my mother at last consented to allow my recitation for a gentleman who was known to have some qualification in the discerning of one's dramatic merits. And though she never wish'd me to fail in anything, I sensed that when all was said and done, she would have been quite relieved to hear that her young Mary's artistic abilities were better suited to the drawing room than Drury Lane.

Five

Enter Garrick

1772 . . . age fourteen

$\mathcal{B}$ecause Mr. Thomas Hull was an actor at Covent Garden, he was well acquainted with Mr. Hussey, esteemed his good opinion, and therefore agreed to listen to me perform for him. This audition was not to take place at Covent Garden itself, but rather within Mr. Hull's apartments in Maiden Lane, a mere stone's throw from the theatre. At the time, Covent Garden was one of only two theatres—the other being Drury Lane—to which the crown had granted licenses, although a summer season was permitted at the Haymarket. It seemed to me that if one did not gain employment at a licensed house, there was little chance of ever making a success upon the stage, for who would see you?

The staircase that led to Mr. Hull's rooms was so narrow that I could scarce mount the steps without crushing my skirts against the dusty walls. It smelled of cat urine as well, and no wonder, for when Mother and I entered the actor's domicile, no fewer than four well-fed felines scampered across my path as I approached the celebrated thespian. I found Mr. Hull, his hair powdered to a shade of pewter, smoking a clay pipe and contemplating the middle distance off to his right hand as though a mysterious object visible only to him—Macbeth's phantom dagger, perhaps—was suspended from the chandelier. As I approached, he kicked away his footstool, which for a fleeting moment I thought might be another puss, and rose to his feet, making a graceful leg. I bobbed a curtsy, and sneezed.

"A pleasure, Miss Darby. Wait, let me fetch my spectacles." Finding them warmed by a cat's underbelly, he dusted them off upon his bisque-colored waistcoat. Jutting forth his little pointed chin, he peered at me. "Ah, then, you are indeed as lovely to look at as Hussey said. I would offer you tea, but I've none on the boil. I hope you'll overlook the incivility. Now, what will you favor me with this afternoon, Miss Darby?"

I had selected Nicholas Rowe's 1714 verse drama, *The Tragedy of Jane Shore*, from which to cull my recitation. My naïvely sentimental heart throbbed to the famous story of Elizabeth Shore, the young and beautiful wife of a goldsmith who became the mistress to a king, and his trusted adviser. After his death, she engaged in dalliances with other noblemen, but was accused of sorcery by the evil Richard III and sent to the Tower. Upon her release, she was forced to do public penance as a harlot, and though she later married well, she eventually died in poverty. Was ever woman so wronged!

By the time the tragedy begins, Richard III has been named Lord Protector and Jane has already fallen on hard times, so frail and despondent one might not recognize her. Such a role naturally suited my attraction for tortured souls.

I began with a few lines from Jane's opening speeches, calculated to appeal to a man whose advanced years—Hull was then forty-two, though still robust—would contrast with those of young Jane.

The actor's indulgent smile gave me the courage to continue; however, I had made the mistake that many novices do, which is to choose a role more befitting to one with a greater experience of the world than their own green years. In performing the passage where Jane describes her lover, the king—lacking all experience in everything amorous, from courtship to copulation—I could only bring my lips to shape the words. The requisite passion and brokenhearted nostalgia necessary to comprehend Jane's lot was far beyond me.

> *He was the very joy of all that saw him,*
> *Form'd to delight, to love, and to persuade . . .*
> *But what had I to do with kings and courts?*
> *My humble lot had cast me far beneath him;*
> *And that he was the first of all mankind,*
> *The bravest and most lovely, was my curse.*

I saw Mr. Hull frown and begin to puff his pipe in earnest. Hoping to redeem my folly, I gave him just a few more lines of Jane Shore. This speech, at least, I could identify with on some level, knowing firsthand how ill-used my mother was by my father.

> *. . . Such is the fate unhappy women find,*
> *And such is the curse entail'd upon our kind,*
> *That man, the lawless libertine, may rove*
> *Free and unquestion'd through the wilds of love;*

While woman, sense and nature's easy fool,
If poor, weak woman swerve from virtue's rule,
If strongly charm'd, she'd leave the thorny way,
And in the softer paths of pleasure stray;
Ruin ensues, reproach and endless shame,
And one false step entirely damns her fame . . .
She sets, like stars that fall, to rise no more.

Now, *there,* I was filled with fervor. Had there been music beneath my words, 'twould have been an anthem. My tears came easily—not only because I related to the text, but because of all the cat hair in the air. Out of the corner of my eye, I noticed Mr. Hull pitching his body forward as if to get closer to my performance.

A bit breathless, I dropped a curtsy after my final sentence. "Well, then, have I any talent?" I asked, with all the exuberant anxiety of youth.

The actor smiled as a cat leapt upon his lap. "It wants coaching."

"I'm happy to take corrections; I absorb learning like a sponge," I said eagerly.

"To begin with, there are simple things you can do, even with the speeches you performed today, to strengthen their impact."

I rubbed my stinging eyes. "Such as?"

"The final speech you gave me. As soon as the last word had left your lips you dropped your hand like a dishclout and then fell right out of character to thank me for listening. There was no transition between Jane Shore and Mary Darby. Assume that final pose and hold it. That is a simple technical note, but without technique, Miss Darby, you shall never rise above the rank of amateur, and that will never do at Covent Garden or Drury Lane. You must also allow each word to live, to breathe—and it must be heard in the balconies. No matter how choked with passion you become when you recite a line, you must take care never to slur your words, to mumble, or to drop below a stage whisper. You have a most pleasant voice, Miss Darby. Use it."

"Thank you, sir." A smile sneaked past my grateful humility.

"I should advise you, in future, to cultivate the roles you can comfortably assay within the scope of your tender years." Mr. Hull drew upon his pipe and exhaled into a kindly smile. "You are not yet a Lady Macbeth, unless you conceal a terrible secret from me, but I daresay Juliet is within your sights. Your Jane Shore wants depth, although you did quite a creditable job with the last speech you presented. Your tears appeared to flow quite naturally. What you have shown me today is by no means dross, Miss Darby. There is ore to be mined, most assuredly. But acting is a craft as much as goldsmithing or tanning hides and you must apply yourself most assiduously to the study of it before attempting to set foot upon the great stages of England."

Hopes now dashed, my face fell. Not one hour previous I had been contemplating a thousand triumphs in my head. I swallowed hard. "I thank you for your time, Mr. Hull. You have been most gracious and considerate."

"I fear I cannot recommend you to the management of Covent Garden at present, but come back to me in a few months' time. Perhaps there will be some roles open with which you can begin a journeymanship."

I quit Mr. Hull's rooms disappointed, but undaunted nevertheless. Mother's comforting embrace was sincerely bestowed. "I shan't give up," I insisted, "for I do believe I can make something of it."

We had moved once again, my mother placing herself under the protection of a lawyer, Samuel Cox, who had apartments at Southampton House in Chancery Lane. My brother and I each had our own room, and mother came and went, though she remained entirely discreet about the nature of her arrangement. She told George and me that she had been engaged to do some copying for Mr. Cox, and I knew not to press her.

On Sunday afternoons the three of us would dine with Mr. Cox, and it came out one day over dinner that I harbored ambitions for the stage. As soon as he learned I had been to see Mr. Hull, Mother's benefactor, a gouty little man, though a kindly one, immediately offered his services if we thought they would be of use.

"What good are one's connexions if not to secure the odd introduction now and again? Dr. Samuel Johnson is one of my acquaintance, Hetty! We've got the same physician for the gout, don'tcha know. Dr. Johnson, of course, is an intimate of Garrick's—"

"You can arrange an interview with Mr. Garrick?" I asked, unable to contain myself. Suddenly, a simple Sunday dinner was as good as a Christmas feast.

"I expect so, Mary. For David Garrick was a pupil of Dr. Johnson's, don'tcha know?"

I shook my head. "Well, no, I didn't know that. Mercy! The greatest actor in all creation—willing to hear me recite!"

Mother chuckled, while my ten-year-old brother kept repeating under his breath, "The greatest—the great, great, *greatest*."

"And I shall become the most famous actress since Nelly Gwyn!"

"You can see the girl's got a natural inclination for the dramatic, Sam."

Garrick resided in a grand home in Adelphi Terrace, over-looking the Thames. Once again, Mother chaperoned my audition, though as things transpired, she needn't have worried about any untoward claims on my virtue, for I was promptly met in the vestibule by the actor-manager's wife, the former dancer Eva Maria Veigel. Miss Veigel greeted me with such warm effusiveness I felt as though I had been her intimate all my life.

"My wife is also very supportive of young actresses," were the first words I heard uttered by the great Garrick, a little man, something on the stocky side, who looked me up and down with the utmost intensity, as if to draw my portrait.

I did not know where to look, for all about me were the most striking objects. Miss Veigel moved about with per-fect grace and her embroidered gown of apple-green silk was the prettiest I had ever seen; the ceilings of the salon had been painted to resemble a pastoral idyll one might find in the mythology of the ancients; and it was difficult to take my eyes off the little man himself, wondering how such an unprepossessing personage could effect such an impact on the last two generations of theatregoers—nay, on the entire business of the Theatre itself.

"You have nothing to fear, Mrs. Darby," said Miss Vei-gel, taking my mother's hands as she escorted her to a table charmingly laid out for tea. "My husband earned his respect for more than his thespian talents. Have you attended the Theatre Royal since David assumed its management?" With a shake of her head, my mother allowed that she had not. "It will please you to know, then, that my husband discontinued the practice of permitting young gentlemen—and I use the word generously—to sit upon the stage. Should a young man wish to enjoy the proximity of one of Drury Lane's lovely actresses, he can do so from the safety of a box or amid the riffraff from a place in the pit. And no longer are such types permitted to roam freely about the backstage rabbit warrens that form the corridors and changing rooms, entering a ladies' dressing room at will or whim." My mother exhaled, audibly put at ease by Miss Veigel's remarks. "And as for my husband himself—David was once a bit of a rake with the ladies, it is true, but since our marriage, he has been a very good boy." Miss Veigel smiled upon Garrick with great affection. "There is nothing with which I can reproach him. How many women, Mrs. Darby, of any stamp, can say that about their husbands?" Mother blushed scarlet.

The "very good boy" was now fifty-three years of age, entering the twilight of his illustrious career, yet with his wife's good assistance he continued to cultivate a select number of protégées, preparing them for a life on the stage.

I wasted no time in assuring Mr. Garrick that such a life was my fondest dream, and that I felt honored beyond all measure simply by his invitation to recite for him. It was true, but in my young heart I'd hoped for ever so much more.

"The Theatre is a demanding mistress, Miss Darby. She expects you to worship her, night and day—body, mind, and soul, and is content with nothing less. She expects perfection in everything, has little patience for illness, and even less tolerance for sloth and slovenliness."

"That doesn't diminish my desire, sir."

"Well, then!" He motioned for Mother and Miss Veigel to draw up their chairs beside his. "What will the spirited Miss Darby favor us with today?"

I had been practicing the speech of Jane Shore's with which I had caught Mr. Hull's attention, proud that I was now able to summon tears without the serendipitous presence of cat dander, and thus I began my recitation.

> *. . . Such is the fate unhappy women find—*

"Stop!" cried Garrick.

"What have I done?"

"I am about to ask the very same thing. What do you think you are doing, child?"

I had remembered Mr. Hull's injunction to speak loudly enough so that every balcony was filled with the sound of my voice, making each word count.

"That is not acting, Miss Darby," said Garrick firmly. "It is declaiming. How can any of the words matter, or mean anything, when you give every one of them an equal weight?" I pondered this. "Now continue, pray, simply and directly as though you were speaking to me, as we are, right in my parlor. Raise not your voice this time, and let the words infuse you with emotion, not t'other way around."

I began again.

> *And such is the curse entail'd upon our kind,*
> *That man, the lawless libertine, may rove—*

"Stop." He had halted my speech just as my bosom was rising with passion over the injustices of the world. "Your natural voice is lovely to hear, Miss Darby. Doesn't she remind you of dear Susanna Cibber, my sweet?" Miss Veigel assented.

I was secretly pleased to hear the same compliment that Mr. Hull had given me coming from the lips of the great Garrick.

Mr. Garrick's eyes met mine. His penetrating gaze nearly paralyzed me. "Now, Miss Darby, *perform*—do not *recite*—the speech from the beginning—wait, don't start until I give the cue. I should like to hear you do it with the same simplicity, the identical intensity of emotion, *but* loud enough to be heard in every one of the eighteen hundred seats in the Theatre Royal."

I swallowed hard at what suddenly seemed a daunting task, then took a deep breath and faced my dragon. 'Twas then I realized that if I obeyed the words, they would take me where I wanted to go; and I was able to forget all, even that I was being judged in my meager efforts by the finest actor to tread the boards since Roscius overtook the Roman stage by storm. I performed my speech and awaited the verdict.

"I confess that your charm and your beauty convinced me from the first that you might have a career, but I needed to know that you possessed talent in equal measure. Mrs. Darby, your daughter shows tremendous promise, and I should like to take her on and present her in due time at Drury Lane."

Suddenly I was a little girl again, laughing and clapping my hands the way I had done when Papa would return from one of his expeditions and place a pretty gewgaw in my tiny hands. "Mother, isn't it wonderful?" I exclaimed.

She was crying too hard to reply. What was it that moved her to tears: maternal pride in my little performance that afternoon, or—ruminating upon the perils of a theatrical career—the dread of so many more to come?

Six

Big Plans

1772 . . . age fourteen

One afternoon a couple of months later, I was leaf-ing through a rare set of Shakespeare quartos Garrick had placed upon my lap. "Why are these beautiful volumes so marked up? I'm dreadfully sorry to have to tell you this, sir, but there are pages where I can scarce read the words."

My tutor shuddered. "With the best of generous inten-tions, that I might aid a dear friend in the compilation of his life's work, back in forty-six I naïvely made a loan of them to Dr. Johnson to use in the research for his diction-ary. I should have recalled that the man had a nasty habit of scrawling all over everything."

"I'm surprised, too, that such a treasure is so dusty," I remarked, blowing away some motes.

"I'm afraid that's not dust," said Garrick, taking the volumes from my hands. "It's scurf."

Ugh. It was my turn to shudder. I hunted for a hand-kerchief to brush away the flakes of dandruff and dried skin that had landed on my skirts.

"Never mind," Garrick added, "I had expected you to become familiar with Shakespeare's text of *King Lear* before we began to work on *my* versions."

Having compared the Bard's quarto to the script we were to play, I noted that the role of Cordelia was somewhat larger than Shakespeare had intended, for Garrick had, in his words, "improved upon the improvements already made to the text by Nahum Tate," giving the tragedy a happy ending where Cordelia marries Edgar!

Having puzzled for days over this decidedly un-Shakespearean finale, I finally summoned the courage to ask my mentor why we were offering the public such imaginative reworkings of the original. His reply was succinct: "No doubt, Miss Darby, you have observed that happy endings are the fashion nowadays. Good must always triumph over Evil."

At Mr. Garrick's insistence, in addition to weeks of study on my voice, carriage, and singing—the last of which I confess myself rather more deficient than my mentor would have liked—I had been attending the theatre as often as I could manage, with Mother as my chaperone. We did see the presentations at Covent Garden, but it was at Drury Lane, sitting in the great actor's private box, where I most felt the magic. For here was a veritable temple to the arts. The interior had recently been remodeled—to Garrick's plans—and it seemed to my young mind that no expense had been spared. Lush draperies the color of garnets and trimmed with gold fringe framed the stage. Elegant plaster medallions festooned the exteriors of the boxes, crimson paper lined their rear walls, slim pillars inlaid with colored glass glittered like rubies and emeralds, candles flickered in gilt branches. I craned my neck to enjoy the to-ing and fro-ing in the upper tier, where the Cyprians plied their trade amid the green boxes, and discovered that these wealthy seats of pleasure were richly painted and adorned with gilded busts.

"Imagine! Here, here is where I shall one day reign," I would whisper to Mother, my head filled with glittering triumphs yet to come. I had been too often in public not to be observed and the word was out that I was the juvenile pupil of Garrick—the promised Cordelia. And as I was fast becoming the heir apparent to many other leading roles of the day, I was treated like the princess royal by many illustrious personages, who would make a point of visiting Mr. Garrick's home in Adelphi Terrace or his box at Drury Lane just to pay a call on his new protégée. The melancholy child had shed her cocoon of morbid and maudlin sensibilities, metamorphosing into a gay butter fly who craved the latest fashions.

I was fiercely determined to make something of myself, and—as our breadwinner had turned libertine and truant—would proudly support our little family on my talents.

I had never been happier. "Surely, Mother, you must find it preferable to spending the latter part of my girlhood hunched over a flame, scribbling tortured verses!"

"Indeed, Mary, you've a fine eye for color and silhouette, and no one knows better what becomes you," Mother agreed. "Fair warning, however: you're playing with fire."

I found myself an object of attention whenever I appeared at the theatre, and I admit I loved the "buzz." It was all a grand game to me, being cosseted and admired, all a prelude to the day when I would leave Mr. Garrick's tutelage for the other side of the pit, where I was already assured of a loyal and devoted following.

It was the end of 1772. I had just turned fifteen, and my little heart throbbed with impatience for the hour of trial. My tutor was most sanguine in his expectations of my success, his encomiums were of the most flattering kind, and every rehearsal seemed to strengthen his flattering opinion.

Never shall I forget the enchanting hours that I passed in Mr. Garrick's society: to me, he possessed more power, both to awe and to attract, than any man I'd ever encountered. Even his smile was fascinating. Yet I confess that he had at times a restless peevishness of tone that so excessively affected me that I shall never forget it.

One morning when we were rehearsing an exchange in the first act between Lear and Cordelia, I had a taste of the frustration that could unleash Mr. Garrick's temper.

He had just addressed me as Lear, and I had replied as Cordelia:

> *Unhappy am I that I can't dissemble,*
> *Sir, as I ought, I love your Majesty,*
> *No more nor less.*

Dismissively waving his hand to halt my speech, the master interrupted. "While you're busy not dissembling, apply yourself to not *mumbling*, Miss Darby."

Endeavoring to retain the simplicity for which Garrick's own acting was much vaunted, I repeated my line with more volume. But my efforts were apparently unsatisfactory, for Mr. Garrick corrected me again, yet this time as King Lear.

Take heed Cordelia,
Thy Fortunes are at stake, think better on't
And mend thy Speech a little.

Frustrated with my inability to get it right, I ended up raising my voice to such a pitch that the contents of Miss Veigel's china cabinet began to tremble.

O my Liege,
You gave me Being, Bred me, dearly Love me . . .

"What the devil do you think you're doing, Miss Darby! Don't shout! Don't *declaim*. Do not *emote*. Whom are you addressing? The empty air? You speak to a *king*, girl. A king who is your *father*. The man who gave you life. *Convince* me of Cordelia's earnestness. You are honest and sincere. Now, speak to me sincerely—*and* loudly. I have expressed every confidence that you shall take the theatre by storm; do not make me doubt my judgment by mumbling one moment and shouting the next like some green girl in a tavern skit. 'Speak the speech, I pray you, as I pronounc'd it to you, trippingly on the tongue.' Now, let's continue the scene. I can't bear to hear you do those lines again. Next time you'll play them exactly as I've schooled you." Mr. Garrick cued me with Lear's next speech, and I daresay I could not tell whether the anger was his own or the ancient king's.

. . . Repent, for know Our nature cannot brook
A Child so young and so Ungentle.

But when I gave my reply, "So young my Lord and True," he again interrupted. "Why did you emphasize the word *young,* Miss Darby? We all know Cordelia is *young.* Is there a better word to accentuate? What is the very essence of Cordelia?"

I blushed. "So young my Lord and *True.*"

"Eureka!"

Whilst I fretted that I might not be up to the challenge after all, Mother worried about my reputation. For her, the fact that I was already wildly popular—and still to set foot upon the boards—nearly palsied her resolution to allow my debut.

My ardent fancy, however, was busied in contemplating a thousand triumphs, in which my vanity would be publicly gratified, without the smallest sacrifice of my private character.

And yet the temptations did present themselves. While nightly I had been holding court in Mr. Garrick's box at the Theatre Royal, receiving visitors throughout the various overtures, main plays, musical interludes, and farcical afterpieces, a number of gentlemen—as well as those of a less moral stamp—had made their intentions known to us.

One professed admirer was a man of splendid fortune, but old enough to be my grandfather. This suit I never would listen to. But there was another man, a naval officer, graceful and handsome of face and figure, who took to following me to and from the theatre.

I was eventually persuaded, through the most ardent letter delivered into my hands by an abigail, that he wished to know me. The writer avowed himself the son of a lady—and offered marriage! I instantly delivered the letter to my mother, and shortly after he was, by an acquaintance, presented to me with decorous ceremony.

Naturally, his proposal came with terms. Any wife of his was not to set foot upon the stage. Mother, who but *half* approved a dramatic life, was more than *half* inclined to favor the addresses of this most accomplished suitor. If she could nip my theatrical career in the bud and couple me with a man of good family, such a consummation was devoutly to be wish'd.

But oh, not all "actors" tread the boards! Some merely tread upon unassuming and innocent hearts. For it came to pass that the acquaintance who paved the path for the handsome captain to inveigle his way into our society became alarmed for my safety and laid open his bosom to us, confessing the captain's secret. It seemed that this paragon of paramours already had a young and amiable wife in a sister kingdom!

Mother's consternation was infinite. But I felt little regret in the loss of a husband, when I reflected that this matrimonial alliance would have compelled me to relinquish my theatrical profession. All my dreams were then focused on a single shining goal. The drama, the delightful drama, seemed the very criterion of all human happiness, and I looked forward to the evening of my debut with all the anticipation of an eager and curious bride on her wedding night.

Seven

Mr. Robinson

Early 1773 . . . age fifteen

"That's enough." Mother closed the lower shutters of our drawing room with an air of finality and a sigh of resignation. "Don't think I'm not aware of your behavior, Mary."

I feigned ignorance. "You fancy every man a seducer and every hour an hour of accumulating peril!"

"I well remember your father's admonition. That young man opposite never misses a moment to come to his window when you're at ours. It's a wonder his employer keeps him on."

The employer in question was the eminent solicitor John Vernon, and the interesting-looking young man, one of his articled clerks. 'Twas true that the clerk did seem somewhat lovestruck, but I rather fancied his attentions and enjoyed what I had believed, until that moment, to have been a covert flirtation. He was handsome in person and his countenance was overcast by a sort of languor, the effect of sickness, I imagined, finding him all the more attractive for having suffered.

Mother was certain she had effected a logjam in the stream of my maiden affections, but some weeks later, after we had moved to the York Buildings in Villiers Street, off the Strand, we received an invitation to form part of a party of six for an excursion to dine in Greenwich the following Sunday. The host was Mr. Wayman, an attorney of whom my mother entertained the highest opinion, his having the patronage of her much-respected Mr. Cox. After a goodly deal of persuasion, my mother consented to go, and to allow that I should also attend her. As it was then the fashion to wear silks, on the day of recreation itself I wore a gown of pale blue lustring, with a chip hat trimmed with ribbands of the same color. Never was I dressed so perfectly to my own satisfaction; with all the vanity of a fifteen-year-old who wished to be thought a lady, I anticipated a day of admiration.

As an amateur sibyl I proved accurate, for on our stopping at the Star and Garter at Greenwich, the person who came to hand me from the carriage was our opposite neighbor from the Southampton Buildings! I stifled my urge to gasp, for now that we stood so close, it was abundantly plain that he was nearly a head shorter than I was.

"May I present my young friend, Thomas Robinson?" Mr. Wayman made the introductions. I was confused, but my gentle mother was indignant. We had been set up like pins!

Our party dined, and early in the evening we returned to London without the company of Mr. Robinson, who remained on in Greenwich. As is so often the case in life, the fantasy was far more intriguing than the reality. Mr. Robinson was nowhere near the creature of my imagination, the mysterious stranger across the lane. I confess, the man made no grand impression on me that afternoon. His manners were tolerable, but his conversation was wanting, droning on ad nauseum about the Law—with which he was fluent—but tongue-tied when it came to discussions of the classics and suchlike. His wan appearance, which before our acquaintance had filled my girlish imagination with romantic notions of the invalid, now seemed merely pallid. His affability seemed his greatest talent.

I raised the subject of Mr. Robinson on the ride home. "Well, Mother, at least you were more impressed than I when he boasted of training with the firm of Vernon and Elderton."

"It bespeaks a promising future," Mr. Wayman interjected, as I pooh-poohed his prospects by fluttering my lips.

"Mary, that's most unbecoming," Mother scolded.

"My young friend would be quite the catch," added the solicitor, pressing his advantage with the woman more likely to favor Mr. Robinson. "Mrs. Darby, Tom is the sole heir of his uncle, a Mr. Harris of Carmarthenshire, and stands to inherit thirty thousand pounds on the gentleman's demise. Tom has a promising career ahead of him—Mr. Vernon sees great things for the youth—which is not to be sneezed at. And of course he's immensely fond of your daughter."

"Pandarus," I muttered under my breath.

"What did you say, Miss Darby?"

"*Bless* us!"

"Exactly! You could do worse than permit Mr. Robinson to pay his addresses."

I confess that at the time I wondered at so effusive an endorsement. Why did Mr. Robinson not speak for himself that afternoon at dinner? But as I knew so little of him, I allowed that much of his languid demeanor might owe itself to shyness, and that he was more comfortable deputizing his wooing to an interlocutor.

But I was mistaken. Mr. Robinson could never be accused of lacking either temerity or tenacity. The route to his conquest lay in first seducing the gatekeeper, and here he excelled. Upon discovering that Mother had a fondness for what we liked to call graveyard literature, Mr. Robinson began making my mother gifts of it. The moat was bridged with the present of an elegantly bound copy of Hervey's *Meditations*. After that, he laid siege to the citadel with daily deliveries of a volume on some moral or religious theme. These tokens were enough to convince Mother—who had closed the shutters upon his flirtations not too many weeks previous—that Mr. Robinson was the kindest and best of mortals.

Yet the hero's greatest trials lay ahead of him.

The scourge that had overtaken so much of the Continent had crossed the Channel and one day darkened our own doorstep. My little brother George, only eleven years old, was suddenly sickened with the smallpox, becoming dangerously ill. For days he lay abed, fretting for water, delirious with fever, sores the size and color of cherry pits ravaging his small frame. There was scarce a patch of unaffected skin on his little legs or on his once-pretty face.

During those anxious and terrible days, Mr. Robinson was indefatigable in his attentions, conduct that offered tremendous consolation to my mother. The second comfort, if one can call it that, which she derived from our domestic catastrophe, was that George's illness took precedence over all, necessitating the postponement of my Drury Lane debut.

I was heartsick, first for George of course, and then for myself. Like Sisyphus, I had been toiling toward the summit of the mountain, only to slide back down to its base.

"No one is sorrier than I at this change in plans," wrote Mr. Garrick, "yet I heartily anticipate the day when your brother will in restored health rejoice at your maiden voyage upon the oaken planks of the Theatre Royal."

And then, while the winter chill of 1773 hardened the ground and George himself was still wrestling with the angels, I succumbed to the disease. Within three days my figure was stippled with a rash, brow to toes, so that I appeared to have a thousand red navels. Yet I felt little terror at the approaches of a dangerous and deforming malady. Though my intended profession depended upon my looks as much as on my talent, personal beauty has never been to me an object of material solicitude.

Mr. Robinson now went full-bore to win my affections by showing his willingness to hazard catching the disfiguring and deadly pox himself, swearing oath upon oath to marry me even if my face and figure should be marred permanently by disease. Every day he attended my sickbed with the zeal of a brother, and 'tis true that zeal made an impression of gratitude upon my heart—an appreciation that became the source of all my succeeding sorrows.

I lay abed for nearly three months. During the worst of my illness, when my fever so overtook me that I was sure that angels and demons danced hand in hand before me, Mother and Mr. Robinson undertook a campaign designed to convince me to relent.

They assumed, at least in my presence, that I would

survive as George had done. "But what condition will you be in for a life upon the stage?" I was asked with the utmost maternal solicitude. "Weakened in body, with the effects of sickness still upon you. . . ." It was evident that Mother thought I would no longer be a beauty should God extract me from the malady's fatal grip, and perhaps no one would want me then. To Mother, Mr. Robinson was as sure a husband as I was ever likely to have.

And Mr. Robinson argued, "The Theatre is no place for such a one as you, Mary. Educated, gently bred, from one of the first families of Bristol. Why chance a flirtation with fame when I offer you a lifetime of security and comfort? I will have five hundred pounds a year and am the sole heir to the fortune of my uncle, Thomas Harris," he reminded us.

Mother invoked her litany. "What would your father say, child?"

Continually evoking Papa's inevitable disapproval of a theatrical career, particularly when a future of comfortable domesticity was being presented as the rosy alternative, was my loving adversaries' greatest weapon. They played upon my filial devotion as well as the guilt that would forever reside within my soul if I disobeyed his wishes.

"But don't you see, I'm just like Papa," I insisted weakly. "Is not my adventurous spirit, my willingness to risk all for what I so dearly desire to obtain more than anything in the world, a shoot from the same tree? Should that not weigh in the balance?"

"Tush, Mary, you're sounding delirious." Mother kissed my brow. "We'll have no more of this silliness," she whispered.

Mother and Mr. Robinson had worn down my resolve

until I no longer had the strength to fight. Lamenting the inevitable sacrifice of my life's ambition before the marital altar, weakened and vulnerable, and hourly reminded of my father's vow, after several weeks of painful squabbling, I at last relented. The banns were to be rung thrice at St. Martin-in-the-Fields while I was yet lying on my bed of sickness, and the day was fixed for our marriage—the twelfth of April, 1773. I was then barely fifteen and a half years of age.

Yet during the three weeks between banns and vows, I remained plagued with regrets, and Mother was no less apprehensive. Despite having so zealously pushed the match, she felt the most severe discomfort at the thought of our approaching separation. Estranged from Father's affections, she had treasured up all her fondest hopes in the continued society of an only daughter.

"Well, then, why not reside with us?" proposed Mr. Robinson. I was most astonished! What prospective bridegroom, so eager for matrimony, would make such an unusual request? And how might we afford this domestic arrangement, for I was certain we should be compelled to set up the most modest of establishments on a clerk's salary.

But Mr. Robinson once more reminded us that his uncle's gift of five hundred pounds a year would enable us to live quite well. "Besides, Mrs. Darby, your daughter is too young and inexperienced to be charged with superintending domestic concerns on her own." I sensed his fear that if mother and daughter should be separated, the cub too soon snatched from the bosom of the lioness, that the entire plan might collapse.

Mother agreed with alacrity to the arrangement, and I

readily consented as well, seeing as I had not been eager from the first to join my hands with Mr. Robinson's. Plans for a simple ceremony proceeded apace until not too many days later . . .

"I should like to keep the marriage a secret!" Mr. Robinson was filled with agitation, coming right to the point without preliminaries. He had rushed into our salon during my daily exercise, a constitutional that consisted of walking from one side of the room to the other until I grew well enough to take the air again.

Astonished to the core, I grew lightheaded and felt my stomach plummet, nearly doubling over. I grasped the arm of a chair to prevent my sinking to the floor. This was an odd demand indeed! "But why? Why did you not tell us this from the outset?"

Mr. Robinson's face colored from rose to crimson and back again. "Two reasons," he stammered, and I silently wondered what he had to hide. "The first is that I still have three months to serve before my articles to Misters Vernon and Elderton expire. . . ."

"And the second?" I rang a little silver bell, which since my illness Mother had instructed me to carry in a pocket, in case I should need assistance. I most assuredly required it now.

Mr. Robinson cleared his throat. "There is a young lady—"

"A what?" exclaimed my mother on entering my sickroom.

"You must hear this," I told her anxiously. "Tell my mother, Mr. Robinson, what you just broke to me."

My suitor paled. "Madam, there is a young lady who entertains the hope of forming a matrimonial union with me." Mother's upper lip began to tremble. "Let me hasten to assure you that the attachment is purely on her side—an affection cherished solely on the lady's part. I am particularly averse to such a marriage. But in three months' time, when I shall attain my majority, my independence will be entirely my own, placing me beyond the control of any person whatsoever."

Curiosity gained the advantage of me. "Who is this young lady, pray?"

But Mother would not permit me to press Mr. Robinson further, claiming that my frail condition should not withstand such undue agitation. A gentleman's word was his bond, and that was good enough for her.

"Well, then, let us postpone our nuptials until that happy date when you are free from encumbrances," I proposed. "I am still too weak to present a pretty picture at the altar, and you are right to think me too young and green to shoulder the cares and responsibilities of running a household." My reasons were genuine, but even more to the point, I felt an instinctive repugnance at the thought of anything clandestine, anticipating in my mind a thousand ill consequences that might attend on a concealed marriage. What if I were to become with child and Mr. Robinson disavow the legality of our union, leaving me (and my baby) the victims of society's degradation? Even to travel in company without being man and wife exposed me to the most vicious censure.

Another thought struck me. During this period, my debut on the stage had been put off so many times that Mr. Garrick had become impatient. Now that George was recovered and I was out of danger, he desired my mother to allow him to fix the night. Garrick had not yet been informed that I had been worn down into relinquishing my dream; however, Mr. Robinson's stunning request for secrecy rang a warning bell and set me to reconsider my too-hasty acquiescence. And I saw opportunity lurking. Now I wavered, telling Mr. Robinson, "Well, then, sir, if you expect me to consent to a clandestine marriage, then I see no reason not to pursue my own ambition. Mr. Garrick has placed his faith in my abilities, and not only do I wish to tread the boards, but I must see that my family and I will be provided for in any eventuality."

"Don't be stubborn, Mary," my mother admonished.

"I'm being practical, Mother. Papa no longer supports us. Your income from copying cannot alone sustain our household. I am willing to assume the obligation of breadwinner out of necessity as well as from the duty a child owes to the parent who has raised her."

Naturally, both Mother and Mr. Robinson pressed me to abandon my folly. Thomas would not have his wife nightly subjected to the lascivious leers and the lecherous kisses and gropings of my person in the names of Thalia and Melpomene.

"And," added Mr. Robinson, "imagine if we were to let you have it your way. For the sake of argument, should you indeed assay a life upon the stage and then evince a wish to marry sometime later, name me another man who would permit you to bring your mother along as well."

For three days was I perpetually tormented on the subject. So ridiculed was I for having permitted the banns to be published and only afterward hesitating to fulfill my contract—though I had assented in the height of fever and before Mr. Robinson had surprised us with his wish to keep the union a secret—that worn down with carping and exhaustion, I relented once more. Unscarred and with my looks intact, I had survived the deadly disease; some might have looked upon my luck as a sign from the Almighty to pursue my fondest desire. Instead, with heart and spirit crushed I gave up all plans for the Theatre and was married, as originally planned, on April 12, 1773, more than seven months shy of my sixteenth birthday. In legal parlance, I was still an "infant." Only three months before I became a wife I had played with waxen dolls, and such was my dislike of a matrimonial alliance that the only circumstance that induced me to marry was that of being able to reside with my mother, and to live separated, at least for some time, from my husband. Tom would remain at the Southampton Buildings until the completion of his clerkship for Mr. Vernon.

"I vow I have never before performed the marriage ceremony for so young a bride," remarked Dr. Saunders, the venerable vicar of St. Martin's. To say that the ceremony was without fanfare is to indulge in understatement. The clerk stood in for my father, who had consented in absentia to the match. As a witness, we had Mrs. Wages, the woman who opened up the pews. Even my wedding ensemble was simplicity itself: I was dressed in the habit of a Quaker—a society to which, in early youth, I was particularly partial, for their freethinking ways.

The wedding breakfast, hosted by a female friend of my mother's, was, however, a sumptuous spread, and at that groaning board I greeted our guests in a gown of white muslin, a chip hat adorned with white ribbands, a white sarcenet scarf-cloak, and satin slippers embroidered with silver threads.

After this lively celebration, the three of us set out for

the first stop on what was to be our honeymoon: the inn at the aptly named Maidenhead Bridge. Mr. Robinson and I rode in his high-wheeled phaeton, while Mother followed in a post chaise.

But I knew not the sensation of any sentiment beyond that of esteem. I was not "in love" with Thomas Robinson. Love was still a stranger to my bosom. When I'd knelt before the gilded altar, try as I might to put it behind me, my mind was filled with the unutterable despair of a lost love. I was imagining myself on the stage at Drury Lane even while I was pronouncing my marriage vow and throwing myself into the role of Wife. I had been close enough to taste the full measure of a life of glamour and independence, with the words of Shakespeare on my lips and thousands of admirers at my feet. A natural-born bluestocking, I'd had my nose in enough books, tracts, and treatises to know that by marriage, the very being, or legal existence, of a woman was suspended—women being considered "children of a larger growth." Now, as "Mrs. Robinson" clad in virgin white, not only was I still a child, I was chattel. I didn't know nearly enough to play the part that was now demanded of me.

Act Two

Marriage Vows as False as Dicers' Oaths

Eight

Caught Out

1773 . . . age fifteen

On our return from my ten-day honeymoon, a house in Great Queen Street, Lincoln's Inn Fields, was hired for Mother and me, whilst Mr. Robinson continued to reside at the house of Messrs. Vernon and Elderton in Southampton Buildings.

The honeymoon lovemaking we had enjoyed, if that word could possibly suffice to describe it, had been perfunctory at best, and had left me wondering why anyone would make such a fuss over the carnal act. I surmised that I had experienced so little of what I had supposed was passion because I did not love my husband. Perhaps things would improve with time.

The stated period of concealment of our marriage soon elapsed, and every day became a trial for me. Mr. Robinson and I had separate abodes, but we had shared a bed as man and wife during our honeymoon at Maidenhead. What if I should become pregnant, and all the sacrifices I had made to enjoy a modest and comfortable life turn to satire? Mr. Robinson, perpetually at chambers in Lincoln's

Inn, evinced no haste to remove the subterfuge. I began to suffer headaches as the days wore on, terrified that Mother and I had been sold a false bill of goods that could never by law be returned.

One blustery afternoon, Mr. Cox paid us a call. After handing his hat and cloak to a housemaid, the solicitor met us in the drawing room, his face a picture of concern.

"My investigations have yielded fruit," he began, "but I fear the taste will be bitter."

Mother began to grow agitated even before Mr. Cox unearthed his intelligence. I clasped my hands so tightly that my flesh began to turn even whiter.

"Where to begin," sighed Mr. Cox. "First of all, Thomas Robinson has already attained his majority, and has been of age for some time. However, he has *more* than a few months of his clerkship remaining. I believe he represented to you both that he had but three months left to serve, and told you as much many weeks ago. In truth, with more than a year remaining, he is nowhere near the termination of his clerkship. The third, and grandest, lie I have caught him out in is that Thomas Harris of Tregunter House, Carmarthenshire, is not Mr. Robinson's uncle. Mr. Harris is Mr. Robinson's *father*."

My hand flew to my breast. "A *bastard*," I murmured.

"Precisely, I'm afraid."

"Then who is Mr. Robinson's mother? Is there a Mrs. Harris? Are there legitimate issue from the marriage?"

"I have not been able to ascertain the answer to your first question, Mrs. Darby," said Mr. Cox. "Mr. Harris appears to be unmarried, and there are at least two other children of his—an older brother of Thomas's, also going by the name of Robinson, and presently employed with the East India Company—and a sister, who resides with Mr. Harris."

"If there is an elder brother . . . then how can *our* Mr. Robinson be the sole heir to Mr. Harris's property?" my mother asked. She looked to Mr. Cox for an explanation but he had none at the ready. "It's all my fault," Mother said, her voice atremble, tears bathing her rosy cheeks. "I encouraged the match with every fiber of my being. I was blind to the signs. My poor little Mary." I knelt at Mother's feet and wept into her lap as I had done when I was but a little girl. "Then what are we to do, Sam?" she asked, looking almost as bereft as she had done when George was at death's door with the pox.

"It is regrettable that you cannot back out of the thing," said Mr. Cox.

I raised my head from Mother's lap. "No. We cannot by law obtain an annulment, for we have lain together after the sacrament of marriage. What's done cannot be undone. I vowed to be Mr. Robinson's, and his I am, till death us do part, and I shall have to stand by him. Although," I added, attempting to inject the somber moment with a feeble bit of levity, "I would have much preferred that marrying *for richer or poorer* most distinctly referred to the *former* option."

At the solicitor's suggestion, Mr. Robinson was requested to attend upon us on the following Tuesday evening.

"For the first time, I confess I now repent the influence I used in promoting your union," Mother said to Mr. Robinson. "I apprehend some gross deception on your part, sir. You may be paying for our establishment in Great Queen Street, but that makes my daughter seem little more than a kept woman. She is your legal wife, sir, and I am firm in my resolution that I can no longer consent to this marriage remaining a secret."

Mr. Robinson's natural affability deserted him. He stammered and spluttered, attempting like a worm to wriggle off the piscator's hook by convincing the fisherman that his part in the affair had been misunderstood.

But my mother was inexorable. When she threatened never more to allow him within fifty feet of me unless he settled things once and for all with Mr. Harris, with much trepidation my husband ultimately agreed. Yet though the truth was out, he stubbornly insisted on maintaining the fiction that the wealthy Welshman was his "uncle."

Mr. Robinson set off first—"to pave the way," he said. George would be left in the company of a neighbor; and Mother and I were to take an excursion to the countryside, stop in Bristol to call on old friends, and eventually meet him in Carmarthenshire. Before he departed, my husband gave me a few guineas for expenses, and bade me write, at his behest, to Mr. King, a well-known money broker in Goodman's Fields, asking him for the finances to subsidize our journey.

Thus began a two-month correspondence with this young and ambitious Israelite that at the outset blossomed into a rather fruitful acquaintanceship. Mr. King was a fine-looking gentleman with none of the hallmarks that characterize the appearance of his tribe. His nose was aquiline, not hooked; his complexion more fair than swarthy; and his hair straight and fine, a rich shade of umber rather than a wiry ebony. Moreover, he was an intellect to be reckoned with, more learned than my husband in nearly every subject. Though his métier was distasteful,

King himself was a man of tremendous sensibility; regarding our tastes, both differing and convergent, in matters of poetry and the Theatre in particular, we found much to discourse upon.

Our first meeting in London was so simpatico that not only did the "Jew King," as he was called, agree to loan Mr. Robinson the sum he had requested, but to eventually accompany Mother and me as far as Oxford. The warm cordiality between us increased as our correspondence continued, flourishing into a flirtation that I confess I should not have been sorry to see become something greater, had my fidelity to Mr. Robinson been less resilient.

But when he dared to imagine my "panting snowy breasts" and "all the restless power of my nakedness," he went too far. My naïve and vulnerable admission of love had unleashed this erotic confession; it both embarrassed and unnerved me terribly. And *then* he had the temerity to scold me, warning that what he viewed as my immoderate desire for material well-being might, if left unchecked, lead me to indiscretion and the life of a profligate.

It was the first—yet by no means the last—time in my young life that I found myself in water over my head, too green to comprehend the consequences of my actions and the effects my conduct had upon others, as well as redounding on my own character.

What a difference the allure of lucre has upon one's reception! Fortune is to common minds a never-failing passport. Mother and I returned to Bristol practically as prodigals. News of my nuptials brought out many of my mother's former acquaintances to congratulate us on having made an advantageous match with a young man of such good prospects. I was invited daily to feasts of hospitality. Fat Mrs. Mannering threw a dinner party in our honor. Mrs. Linton hosted a tea. Even frugal Mrs. Abercrombie invited us to a breakfast.

Though it seemed, socially, as if little had changed from the time we dwelled in the city as a happy family, the home wherein we spent those felicitous years was no more. The edifice was cracked and crumbling, and the glass in the nursery windows had been shattered, leaving jagged holes that birds now used for portals. In mourning for more innocent days, I wandered pensively about the churchyard, coming across the grave of William Powell, the first professional actor I had ever seen perform, and shed a tear upon his tombstone. What would this once-proud Lear have thought to learn that little Mary Darby, grown tall and slender, though not much older, had almost become a Cordelia?

While outwardly I rejoiced with Mother's former friends at my good fortune, in truth I was plagued with fears. What if Mr. Harris should reject his illegitimate son, and the open recognition of our marriage never materialize? Where would that leave me? I had indeed agreed to marry Mr. Robinson; no one literally dragged me to the altar, and the union had been duly, if not dully, consummated. I was still not yet sixteen years old, and though there were times when I fancied myself quite the lady—particularly by virtue of being made a matron at so tender an age—I was in many ways still a schoolgirl with much to learn about the ways of the world.

Wishing to recapture the solace I had experienced when, as a child, I would slip inside the minster and crouch under the wings of the enormous brass eagle, I returned to my former hiding place. The minster seemed empty now, my footsteps echoing on the slate. No one saw me settle in, wearing an expression mixed with both mischief and melancholy. Language cannot describe the sensation that coursed through my veins when suddenly the organ rang out, its tones at once sonorous and mellifluous, soothing my troubled soul. Curled up in as small a ball as my adolescent body could manage inside voluminous skirts, knees pressed against my bosom, I clutched my legs and wept.

On his arrival at Tregunter Mr. Robinson dispatched a letter to Bristol, informing me that his *uncle* seemed disposed to act handsomely.

My mother was visibly relieved. "Well, that is good news indeed."

"But it's not quite all. It appears that Mr. Robinson only disclosed to Mr. Harris his *intention* to marry. He hasn't told his father that it's a fait accompli! Listen." I continued to read my husband's letter. "He writes that he was fearful of abruptly declaring the truth of the thing; that he has been for some months a husband. ' "I hope the object of your choice is not too young," says my uncle. "A young wife cannot mend a man's fortune." "She is nearly seventeen," I lied. "I hope she is not handsome," was the second observation. "You say she is not rich; and beauty without money is but a dangerous sort of portion." ' "

My stomach plummeted and I forced myself to read on. "No—no—wait! He has indeed done it after all." I read aloud the news we had been so eager to hear. " 'It was then that I made a clean breast of it and confessed our nuptials, which occasioned his request that I send for you.' "

Mr. Robinson came to fetch me some days later.

"Perhaps it might be better if you remained in Bristol, whilst I journey on to Wales," I suggested to Mother. "If I am to prove my maturity as Mrs. Robinson, I should not present such a wifely aspect with my mama in tow!"

She reluctantly assented; and wishing me luck, my mother bade me an anxious farewell. There were tears in her large gray eyes.

"I'll see you as soon as I can," I assured her, my trepidation mirroring hers. Pressing her to my breast, I whispered, "Pray for me."

Nine

Tregunter

1773 . . . and nearly sixteen

M y husband and I crossed the Severn to Chepstow in an open boat. The distance, though not extended, was extremely perilous, for we found the tide so strong and the night so boisterous that we were apprehensive of much danger along the way. Had it not been real, the dark and hazardous journey would have seemed a scene from one of the popular gothic novels. The rain poured and the November wind blew tempestuously. Even in oilskins, we were not adequately protected from the elements and I feared catching a chill so soon after my recovery from the pox. My trepidation was all the greater for Mr. Robinson's frequent exhortations during the voyage that I be prepared to overlook his "uncle's" incivilities and any harshness in the man's manner.

Yet, it was one of Mr. Harris's coaches that transported us overland, across the rugged landscape of the Black Mountains to the fecund Wye Valley pastures. We passed through a thick wood, eventually reaching the parkland of Thomas Harris's Tregunter estate just as the sun began its slow descent behind a mountain resembling nothing so much as a sugar loaf. I should have been content forever to gaze upon the lofty peaks covered with thin clouds, and rising in sublime altitude above the valley. A more romantic space of scenery never met the human eye.

The view from the terrace, under construction in front of the grand house, was unparalleled for its grandeur. I imagined what it might be when the trees were in full bloom, or in the pride of early autumn when the foliage would be resplendently russet, vermilion, and gold. The air, now and again pierced with the cozy aroma of burning wood, smelled sweet and fresh and the quietude did much to settle my nerves. During our journey I had endeavored to keep up my spirits, but my mind was preoccupied with the thought that I should not be accepted by Mr. Harris and my marriage permitted to indefinitely remain a dirty little secret.

A salubrious breeze caught a bird on the wing; in her struggle to freely follow her own course of flight, I saw my own plight. Mr. Robinson stood behind me, his hand resting upon my shoulder as I stood beneath the portico admiring the mountain. "It's quite the thing, isn't it?" he remarked. I nodded in agreement, and he stretched forth his arm like Moses leading the Israelites across the desert. "Just about all of it—from here to there—belongs to my uncle."

I had given great thought to my ensemble so that my first meeting with Mr. Robinson's family should show me not to appear to be a fortune hunter—if that was what they feared—but rather to present the image of a stylish young lady who already possessed an income. I arrived in a claret-colored riding habit with a white beaver hat trimmed with feathers, which showed off my auburn hair and blue-green eyes to perfection.

But before I met the master, I was greeted, if such is the word, by Mr. Robinson's younger sister Elizabeth and their sour-faced housekeeper, Mary Edwards. The latter had such a run of the place that I surmised her familiarity with its rooms extended well beyond the kitchens and the parlors. Had her brother presented the most abject being to her, Miss Robinson could not have taken my hand with a more frigid demeanor.

"Come, miss," commanded this low and clumsy woman, barely glancing in my direction. Obediently I followed the gaudy-colored chintz gown, the pretentious twenty-year-old head attired in its thrice-bordered cap with its profusion of ribbons. We entered the drawing room, where the master was seated, pipe in hand, with a dozing mastiff by his side.

"Why, deuce take all, she's damned lovely, Tom!" exclaimed Mr. Harris, nearly tripping over the immobile bulk of his hound as he rose to greet me, and kissing me on both cheeks with excessive cordiality. Sizing me up in an instant, he declared, "By gad, I should have liked you for *my* wife, had you not married Tom!" As Mr. Harris's age was somewhere between sixty and seventy, I masked my shudder with a smile and cordially thanked him for so liberal an encomium.

I had made a conquest of the most unlikely of souls. Determined to remain in his excellent graces for the sake of my husband's inheritance—and realizing that this deportment was in fact required of me—I donned the mask of cheerful satisfaction and played the role of the fascinated and fascinating young miss for all it was worth.

But the scowling housekeeper, "Mrs. Molly" they called her, and Tom's sister, Miss Betsy—with her squat figure, snub nose, and a complexion too ruddy to be the product of country air alone—made it clear at every turn that a poor lawyer's wife had no business having airs about her.

"Might I avail myself of your father's harpsichord?" I asked Miss Betsy.

She laughed, exposing her little yellow teeth. "What use have we for a harpsichord?" Betsy scoffed. "The devil finds work for idle hands."

"And you consider music one of his chief methods of employment, then?" I replied. Miss Betsy sniffed imperiously. "Ah. Then will you kindly direct me to Mr. Harris's library so I may borrow a few books to read during my visit?"

This query was met with a guffaw from my rosy-cheeked hostess. "Would you prefer the Bible or the Almanack? We're good Methodists here. A library! Who needs a library?"

Clearly there was not to be any amity between us. Miss Betsy had deemed me an enemy on sight and treated me as such until the day I departed.

Though the companionship of Mr. Robinson's coarse "uncle" was scarcely tolerable as well, it was the sunshine after a rain compared to the society of the other principals of his household. As the days passed I was condemned either to drink ale with him and make the best of it or else ride out to the Methodistical seminary on his estate.

Yet the acquaintance had its perquisites from time to time. Mr. Harris was in the process of making improvements to his house and many embellishments for the establishment were submitted to my taste and choice. There he was, one drafty morning, giving orders for the marble chimneypieces. He greeted me with a violent embrace, crushing my frame within a suffocating cloud of civet and tobacco smoke.

"Choose them as you like, my dear, as they are all for you and Tom when I am no more!"

I thanked him profusely between sneezes.

He frequently assured me, while I was at Tregunter, that the estate should be my husband's; and I do believe Mr. Robinson was impatiently, if quietly, counting the hours until the gentleman met his maker.

Whilst I had become the object of the squire's attentions, Miss Betsy and Mrs. Molly observed me with jealous eyes. It was abundantly evident that they considered me an interloper whose manners attracted Mr. Harris's esteem and who was likely to diminish their divided influence in the family. I found them daily growing weary of my society, perceived by their sighs and sidelong glances when I was complimented by the visiting neighbors on my looks or my taste in the choice of my dresses. Envy at length assumed the form of insolence. The women perpetually taunted me on the folly of appearing like a woman of fortune, with a fondness for fine clothes and leisurely pursuits, such as music and reading.

For three weeks I endured these constant jibes with patience. Knowing that Mr. Harris was still disposed to think favorably of me, at last I thought it most prudent to depart Tregunter, lest through the machinations of Miss Betsy and Mrs. Molly I should lose the share I had gained in his affections. Yet imagine my surprise when the squire insisted that he should meet my mother! Quite like the worthy gentleman, he saw me safely returned to Bristol, accompanying me back across the Channel, and riding with Tom and me all the way.

My gentle mother received him with her customary grace and cordiality. Now that she was alert to Mr. Robinson's penchant for dissembling and untruths, his "uncle" had scarce been in Bristol for a day when she called my attention to a most intriguing detail.

Mr. Robinson and Mr. Harris had quit my mother's apartment to avail themselves of a morning stroll. Mother had suggested that they might like to view the hustle and bustle of the wharves, and Mr. Harris, a ship fancier, had responded with alacrity.

Mother drew me into her boudoir and sat beside me on her divan. What she told me was nothing short of startling.

She called my attention to the fact that the squire's physiognomy, in addition to its more than passing ruddiness, owing to the great amount of time he spent out of doors, was somewhat marred and pitted: proof positive that he had survived the pox. Mother posed a question concerning the mendacious Mr. Robinson: Had my husband been exposed to, and escaped unscathed by, the disease before he'd even met our family?

Once I set my mind to solving the riddle, it took me no more than a few moments to figure it out, and my conclusion was exceeding unpleasant. We had been duped again, the victims of another of Mr. Robinson's deceits. "No wonder he was so attentive during my illness—and George's," I exclaimed. "In playing the martyr, he played us for fools! I'll wager—"

"Don't speak like a gambler, Mary dear; it's vulgar."

I jumped up from the divan and began to pace. "But

don't you see? 'Tis certain then, he was variolated when his *father* was suffering from the malady. The inoculation would have given Tom but a mild case of the pox, and therefore, he couldn't catch it again."

Mother was unable to hide her look of dismay. It pained her that I continued to be the subject of a husband's deception, a fate she knew too well. "But now that father and son are reconciled regarding your marriage and Mr. Harris is truly well disposed toward Mr. Robinson, let us pray the young man has learnt to mend his ways and has put an end to his falsehoods."

As it appeared to be a certainty that I should one day be châtelaine to Tregunter House and its vast estate, the boisterous and vulgar Mr. Harris was introduced to Mother's respectable friends and partook with us of many dinner parties and dances. I was his idol. He would dance with me, stand by my shoulder and sing with me whilst I played upon the harpsichord—in short, I was to him the most delightful of beings. My husband was now thoroughly convinced that in his pretty, clever wife's abilities to charm his "uncle" he had made a good match indeed, no doubt counting the months until a grieving Mrs. Molly presented him with the iron keys to Tregunter. Silently, I counted my single blessing over and over again: owing to his consultation of my advice in every little improvement, and his myriad attentions to me, the squire had most certainly made us believe that our position was assured and an affluent and prosperous future was just on the horizon.

Ten

Making an Entrance

1774 . . . age sixteen

After passing many days at Bristol, Mr. Harris returned to Wales and my husband and I set out for London. Mr. Robinson's mind was easy, and his hopes were confirmed by the kindness of his uncle. Our marriage was no longer a secret and he now considered himself the happiest of mortals. On the heels of Mr. Harris's hearty welcome, we had earnestly set about our duty to beget the next generation of heirs to Tregunter.

Back in London, we moved into a new residence at number thirteen Hatton Garden, furnishing our marital abode with liveried servants and peculiar elegance, sparing no expense. In addition to our domestic establishment, Mr. Robinson had purchased a handsome—and spanking new—phaeton, with saddle horses for his own use.

"Where is all the money coming from?" I marveled, as highboys and candelabra, a Kirkman harpsichord (to replace the one we'd had to sell when I was a child), Turkey carpets, and mahogany bedsteads were installed.

"Fear not, Mrs. R.!" exclaimed my husband. Pecking

me on the cheek, and pressing my hands into his, he assured me that his finances were in every respect competent to his expenses.

Thus situated and provided for, I now made my debut in the broad hemisphere of fashionable folly. As for my husband, after all his years of study, all thoughts of becoming a lawyer evanesced in favor of something far less prosaic: that of cutting a dash in society. And if Mr. Robinson was determined to become one of the grand young bucks, then I, too—as my theatrical career had been rudely aborted—might recast myself in a role of my own making: the society belle. If I was not to shine on the stage, I would use my talents to glitter off of it. It then became my intent to assiduously observe the influential female members of the bon ton as if I were to play *them* at Drury Lane. As a sixteen-year-old bored wife with few responsibilities, dress, parties, and adulation occupied all my hours. I contrived my appearance to gain the attention of Those Who Mattered.

A pretty new face was sure to attract attention at places of public entertainment, and it was here that Mr. Robinson and I began what we laughingly called our conquest of polite society—too green to realize that polite society more often than not shunned the venues in which we sought to triumph. Though I'd been married for several months, I had yet to "fall in love with" Mr. Robinson. Such sentiments remained foreign to me. I found him deficient in matters of the intellect, but his affability and generosity, and his desire for music and gaiety, made him an entertaining companion at parties, dances, and public spectacles. At least I had not been married off to a doddering codger who never wished to leave the fireside, except to attend his club.

The first time we paid our half crown apiece to enter Ranelagh Gardens, my habit was so singularly plain and Quaker-like that all eyes were fixed upon me. I had spent hours to create the artifice of a study in simplicity. The gown of light brown lustring was finished with round white cuffs, though ruffles were all the fashion; and I left my auburn hair unpowdered, adorned only with a plain round cap and a white chip hat. When I strolled through the Chinese temple and along the gravel walks or enjoyed the singers in the glorious candlelit rotunda, I turned every head, for I looked nothing like my compatriots. We were social fishermen casting our nets, my husband and I; and that very night we supped well.

Having scored a triumph on our maiden voyage, Mr. Robinson determined that our next public airing be a concert at the Pantheon. This was London's most spectacular of pleasure palaces, then the most fashionable assemblage of the gay and the distinguished. I never shall forget my first impression when, goggle-eyed, I entered the Pantheon rotunda. A thrill went through my body; I felt as though the music and the illuminations were just for me, the colored lamps ensconced in the niches and dome shining not on the statuary but on my gown of pale pink satin trimmed in sable—enhanced by a present from my dear mother: a suit of rich and valuable point lace. At the Pantheon it was the fashion to wear court dress—enormous hoops and high feather headdresses. I'd spent nearly the entire day in preparation. My figure at that period required some arrangement, owing to the visible increase of my domestic solicitudes, for I was now expecting; and it took hours for the friseur to dress my hair in the high style required of these lavish soirees.

"Will you have the nightingale or the caravel, madame?" he asked, as he teased my tresses over the wire cage that would support my voluminous coiffure.

"Ouch! Must you pull so hard? I'm getting a headache."

"I am fixing madame's coiffure in the most fashionable style. What is a little pinch and tug to become absoluement à la mode?"

Suffering for vanity's sake, I endured the pain of having my long hair yanked skyward, against Nature's plan, and permitted the friseur to affix the caravel to the summit, where it bobbled over my pomaded and powdered locks a full three feet above my scalp, the way I imagined my father's ship bounced upon the waves to America.

Having made a study of the numerous daily papers and broadsheets, a devotee of the *on-dits* and caricatures, I recognized at once, as we took a turn about the Pantheon rotunda, at least one marchioness, a countess, and other titled ladies peering at me from their quizzing glasses and turning to their neighbors to whisper behind their fans, "Who is she?"

Just a few weeks previous, I was lithe and not very bosomy, with the body of a coltish girl. Now four months pregnant, my figure resembled the beau ideal of the day, voluptuous and pulchritudinous.

With some glee, I realized that the buzz was about me, and was then delighted to notice, out of the corner of my eye, that I was being observed by two men of the most fashionable ilk. "I think I know her," a third murmured. He went on to remark that he was certain I was his father's godchild.

"Miss Darby, I believe. Lord Northington, at your

disposal, madam," he said, introducing himself with a bow of marked civility.

"Heavens!" I stifled a gasp as I dropped a curtsy to his lordship. "I am sorry for your loss, sir." Turning to his companions, I added, "The late Lord Northington was indeed my godfather, though I was presented to him by my father on but a few occasions." I smiled at the son. "He always made me a gift of a pretty ribband for my hair." I added that my name was now changed to that of Robinson, and to prevent any awkward embarrassment, presented my husband, on whose arm I was still leaning.

Mr. Robinson received his lordship's felicitations on our nuptials, and then excused himself to fetch a glass of punch—whereupon Lord Northington made swift work of my unprotected state to make his two confederates known to me. They asked leave to pay their respects to the newlyweds, a boon I was only too pleased to grant, as I was eager to enter society as quickly as possible. The following day, both Captain Ayscough and his cousin Lord Lyttelton—the gent from the previous eve with the misbuttoned waistcoat and unkempt appearance—paid a call at Hatton Garden, where I endeavored to entertain them, though my husband was not at home. From that day on, Lyttelton was a frequent visitor.

Had I known that night at the Pantheon what I was soon to discover about Lord L., I should not have been so quick to open my house to him. Too late I learnt that for a woman to be seen in his company was to compromise her reputation, for people suspected only one thing. How naïve I had been! At the pleasure gardens, words of warning were whispered in my ear by well-meaning acquaintances, but I had hastily dismissed these cautions, assuming they were born of envious motives. Yet even my maidservant seemed to be aware that he was known as the "wicked Lord Lyttelton," a notorious libertine. He was twenty-nine years old to my sixteen, and only the previous year—1773—according to Caroline, my abigail, he had left his wife of but a few months and absconded to Paris with a barmaid. "It was in all the papers!" she said. "Not only that—he'd a mistress, too, at the time!" Caroline told me. "A Missus Dawson he was keeping over in St. James."

The fabulously wealthy—and equally unappealing—Lord Lyttelton simultaneously courted the friendship of both myself and my husband, who insisted that I continue to admit him to our home, despite my abhorrence of the man. His lordship's manners were overbearingly insolent, his language licentious, and his person untidy even to a degree that it was disgusting. Had he no valet? Though Mr. Robinson was deficient in his own ways, he was at least in every respect the reverse of his new companion: unassuming, neat, and delicate in his conversation. Yet my husband was too much pleased with the society of a man whose wit was only equaled by his profligacy, to shrink from such an ambitious association.

One might wonder, as did I at first, how a man whose appearance is slovenly and manners are impertinent has even the remotest chance of succeeding as a seducer, let alone become one of the masters of the art. Lord Lyttelton's approach was singular, the Trojan Horse of Lotharios, for the very things that put one off about his person were those qualities that eventually gained him access to the boudoir.

Clever the man whose true prey is the young wife, for

this sharper, while keeping company with Mr. Robinson night and day, took pains to ascertain my own pleasures. Upon learning that I dedicated my leisure hours to writing poetry, but a few days into our acquaintanceship he presented me with a rare volume, also penned by a woman.

Recalling too well that Mr. Robinson had used much the same stratagem in weakening my mother's resolve to forfeit her daughter to him, plying her with copies of sermons and her beloved graveyard literature, I asked Lord Lyttelton if his design was not to seduce *me*, rather than befriend my husband?

"Heavens, no," he drawled, feigning indifference. "What would I want with you? Your figure is tolerable to be sure, your face a picture of the buds in May . . . but no woman under thirty years is worth admiring. I'faith, even the antiquity of forty is preferable to the insipidity of sixteen." I glanced at him darkly. "Tut, tut, I hope I have not made the pretty child angry."

Had Lord Lyttelton himself not been a talented amateur in the field of poetry, I should not have been able to abide him at all.

I knew that he frequently led my easy-tempered husband from the paths of domestic confidence to the haunts of profligate debasement. Many were the nights that Mr. Robinson returned to Hatton Garden reeking of brandy, vomit, and those bodily effluents nocturnally exchanged twixt man and maid.

His intercourse with Lord Lyttelton produced a very considerable change in Mr. Robinson's domestic deportment. Every hour he seemed to sink more deeply in the gulf of dissipation. At length, I confronted my wayward husband. "You are not the man I married," I said sorrowfully, endeavoring to keep the scold out of my voice. "You are constantly together with his lordship, whilst I am left at home with nothing but quill and parchment to entertain me. Is the society of a clever, pretty wife so repugnant to you that you prefer to spend your evenings with gamblers and whores?"

I thought he might strike me. "I am doing this for *us,* Mary," he insisted, dismissing out of hand the neglect with which I charged him. He had become not only careless of his wife and unborn tot, but of his pecuniary finances, whilst I—"the child," as Lyttelton called me—was kept in total ignorance as to the resources that supported his increasing expenses.

The licentious activities of my languorous, and increasingly laconic, husband did not yield enough red meat for the gossipmongers who provided fodder for the morning papers, so the editors found fresh blood in traducing *me* for our new association! At least once a week did I read an anonymous *on-dit* that referenced myself and Lord Lyttelton. Speculation over whether a notorious rake had added to his list of conquests the latest pretty newcomer to the social scene was too delicious to ignore.

One rumor might have amused me, had I not given a fig for my character: The *Morning Post* reported that his lordship and I had made violent love numerous times during one rather jouncing carriage journey while Mr. Robinson rode alone on horseback, a distant postilion some half mile behind the exuberantly prolific fornicators. One who had any interest in the truth of the thing might have asked themselves how any gentleman, even a libertine as practiced as Lord L., could gain access with his prick to that most perfect treasure—in the confines of a coach—with so many yards of fabric and underpinnings, including my crinoline cage, impeding the attainment of his goal. But of course, no one was concerned with verisimilitude, least of all the morning papers. It made a good story.

Lord L. did, however—though it had never been his design—make an excellent foil on which I could perfect the age's all-important art of flirting. Clearly, I had much to learn about this particular social skill if I was to take the ton by storm.

Truth be told, my newlywed life was at times quite exhilarating, if not entirely Edenic . . . until the day Lord Lyttelton revealed himself to be none other than the serpent in number thirteen Hatton Garden.

Eleven

Two Startling Confrontations

1774 . . . age sixteen

"*L*ord Lyttelton, ma'am."

"Thank you, Maude." My maidservant dropped a curtsy and went about her business, closing the door to the pale green paneled drawing room.

I remained seated whilst I received his lordship. "My husband is out," I told him.

My daily caller appeared in much distress. "I am aware of that, madam. In fact, that is the nature of my business. I have a secret to communicate to you, Mrs. Robinson, that I believe is of considerable moment both to your interest and your happiness."

I started at this news. "Nothing I trust has befallen my husband," I said, with a voice scarcely articulate.

Lord Lyttelton hesitated. The room was so quiet that I could hear the mantel clock as the seconds loudly ticked by, each one an eternity, while I waited for him to come to the purpose. "How little does that husband deserve the solicitude of such a wife!" he at last exclaimed. "I fear that I have in some degree aided in alienating his conjugal affections. But I could not bear to see such youth, such merit, so sacrificed—"

"Speak briefly, my lord." My nerves were aflutter.

He paced the rose-patterned carpet for several moments, and stationing himself at the mantel, outstretched his silk-clad arm along the marble and declared, "I must inform you that your husband is the most false and undeserving of that name."

"Are *you* not to blame, sir, for introducing him to the bawdy houses?"

His lordship's tone softened. Lowering his voice as if to speak more confidentially, he told me, "Mr. Robinson has formed a connexion." I raised an eyebrow, endeavoring to maintain my composure. "With a woman of abandoned character. He lavishes on her those means of subsistence which you will shortly stand in need of."

Though I suspected my husband's betrayal, I keenly felt the importance of preserving my own dignity as well as the sanctity of my home and hearth. "I don't believe it."

"Then you shall be convinced," answered his lordship. "But remember, if you betray me—your true and zealous friend—as the means by which you obtained this intelligence, I shall be forced to fight your husband, for he never will forgive my having discovered his infidelity."

"It cannot be true. You have been misinformed. And dueling is illegal, sir."

"There are many things that are illegal; it does not mean that they aren't done. And if I am misinformed, it is by the selfsame woman who usurps your place in the affections of your husband."

"Who is she, then?"

His lordship availed himself of a pinch of snuff. "Her name is Harriet Wilmot," he said, turning his head to sneeze. "She resides in Soho. Number four Prince's Street. Your husband daily visits her."

"As you do me."

"You continue to disbelieve me?"

A dreadful silence hung in the air and suddenly, as if a floodgate had been thrown open, a torrent of tears descended down my cheeks.

"If you are a woman of spirit, you will be revenged!" said Lord L., his voice a threatening rumble that hinted at dire consequences. I shrunk with horror and would have quitted the room had he not held out his hand to stop me. "Hear me, madam." His countenance became quite earnest. "You cannot be a stranger to my motives for cultivating your husband's friendship. Mrs. Robinson, fair creature, my fortune is at your disposal—"

Should I become the poorest wretch in Christendom, I would never stoop to become his mistress. "Despicable man!" I flung the words in his face.

But he thought I was speaking of my husband and continued to press his advantage. "Mr. Robinson is ruined; his debts are considerable and nothing but destruction awaits you. Leave him! Command my powers to serve you!"

I would hear no more. "My maid shall see you to your carriage, sir!" Shaking, seething with hurt and rage, and nearly blinded by my tears I fled the house, leaving a stunned Lord Lyttelton alone in my drawing room. At the end of the street I spied an empty hackney coach, flagged it down, and flung open the door. "Prince's Street, please!"

The coach lurched and clattered through the rutted streets. How would I summon the courage to confront my rival? And what would I say? My world had turned upside down in a matter of minutes. I knew from the haunts he had frequented in Lord Lyttelton's company that Mr. Robinson had not been faithful to me, but there had been no names, no faces. I had willed myself to see those trans-gressions against me and our marital vows as something somehow surreal, because they did not exist to me in flesh and bone, in garters and petticoats, with painted faces and perfumed limbs. But this was different. I had not in-structed the hack driver to race hell-for-leather to a bawdy house but to a home my husband paid for, the home of a woman who shared his bed as often as I did.

I felt as insignificant as a fruit fly. Had my swollen belly repulsed him? Or had Mr. Robinson been born with a pair of roving eyes? If his mention of a one-sided entanglement had been a falsehood, perhaps he had been keeping Mrs. Wilmot since we met, when with fervent oaths over my sickbed he promised to see me well provided as his wife. I'd had neither dowry nor position—nothing to tempt a young clerk to matrimony. What had he wanted of me other than to torment me?

I rapped on the roof. "Pull over!" When the driver reached the curb, I opened the door to vomit into the street. I wiped my mouth with a handkerchief scented with rosewater and tossed it into the gutter when I was done. Then I shut the door and told the driver to move on.

In Prince's Street I gave him a guinea to knock at the door of number four whilst I remained inside the carriage. A dirty-looking servant girl answered his summons.

"Does Harriet Wilmot live 'ere?" the driver asked her.

"My mistress is not at 'ome, sir."

I quitted the coach and paid the driver.

"You will show me in," I insisted in a tone that brooked no denial. A raging fire consumed me, but if I had any shred of dignity or pride, I could not permit myself to reveal my weakness, certainly not to a serving wench. She would not see my tears.

"Follow me, miss." The girl led me into the front parlor and motioned for me to sit in a slipper chair. I began to tremble and choked back a sob. The chair was covered in red toile de jouy, the identical fabric our upholsterer had used to fashion my bed curtains.

"Wait here, please. My mistress will be back shortly." The servant closed the door behind her. I was left alone. Left to look about the flat and see where my husband of less than half a year was spending his money. I had begged for chinoiserie paper on my own drawing room walls and Mr. Robinson had denied me, citing its exorbitant cost, yet Mrs. Wilmot had a fashionable pattern of bisque-and-blue-hued bamboo. The mantel had been faced with marble. I rose and began to touch things. Although there was dust on the festoons, the mustard-colored drapes were a good grade of silk.

I opened the door that led from the drawing room into the next chamber. "Ah!" I could not stifle my shock when I spied a fine petticoat and a new sacque gown of fine white lustring lying upon the bed. A loud knocking at the street door caused me to nearly jump out of my skin. I tiptoed back into the parlor and waited with a palpitating bosom until the being whose triumph had awakened both my pride and my resentment appeared before me.

Her manner was timid and confused. "Do I know you, miss?"

She caught me off guard. I had prepared myself to meet a young flibbertigibbet, a painted creature as hard as she was silly. Instead, my eyes met a handsome woman with a pleasing countenance, some ten years older than I. A million things flashed across my mind within a single moment: Was her dress of printed Irish stuff more costly than my morning dishabille of India muslin? Her black gauze cloak finer than my white lawn one? At least mine was trimmed in lace. Did her chip hat trimmed with lavender ribbands better become her than my straw bonnet did me? Was this woman the entanglement Mr. Robinson avowed he would be rid of once he came of age, and a chief reason for our marriage to remain clandestine? That, too, had been a lie. I was up to my elbows in them.

I motioned for her to sit. She looked distressed, her lips pale as ashes, their color drained. "You are Harriet Wilmot?" She nodded. "I came to inquire whether you are acquainted with a Mr. Robinson."

"I am," she replied. "He visits me frequently." Mrs. Wilmot drew off her glove as she spoke and passed her hand over her eyes as though she was suffering from a headache. I nearly started when I observed upon her finger the ring that I had given to my husband for his birthday. It took every ounce of bravery I had to retain my composure and my dignity.

"I have nothing more to say," added I, "but to request that you favor me with Mr. Robinson's address. I have something that I wish to convey to him."

My rival had seen me notice the ring. Her gaze shifted to my dress, my undeniably swollen belly. "You are Mr. Robinson's wife," she said, her voice trembling. "I am sure you are, and probably this ring was yours; pray receive it—"

"No." I looked away and made to take my leave of her. I had not expected kindness.

"Had I known that Mr. Robinson was the husband of such a woman—madam, I will never see him more—unworthy man. I give you my word on it—I will never again receive him!"

I know not which of us was more pitiable then, and somehow . . . I cannot say why, but I believed her. Something in her manner . . . she had been tenderhearted and had relinquished all claims to my husband so immediately and with such earnestness that I found I could not hurl insults or abuse at her. If I had said another word I should have burst into tears and most likely found myself sobbing on Mrs. Wilmot's bosom, and so I gave her but a cursory nod and descended into the street.

On my return to Hatton Garden I found Mr. Robinson awaiting dinner. I masked my chagrin, biding my time. We even made a party to Drury Lane that evening, and from thence we planned to attend a concert at the home of Count de Belgioso in Portman Square. Lord Lyttelton was to join us in both places. Throughout the play he watched me with barely concealed curiosity. But my agitation produced such a headache that I insisted on being driven home as soon as the curtain was rung down on the afterpiece and was obliged to send a letter of apology to the imperial ambassador.

A few lavender drops eased my anxiety enough to let me sleep, and the following morning at breakfast I asked my husband, "Do you know of a person named Harriet Wilmot?"

Unblushing, he replied that he did, and did not deny that he had visited her frequently. "But you must not reproach me for these indiscretions, my dear." He made to take my hands, but I pulled away.

"My God, who then deserves the blame?"

"Who else? Lord Lyttelton!"

"You must think me a fool. I have no great affection for his lordship—quite the reverse—but you cannot expect me to fault an unscrupulous shepherd when the sheep strays."

Mr. Robinson grew defensive. "Who told you about Mrs. Wilmot?"

"That's none of your affair." It fascinated me that he had such a high opinion of his associate that he did not even suspect him of treachery.

My lot was no different from that of many other wives bound lovelessly to philandering men. Yet now my trust in Mr. Robinson was irrevocably shattered. And now that I had firm proof of what sort of life he led outside our home, I wondered about so many other things—chief among them how he came by all his money. I resolved henceforth to take a keener interest in his activities. My own hearth, and my future happiness—not to mention the welfare of our unborn babe—were at stake.

It was at Vauxhall one evening that I could no longer restrain my curiosity—and my tongue. I had been craving a visit there not merely for the gay entertainments, but— since I had become enceinte—for the celebrated Vauxhall ham. Sliced so thin, the meat's iridescent translucence was, for me, part of the venue's magic, and in my condition I could never seem to eat enough of it.

I wore a new gown of pale blue satin with slippers to match, only one of a number of recent expenditures. Perhaps it was my pregnancy that rendered me far less patient and my emotions far more unpredictable, for the words just tumbled out of my mouth. "Where are the funds coming from?" I asked Mr. Robinson, drawing him closer as we strolled through the rotunda in search of a place to sit. "Is Mr. Harris financing our lifestyle?" There was no reply.

I pressed on. "Why is our house filled with Jews nearly every morning?"

"In my profession I am obliged to be civil to all ranks of people."

"But you have not returned to Vernon and Elderton since we were wed. How are you paying for all of this?"

"Do you want for anything, my dear?"

"But for the lack of love and respect, I do not."

"Your condition makes you most trying, Mary. Not to mention irrational."

"My vexation is not born of my condition, I assure you. But I do fear what may befall us when the child comes into this world. To my knowledge you have no income beyond the salary of a clerk, and I am not even certain you continue to draw it. Yet we live like the Duke of Bedford!" Biting my lip, I added, "I fear we so outlive our means that perhaps it might be for the best if we were . . . to retrench." I was met with another stony silence. How I wished to have benefited from my mother's hard experience in the selfsame matters, but she had returned to Bristol, leaving me to stand on my own two feet as a married lady. "Good heavens, all I ask is an explanation!"

"Egad, woman, quit being so meddlesome. It is none of your affair. Before God I vowed to provide for you, and I am doing my duty by Him and by you." This utterance was punctuated by the sharp inhalation of a pinch of snuff. "I beg of you not to plague me with questions. Enjoy your gowns and your footstools and your perfumes and don't quiz me like a fishwife."

"A fishwife? I was merely—"

"Ah, the newlyweds." Lord Lyttelton bowed, and it would have been rude of me not to have returned the courtesy of a curtsy. His manner, so arch, so unctuous, made my skin pebble with revulsion. "Mr. Robinson, may I have the loan of your pretty wife for a moment or two?" I had no say in the matter, and reluctantly permitted his lordship to escort me along one of the illuminated allées.

"You look unhappy, child."

"Pray don't call me 'child.' "

"My apologies." Lord Lyttelton brought my fingers to his lips. After he released my hand, I wiped it on my skirt when he wasn't looking.

"Mr. Robinson greatly insulted me when I had the temerity to inquire as to the provenance of his funds. He spends money like water, I am quite sure that his 'uncle' is not the benefactor he was advertised to be, and my parlor is almost as much frequented by Mr. King and his bearded friends as though it were their synagogue." I had been avoiding the Jew King ever since our correspondence had so unpleasantly concluded.

"It was not ladylike of you to make such a request of your husband. The child wants schooling."

"If you continue to sneer at me, I will not walk with you, nor ever receive you again."

"Then you will never discover the depth of your husband's difficulties. He is in debt to his eyeballs, a situation which is not ameliorated by the expenses of Mrs. Wilmot's rooms in Prince's Street."

"With tears in her eyes, she vowed to me that she would no more entertain him!" Suddenly I felt terribly dizzy, as though the earth had been yanked out from under my feet. "I—I must go!"

Lord Lyttelton caught my arm before I had traveled two footsteps. "Mr. Robinson has taken me into his confidence. Previous to your union, he was deeply involved in a bond debt of considerable magnitude. He has continued to borrow money on annuity—one sum to discharge another—taking from Peter to pay Paul, one might say." He waited for my reaction but I refused to favor him with the depths of my dismay on hearing my deepest fears confirmed. "Will you not hear my entreaties, Mrs. Robinson? Your husband can do nothing but drag you down with him. I am entirely at your disposal. If you would only—"

"I beg of you, let me go." Fighting back tears, I wrenched my arm from his grasp and raced as quickly as I could toward the light. But I nearly stumbled when a bit of golden gravel bounced into my shoe. Balancing precariously on one foot, I removed my slipper and shook it free of the offending stone, dropping it on the pathway among its gilded brethren.

Rage blinded me. My ears filled with a rush of sound. The melody that turned all of Vauxhall into a vast symphonic wonderland became a cacophony of shouts and shrieks. All that only moments earlier had been beauty to me was now discord. I wished to go home. I began to search for my most blameworthy husband, head down, charging like a bull through the twinkling allées toward the pavilion.

My eyes were blurred by hot tears, but I was too angry to take the time to stop and blot them before they made ugly trickles down my face. The telltale lines marring my maquillage like so many rivers on a map would confess my sorry state.

Ouch! I stubbed my toe and fell forward, my body pitching into a rather formidable obstacle.

"And where might ye be runnin' off to?"

Oh, dear. My near fall had been broken by none other than the man known as Fighting Fitzgerald, a notoriously charming Irish libertine and duelist. Which of these talents was the more lethal was a matter of opinion.

I counted George Robert Fitzgerald among the most dangerous of my husband's associates, not because I feared his impact upon my husband's character, but because I was affrighted of my own when I was in his presence. Can a snake be compassionate and understanding? The person of Fitzgerald, so handsome with his tawny coloring, his hazel eyes so solicitous of a lady's anguish—particularly my own—answered this question upon our every encounter. Whether at the theatre, opera, or pleasure gardens, his conduct was always impeccable, his attire *comme il faut* without calling attention to itself, and his manner one that consistently encouraged me to favor him as a confidant. It was a seductive trap I endeavored to avoid at all costs.

"Ah, now I perceive the cause of your distress." He nodded in the direction of Lord Lyttelton. "Yet I hear that you and he are quite *intime*."

"Believe me, sir, his lordship is the last man on earth I could be persuaded to fall for."

"I am glad to hear it. Though I call the man my friend, I know he has had a pernicious influence upon your husband. Were I Mr. Robinson, I should kneel on the cold floor every morning and thank God for such a charming and intelligent helpmeet. Come now, you're trembling. What has the brute done to upset you so?"

Fitzgerald's manner was so solicitous, his voice so soothing and gentle, that against all reason I felt comforted by him. Weeping, I confessed the gist of my conversation with his lordship, the extent of my husband's financial encumbrances, and my despair over his betrayal of our vows, as well as the steep pitch of our descent into an uncertain, and degrading, future.

"Poor lady," said he, proffering his arm, "to be merely on the brink of womanhood, and bound forever to a man incapable of estimating your value—one as far beneath you as a Covent Garden flower seller is to the Prince of Wales. I do not envy the destiny that has befallen you. And in your condition, too," said he, glancing at my belly.

Offering me his monogrammed handkerchief of fine Irish linen, he insisted I dry my tears before escorting me into the rotunda for a cool drink.

"It's late—I should be getting home. I should find my husband . . . and return to Hatton Garden."

"I should not think, as Robinson does, to sully myself with the companionship of others," added Fitzgerald, his countenance open and earnest, his lilting cadences gentle and sweet.

Under the bright illumination of the high-ceilinged pavilion, Fitzgerald played my *cavaliere servente*. After seeing me comfortably seated near the statue of Handel, he returned with a glass of punch and a plate piled high with ham.

"What you require is a champion," he confided, taking the chair beside me. "Ah, he sees us."

Moments later, we were joined in the box by my husband. I was in no mood to affect a smiling countenance, but managed to don a mask of complacency in its stead. Neither Fitzgerald nor I gave any indication of the intimate nature of the conversation we had just shared. But Fitzgerald, in his own silky way, did caution Mr. Robinson against leaving such a charming woman unprotected whilst he made his own way about the gardens. "People's talk can be even more dangerous than what may actually transpire, sir."

Before Mr. Robinson could consider mounting his defense, a great commotion in the vicinity of the orchestra caused many to rise from their seats to observe the hubbub. Easing myself to my feet, I spied two gentlemen with their fists in the air quarreling furiously by the podium. Fitzgerald and my husband ran out of the box toward the stage and I made to follow, but lost them amid the throng. Thinking the only way for us to be reunited was for me to return to our table, I did so, and had not been seated for more than a minute when Fitzgerald reappeared.

"Oh! Mr. Robinson has gone to seek you at the entrance door. He thought you quitted the box." After I explained the situation, he concluded, "Let me conduct you to the door, my dear; we shall certainly find him there. I know that he will be uneasy for your safety, as the fisticuffs may soon become something far worse."

As I clutched Fitzgerald's arm, we pressed our way toward the entry on the Vauxhall Road, but Mr. Robinson was nowhere to be seen. "I'll look for our carriage," I suggested, and eventually, much puzzled, spied it amid the line of waiting coaches some distance away. Suddenly, both distressed and bewildered, I realized that something was amiss.

"Don't be uneasy," soothed Fitzgerald, making to hurry

me along, "we shall certainly find him, for I left him here not five minutes ago." As he spoke, he stopped abruptly in front of one of the chaises. A servant promptly opened the door. There were four horses harnessed to the carriage, leading me to ascertain that a journey of some length was planned; and by the light of the lamps along the footpath I perceived a pistol peeking out from the pocket of the open door. As the servant maintained a discreet distance, Fitzgerald protectively placed one arm about my waist, the other beneath my elbow, and endeavored to lift me up the step and into the chaise.

"What are you doing?" I cried out, much alarmed. "What means all of this?"

His hand trembling as much as did his voice, Fitzgerald at last confessed himself my most ardent and devoted admirer. "Robinson can fight me for you," he said in a low voice that struck terror into my heart.

"Are you mad?" I shouted. With much difficulty I wrested my arm free of his grasp and, my heart pounding a furious tattoo, ran hell-for-leather back toward the pleasure gardens' entrance, the gravel flying as it crunched beneath my footsteps.

We both now perceived my husband coming toward us, his face the picture of confusion. "Why, here he is," exclaimed Fitzgerald with such easy nonchalance, as though all along he had been my gallant protector instead of a would-be abductor. "Egad, we had found the wrong carriage, Mr. Robinson. All this while, we have been looking after you! You can see that Mrs. Robinson is alarmed beyond expression."

"Oh, I am indeed alarmed!" I retorted, thinking I should like to spit upon him and ruin his green silk waistcoat.

We stepped into the proper coach, Fitzgerald following. In fleeing Lord Lyttelton for the sympathies of Mr. Fitzgerald, I had leapt out of the leaking boat into the lake, and silently cursed myself for having permitted my attraction to the latter to render my character so vulnerable. I'd have been ruined utterly if Fitzgerald's scheme had succeeded.

"It was indeed providential that you happened along when you did," I told my husband. "But five moments of hesitation, and we should both have been at the center of a crim-con trial."

Mr. Robinson assured me with oath upon oath that he'd no inkling of Fitzgerald's sinister motives, and I felt compelled to believe him—for though his own conduct was reproachable, I did not think him so low to wish me cast out of the society we strived so hard to join.

Along the road to Hatton Garden the night sky, though cloudless, flashed with lightning. I took it as a portent from the Almighty to shun the Irishman's future society. Though I had myself to blame in part, it did not lessen the humiliation to which a husband's influence had dangerously exposed me.

Twelve

Flight!

1774 . . . age sixteen

At length I persuaded Mr. Robinson to remove his head from the sand and confront the truth of our situation. "With great success you talked me out of a means of independent income, Tom. Our fortunes rise or fall as one. If you will not think of me, or even of yourself, consider the life I carry within me and our responsibility to her—or his—welfare."

This argument won me the retrenching I had suggested. My young husband at length concluded that Hatton Garden was too costly to maintain and moved us to the home of a friend of his on Finchley Common. This was a greater sacrifice for me than for Tom, for his business took him daily into London, whilst I languished alone, far from the city.

Though horribly lonely at first, I soon grew acclimated to the solitude. I endeavored to use my time wisely, reading and composing poetry; and as I was near my confinement, I devoted many hours to making my infant's little wardrobe, the sweetly pleasing task of stitching dozens of tiny muslin dresses converted from the fabric of my own frocks and trimming them with the finest lace.

My mother had returned from Bristol and was again living with us, so I had the consolation of her society. Her soothing pragmatism solaced my mind against my misfortunes. If the sale of much of our property and the *déménage* to Finchley Common was the worst that had befallen me, I could count myself a lucky woman. Little did I know, or could have imagined, the dark perspective that destiny had in store for me.

As Mother was back within the domestic picture, my brother George, still shy of adolescence, now lived with us as well, often accompanying my husband on his errands into the city, riding on a pony. After one such visit, he came back to Finchley Common quite agitated, running into the parlor where I was sewing, and drawing me by both hands toward the dish cupboard, exclaiming, "I must tell you a secret!"

"However do you expect me to fit in here, with my belly and petticoats?"

"It is no laughing matter, Mary," said George, his face so pale and grave. "It is about Mr. Robinson."

I took my brother into my dressing room and locked the door behind us. "Whatever has he done that has you so excited?"

"Your watch—the enameled one with the musical instruments on it and the long silver chain—I saw it today!" George said breathlessly.

"Where?" I had given it up for lost among many other possessions during our removal from Hatton Garden.

"We went to the house of a lady today . . . and Mr. Robinson asked me to wait outside whilst he went in

to speak with her and told me not to tell anyone why I
was there or who I was with—today or any other day I
accompany him—or he should never permit me to join
him in future . . . but I got thirsty and had grown tired
of waiting so long, so I went looking for him. And there
he was with the lady, and your watch was hanging on
the wall."

The bastard. "Was the lady dark-haired?"

"No, fair. And not near as pretty as you."

Not even Harriet Wilmot, then. Someone else. How
many someone elses were there? And even a boy who was
not yet twelve had drawn the inevitable unfavorable conclusions. I considered asking George what other items,
once mine, he might have spied, but bit my tongue. My
brother was an innocent, and not to be dragged into my
matrimonial contretemps.

Later that day, when I confronted Mr. Robinson upon
his return to Finchley Common with the news regarding
the stunning reappearance of my treasured timepiece, he
did not even attempt to deny his infidelity.

"I won't be seeing her again. I can promise you that."

I was startled by his response. Was it possible that my
victory could have been won so easily? Then again, after I
had visited Mrs. Wilmot in Prince's Street he had promised to see no more of her—or the other way around—yet
Lord Lyttelton had informed me at Vauxhall that the connexion had not in fact been severed.

I was, however, immediately disabused of the rosy
notion that my husband had performed an astonishing
volte-face, agreeing to cast off his latest conquest simply
because I had caught him out once again.

"We must depart for Tregunter as soon as practicable,"

he said. "I fear for our safety here, and our personal liberty is much endangered if we remain."

In the one breath I deciphered that his—our—creditors would soon be on our heels with brickbats, and in the next I concluded that if we did not decamp immediately, our next home would be a debtors' prison!

"What have you done?" I sobbed. "We are ruined!"

"Not if we can make our escape. Bid your mother and brother farewell and have Dulcy and Joseph pack your things."

"What will happen to them?"

"It is none of my concern, now. We must look to our-selves and leave the servants to fend on their own. You can't imagine that we could possibly afford to bring them with us?"

"I—I—I don't know what to think anymore."

"You don't want our child to be born in a cell, do you?"

"No, nor a stable neither," I muttered. Our babe was due in a little more than a month. "Must I leave my mother?" My agony at the thought of parting from her was extreme. We had resided in Finchley Common for less than a quarter of a year. Now we were to take to the road whilst Mother and George would be compelled to return once more to Bristol. I fancied that if we should part company now, I should never behold her more, and that the harshness and humiliating taunts of my husband's kin would send me prematurely to the grave, perhaps tak-ing the innocent life within me as well—and if not, that the infant should be left among strangers, and my poor grieving mother would scarcely have the fortitude suffi-cient to survive me. Placing my hands upon my belly for emphasis, I added, "Now, more than ever, is when I most stand in need of my mother's attention."

"But it is impossible for the moment," said Mr. Robinson, his voice rising to a panic for the first time since the ugly subject of flight had been broached. "I suggest you begin packing, Mary."

Mr. Robinson had borrowed liberally, mortgaging his hopes on the plan that Tregunter and all its wealth would one day be his, but his creditors had proved inexorable. With a thousand tears and tender regrets I said good-bye to my relations. Though she was disconsolate, Mother understood too well that where the husband journeyed, as long as he wish'd her by his side so went his wife, no matter the road he traveled.

Mr. Harris was away from home when we arrived at Tregunter in mid-September.

"Well, well, the prodigals have returned," said Mrs. Molly.

"With their tails between their pretty legs," sneered the snub nosed Miss Betsy in rejoinder. She could hardly have been less pleased to see her brother.

The housekeeper regarded me insolently. "I suppose you'll be wanting us to be at your beck and call. This ain't the City, you know. And you're not the first woman to be in the family way. You'll have to rely on your own maidservant to do your fetching and carrying; we've got more pressing duties, ma'am." She extended a muscled arm toward the interior rooms of the manor, from whence emanated a clattering of hammers.

"I was compelled to dismiss my maidservant, Mrs. Edwards," I mumbled, already feeling browbeaten. I knew this interview was not to be a pleasant one, but the benign musings of my imagination were not equal to the cold reality. It was time to consign myself to the fact that my child would be delivered among hateful monsters. Ironically, the rude treatment we received upon our arrival from the distaff members of clan Harris had a way of shaking loose whatever tender sensibilities I bore my husband. He had used me ill, there was no doubt of it, but being ill-used himself by his own relations softened my compassion for the man.

On Mr. Harris's arrival a few days later, his greeting could scarce have been considered a welcome. "Well!" he exclaimed, tossing his muddy spatterdashes into a corner of the parlor. "So you have escaped from a prison and now you are come here to do penance for your follies?"

Silence. We had indeed been one step ahead of my husband's creditors. There was no excuse, nor explanation, for our predicament other than the truth: we had exceeded our means.

"Well!? And what do you want?"

I glanced at Mr. Robinson, but he was too cowed in the presence of his irate "uncle" to provide a reply. I had been the favored one on our previous visit to Tregunter. And my condition merited compassion. "We want shelter from the storm, as it were, sir," I said quietly.

"What business have beggars to marry?" retorted Mr. Harris in disgust. Looking his son squarely in the eye, he added, "I should never have given you my blessing. How long do you think I will support you throwing my money to the winds like a couple of unruly, overindulged children who don't know the value of a day's hard work?"

My husband shrank into himself as his father's words

clouted him about the ear. We took our lumps, unpleasant as they were, for they were not entirely undeserved.
But the following morning, after an anxious night's sleep,
due to the stresses of travel, our mean reception, and the
baby within my belly no less active than a prancing pony,
I found myself subjected to renewed torment.

"Mr. Harris has instructed me to inform you that we
will be unable to accommodate your lying-in," said Mrs.
Molly, her grin a triumphant rictus. "You arrived at a
most inopportune time, as the house is undergoing reno-
vations. I am certain that, what with the clamor and the
dust, you would prefer to avail yourself of a more conge-
nial atmosphere."

She spoke with the words of a diplomat, but her errand
had been to banish us from Tregunter to another property
on the Harris estate. A carriage arrived soon after breakfast
to take us along the two-mile journey to Trevecca House,
which contained the most modest of living quarters, in
addition to a flannel manufactory. "Well, at least our baby
will have plenty of swaddling," I joked, hoping to lighten
my husband's spirits, but he would not be coaxed out of
his moroseness. His father's conduct had convinced him
that there should never be a reconciliation between them
and that all hope of ever inheriting Tregunter had vanished
on the chill wind that had blown us across the Severn.

Though it had been intended as a punishment, our
removal to Trevecca House was, to me, a blessing. There
I did not have to endure the perpetual slings and arrows
aimed to wound by Mr. Harris's distaff ménage. Left to
my own devices, I roamed freely—though slowly in my
advanced condition—amid the long violet shadows of
Sugar Loaf Mountain, inhaling the crisp autumn air and

reveling in the heaven-sent vistas of russet and orange and gold, brought about by the changing seasons. I would take my constitutionals while the grass was still spangled with the dew of morning, my soul soaring as my mind remained exceeding tranquil amid all the sublime glories of God's creation. My sallies became a respite from the realization that I had formed a union with a family who had neither sentiment nor sensibility, both of which I had felt acutely since earliest childhood. In this soulful aspect I favored my mother, though we were most decidedly not of one mind on many things.

I had been enjoying my solitary strolls for two weeks, when one afternoon as I crested a gentle hill from which I often reposed, gazing at Nature's bounteous scenery, I found myself suddenly deluged with water.

"Help me!" My voice echoed through the valley. "Mother!" I knew my mother was back home in Bristol with George, but she was the first and only one I thought to shout for. "Mama!" The reverberation mocked me. How would I get home in my drenched state, doubled over, and fearful that the baby would drop out of my womb as an overripe apple plops from its lofty branch?

I trudged across the valley to Trevecca House, my fluids filling my boots, and collapsed on the flagstone steps. The next I knew it was night, and I was lying upon my bed, propped up on my side against a linen-covered bolster. Candles flickered about me, casting ghoulish shadows on the concerned faces of what seemed a bevy of onlookers. Beside the bed a basin and a pair of forceps glinted ominously.

"Must the servants see me thus?" I demanded, both weary and afraid. The doctor shooed them from the room as I yowled in pain.

"Push, my child!" He exhorted me to push as though my life depended upon it. I knew the life within me did so. I screamed for laudanum, but the physician, whose large hands frightened me, refused to grant my wish.

"We need you conscious, mum; the little one won't come out on his own, otherwise," he insisted. I felt as though I was trying to shit out a melon, though from the other orifice. I hollered for Thomas and even louder for my mother, cursing them who had conspired to bring me to this pain, first dashing my hopes of a theatrical career and then rending my body in two in the birthing of a child.

Daylight had long waned, the room becoming tomblike, illumined only by the flicker of lamps, when Maria Elizabeth Robinson—her middle name an homage to the elder sister I had never known—beheld her first glimpse of humankind through encrusted eyes and was too briefly laid against my breast before being handed off like a fragrant parcel to the wet nurse, a clean, Christian woman named Mrs. Jones. The date was October 18, 1774—I was just five weeks and two days shy of my own seventeenth birthday. What had, hours earlier, been naught but a reason to rage and curse suddenly became my only consolation in a world of precariousness and uncertainty.

Something had overtaken me during that most perilous event; a new and tender interest awoke within my breast. My child! My Maria! I cannot describe the sensations in my soul at the moment when I pressed the little darling to my bosom—my maternal bosom. When I kissed her hands, each of her tiny pink fingers, her damasked cheeks as soft as rose petals, her sweet-smelling brow—when I nestled her to my heart, this tiny miracle claimed that affection which has never faltered since.

"Is she not the most beautiful of infants?" I murmured. "Oh, look—her first smile!" It was the most celestial thing I had ever beheld.

Truly, Mrs. Jones agreed with me, for not two days after Maria was born the wet nurse was eager to gratify the wishes of the manufactory workers by presenting to them "the little heiress of Tregunter," as they had been calling her.

"But it's October," I protested, noting the autumnal nip in the air.

"Pshaw," tutted the wet nurse dismissively. "In these parts, Mrs. Robinson, it's no surprise to see infants carried into the open air on the very day they open their eyes on the world. 'Sides which, you don't want to go a-disappointin' all them honest, hardworking factory folks as been waiting to catch a glimpse at their new little mistress. You don't want to be committing the sin of pride, which is what they'll all be thinking if you refuse to take little Maria Elizabeth for a visit."

The birthing had left me feeble and exhausted. As I was not yet able to be up and about, Mrs. Jones brought my sweet delight down to the factory. Maria's absence seemed an age. But when the nurse reported how fondly my tiny girl was doted upon by the flannel workers, and the effusive praise that was sprinkled like holy water upon her tiny blond head, my heart was filled to bursting with the fondest gratification and delight.

I was not to enjoy my euphoria, however. Amid these warm and never-to-be-forgotten sensations, Mr. Harris and Miss Betsy entered my chamber, unannounced.

"Well, what do you mean to do with the child?" demanded Mr. Harris of the precious bundle in my arms.

Stunned to the quick, I made no answer. How coarse of him to speak so brusquely, and of intimate family matters, in the presence of Mrs. Jones, whom he scarce knew, and who was nearly a stranger to me as well!

"I will tell you," added he. "Tie it to your back and work for it."

Did he truly expect me, a gentlewoman, to become a laborer? I shivered with horror. But the man's greater insult was to my daughter. "It? *It?* We are talking about a girl. Not an it. A sensate human being, not a bundle of turnips!"

"Prison doors are open," my father-in-law continued crudely. "Tom will die in jail, and what is to become of you?"

"*I* know what will become of her," tittered Miss Betsy. Shaking her head with mocking dolefulness, she glanced at tiny Maria Elizabeth, her tiny dimpled hands curled up to her mouth, the placid features of her innocent sleeping face, and added, "Poor little wretch! It would be a mercy if it pleased God to take it."

I summoned every dram of energy within me. "Out!" I cried, intending a shriek that I fear carried no more weight than a whisper.

I saw them no more during my recuperation. The very sound of their footsteps would have been enough to curdle my milk.

Three weeks hence, Mr. Robinson came to me wringing his hands. "We must leave Trevecca House at once. My creditors are on our trail!"

The amiable Mrs. Jones cautioned against my undertaking such an arduous journey—and where were we to go?—in my debilitated state. "Could you not begin the trip in another week or so, at the very least?"

But I argued that my husband's liberty was in danger, and with it my own, that my place was with him. "My own life is of little consequence to me now," I told the nurse.

"But what good will it do the poor mite to be mother-less?" averred the pragmatic Mrs. Jones.

Yet I would not be dissuaded from my purpose, even though it meant leaving the good Mrs. Jones in Wales, as she was a widow with two small daughters of her own in Brecon. I would nurse Maria myself, though such devotions would undoubtedly scandalize our gently bred family and friends. But I saw no alternative. We were in no position to engage another wet nurse. Still, I feared for my own maternal abilities. Would I have them? Would I know what to do? As a girl, I had been schooled in the masculine mode; I had learnt but little of the domestic occupations.

"Nature will tell your body what your heart already knows," said the nurse, as we parted from one another tearfully and with great regret. "You will be a splendid and devoted—and quite capable—mother."

With the reassuring words of Mrs. Jones a tonic to my nervous ears, just a step ahead of his creditors, Mr. Robinson, Maria Elizabeth, and I set off for Monmouth, to visit my mother's kin. There we were received with genuine affection and the kindest hospitality—such a welcome change from the harsh treatment we had met with at the hands of the Harris clan.

I wept with joy to see my grandmother, still looking as my memory had fixed her, always attired in brown or black silk, her countenance mild and pleasant, her manner ever gracious. And how she beamed at the presentation of her great-grandchild!

"You must take regular airings," Grandam insisted. "You'll lose your health entirely if you remain a shut-in. Remember how you always used to love to wander about the ruins of the castle?" She pointed to the crumbling battlements just beyond her garden wall. Her pale blue eyes sparkled with amusement. "They're still there, you know."

What a balm it was to be treated with respect, to be greeted like a proper gentlewoman with smiles and words of kindness.

I passed many happy hours with my infant in Grandam's paneled library, reveling in her finely bound collections of poetry and philosophical essays. I breakfasted on fresh eggs and porridge in her print room, which, though the lavish wall coverings were now somewhat faded, had once been the height of fashion. And I strolled with little Maria Elizabeth in my grandmother's garden where, come springtime, a riot of color would confirm God's presence in Nature's hand.

We had been residing in Grandam's well-appointed home at Monmouth for about a month when Mr. Robinson and I were invited to a ball. By this time my spirits and strength had been greatly rejuvenated by the change of scenery and I felt I was up to the exertions of a dance floor. But as I had undertaken to feed little Maria Elizabeth myself, how would I make it through the evening without giving my daughter her nourishment?

"You tread the measures like a sylph," one partner commented, and I blushed at the compliment that made me give myself over even more to the music. Thus it was that heated and flushed I took Maria from the arms of a young miss who had expressed a wish to cradle and dandle her as I danced, and brought her into an antechamber where I could give the babe the only succor she had ever yet taken. If anyone had chanced to come upon us, they would sure have been appalled by the spectacle of a gentlewoman breast-feeding her own babe, a notion that paled in comparison to little Maria's presence at a ball.

How could I know of the dangers inherent in such an activity? My body had been agitated by the violence of exercise, and the stifling heat in the crush of the ballroom had not ameliorated matters. On the carriage ride home, Maria became convulsed.

I panicked. "What do I do? Stop the coach! No—don't stop—drive on—faster. We must make it home post-haste!" My state was frantic to the point of not being able to stimulate any milk, even when Maria's little mouth was parched for the refreshment. All the night I sat up with her, awaiting the arrival of a medical man. I felt so foolish, embarrassed that I had brought my daughter to this danger, and all because I did not know of the perils of dancing whilst I was a nurse.

"If the Lord takes her, I pray He takes me too," I wept. All through the night the convulsions continued with little abatement. A clergyman arrived and counseled the infant's removal, but I resisted all attempts to displace her from my lap.

At long last, the doctor presented himself, and after examining Maria and observing the nature of the convulsions, assayed a recipe that had benefited one of his grandchildren. He mixed a tablespoon of spirit of aniseed with a small quantity of spermaceti and gave it to the poor mite to swallow. She took it with the saddest and most awful face I have ever seen, but in a few minutes' time the spasms abated, and in less than an hour the brave little one lapsed into a sweet and tranquil slumber.

"The anise is beneficial in cases where expectoration is difficult," the doctor explained. And though his remedy availed, he could not determine the precise cause of Maria's convulsions, suggesting only that they were due to a bout of infantile catarrh.

To this day I blame myself for undertaking such festive exertions at the time, and thank God that Maria recovered fully from this prodigiously frightening episode.

Two days later, with the sun scarcely risen, there was a brusque knock at our door. "Sheriff! Open up in the name of the law!"

Clutching Maria Elizabeth to my bosom, I looked to Tom for guidance, but Mr. Robinson, his face ashen, was trembling with an even greater ferocity than was I. "What is to be done now?" I asked him fearfully.

With no choice but compliance, we admitted the sheriff's man, who carried with him an execution for a considerable amount. With all hope vanished of ever again being well received at Tregunter, Mr. Robinson's expectations for obtaining the vast sums he owed to his dunners were nonexistent.

Like the *deus ex machina* in a Greek tragedy, Grandam entered the room, having had her toilette discommoded by the ruckus. "Why, Mr. Wainwright," she said charmingly, "whatever brings you calling at this early hour?"

The sheriff's man stated his business, and to our utter astonishment Grandam invited him to sit down and enjoy a cup of tea and a plate of caraway biscuits.

"Dear heavens, I have known your employer for eons!" she exclaimed as she poured the tea. "I'm certain the sheriff would appreciate the embarrassment attendant on taking my granddaughter's husband into custody in a town where our family is so well known and our connexions so extensive."

Within minutes my elegant and doting grandam had convinced Mr. Wainwright that it would be better for all concerned if the sheriff were to grant us an escort who might accompany us down to London, where the matter might be resolved more anonymously.

Arriving there, we took up modest lodgings in Berners Street, but every moment of freedom managed to increase our fears, for the sword of Damocles still dangled above our heads.

A four-handled oblong basket of osier with a pillow and a small bolster was Maria's bed by day. Placed near my chair and writing desk, she enjoyed the sleep of the innocent, her gurgled, soft cooing the sweet accompaniment to my poetic compositions. My table was spread with papers, and everything around me presented the mixed confusion of a writer's study and a nursery. From the time Mrs. Jones had quit our presence back in Abergavenny, I had made it an invariable rule always to be the one to dress and undress my infant, and never to suffer her to be placed in a cradle or to be fed outside my presence. At night my daughter slept with me, for I had too often heard of the neglect that servants show to young children; and I had resolved never to let an infant of mine fall victim to their ignorance or inattention.

"I am becoming like you," I wrote to my mother,

much amused. "I despair of my daughter's ever quitting my sight!"

She was concerned that as I was making a return to London society I should fall under censure for my maternal devotions. "None of the middle classes feed their own," she reminded me. "I should hate to see you an object of mirth, or worse, derision. But you will make your own way, I daresay, and there's no use my suggesting otherwise to you. You are indeed very like myself."

I thought of my mother's refusal to board me at the Miss Mores' and how it affected her marriage, as she was unwilling to either uproot us from a proper Bristol education or accompany my father to the Americas without us. Yet I was certain that I might have it both ways: my life was bound up in my husband's, my fate and future his—but I would sacrifice neither maternal affection nor my child's schooling to follow his drummer.

So when Mr. Robinson was arrested for debts amounting to twelve hundred pounds—chiefly the arrears of annuities and other demands from his Hebrew creditors—and spent three weeks in the custody of a sheriff's officer, I refused to separate our little family for a single hour.

And on the third of May in 1775, when Mr. Robinson was remanded to the Fleet, thrust into the confines of a debtors' prison, for the love I bore my daughter and the duty I had to my husband, I gave myself no choice: I, too, was obliged to submit to the perils and the privations of an extended captivity.

Thirteen

The Fleet!

1775 . . . age seventeen

I had now been married just upwards of two years; and though love was not the basis of my fidelity, honor and a refined sense of rectitude attached me to the interest as well as to the person of my husband. For the astronomical sum of one shilling threepence a week, we obtained a gloomy two-room apartment on the building's third floor, with the rare perquisite of a fireplace, and an even rarer window. Removed by the altitude of thirty feet from the fetid stench of the moated area surrounding the jail, our quarters overlooked a racquet ground, the courtyard being a popular venue for the inmates' physical exercise. Whilst Mr. Robinson partook of such athletic amusements I consoled myself in our dreary habitation—where the walls bled with a rusty ooze every time it rained—in the company of my beloved daughter and in readying a collection of my poems in the hopes of finding a publisher who might print and distribute them.

For a change of scene, I would pick my way down the dark and narrow stairways, holding my skirts that they might not touch the treads or the dirt-encrusted walls. Belowstairs were the prisoners' amenities, such as they were. I once visited the taproom, but alcoholism was so rampant in the Fleet that I could not bear to be amid such a vulgar, leering, often violent, lot. I endeavored to keep the Sabbath on Sundays in the tiny chapel, and on occasion would enjoy a pot of cocoa and the morning newspapers in the prison's coffeehouse, where I listened to the local gossip. Still, in the main, I seldom quitted the apartment, and never till the evening, when I walked on the racquet ground with Mr. Robinson and envied the freedom of the stars.

After a period of several days had elapsed, having gleaned some intelligence from the warden, who would dispense with his knowledge for coin, I told my husband: "I understand that the inmates are permitted to obtain some form of employment during their incarceration."

"Why should I?" he inquired lazily, puffing upon a clay pipe, a newly acquired habit of his.

"The sooner to discharge your debts," I replied, endeavoring not to sound as exasperated as I felt. How could he be content with his lot, lolling about in a squalid, nearly airless room, with no liberty in sight unless he obtained the means to be released from his obligations? An incarcerated debtor was like a dog chasing his own tail, an endeavor that would always prove fruitless. By the very dint of imprisonment he had no means, yet was compelled to find a way to afford his food and lodging, plus a garnish, or remuneration for his jailer. While imprisoned, he was expected to earn enough in addition to settle the debts that led him there, and thus obtain his freedom.

Still weak from the exigencies of childbirth, I had willingly agreed to accompany Tom to prison, to cast my lot in with his, but it had never been my intention to *languish* there. So I took the reins in hand and procured for Mr. Robinson a copyist's employment. And then I feared turning shrew as he refused to lift a quill, jeopardizing the deadlines for which the work was due, and for giving so little care to the welfare of his family.

"Right, then, I'll do it!" I declared, and volunteered to undertake the copying work myself. "We need the money, Tom." My eyes welled with tears. "We'll never have enough to pay off our creditors otherwise." He hadn't even had the money for the doorkeeper's garnish; he'd had to provide his overcoat as surety instead. "And we have to keep up the payments for our food and lodging in here as well." As it was, my back was near to breaking from the other employment I had taken on—that of a charwoman at the prison, scrubbing and mopping for hours on end—and still I could not rid the walls, floors, and staircases of years of stench and filth.

Had I not undertaken this drudgery, we could not have afforded to lay our fire that winter, and we all might have frozen to death. The months of January and February, 1776, were fierce, and unusually inclement. Howling winds whipped across the racquet court, blowing the unceasing snowfalls into prodigious drifts. It was far too dangerous to venture out of doors. The streets grew strangely quiet, for the carriages that were able to function moved noiselessly through the city, so deep and thickly bedded was the snow beneath their wheels. And the clip-clop of horses' hooves was muffled entirely.

Yet I could never have anticipated that the least of the tribulations of incarceration would be the imprisonment itself! Whilst we were ensconced in the jail I received numerous messages and letters from those bon vivants of my pre-Fleet acquaintance: Lords Northington and Lyttelton, and Mr. Fitzgerald among them. Excepting the notes from Northington, the other missives were written in the language of unctuous gallantry, with honeyed words of love expressing a dismayed heartsickness at my predicament, adding if only—if only—I could see the reason in committing myself to their protection, I would soon see the last of my unpleasant and humiliating situation.

Though I burned their letters, giving no thought at all to violating my marriage vows, these gay blades could not begin to know just how unpleasant and humiliating my life had become! Mr. Robinson had fallen in with a bad lot, who condoned, even enabled, his participation in all of the licentious and lascivious behavior he had previously enjoyed outside the dank and rancid walls of debtors' prison. And it became my lot to share the unhappy tales of his vile comportment with a most unlikely pair of ears.

Georgiana, the newly minted Duchess of Devonshire, now mistress of the spectacular Chatsworth, was the same age as I. On hearing of this vivacious young patroness's penchant for literature, my sweet brother George, now apprenticed to a London merchant, demanded a copy of the volume of poems I had been preparing.

I clapped my hand to my bosom in amusement. "What makes you think she will admit you to Devonshire House?" I asked him.

"Because I'm charming!" He grinned. "Charming and clean. And I ask for nothing on my own behalf. All I wish to do is make a gift to her. And," he added, with all the swaggering confidence of a youth of fourteen years, "I don't think she's half so inaccessible as people make her out to be, even if she is the most popular and fashionable girl in London." George pressed his point. "Take a chance! What have you to lose?"

"Very little, indeed—though I'm no gambler," I agreed. "Apart from my enduring a lifetime of mortification should she refuse you, or worse, detest the contents of this little parcel." In an effort to mitigate what might have been an unkind reception—or, more likely, a blow to my own vanity as to the little volume's artistic value—I penned a brief note to the duchess, apologizing for the verses' defects and pleading my age (or the lack of it) as the only excuse for their inadequacy.

All that day, I was filled with agitation, wondering how such an illustrious personage would receive one such as I, let alone praise the humble efforts of my busy pen. I scrubbed the prison floors with an added vigor to relieve my mind from anxiety. I paced my tiny quarters until my slippers were scuffed, and gazed out our narrow window at the courtyard below, my only connection with the world outside, as if the duchess's reaction to my poetry would be borne to me on a breeze.

At length the jailer rapped upon my door. "Your brother to see you, ma'am." He held out a grubby fist for a guerdon. "And in 'igh spirits 'e is, too!"

"Good news! Oh, the most wonderful of news!" My young brother bounded into the room like a stag. "Her Grace wishes to see you! Tomorrow!" He wrinkled his nose at the sour odor that pervaded our room. "Someone needs her linen changed."

I glanced at Maria's basket. "No, the rooms always smell this way, I fear. But tell me"—I grabbed his hands—"what did she say? How did she look? Did she read my poems?"

George recounted their meeting in chapter and verse. Her Grace had been most amiable and gracious indeed; and, as my brother had accurately predicted, she had also been quite taken with his exuberance. She had paged through the slender volume, her eyes lighting on one or two of the poems, which she read to herself as her lips mouthed the words.

"As if to taste them," George told me. "And then she inquired after the particulars of the situation of the young woman—nay, not more than a slip of a girl, she said—who had written the stanzas." George lowered his eyes, his long light lashes nearly brushing his cheekbones. "I confessed all, I'm afraid." Her Grace had been most especially impressed, as his errand showed the extent of a brother's love for a sister in dire straits. "It was then she pressed my hands in hers and with the sweetest expression, told me, 'She must come to call upon me tomorrow. I will not admit any refusal.' "

My brother's eyes shone with admiration—yet whether they were for me or for the fair duchess, I could not say.

I ran to Maria's basket and picked her up in my arms. "She'll see me! She'll see me!" I crowed, dancing about the room with her and planting kisses on every feature of her little face.

That evening as I strolled about the perimeter of the racquet court, eyes tilted skyward watching the clouds scud across the moon as if on some urgent errand to the other side of the atmosphere, I fretted about what I should wear on the morrow. The sartorially minded Mr. Robinson was of no use as a sounding board, for as usual he was nowhere about. During my seclusion from the world I had adapted my dress to my situation, a form of "costuming" I would continue throughout my life, both onstage and off. Neatness was at all times my pride, but now plainness was the conformity to necessity; simple habiliments illustrated my adversity. Thus, the brown satin gown I wore on my first visit to the Duchess of Devonshire was as strange to me at the time as a birthday court-suit would be to a newly married citizen's daughter.

As Maria and I were not responsible for Mr. Robinson's debts, we were free to leave the Fleet at any time; but it had been my choice to keep our little family together and reside with my husband in debtors' prison. Despite the degradation, I was shielded from the temptations of the city as well as from any malicious slanders attendant on my unprotected state. Whither went my husband, however unpleasant, I felt duty-bound to follow, remaining a stainless wife and mother.

Perhaps that's why this excursion to the duchess was doubly sweet, for it was my first foray outside the prison walls since Tom's incarceration.

The heavy door thudded shut behind me as I stepped into the street. Every gray uneven cobblestone was suddenly a thing of beauty to me!

Oh, to taste the air beyond the Fleet! Now and again I could make out a patch of blue muscling its way through the miasma, and I wished to be able to kiss it. Someone's kite soared high into the sky, its tail a knotted strand dressed with bows as colorful and gay as butterflies. As I picked my way along the ruts of Piccadilly on my way to

Devonshire House, the trees in the Green Park had never seemed more verdant.

I found the wooden gate within the stone wall that George had mentioned to me, and curtsied to the sentry. "I am Mrs. Robinson, poetess," I said proudly, mustering as much dignity as I feared my state would allow me. "Her Grace expects me."

The guard bowed politely and the gate swung open. Before me was a splendidly imposing stone edifice. Behind which of the windows—there must have been a dozen on each of the three stories—sat the young duchess? I wondered what she did with her days. Did she sit at her needlework frame, or compose letters? Did she draw, or practice dancing? I traversed the wide courtyard to the main entrance, where another man, liveried and periwigged, stood stiffly at attention. I stifled a giggle, for with his chest so puffed out he resembled a grand guinea fowl all trussed up for a gentlewoman's supper.

I reiterated my errand and the popinjay of a servant let me enter. My pen cannot adequately do justice to the opulence that greeted my astounded eyes. The gilt, the frescoes, the statuary, the damasks!

But this majesty and splendor was nothing to the mistress of the manor. I had been shown into the back drawing room, into which I might have trebled the largest of chambers I have ever dwelt in. Here I had not remained long, when the most lovely of women entered the room, her cheeks rosy with the effects of nature displayed by the gentle swelling of her belly. She was carrying my little book of poems, and stopped a few feet from me as if to draw my picture.

"Mrs. Robinson," said the duchess with the warmest

effusiveness. "Let me see if the image matches the verses!" She studied both my figure and my countenance, and sighing, said, "Ah, yes, I can see it; the sadness as well as the sweetness." A tear of gentle sympathy formed in the corner of her bright blue eye. "And so young! Too young to have encountered so many of fortune's vicissitudes. A destiny too little proportioned to what I am pleased to term your desert," she added, as she gestured with my volume toward a gilt sofa. "Fate has not seen fit to reward your merits, madam."

She then approached me and took me by the hand, leading me to this most sumptuous divan. "We must sit. I find I cannot stand for long in my present condition. It has quite altered my capacity for dancing, too! But—oh, I'm to be a mum! Isn't it the grandest?" She held my hands and beamed like a little girl about to open the yuletide gift of her fondest dreams. "Your brother tells me that you are a mum as well. And so fond of your little girl! Do tell me all about her, for I love children so!"

To describe the duchess's look and amiable manner as I gazed upon her that first afternoon would be nigh impracticable. Her eyes shone with intelligence, mildness, and sensibility, and her vivacity, even in repose, was to be wondered at.

"I am ever reluctant to quit my baby's sight," I told the duchess. "But as one of us must pay down my husband's debts somehow, and earn the means as well to pay for our food and lodging at the Fleet—how the devil is a debtor supposed to free himself from his encumbrances where even in the jailhouses one must pay for everything! Since I must leave our quarters to attend to my charwoman's duties, I have been compelled to engage a girl named Dorcas, one of the cook's daughters, to look after Maria Elizabeth. Thank heaven Dorcas adores her; in fact, she begged me to leave Maria with her today. What Mr. Robinson has got up to this afternoon, who can say, but then husbands never look after children."

Her Grace cocked her head sorrowfully. "Husbands," she sighed. "Children, I believe, must be the only thing that makes the creatures worthwhile." She smiled, indicating to me that she was at least half in jest. "I have been married for eighteen months, and I have yet to understand mine, and I daresay Canis doesn't comprehend me in the least. What can one expect, I suppose, of a husband whose pet name evinces his preferences for his dogs? Everyone, of course, said it was a brilliant match; it never occurred to them that I'm as blithe as my husband is boring. He couldn't give a fig for fashion. But talk to me of sweeter things; talk to me of little Maria Elizabeth."

I confess that I went into raptures relating an event that had touched my heart beyond measure. Two nights previous I had taken Maria on one of my night walks about the racquet court. It was a clear and moonlit evening, and as I held her, she kept reaching for the sky, dancing up and down in my arms until I feared that she might bounce right out of them. Her dark eyes were fixed upon the moon, to which she pointed with her tiny forefinger. Suddenly, a cloud scudded past, obscuring the celestial orb from view—and Maria dropped her hand from her eyes with the saddest sigh of resignation. "All gone," she murmured.

"All gone," I repeated. "She says that when she plays peek-a-boo with Dorcas. If Maria wants a toy, or more

milk or a biscuit or reaches for something it would be better not to eat or play with, Dorcas will hide it, like this."
I made a snatching movement with my hand and shoved
the imaginary forbidden fruit behind my back. "All gone!
And every time that night when a cloud would hide the
moon, Maria would hold her hand up to the sky and
say, 'All gone.' She's but eighteen months old and already
so . . . her mind is so quick."

"Like her mama, I expect," said the duchess, the volume of poetry nearly hidden in the silken folds of her
skirts. "You must come back to see me again. And soon,"
Her Grace insisted. "And next time you must bring Maria
Elizabeth. I would so love to meet such a darling."

Somehow from the depths of her magical pockets, the
duchess produced a small purse. "I wish I could do more
to soothe your troubles."

I tried to refuse the gift, but she ever so delicately referred to my impecunious state and pressed the coins upon
me more urgently.

"It will give you more time to write your glorious poetry. We must speak more of it—but I—" I noticed that
the high color had begun to drain from her face. She caressed her rounded belly. "I fatigue easily these days."

I returned to the Fleet filled with pride in the promise
of a friendship with the vivacious duchess. What an honor
I had been granted in her condescension of an interview!
And to hear her praise my poetry—even the degradations
of a debtor's incarceration could not have dampened my
spirits.

"Good news!" I exclaimed as I unlocked the door to
our meager rooms.

I heard my husband's voice coming from the direction

of our bedchamber. "Blast!" he swore. "Are you back then, Mary?"

"Who else?" I asked gaily, breezing into the room. I halted, mid-step, at the sight before me. For there was my husband, naked as a plucked guinea fowl from the waist down, in the arms of a siren I knew too well.

I knew that Mr. Robinson had not been faithful to me, even whilst we languished in prison; but evidently his affairs were being conducted nearly under my nose. Now it was abundantly apparent that at every opportunity he availed himself of my absences, when I undertook my charwoman's duties—and even during my visit to the Duchess of Devonshire.

"How dare you!" I said, keeping my voice low, "with our daughter slumbering in the very next room!"

My husband, and his inamorata, an Italian woman named Angelina Albanesi, whose husband was also imprisoned in the Fleet, regarded me with only the mildest interest. They did not even have the compunction to be affronted by my discovering them in flagrante.

I knew of Signora Albanesi's reputation. She had not chosen, as had I, to reside in the Fleet with her husband, Angelo, an artist, but visited him with regularity. In the course of such conjugal excursions, she made so free to visit other men as well—and one of them was Mr. Robinson! I had been given to understand that Signor Albanesi, who I heard had been an artist of some renown, not only winked at his wife's conduct, but—and I can think of no other term as appropriate—was her Pandarus. Purportedly he procured women for the other inmates as well.

Signora Albanesi disentangled her limbs from my husband's body and straightened her violet silk petticoat.

"What monsters you are," I said, my voice aquiver with rage. "To make a mockery of our marriage and a fool of me—I, who have willingly been the partner of Mr. Robinson's captivity, the devoted slave to his necessities—while he engages in the lowest and most degrading intrigues imaginable."

A bitter laugh strangled itself in my throat. "Why ever did you wish to marry me and consign me to hell when you never had any intention of honoring your vows? It is certainly not your first time, or even the fourth where another woman is concerned." I lowered my eyes, ashamed to cry before the glamorous signora. "It seems I have always been the dupe of your affections." I picked at the lace threads of my handkerchief so I would have somewhere to look that was not the lovers' eyes. "Perhaps, Tom, if you loved another with constancy—if *one woman* had so captured your heart that you could never bear to see it released and therefore had none to give another, regardless of the state of wedlock—this, perhaps, I could understand."

Signora Albanesi kissed my husband on each cheek, in the continental fashion. Then, crossing the room and clasping hold of my unwilling hands, she looked deeply into my eyes and said, "You are so young, my dear; you have much to understand about men—and women. It is the very least I can do to tutor you in the ways of the world."

"I have no wish to con the lessons you might inculcate, madam," I replied stiffly.

"Then you are a little fool," she said, absent any trace of malice.

Despite my better judgment, some days later I found

myself inviting Signora Albanesi to visit our rooms, whilst Mr. Robinson whiled away the afternoon in the prison's coffeehouse.

I had to admit that La Albanesi did possess a certain magnetic exoticism. Though she was quite a bit my elder—between thirty and forty years old, I supposed—she was a handsome woman. Part of her allure was that she never powdered her abundance of raven hair, and never did I see her when she was not dressed in an extravagant ensemble of richly embroidered satins, or brocades trimmed with point lace. The signora was a woman who knew quite well that she caused heads to turn.

Her colorful presence seemed to suck the air out of the room; I felt faintly queasy. "You know, Mrs. Robinson, I had *intended* that you should catch us out!" she said brazenly, referring to her interrupted liaison with my husband.

"And why might that be?" I asked her, utterly appalled.

"Because I have observed you. You do not know how to hold on to a man, child. And yet, you have too much to offer such a one as Mr. Robinson, but neither of you knows it. You deserve better than he, and I will teach you the way to obtain it."

She drew my chair away from my desk and seated me in the center of the room. Slowly circling the chair, she said, "You must always scintillate. Fascinate. Use them. Your beauty is a tool, your figure a weapon. Look at you—dressing the penitent! Somebody must instruct you in the ways of the world or you will be squashed like a water bug," she declared in her most melodious accent. "Now watch me," she commanded. "Watch me walk. Watch me sit. Watch me look at someone in a way that will make them do anything it is I may require of them. How do you think I became the mistress of the Prince de Courland? I will do for you a far greater service than I provide for your husband. Your husband is nothing to me—a diversion only; you are welcome to him and your silly romantic domestic attachment. But I will instruct you on how to do far better. To use your beauty to advantage, rather than squander it on the undeserving. If you do as I have done, you, too, may command the attentions of the nobility." She lowered her voice and told me, quite confidentially, "I have already spoken of you to the Earl of Pembroke. He has assured me that he would be happy to offer you his protection."

"Believe me, signora, I am no stranger to the most licentious of lordlings offering me his protection, if that is what I desired!"

"Tut, tut, child, there is a world of difference between a man such as Lord Lyttelton and the Earl of Pembroke. The former is to the latter as dross is to gold."

Thank heaven my view of womankind was not entirely sullied by this siren. For the Duchess of Devonshire, as kind as Signora Albanesi was calculating, extended the courtesy of inviting me to frequent her establishment as often as I could. Georgiana's company brought my aching bosom tremendous solace, and as the weeks and months progressed we became confidantes, unburdening ourselves about our marriages and the husbands who could not be bothered to know our hearts.

I confessed to her that Mr. Robinson had been com-

mitting frequent and disgraceful infidelities, admitting
the most abandoned of my sex, not only Signora Albanesi,
but other women whose low, licentious lives were such as
to render them the shame and outcasts of society.

"After I discovered him with Signora Albanesi, he did
not even scruple to make a defense," I told her. "I cannot
say that he was brazen about their affair, but he most certainly did not appear the least bit contrite."

"How can he not realize he has more loveliness, more
animation, more grace under his own roof than he could
ever hope to find elsewhere? What does this Signora Albanesi have that you do not?"

I lifted Her Grace's spaniel pup into my lap. "You do
not think me plain then?"

"Heavens, no!"

Almost absentmindedly, I stroked the spaniel's silky
coat. "Yet I realized that this serpent in the garden walked
with dignity and grace. I did envy her confident mien
as well as her fine clothes and her dark, exotic beauty. I
resolved to listen to her, if only for a minute or two. I
found myself appalled and disgusted at her vulgarity, and
yet I could not help but admire her. As Angelina Albanesi
promenaded about the room, using her face, her fan, and
the movement of her skirts to allure and entice, how I
wished to hurl something at her regal raven head! A tutor
indeed, to teach me the art of seduction!

"At that moment, I admit to thinking of nothing but
revenge on Mr. Robinson. But it was envy talking, the
open, running sores of wounded vanity and pride. I did
not fancy myself a siren whose aim was to seduce men and
discard them for sport, in the mold of Signora Albanesi.

Though I do not love my husband, I am *devoted*. And I view our wedding vows with all due solemnity."

At length, after pouring herself a cup of tea and sipping it with great rumination, the duchess remarked, "At every turn the prison presents an evil influence. You made the brave choice to accompany Mr. Robinson in his captivity, Mary, but I am quite certain that his incarceration will not only fail to rehabilitate him—so he may be forever released from a debtor's shackles of writs and decrees—but it will destroy you."

"Though I have confessed much during our visits, were I to describe one-half of what I have suffered during these nearly fifteen months of imprisonment, the world would consider my confession as the exaggerated inventions of a novel!"

A sweet smile suffused the duchess's lovely countenance. "If not a novel, why not poetry?" She surprised me by taking my little volume of verses from the depths of her embroidered skirts. "I carry this everywhere, you know. Whenever I find myself idle or discomfited, and in need of the balm that poesy brings, I choose one of your verses and read a few stanzas to myself—or to Charles," she said, indicating the spaniel that had fallen asleep in my lap. "I believe you have a genuine gift for poetry, my dear companion. And I should not bear to see the world deprived of it." And before I could reply, she had declared that she would be the happiest of mortals to become my patroness, seeing that the little volume was published and sold by subscription.

"An imprimatur from His Grace or me is as good as a royal warrant," she giggled. "I have not the slightest doubt that when I tell those in our circle that I have found the female Dryden, they shall clamor for a copy."

I blush to write that I removed the dozing spaniel from my skirts and prostrated myself at her feet. "My admired patroness, the best of women!" I wept, the tears of joy—and relief—staining my brown silk bodice.

The duchess was, as ever, true to her word. In the summer of 1776, *Poems by Mrs. Robinson,* a 134-page octavo volume, was published. In a slender twist of irony, the frontispiece was drawn by Angelo Albanesi.

The contents were mostly moral elegies and pastoral verses featuring numerous rhymes twixt "bower" and "flower," "heart" and "art"—youthful efforts containing tumbles of words as purple as irises and phrases as torrid as a November tempest. But such was the popular poetry of the day, and I was confident that my style would improve and mature, ripening with time, until it became truly my own and not derivative of other poets' odes to Phyllis penned during the seventeenth and early eighteenth centuries.

But my slender volume sold. And sold!

And on the third of August, 1776, Tom Robinson was discharged from the Fleet. Thanks to the patronage of the Duchess of Devonshire, sales of my little volume of poetry garnered enough money to enable the settlement of my husband's debts.

On our release, I made straight for Vauxhall. How I had missed its magic! I had frequently found occasion to observe a mournful contrast when I quitted Devonshire House to enter the dark galleries of a prison; but the sensation I felt on hearing the strains of the pleasure gardens' orchestra, and on beholding the gay throng during this first visit in public after so long a seclusion, was indescribable.

Adding to my delirium was the giddy knowledge that my talents as a poetess had provided the golden key that turned the clink, setting us free as a family to hear the nightingales from a moonlit walk, and picnic by the bankside in the summer sun.

Act Three

All the World's a Stage

Fourteen

A Second Chance

1776 . . . age eighteen

Now that Mr. Robinson had obtained his liberty—thanks to my pen and Her Grace's patronage of it—how would he provide for his family, assuring that we would subsist honorably and above reproach? My husband had never completed his legal studies. My literary efforts did not produce a steady stream of income on which we could rely. Mr. Robinson had applied to his father for some form of allowance, but every request for aid was refused. Mr. Harris, whom my husband persisted in referring to as his "uncle," had provided us a pittance on which to man age whilst we languished in prison, but it was an amount so low that it might better be deemed an insult than an income.

Although the American colonies declared war against us that summer, my thoughts had been focused on our release from the Fleet and I'd had precious little time to read the papers. Now, as autumn leaves waxed russet and gold in St. James's Park, and across the ocean the fatal volleys were exchanged twixt rebel and redcoat, my mind was fixed upon the duty of providing for my family, whose number would soon increase again.

Not too many weeks later, during our daily constitutional amid the park's graceful groves, we chanced to meet William Brereton, one of the luminaries of Drury Lane, whose acquaintance I had made nearly four years previous when the illustrious Garrick presumed to tutor me as his protégée.

"Well, damme—Mary Darby, is it?" exclaimed the actor.

"Robinson now." I curtsied prettily and introduced my husband. From Mr. Brereton's reaction, I think he was surprised to see me wedded to so diminutive a specimen of manhood.

"Well—my felicitations," Brereton gushed, pumping my husband's hand. "Tell me, *Mrs. Robinson*—what have you been getting up to since we last met? I daresay the stage was deprived of one who might have been among its brightest ornaments when you broke off your connexion with Mr. Garrick."

I glanced at the actor, a fine example himself of thespian talent. Was he quizzing me, or did his earnest expression speak his mind truthfully? At that moment, gazing into Mr. Brereton's gravely handsome face, my thoughts turned once more to the pursuit of a dramatic life—the idea rushed like a bolt of electricity through every fiber of my being.

"Do you really think I could make another go of it?" I asked him, the color rushing into my face. I had not felt more excited about a thing since my first, and last, sally toward the boards.

To my astonishment, Mr. Robinson answered for him. "And why not!" Well he knew, of course, of our pecuniary constraints. And ever since the publication of my first volume of poetry I was convinced of the possibility that my artistic talents might win me an honorable independence—which seemed my only recourse, as my husband appeared congenitally allergic to any form of employment that did not feature a baize-covered gaming table.

Not too many days later, Mr. Brereton surprised me by calling at our lodgings in Newman Street. I had not been well; my condition had weakened my constitution, exacerbated by having continued for so long to attend to my devotions as a mother by nursing Maria, who was now past the age of two.

My mortification was complete when Mr. Brereton appeared with a companion, catching me in a state of maternal dishabille, my pink silk dressing gown askew, my hair unpowdered, and my face unpainted and natural as a milkmaid's. My mind, too, was somewhat distracted and disoriented. During this second pregnancy I seemed to have developed an odd sort of occasional memory loss. I would be in the middle of a sentence and suddenly need to search for the next word, my brain being faster than my tongue. "Yes, Maria still sleeps in a . . . *wooden rocking* . . . *thing*," I would say, the word "cradle" suddenly evanescing from my mind. Not an auspicious beginning for an actress, particularly when the profession demanded such retention skills as to have in one's memory the roles of an entire repertory season.

Thus, it was with the utmost trepidation, despite my every desire to realize my fondest dream, that I greeted Mr. Brereton and a tall man with regal bearing whom he introduced to me as Mr. Richard Brinsley Sheridan, newly part-owner of Drury Lane, and a dramatist in his own right. Sheridan's comedy of manners, *The Rivals,* a semi-autobiographical account of his own amorous shenanigans in Bath, had been performed to great acclaim.

Sheridan's keenly intelligent eyes and lively wit immediately bespoke his Irish heritage, which I, too, claimed through my father's ancestors. His manner was kindly and solicitous of my condition, and yet thoroughly professional when it came to matters of the theatre.

"I . . . I must change into something more proper," I stammered, begging a hasty retreat.

"Your wardrobe is of no consequence," replied Mr. Sheridan gently. He dismissed my appearance with a wave of his uncommonly delicate hand. "Your beauty and grace are apparent without the addition of silken flounced panniers. I should be gratified merely to hear you recite a bit. Something of Shakespeare, if you can recall it."

Good heavens! How would I, who had but yesterday referred haltingly to Maria Elizabeth's "little white . . . frilly head-cap-coverer," when I simply meant to say the word "bonnet," be able to navigate my tongue through the rills and rooks of Shakespeare's rhymes?

Somehow I managed to recollect Juliet's speech exhorting the heavens to "Gallop apace, you fiery steeds toward Phoebus's lodgings" and bring my Romeo to me. It was not a phantom Romeo I thought of when I invoked him, but an image of the theatrical career I had so desperately coveted and might once again achieve, should fate and my judges so decide.

Messrs. Brereton and Sheridan quite approved of my Juliet. Then Mr. Sheridan, requesting something from a comedy, was impressed with my Rosalind and my Viola—

trouser parts that I surmised would also suit me well, for my slender hips and long legs comprised just the sort of figure that was sought for these cross-dressing roles. Of course, in my present condition, though barely four months advanced at the time, my shape hardly resembled that of a stripling!

My recitation that morning did prove, however, to be an audition; for at the end of our interview, Mr. Sheridan invited me to attend upon him in the Green Room at Drury Lane. The date was fixed, and Mr. Robinson accompanied me on this appointment, where I was astounded to see my dear Mr. Garrick himself—come back from his retirement—to hear me recite the principal scenes of Juliet. Mr. Brereton was my Romeo, and Mr. Sheridan, in his bright red waistcoat, sat beside Mr. Garrick exchanging glances and whispers with my former mentor.

"Well, young lady, as the greedy undertaker once said, 'Better late than never!' " Garrick quipped. "I have been waiting these past four years to see you make your debut, and my only regret in its lengthy postponement is that I can no longer be a Lear to your Cordelia." Garrick nodded to Messrs. Sheridan and Brereton and said, "Juliet it will be, then! And I will coax this infirm body of mine out of bed every morning to coach her myself."

"Oh, sir, you are kindness itself!" I fairly threw myself at his feet and hugged his knobby knees to my chest.

Garrick paternally patted my hair. "But I think we should not dally in fixing the opening night, for Mrs. Robinson's *own* body will not wait on our rehearsals."

The tenth of December, 1776, was to be the night. The broadsheets proclaimed simply that "a young lady" would mark her stage debut in the role of Juliet. My novice's salary of two pounds a week proclaimed my own declaration of independence; if I was any good, I would rise within the company ranks and so would my earnings, perhaps one day topping the twenty-six pounds a week paid to Mrs. Yates, Drury Lane's premier tragedienne. I was nineteen years old, and a little more than four months pregnant with my second child.

We engaged Dorcas to be Maria's nanny, for Mr. Robinson could not be relied upon to superintend our daughter whilst I was at the theatre for rehearsals and performances.

I feared I should never master my nerves. As my dresser, Mrs. Armistead—who was far too flirtatious with the gentlemen for her own good—laced me into my gown of pale pink satin trimmed with crape, I had to grasp the back of a chair to keep my wobbly knees from knocking together. My fingers fiddled with the frock's ornamental silver spangles.

When I entered the Green Room, it was filled with fashionable spectators there to wish me well, or to watch my debut from the wings. The Duchess of Devonshire stepped forward and presented me with a beribboned posy. Mr. Garrick himself kissed me upon each cheek and then left to take his place in the orchestra amid the critics—those discerning eyes whose pens would either eviscerate or ennoble me in the morning papers.

His uncannily lustrous eyes sparkling with excitement, Mr. Sheridan clasped me about the waist, careful not to muss my hair, nor the stage maquillage I had so carefully applied—the carmine, kohl, and alum paste that gave me the complexion of a china doll. "You look a picture, my dear. I am certain you will win their hearts tonight. Not an eye will be dry when such a lovely creature breathes her last."

Of course no one dared to comment on my talent winning the day—or the evening, as the case was—for they all knew me to be utterly untested. And no one was more terrified than I at the prospect of stepping upon that stage, in front of nearly two thousand boisterous souls who lacked no compunction about delivering their reviews on the instant with catcalls, hisses, and missiles of tankards, goblets, and rotten fruit.

Perhaps the prostitutes who plied their trade in the "green boxes" in the theatre's uppermost tier would take no respite from their trolling to look upon the stage; but otherwise, conversation briefly ceased while all attention was fixed toward the proscenium. From behind the scenes as I waited for the bellman, I could hear the heated conversations of the dandies in the pit, the titters of the quality in the side boxes, and the hearty laughter of the middle classes in the center boxes amid the cries of the orange sellers picking their way among them.

My heart throbbed convulsively as I approached the wings. *What was I thinking?* echoed in my poor brain; suddenly I forgot all my lines. My mouth was as dry as if I had stuffed it with cotton wool. Fearing that my resolution would fail, I leaned upon the Nurse's arm, almost fainting.

"Buck up, love," my colleague whispered reassuringly. "I felt this way, too, on my first night. But I was there with you in the rehearsals, remember? You'll take to it as a duck to water, dearie."

"Go, child," urged Mr. Sheridan. "Show 'em what you're made of!"

And then we were on! With trembling limbs and fearful apprehension I approached the audience, not daring to look at them. The thundering applause that greeted me nearly overpowered all my faculties. I stood mute and bending with alarm, and the stage fright did not subside until I had feebly articulated the few sentences of the first short scene. Fear had palsied both my voice and action. *Oh, dear God,* I thought, *I'm certain they cannot hear me. Mr. Garrick will have my head.* If he had told me ten times, he had told me a thousand that I must still project my voice to the rafters or all the naturalness he'd taught me would be for naught *if no one could hear a bloody word I said.*

On my return to the Green Room after my first scene, I was again encouraged, as far as my looks were concerned, by a plethora of compliments. "But you must speak up, girl," exhorted Sheridan. "The conversations in the pit were louder than you were. And sure they won't hush up if you don't give them a good reason. Playgoers come to the theatre to see *one another* first; the players take second fiddle unless they offer a livelier tune."

The second scene being the masquerade, I had time to collect myself, and stepped more confidently upon the boards. And what a sublime sensation coursed through my bosom when I dared to take my first look toward the pit and saw the gradual ascent of heads. All eyes were fixed upon me—most thrilling indeed—but to me the most impressive response was the keen, penetrating gaze of Mr. Garrick, seated in the center of the orchestra. His approbation, above all, was the finest imprimatur any actress could hope for.

As I acquired courage, I found the applause increase,

and the night was concluded with peals of admiration. By the end of the final act, the audience held their breath as one when the stagehands laid out the green carpet, that I should not dirty my white satin gown—the customary costume for characters about to die. Crowning my powdered auburn curls was a veil of the most transparent gauze that fluttered to my feet, whilst about my waist a string of beads and a little penitent's cross of wood completed the portrait of the tragic Juliet.

I took my bows to the most thunderous applause; my heart throbbed with inexpressible happiness. I had done it! I had conquered my temporary fears and achieved my lifelong dream. Of all the places I had ever set foot in, I was certain now that not only was the Theatre my temple: it was my natural home.

After my performance I was complimented on all sides, but the praise of Mr. Garrick—one of the most fascinating men and most distinguished geniuses of the age, and the one object I most wished to please—was a gratification that language cannot utter. Only sighs and tears and smiles can begin to express what was in my heart. I had made him proud of me. And yet, inside my brain the single thought niggled me: If my own father had been able to know me then, would he have been half so pleased with my efforts?

I was offered a contract to appear at Drury Lane for the remainder of the season, assigned a number of roles in the repertory both leading and supporting, from tragedy to comedy, from trouser parts to comely lasses, from swaggering swains to sighing ingénues. Truth told, I found it highly amusing that I should have any credence in the trouser roles that season, for by then, in such habiliments, my domestic condition was quite apparent. Nonetheless, Sheridan felt that I was up to the task, and who was I to contradict him?

My second venture on the boards was in the role of Amanda, a duped young wife, in Sheridan's own *A Trip to Scarborough*. It had been billed as a brand-new comedy, but when we began to play, the canny crowd realized at once that the script was merely a watered-down rewrite of Sir John Vanbrugh's lusty Restoration romp, *The Relapse*—only without all the lust, which present tastes deemed indecent. Regardless of the tamer incarnation, the experience was, of course, a great disappointment to those who had paid good coin to see a new work.

Feeling as betrayed as the hapless Amanda, the audience began to hiss and shout at us, their disapproval reaching fever pitch during the scene between myself and Mrs. Yates, who played Berinthia, the object of my stage husband's licentious attentions.

My colleague, distracted beyond measure by the shouting from the pit, clasped my hands in hers and gave me the inexorable look of a rabbit gazing at a gun muzzle. Her mouth opened and closed, gaping and flapping, but no words would come, at least none that I could hear. I realized suddenly that the disapprobation had so greatly put her off that she had gone up on her lines, forgetting her part!

"Never have I been treated so poorly," she exclaimed— this much I could hear—and dropped my hands, all pretense at playing the scene totally cast aside.

"I am a tragedienne!" she announced, though none could hear her but I. Mrs. Yates made every attempt to retain her dignity as she dodged a flying dinner roll, exclaiming, "Good God, they'll kill us all!" But she retreated from the stage, leaving me alone to encounter the critical tempest.

I stood stock-still for some moments, fearful that the dinner roll might be followed up by something more damaging, unsure of what to say or how to salvage the situation. Sheridan, whose play it was, called frantically from the wings, "Mary, hold your ground!" as if I were a general under attack from enemy fire.

I looked about me for a friendly face, but encountered mostly angry snarls. Yet in the royal box right above the lip of the proscenium sat His Majesty's libertine brother, the Duke of Cumberland.

"Take courage, young lady; it is not you but the play they hiss," said His Royal Highness.

Perhaps because of where he sat, I could make out his voice above the din. I curtsied most gratefully, and to my utter astonishment, that curtsy seemed to electrify the whole house—for a thundering appeal of encouraging applause followed. Even more astonishing was that the comedy was suffered to go on—and became a stock play at Drury Lane.

After this, Sheridan was determined that I should play more comedies, offering me the greatest compliment by penning one of the supporting roles in *The School for Scandal* for me. Though Sheridan was one of them, his play positively skewered the Devonshire set; in fact, the leading character of Lady Teazle was rumored to have been modeled on the duchess herself.

My delight was immense at such an honor. How many actresses can say that one of the greatest dramatists of their day has found in them a muse? Yet, alas, it was not to be. With heavy heart I admitted that I was by now so unshaped by my increasing size that I should probably be confined to my chamber at the period when the opus should receive its debut.

My final performance of the season was fixed for April 10, 1777, but five months since I had first met Mr. Sheridan. Coincidentally, it also was to be my benefit performance—an annual tradition among thespians. Though my burgeoning figure had made quite the comical silhouette a few weeks earlier when I played Sir Harry Revel in Lady Craven's *The Miniature Picture,* I did not wish to provoke laughter for all the wrong reasons. Therefore, given my condition, I chose my benefit role sensibly, portraying the pregnant Fanny in Garrick and Colman's comedy *The Clandestine Marriage.* The boxes were filled with persons of the highest rank and fashion, a thrilling and flattering assemblage for my temporary swan song.

It was painful for me to abandon the adulation I had received for the past several months. Just as dear to me was the camaraderie—even the rivalries—that went on in the warrens behind the scenes, amid the tiny, cramped dressing rooms, and after hours in the noisy taverns and fashionable salons; for theatre folk have the biggest, grandest hearts of any you'll meet. Though they may sulk and fuss when another is preferred for a plum role, they are also the first to lend a hand or a shilling when one of their own has fallen upon hard times, and they never fail to bolster the kindred spirit wounded by a fickle critic.

Sheridan was one such soul. He would visit me almost daily during my confinement, despite the enormity of his responsibilities at Drury Lane. Aside from selecting the theatre's repertoire and overseeing the casting and the rehearsals, he juggled the delicate egos of eighty-five actors and actresses, twenty dancers, and the thirty dressers who saw that we got onstage in the proper costumes, not to mention the men of the orchestra and an army of backstage staff—prompters and carpenters, and the artisans who would design the set pieces and the lighting, for colored gauze reflecting off of an illuminated tin screen was now the latest thing. Even the men who swept the peanut shells from the floors, and the orange sellers who hawked their wares in the aisles, fell under Sheridan's managerial purview.

"Well, now, what is it today, my gazetteer?" I would ask him, eager for the news from the stage. "The morning papers have *their* opinions; now what's *yours*?"

And Sheridan would laugh and those Irish eyes of his would twinkle. "While Mrs. Yates dithers about whether to do Jane Shore or Lady Macbeth for her benefit, I waste time scolding Miss Farren for neglecting to purchase her own white stockings. Actors! They know bloody well the theatre doesn't supply one's hosiery. Egad—the minutiae of wardrobe expenses is the sort of thing Mrs. Linley should be worried about. The Farren had to go bare-legged as Ophelia the other night. I daresay her flightiness, or her parsimony, started a new fashion for the mad scene."

I cradled my belly, near to bursting with child. "She's playing my roles."

"She always has," Sheridan replied pragmatically. "And mayhap she always will. Some manager I'd be if I had only one performer in the company who knew a given part." He glanced at my stomach. "All it takes is a simple indisposure and the schedule goes to hell."

Though I often flinched to hear the news of the day, I cherished Sheridan's visits. I was too much alone in my thoughts, which in my solitude have always tended to melancholy. Absent the gaiety of the theatre, my time was occupied chiefly with reflection, unless I felt strong enough to entertain little Maria Elizabeth. I missed Mother, who was home in Bristol; and though I should have liked her to come down to London for my lying-in, we both knew that I was of an age where it was meet that I superintend my own establishment.

Besides, I knew too well how she and Mr. Robinson could take advantage of my weakened state and conspire to ambush my better judgment. Perhaps that should not have been a concern, for Tom was rarely at home, preferring to spend his days gambling in the clubs and carousing in the coffeehouses. His nights removed him from our hearth as well. I could only imagine that his winnings at the faro tables—in addition to the money that as my husband he was legally entitled to leech from my earnings—funded his rakish conduct. Our household was managed entirely on my salary from Drury Lane.

On May 24, 1777, my second daughter, Sophia, was christened in the actors' church, St. Paul's Covent Garden. But the brief labor and easy delivery did not augur a charmed life. She wouldn't take my breast and no one could fathom why. She grew frailer and sickly. I blamed myself. Had I nursed Maria Elizabeth for too long? Were my bosoms, never very ample to begin with, too inadequate somehow to give suck?

At the end of only six weeks, I lost her. Numb with disbelief was the state in which Sheridan found me when he called on me that day, the little sufferer still on my lap, her soul flown up to God. Only minutes earlier, Sophia had expired in my arms in convulsions. My distress was indescribable. I cursed myself, recalling the time when as an infant Maria had endured similar convulsions whilst, overexerted and overheated from dancing, I was nursing her. What had I done this time? I had led a quiet confinement, no parties or balls, and yet my tiny daughter was taken from me.

I was gazing upon her lifeless body with agonizing anxiety when Sheridan tiptoed into my chamber. "She's gone," I murmured. "Just now." My hot tears baptized her soft, colorless cheeks with my shame, guilt, and incomprehension. "And I don't know what to do."

"May I?" my friend asked, with exquisite sensibility. I nodded mutely and he approached me, stopping to rest his eyes upon the little dear resting in my lap. "Beautiful little creature," he breathed, sighing with such a sympathetic sorrow that I thought my heart would burst from my breast. Had I ever heard such a sigh from a *husband's* bosom?

Sheridan's gentle solicitousness released from me a torrent of emotions. I wept for poor tiny Sophia, and for the knowledge that I never was beloved by him whom destiny allotted to be the legal ruler of my actions. And yet, I could not condemn Mr. Robinson, for too well I know that we cannot command whither our affections wend. One can no more choose to fall in love with someone than they can select the color of their skin. And marriages were almost always pecuniary arrangements.

As if he read my mind, Sheridan asked softly, "Where is Mr. Robinson?" It was kind of him to make inquiry as if he were ignorant of my husband's conduct, for everyone knew that he kept two mistresses, one of whom was a figure dancer at Drury Lane—my own backyard, as 'twere—and the other a fancy woman of professed libertinism near Covent Garden. Whilst he continually gratified his own caprice, Mr. Robinson observed no decency in his infidelities, exposing me perennially to the most degrading mortification.

"I will summon a doctor," said Sheridan. He bent over me and kissed my brow. "You know that you will be welcome at Drury Lane whenever you are able to return. Let me know so I may arrange the schedule to accommodate your performances. Mayhap the work will soothe your troubled soul." He turned to leave, with a last glance at the lifeless form nestled in my skirts. "When these rooms afford you no comforts, take solace in the knowledge that the theatre is your home."

"I cannot now," I mumbled. "I should not be able to summon a dram of wit or gaiety, even in sham. Forgive me . . . I cannot honor the remainder of my engagement this season." After several moments of silence I said, "Permit me to depart for Bath that I might recuperate my health and spirits. From there I should like to make the short journey to Bristol to visit my mother's home. Wandering the haunts of my birthplace always seems to make me whole, somehow."

Sheridan granted my wish; and after some weeks in Bath, and a pilgrimage to Bristol's antique minster, in whose shadows I used to hide when a child, I returned to London, still restless, still perplexed with painful solicitudes.

Perhaps I was more like my mother than I'd been willing to admit; I saw her with new eyes during our visit in Bristol. She, too, had lost an infant daughter.

Sophia's death made me wish to keep little Maria even closer to my bosom. Though I'd always been quick to acknowledge our differences in temperament, it surprised me to realize that I was stitching the same picture Mother had made when she feared to let me stray too far from her hem. And yet she had dashed my dreams to wed me to a deceiving rake, for which I remained unable to forgive her. Those traitorous colors I vowed never to sew into the fabric of my surviving daughter's life.

There was much to condole and much to consider.

I was not yet twenty years old.

Fifteen

Marked Attentions

1777 . . . age nineteen

$\mathcal{B}$y the time I returned to town, the two licensed theatres, Drury Lane and Covent Garden, were closed for the season. But the Haymarket had a royal patent to operate during the summer months; and it was there, under the direction of Mr. Colman, that Sheridan proposed I seek employment—after I nixed his suggestion to tour the provinces, which had never been my ambition. While the work might be gainful, I had an outright aversion to the notion, as the artistic quality of these touring productions was often spotty at best, and an actress's reputation—poor enough in the city—was deemed downright licentious once she was labeled a strolling player.

I met with Mr. Colman in a coffeehouse on the Strand and told him that I would prefer a limited engagement, with the right to choose the roles I would play. His disposition was amiable, and in retrospect, his ready assent to my terms seemed too easy.

But thus began my employment with the Haymarket.

The first part I was to assay for Mr. Colman was that of Nancy Lovel in the popular comedy *The Suicide*. I received the written character and was hard at work in our family's new lodgings in Leicester Square, awaiting notice of the rehearsal schedule. Imagine my astonishment when one morning I opened the *Post* and saw the name of *Miss Farren* announced on the bill for that night in the very role I was to perform!

I marched down to the theatre and demanded an interview with Mr. Colman. After letting me cool my heels for several minutes, he timidly stepped out of his office and into the dingy corridor. I rose to my feet and shoved the morning paper under his snub nose. "What is the meaning of this?" I inquired.

"Of what?" replied the manager stupidly.

"Miss Farren is to play Nancy Lovel tonight—evidently. This is one of the roles we agreed upon when you tendered me a contract."

"Well—b-but I had promised the role already t-to Miss Farren before we met," Colman stammered, his face reddening without benefit of drink.

Though my knees were shaking with nerves, I compelled myself to hold my ground, playing the role of my own advocate, for who else was there to speak for me? "That is none of my concern, sir. You never informed me of any prior commitment to the part during our original interview." I felt myself keenly insulted. "I have sat in my rooms for the past several days, studying the role with my customary diligence. You, sir, have not supplied me with the same courtesy I have extended to you."

"B-but I *promised*," insisted Mr. Colman, showing me inside and offering me a seat. "Miss Farren is one of my regular company; this is her second season at the Haymarket. I dare not offend her by changing the casting at such short notice; and I cannot, nor will I, cancel tonight's performance. What would you have me do?"

I could ill afford to break my contract with him. I desperately needed the income, for our bills were ever mounting, and apart from Mr. Robinson's occasional winnings at a hand or two of Ecarte, I was the family breadwinner. "Fulfill the engagement or give me leave to quit London and seek theatrical employment elsewhere," I told Mr. Colman.

He refused to grant me the liberty of either option.

"Then you must tell Miss Farren that we have an agreement," I said, taking his signed contract from the deep pocket cleverly hidden by a slit in my skirt. Wounded and jealous, I wanted to cry, but willed myself to check my tears. "Sir, by this agreement, my first appearance at the Haymarket Theatre is to be Nancy Lovel in *The Suicide*. Your partiality for Miss Farren evidently precludes you from honoring this notarized bond and restoring the role to me. Therefore, though my heart is heavy and regretful that I will not tread the boards tonight, you have left me little alternative but to abide by the representations made in this legal instrument. I will refuse to play at the Haymarket until I have given the public my Nancy Lovel. And it would seem"—I laid the document before him—"that by the terms of this contract, you are bound to pay me my salary, regardless."

I held my breath, awaiting his response. To my total shock, Mr. Colman was more loyal to Miss Farren than to the contract we had drawn up! "M-my treasurer will see to the details, Mrs. Robinson."

And so it was that I was engaged at the Haymarket for the summer without once performing—and my salary was paid weekly and regularly!

Left with much time on my hands until the autumn performances recommenced at Drury Lane, I occupied myself with daily shopping trips to the popular milliners and mantua makers, and with various entertainments both at home and at concerts and pleasure gardens. Before long, my bills mounted quite in excess of my earnings. I found that my future stage appearances were much anticipated by people from all strata of fashion, from the Conduit Street mantua makers' assistants to a marquis of some renown who had passed a note to one of the mercers I frequented, suggesting that he would be willing to relieve me of my pecuniary distresses for a certain consideration. The shopgirl awaited my reply. "I'm to give him an answer by week's end, miss," she said to me.

I tucked the note into my busk. "Tell him it will be a chilly day in th' Antipodes before I should accept such a bargain," I said, and turned on my heel, leaving the emporium with the yardage for a fine woolen cloak.

Such offers of protection continued to plague me after the theatre season recommenced and as I gained more approbation and attention at Drury Lane. To my personal repertoire of contemporary roles, many of them penned by Sheridan, I added those from Shakespeare's canon: Perdita, Ophelia and Rosalind, Viola, Imogen, and Lady Anne, as well as the deliciously wicked Lady Macbeth, which I planned to perform for my next benefit when the time came.

My pious mother was now in town and visited me

daily, though it broke my heart that no matter how great the applause, she always watched my performances with the utmost consternation, the knowledge of which always remained a source of distress to me.

"Why can you not be happy for me, Mother?" I had asked her this on more than one occasion. Now she sat on a rather worn divan in my dressing room at Drury Lane, sipping my extravagantly costly Darjeeling whilst I applied my makeup.

"Oh, Mary," she sighed, "do you expect me to evince delight when you nightly expose your person to the world to ogle as they wish?"

I dipped my finger into a pot of crimson and dabbed it on my cheeks, studying my reflection in the glass. "My conduct has always been quite respectable, ma'am. Both on and off the stage. But for my love of fine things and the pleasure I derive from attending routs and ridottos, I should say I am quite stainless. I abjure cards; and I flirt no more nor less than anyone else, man or woman—but such behavior is *comme il faut* among the fashionable! The furtive wink behind a fan, the nod, the encouraging smile, the sly bow or curtsy—it is common conduct here, and I'm told I've become rather adept at it. It may appear to signify everything at the time, but in truth, the behavior means nothing. It is all a game people play, and to be accepted as much as any actress can by society's diamonds of the first water, I must play it, too."

"It is because your profession condemns you as an outcast, no matter how cleverly you play the game, that I fear all the more for your character. I cannot help but recall your father's admonishment." Mother shivered.

She never failed to hit my Achilles' heel with one of

her baited arrows. I knew she would invoke Papa's name at some point. She always did. "Nicholas Darby. A fine example of high feelings and proper manners *he*!" I retorted. "Should I imitate the sort of conduct exemplified by my father and my husband, I would have the blackest character in Christendom!" I assured her that I still had the consolation of an unsullied name and enjoyed the highest female patronage—a circle of the most respectable and partial friends, which included the admirable Duchess of Devonshire, the very avatar of fashion.

Had I mentioned to my mother the names of those who had dangled before me the temptation of fortune, it would have cast in marble her unfavorable impression of the set in which I moved. I daren't tell her that no less a personage than the Duke of Rutland had—via the supercilious silk merchant at Hinchcliffe and Croft in Henrietta Street—offered me a settlement of six hundred pounds per annum as a means of estranging me entirely from my husband. My mother would have remained just as anxious if I had told her the truth—that I refused the offer. Though an acceptance of such protection might have solved my pecuniary predicament, I wished to remain, in the eyes of the public, deserving of its patronage. Mother, like much of the rest of society, particularly the rising middle classes from which we sprang, equated all actresses with those females of a distinctly lower stamp for whom artifice is also a chief weapon within their personal arsenal, and who exhibit their charms for the exchange of coin.

The fact that I had a husband, however wayward, was an enhancement, rather than a detraction, to my good reputation. And for better or worse, Mr. Robinson and I were bound to one another. In our station of life, divorce was a near impossibility.

How delighted I was when John, my elder brother, whom I had not clapped eyes upon in years, came to London and expressed an interest in attending one of my performances. That night I was to do Jacintha, a trousers role, in *The Suspicious Husband,* and with great excitement I was helped into my red velvet suit by my new dresser, Mrs. Bates. "My brother is in the house tonight," I told her. "He's a merchant—in from Leghorn on business."

"Sure, he's very proud of you, Mrs. R.," Mrs. Bates said cheerfully. She gave my cuffs a tug to adjust the lace. "You break a leg out there this evening and I'll see you at the interval."

My nerves were aflutter, so eager was I to shine for my brother. But the moment I stepped out on the stage, I saw John rise and quit his box immediately. With the audience as illuminated as the actors, it was sometimes all too easy to discern a familiar face. My mother, who had been seated beside him, hid behind her fan when she met my gaze. I was so wounded, and so mortified by their reaction, that it seemed an eternity before I could recover myself and slip back into the personage of Jacintha. So unconquerable was his aversion to the notion that his sister had sullied herself by treading the boards—and in trousers—that my own brother declined to remain, refusing to see me in the profession I had sought so long to achieve, and in a role for which I was quite renowned. That night I had intended to host a supper in John's honor, but when I arrived back at my rooms, Maria's nanny, Dorcas, informed me that my brother had desired to return to his hotel, expressing the wish that I not call upon him.

I knelt down and took my little girl in my arms, bursting into sobs. "I hope, if I should give you a brother, Maria, that he will never deny you his respect and withhold his devotion, regardless of the path you choose."

She regarded me uncomprehendingly. "Don't cry, Mummy." With her tiny finger she smudged away my tears. "Besides, I'd rather have a pony. Can you give me a pony instead of a brother?"

My life was becoming quite fantastic and gay. I was stopped in the street wherever I went by people eager to meet me. They would follow me into the shops and note what I purchased. Those with the funds to do so endeavored to copy what I wore, no matter how grand or outlandish. But two seasons on the stage and already I was becoming a celebrity!

My home had become a salon. "Can you imagine, my morning levees are as well attended as the queen's," I crowed to Georgiana. "They're so crowded I can scarcely find a quiet hour for studying my roles or playing at jacks or dolls with Maria. My house is perpetually thronged with visitors!"

Having enjoyed her patronage on two occasions, I had begun to move on the fringes of Her Grace's social circles, content to bask in the warmth of her reflected effulgence. Through the duchess, I was introduced to a number of the nation's brightest luminaries, from the wellborn to the well-read, nobles and nabobs, poets and politicians, including the rising Whig firebrand Charles James Fox. Sheridan, too, was a prominent member of the Devonshire House set. This circle was known throughout London for their Whig sensibilities as well as their peculiar way of speaking to each other—a sort of precious, haute ton baby talk, where their *R*s and *L*s were transformed by the tongue into *W*s—a tic I promised myself never to adopt no matter how "cwose" I "gwew" to "Her Gwace," the "pwetty wittle" duchess and her clique.

Yet this ascendance in society came at a steep price for one so situated as I. My salary—though better than modest, owing to my popularity on the boards—was at times inadequate to the expenses incurred by our having such an enlarged acquaintance, some of whom were connexions that Mr. Robinson had formed since my appearance on the dramatic scene. His passion for gaming was now boundless; card parties could last through the night or go on for several days, and an entire fortune could easily be lost in a single trick. I detested the gaming even more than his other passions, reserving for cards a special brand of vehemence, but I was powerless to halt his play and forestall his losses. The bond creditors became so clamorous that the entire proceeds of my benefits were appropriated to their demands.

Still, my popularity increased every night that I appeared on the stage, and my prospects—both of fame and affluence—began to brighten. Even off the stage, I gained attention. I loved to visit the pleasure gardens after a performance still attired in my costumes, causing a scandal whenever I appeared in my breeches.

My quill brought me notoriety as well. In 1778, following my benefit performance as Lady Macbeth, the afterpiece, an operatic farce titled *The Lucky Escape,* was penned by me. At the bookstores in Paternoster Row, and all along the Strand, copies of the libretto were available for a few shillings, and sold as quickly as did the tickets to my performances. I had found another avenue through which to fill my perennially empty purse.

In proportion, as play obtained its influence over my husband's mind, his small portion of remaining regard for me visibly decayed. He let separate quarters in Covent Garden, nearly adjacent to our marital residence, where he entertained his acquaintances, since I would certainly not conscience his bringing his tarts into my home, particularly where they might be seen by our daughter, now four years old. Though I did not edit my own guest lists for Maria's sake, Mr. Robinson's were most definitely of an unsuitable caliber for the prying eyes and curious ears of a small child.

Mr. Sheridan was still my most esteemed of friends, and his concern for my welfare was always so kindly and solicitous that it was almost paternal. One afternoon, when we two alone sat in my front parlor, the dramatist drew up his chair and pressed my hands in his. My heart began to thrum wildly, for I feared he was about to make some sort of declaration, and though I had such regard for him—his fine mind, pleasing face, and rather tolerable figure, made all the more attractive by his ever-gentle attentiveness to me—he was nonetheless my employer.

"If you will listen to no other, you must hear it from my lips," Sheridan began. His eyes imparted the utmost sincerity. "I know that we often travel in the same social spheres, but I fear that you are flying too close to the sun, and its heat can only destroy you. It gives me great distress to see you turning profligate." His expression was so earnest, I found myself near to tears. "Mary, you can ill afford it on every level. After the performances, you frequently attend masquerades and ridottos, when you might be studying your parts or getting a good night's sleep—especially when you have a rehearsal the following morning and a premiere that same evening. Your every penny is spent on horses, ponies, a phaeton, your clothes and accoutrements—and the more you part with, the more you will need to fill your purse again. You can never hope to catch up with your creditors this way. I know you are thick with the duchess, but you have not Her Grace's income. And I fear you are chasing the fashions—and devoting your energies to questionable liaisons—at the expense of your dramatic reputation."

At this I bristled. "I already have a father, sir, who felt it his office to scold and condemn me even before I set one kidskin slipper on the stage." The man before me was not the Sheridan I had near to fallen in love with, not the man whose brilliant conversation never failed to fascinate me and whose charm was near irresistible. Where was his usual *solicitousness* for my regard? Instead of kindness, I received a tongue-lashing.

"Are you jealous?" I laughed, struck quite suddenly by that possibility. "What parties comprise these 'questionable liaisons' you speak of that so distract from my dramatic devotions?"

Sheridan's piercing gaze trumped his discomfiture. "It is the talk of every coffeehouse—not to mention the Green Room—that these days you are squired about by Sir John Lade, the brewer's son."

"Sir John is a most amiable gentleman—and more frequently appears at my husband's gaming tables than as my chaperone—but what of it, Mr. Sheridan? I find the brewery baronet amusing—and he and I are of the same young vintage. Confidentially," I added, leaning toward him and lowering my voice to a whisper, "Sir John is a most dreadful card player. Though my husband plays far more deeply than is discreet, we should never have afforded my new vis-à-vis were it not for Sir John's appalling luck at the faro tables! It appears to me that you would deny me not only my pretty little carriage, but my popularity, Mr. Sheridan, even as you advance it, and even as it increases the company's coffers."

The dear man looked wounded by my words and I instantly wished that I might have taken them back, erased them from the air that had borne them from my lips to his ears.

"You know, I am quite confounded myself by all the attention I now derive, from the highborn to the low. It is not merely the honest Sir John Lades or the unprincipled Lytteltons who pay court to me. The Duke of Rutland is not the only one eager to buy what I have. Now—imagine this, Richard. Tuesday last I was trying on a yellow bonnet at a milliner's near Covent Garden market. No—first I must tell you that a coterie of women, both old and young, must have been camping underneath my window for hours, for they followed my footsteps like ducklings, and the moment I stepped inside the shop, they did the same. All during my brief walk, I could overhear them commenting to one another on my gown, my shoes, my parasol—wondering where I had purchased the trimmings that they might do the same, who my modiste was—even the color of my hair was roundly discussed.

"And no sooner did I settle upon that bonnet, which quite resembled a lemon meringue tart, only got up with pale green ribbons at the chin, and the shopkeeper extended me the credit of the house for it, than did every single duckling ask for the very same confection, that they might copy Mrs. Robinson's taste! Nowadays, should I wish to slip out of the theatre unnoticed after a performance and enjoy an hour of blissful anonymity, I need not contrive a disguise, for there are easily a dozen women in the audience who are wearing nearly the same ensemble I did when I entered my dressing room." With a hearty laugh, I said, "I cannot tell you how amused I have become by such flattery. Truly, I am tickled by it all."

Sheridan frowned. With the gentlest anxiety, he cautioned me to beware these sycophants. "You are on every side surrounded by temptations," he said, with a wave of his hand that encompassed the little luxuries I had accumulated—gilded candelabra and porcelain figurines—trophies all acquired on credit or from my husband's occasional winnings on the field of green baize. "My dear Mary . . . you are still so—dare I voice this—ignorant . . . in many respects . . . to the ways of the world. With the Rutlands, it is easy to see that no one offers something for nothing. But with other species of flatterer, their motives are obscured and by the time you have sussed out their intentions, it may be too late to salvage your reputation." He took my hand and held it until I felt the warmth from his palm penetrate my own. "Dear child, I watch you move through the world and I fear that you are destined to be deceived, particularly if you choose the path of greatest temptation. You have within you the makings of a fine artist. If this is your dream, then let your popularity soar because the public clamors for your theatrical talent—and not because they have conspired with you to manufacture a celebrity. For one is your eternal gift from God and Mr. Garrick; and the other, a matter of public taste beyond your control, as fickle as vows made in wine."

I shook my head and blinked back a tear. I did not wish to believe him.

Sixteen

Enter Prince Florizel, Stage Left

1779 . . . just past my twenty-second birthday

On December 3, 1779, Londoners might have perused any one of the morning papers, of which there numbered over a dozen at the time, and read the following item amid the theatrical announcements:

> *Drury Lane,*
> *By Command of their Majesties*
> *The sixth time these ten years*
> *At the Theatre Royal in Drury Lane*
> *This Day will be presented*
> The Winter's Tale
>
> *(altered by Garrick from Shakespeare)*

So altered, in fact, was this production that Garrick had the title published under the name *Florizel and Perdita,* for the entire crux of my mentor's tale was the relationship between the lost princess raised as a lowly shepherdess, and the son of her father's greatest rival. And it was as

Florizel and Perdita that we theatricals referred to the play backstage at Drury Lane.

I confess I felt a most strange degree of alarm when just two days prior my name was announced to perform the role of Perdita. When I curtsied deeply to Mr. Sheridan to thank him for such an honor, it was all I could do to rise to my feet with any semblance of steadiness.

Miss Farren had been the first to offer me a kiss on the cheek. "Congratulations, Mary. The Perdita for Their Royal Majesties. Such an honor does not make you tremble, does it?"

Such solicitude! No doubt she wished me to tremble so mightily that I should have to be replaced in the role by none other than herself. And if the encomium did indeed paralyze my nerves, Betty Farren would be the last to know of it.

"I'm quite surprised, you know," Miss Farren continued. "Their Majesties much prefer Covent Garden to Drury Lane."

"And why should that be?" I had demanded, fiercely proud of our company, and wondering whether Miss Farren was just as loyal.

"Why, Covent Garden is managed by a staunch Tory— and everyone knows Mr. Sheridan's political bent leans most decidedly for the Whigs. And it's common knowledge that King George and Queen Charlotte, no matter how proper she is, and how little she appreciates entertainments that do not uplift the general moral tone, prefer the popular contemporary comedies to Shakespeare. I should wonder at His Majesty's selection of *Florizel and Perdita*."

She was trying to unnerve me then, and I own she was having some success. I had never performed before the royal family, though I had frequently played the part, with more than one actress, including Miss Farren, in the supporting role of Hermione.

I could not sleep a wink during the night that preceded the command performance. Poor little Maria Elizabeth was fussy with toothache and I spent half the night awake with her and rubbing her gums with brandy to soothe her pain. At least her discomfort distracted my mind from all thoughts of mortification before Their Majesties.

Yet as soon as I departed for the theatre in the morning, I could fix upon nothing else. As I picked my way through the rutted streets of Soho, muttering aloud to myself—I was running my speeches—the coterie of admirers tracing my steps must have thought me a madwoman. For the next week there would doubtless be legions of women dashing about the streets of London talking aloud to themselves!

The mood behind the scenes at Drury Lane was no less enervated. The actors could talk of nothing but the performance, fearful they might not be up to the task though they'd played their roles a hundred times, and eager beyond all measure that the royal party should single them out for their merits. The backstage warrens, from corridors to dressing rooms, received a thorough scouring, personal items deemed a bit too personal were removed from dressing tables, and the front of the house—from the uppermost boxes to the benches in the pit—was attacked by an army of charwomen, who swept and scrubbed and dusted the walls, chairs, and floors as though their very lives depended on its cleanliness.

Because I had neither the clout nor the salary to have my own costumes constructed, I relied upon the company's vast wardrobe. Yet since I was playing a principal role, I had the right to select my own garments. Rather than choose the usual pastel confection, which I deemed unbefitting a girl who has spent a lifetime as a lowly shepherdess, I decided to present a more rustic prospect. Evidently, I had chosen well, for dear Mr. Smith, our Leontes—an actor whose gentlemanly manners and enlightened conversation rendered him a credit to our profession—applauded upon seeing me in my fitted red peasant jacket, my hair ornamented with matching ribbands that danced fetchingly when I moved about. "By Jove, Mrs. Robinson, you will make a conquest of the prince, for tonight you look handsomer than ever!"

I blushed and twirled a bit. Though outwardly it may have seemed bravado, it was all a screen to mask my anxieties that I should not be adequate to the task ahead of me, for in Mr. Garrick's script, Perdita is the most important role.

Finally—the spectacle commenced. Their Majesties were seated in their box, just above stage right, with His Royal Highness, the Prince of Wales, ensconced in his own box, just across the pit, from which he had quite a clear view of the performers waiting in the opposite wings. "He marks you!" whispered Mr. Smith in my ear. "Look how he marks you!"

Mrs. Hartley, who was playing Hermione, nudged me smartly in the ribs. "It's true. His Highness is far more interested in our conversation than the one taking place onstage. He has not taken his eyes off you."

I pretended not to look, but out of the corner of my eye, I could most certainly see the prince observing me through his quizzing glass. "And I have not even made my first entrance," I murmured to Mrs. Hartley. "Hallo, we have company," I added, noticing a short, stout buck but a few feet away, whose rose-colored coat and heels complemented his floridly hued cheeks.

It was not unusual for men of quality to linger in the wings with us, and even engage us in conversation between our entrances. After all, with the audience as illuminated as the actors, most theatergoers behaved as though they were attending a ridotto, paying far more attention to one another than to the entertainment—but I had not seen this man before. "He's not a regular," Mrs. Hartley said. "Probably with the prince's party. He looks to me to be the proper vintage."

Just then, Mr. Ford, the manager's son, led the pink-tinted gentleman to where I stood with Mrs. Hartley and made the introductions. "Mrs. Robinson, allow me to present you George Capel, Viscount Malden."

I curtsied respectfully. "A pleasure, sir." Such encounters wreaked havoc on one's concentration but did wonders for enlarging one's social sphere. "I hope you are enjoying our play."

"I will enjoy it all the more when you step out upon the boards," he said, smiling broadly. His teeth were quite tobacco-stained. "Tell me, do you enjoy your profession?"

I noticed that the prince was intently observing our tête-à-tête; he had not marked a word of what was transpiring onstage in Bohemia. "It is everything I have ever aspired to," I told the viscount. "I have desired nothing else all my life."

The nobleman raised his lorgnette. Pretending to scrutinize me as though I were a scientific specimen or circus oddity, he replied, "Not so very long a life, though."

I smiled. "I am just twenty-two, your lordship." Suddenly, I felt dreadfully ancient. I guessed that Malden was about my age, but His Royal Highness, only seventeen, was still four years shy of his majority. "Oh, good heavens, that is my cue!" I exclaimed and rushed out onto the stage.

What a monumental task not to be distracted! I hurried through my lines, displeased with my efforts, and yet, owing to the proximity of the prince's box—which was right above the stage—I could hear everything he uttered as clearly as I could hear my colleagues' lines.

"Breathtaking! The beau ideal!" remarked the prince. I found myself torn between playing directly to him—was I supposed to do so?—and focusing on the other actors in the scene.

"The nonpareil of natural beauty! Such grace! Oh, Perdita!" he sighed, loud enough for all about to hear him. I stole a glance at His Highness's countenance and read there an expression of sublime delight. Truly, he did seem transfixed by my person. I felt acutely embarrassed by such attentions, made all the greater only moments later, for now the entire house was gazing at the heir to the English throne gazing at me! I was overwhelmed with confusion. Was I expected to acknowledge His Highness's approbation in some way? A glance? A smile? A curtsy? Certainly not a *word*—one did not speak to a member of the royal family unless most distinctly addressed. My thoughts were all a-jumble. *Oh, dear. The ghost of my dear mentor Garrick would have my head in Shakespeare's name if I did not make him proud and play my part to perfection!*

Each time I would make an exit, there was Lord Malden in the wings, eager to resume our conversation. "The prince is quite taken with you," he remarked.

"I am honored beyond all measure; but I know not how to respond," I admitted.

"As he favors you, so you favor him," said the courtier. "Smile for smile."

Lord Malden said a thousand civil things to me between scenes, evoking everything from the weather to politely inquiring as to whether I had family in London, to queries about whether an actor's mind was better honed than others' brains, for how did we manage to cram so many lines and scenarios in our heads all at once without ever making a single mistake?

"Oh, we make mistakes from time to time," I laughed. "One night last season our Mr. Smith began the play with the opening monologue from *Richard III*—you know, 'Now is the winter of our discontent . . . ,' and he acquitted himself marvelously—but the company was performing *King Lear* that night! Confidentially"—I leaned toward the viscount until I was so close that I could smell the pomade on his wig—"I daresay the audience was so busy talking amongst themselves, as is their wont anyway, that I doubt they noticed the difference."

I rallied my nerves to perform my final scene, and we actors took our bows. To my amazement, the royal family then rose from their seats, and with the greatest condescension that had us all starry-eyed with triumph, returned a bow to the performers! They had liked us! And—just as the curtain was falling, my eyes met those of the Prince of Wales. With a look that I shall never forget, he gently inclined his head a second time. I felt this compliment from the summit of my coiffure to the tips of my boots; it was as though the god Apollo had shone his light directly on me and I keenly sensed the glow travel through the very core of my being.

The royal family then descended from their boxes and crossed the stage as the actors were making their exit. I was headed for my sedan chair, which was always waiting for me outside the theatre, when I met the royal party in the wings.

Once more, the prince's gaze met mine, and he honored me quite attentively with a very marked and low bow.

Their Royal Majesties stopped in their tracks and regarded their heir. In fact, it seemed to me then as though the entire assemblage drew in their breath as one and held it until His Royal Highness straightened his back again. My face was flushed, and not only from the exertions of a performance. I could feel my heart race within my breast, and had no desire to catch it.

The Prince of Wales! Me! What a time we had at my supper party that evening, back at my apartments. No one could speak of anything else but His Highness's attentions to me.

"One never knows what might come of it," said Mr. Smith.

Mrs. Hartley remarked, "Did you observe His Highness's manners? Such grace! Such amiability! And such a genuine smile. Rather a nice-looking young man, wouldn't you say, Mary? Tall, well formed—"

"Yes—he makes quite the dashing picture," I agreed, fearful to act like a blushing schoolgirl in the presence of my professional colleagues, who had all seen and heard far more of the world than I had.

"Nell Gwyn's eldest son was made a duke, you know," said Mr. Smith with a wink.

"Oh, come, come now. It's *hardly* a royal intrigue. His Highness merely bowed and smiled at me."

"You're such a green girl sometimes! He could not take his eyes off you during the entire performance—even when you weren't on the stage. Everyone watched him watch *you*," said Mrs. Hartley good-naturedly. She washed down a forkful of pheasant with several sips of claret. "I could have stood on my head and recited Virgil—if I knew any—and no one would have noticed."

"They would if they'd gotten a gander at your legs, Mrs. Hartley," chuckled Mr. Smith.

"I'm not certain whether that was a compliment, sir," Mrs. Hartley replied, knowing full well that it was.

The following morning, Lord Malden paid me a visit. Mr. Robinson was not at home, having spent the entire night elsewhere, in the arms of some trollop, or wallowing in drink. My frequent admonishments to set a proper fatherly example for Maria fell on consistently deaf ears; I had come to realize there was no curing him of his vices. The domestic duties attendant on being the head of a family meant nothing to him but a means by which he might prove worthy of an inheritance from Mr. Harris.

I had learned my lesson with Lord Lyttelton about the dangers of receiving calls from gentlemen, however titled, when I was home alone. And yet I could not turn away the prince's companion; it would have made for a most awkward situation. As it stood, things were already awkward enough. I stammered a welcome to the viscount, noticing that he seemed younger in the natural light of my drawing room. The lamps backstage, masked with lengths of colored fabric so that they would cast a subtly hued glow upon the players, often lent a harsh glare to the physiognomy of one standing in the wings.

"I—I am sorry to intrude upon you so," said Lord Malden, glancing about with evident discomfort. "I have—I have come on a particular errand, you see." He bowed politely. "I am most embarrassed." He saw little Maria playing at my feet with a pull toy on a string, a little lamb I had given her in honor of my command performance as Perdita. I scooped her onto my lap and introduced her to his lordship. "I—I am afraid I have come at rather a bad time."

Endeavoring to put him at ease, I assured him that on *any* morning a visitor would encounter me at play with my daughter. "It is our special time together, for the life of an actress can often be quite pell-mell."

"Nonetheless, I am truly sorry to have incommoded you, Mrs. Robinson." Lord Malden's countenance reddened to the rosy shade I had noticed the night before. "I come on a most discreet mission—you must pardon me—and—and I must ask of you never to mention it to anyone."

How intriguing! "On my honor, then, I shan't." I gave my little girl a sweet kiss upon the lips, promised that Mama would play "shepherdess" with her very soon again, and rang for Dorcas, who came to take her from the room.

"It's something of a delicate situation." His lordship dabbed at the moisture on his powdered brow with a monogrammed handkerchief. "Please do me the honor of hearing me out, and then do as you think most proper."

"It's all something of a mystery then, isn't it?" Receiving no answer, I pressed on. "You'll forgive me if I don't comprehend your meaning, sir. You will not offend me if you speak explicitly."

Lord Malden hesitated, reached into his pocket, drew his hand out empty, then blotted his brow again. After some moments of evident rumination, he tremblingly withdrew a small letter from his pocket. The paper shook like a bough of quivering aspen as he handed it to me. I took it, and upon reading the name on the fold, knew not what to say. It was addressed to "Perdita."

Turning away from his lordship, I opened the billet. It contained but a few words, which went quite beyond the bounds of common civility: "My Perdita, you have enchanted my heart and bewitched my soul." The note was signed merely "Florizel."

I smiled a bit sarcastically. No wonder he had quizzed me so assiduously the night before as we conversed in the wings—it had been an overture in preparation for this morning's symphony! "Well, my lord, and what does this mean?" I confess I was half angry at such boldness.

The viscount appeared somewhat taken aback. "Can you not guess the writer?"

"Perhaps yourself, my lord," I said gravely, believing full well that he was the author of the *billet-doux*.

"Upon my honor, no!" exclaimed Lord Malden, clapping his hand to his peacock-blue bosom. "I should not have dared to address you on so short an acquaintance."

"I am sorry then, if I have offended you. But if you are not the progenitor of these words, I must beg you to tell me who penned them."

The viscount rocked back and forth on his powder-blue heels. "I—I am . . . egad, this is most awkward . . . I should not have come here today, ma'am. I regret now my acquiescence in undertaking to deliver this epistle. I hope I shall not forfeit your good opinion, but—"

"But what, my lord?"

"I could not refuse my commission—for the letter is from the Prince of Wales."

You could have knocked me over with the tip of an aigrette. If this was true. . . . How my heart began to beat! And yet, I could not take Lord Malden's confession on faith. He had himself acknowledged that we scarcely were acquainted. How could I know that this was not an elaborate ruse to entrap and seduce me by using the name of another? I resolved therefore to consider the love note as an experiment made by his lordship, either on my vanity or on my propriety of conduct.

The viscount called on me again the following evening, whilst I was hosting a small card party of six or seven. I had not spoken to my colleagues, even to Mr. Sheridan, about the lovelorn billet; and even before Lord Malden's nocturnal visit, the talk was of nothing but the prince— his manners, his appearance, and another blow-by-blow recitation of his comportment toward me both during and after the performance of *Florizel and Perdita*.

Malden then joined my other guests in their unbounded panegyric of His Royal Highness—expounding, from his firsthand knowledge of the princely mien, on how the youth's nature was remarkably unaffected for one so high-born, his temper mild, his conversation engaging—even his gentleness toward animals was touched upon by his lordship. I heard these praises and my bosom throbbed with conscious pride, while my memory turned to the partial but delicately respectful letter I had received the previous morning.

The next day, Lord Malden arrived with a second letter purportedly from the heir apparent. I accepted it tentatively. With equal anxiety, the viscount assured me that His Royal Highness would be most unhappy indeed if I had taken offense at his conduct.

"The prince desires me to tell you that if you will attend the Oratorio this evening, he will offer a signal by which you will know that he is the true author of these letters, laying aside all skepticism you may have as to their authenticity."

"If I do, I must inform you that Mr. Robinson will be with me." Even then, though we now dwelt apart, I had no wish to offend my husband or upset our domestic apple cart, however rickety it may have been.

Our marriage was then little more than a sham. Mr. Robinson visited me when he needed money, and for little else, though he could always be counted upon to dress grandly and affect his most polished manners when it came to any entertainments in the offing, from concerts to theatre to ridottos to card parties—most *especially* card parties.

That night, Mr. Robinson and I took our places in one of the balcony boxes at the concert hall. He had no notion of why I had suggested we attend the Oratorio. Immediately, he withdrew his quizzing glass from his pocket and fixed his attention on a garishly attired lady seated across the auditorium. I made use of this opportunity to glance toward the royal box, from which the prince almost instantaneously observed me. He held the printed bill before his face and drew his hand across his forehead, still fixing his eye on me. I had absolutely no idea what he was about. Unable to fathom his semaphore, I frowned and discreetly raised my hands as if to convey that I had not comprehended him.

His Highness continued to make signs, but I could make neither head nor tail out of them. Finally, he laid his arm across the edge of the royal box and moved his hand in pantomime, as if writing a letter. This sparked the attention of the prince's next youngest brother, Prince Frederick, then Duke of Osnaburg, who was sitting in the box beside him. The youths exchanged words, and Prince Frederick then looked toward me with particular attention.

How should I react? I wondered. Subtly enough to acknowledge their attention without raising my husband's suspicions—and perhaps worse, arousing the attention of the audience, who was fixated upon the royals in their midst. I had learned from our command performance at Drury Lane that where the royals looked, there too focused the rest of the house.

One of the gentlemen in waiting brought the Prince of Wales a goblet of water; before he raised it to his lips, he looked at me, almost as if to toast me with it. By now, so marked was His Royal Highness's conduct that several persons in the pit turned to direct their gaze at me.

My vanity was gratified in the extreme to know that the most admired and accomplished prince in Europe appeared to be devotedly attached to me; yet I was as discommoded as I was flattered, for surely now the wags at the morning papers would fall over themselves to mention it. Our London dailies never permitted the truth to get in the way of a good story. Everyone knew that people paid the editors good coin to publicly puff themselves or level a jibe at others. Never mind if the stories weren't true and the items not genuine—scandal and gossip sold papers.

*   *   *

I had to know more. I requested an interview with the Duchess of Devonshire as soon as she could see me. She was the very pinnacle of smart society and her connexions were both cultivated and extensive. In between remarks about whether or not children got too much fresh air or not enough of it these days, I breezily asked her, "What think you of the Prince of Wales?"

"Don't think I don't read all the papers, ma chère; I know why you're asking me. Frankly," she added, offering me a meringue with my tea, "I've never met him. Odd, isn't it?" The duchess cocked her head prettily. "Though perhaps not. Their Majesties keep the princes of the blood terribly sheltered—and the princesses even more so." Confirming what Betty Farren had told me, she added, "Only entertainments that will expand the mind are permitted, and if the events are of a religious nature, such as the Oratorio, so much the better. Unless the king wishes to attend the theatre, they never go to such frivolities. Once he attains his majority, of course, Prince George is free to go where he pleases. I shouldn't blame him if the moment he turns twenty-one he joins a regiment and dashes off to fight in the colonies, just to escape his parents' domestic tyranny. I don't envy the four years of Hanoverian repression still ahead of him."

"Hush! You mustn't talk like that, Your Grace! It's practically treasonous." And I had nearly forgotten that he was so much younger than I. Good heavens, what would Their Majesties think if they learned he was sending *billets-doux* to an actress at Drury Lane.

"I can only tell you what I hear of him, which perhaps is not much more than you have heard yourself, though I move with some of his intimates. They say his jokes sometimes have the semblance of genuine wit—which is all to the good. And he appears to have an inclination to meddle with politics, so heaven help us all if my dear friend Fox—or your Mr. Sheridan—takes him under his wing, for then His Highness and His Majesty might come to blows. By all accounts, the prince wishes at all times to be considered a person of consequence—"

"But he *is* such a one," I interjected.

"—whether it be in intrigues of state or matters of gallantry. I thought you desired to learn all that I know of your most besotted swain, yes? Then you mustn't interrupt me," she teased. "Already it is spread about that His Royal Highness often thinks more is intended in such instances than really is the case. A form of aggrandizement, I suppose one might call it."

If this was true, I was glad to be erring on the side of caution and practicality where the prince's infatuation with me was concerned. "But what think you of his *person*. Do you not find him handsome?" Truth told, I wanted corroboration from the very avatar of elegance, for I found His Highness most pleasing to look upon.

My good friend pursed her rosy lips into a pouty moue. "I would say he has a figure that is striking, though not perfect. In my view, he might have the tendency to run to fat if he doesn't check himself. But he certainly loves fashion—I can say that, too." She let out a peal of laughter.

"What? What the devil is so amusing?"

Georgiana clasped my hands in hers, laughing so hard that she gave herself the hiccoughs. "Oh—I shouldn't say it."

"Say it!"

"And if there were anyone else in the room, I wouldn't dare."

"Say it!"

"And if it ever comes back to me, I'll deny I ever uttered the words."

"Say it!"

"Well . . . oh, may God forgive me . . . egad, I'm laughing so hard I fear I'll burst a stay . . . all right, then . . . I do think His Royal Highness looks too much like a woman in men's clothes!"

As the days became weeks, and the weeks turned to months, the prince's infatuation with me proved to be no mere passing fancy. He was positively smitten, and utterly devoted, daily professing his adulation—nay, his passion—for me in a flurry of wildly romantic letters. He pressed me for an interview, a meeting, however fleeting, that he might fix his adoring gaze upon my person and drink me in, *if only for a moment, that my eyes might feast upon what my hopes dare to dream is a taste of Elysium.*

"I am not insensible to his powers of attraction," I confessed to the duchess that spring. During the whole season, till the theatre closed, His Highness's correspondence continued. "Every day he gives me some new assurance of inviolable affection," I told her. "Whilst I counsel caution. 'Wait until you attain your majority, when your will is your own,' I've written to him. 'Be assured that your every word is cherished in my bosom, and every thought behind them a glimpse into the pleasures of golden days to come. But be prudent. It is unwise to offend, or even aggravate Their Majesties, for their tether upon your activities may tighten even more.' I must admit, he will not be dissuaded in any way from his pursuit, which each day grows in ardor. Lord Malden tells me that the prince is most wretched on my account, for I will not see him, no matter how many times he implores me."

Georgiana smiled knowingly and edged away a turquoise velvet footstool with the toe of her brocaded slipper. We were sitting in one of her salons, painted to resemble an exotic oasis with gilded palms adorning azure-colored walls. "Our royal Apollo's pursuit of the theatrical Daphne is the talk of the town. Society can scarcely find another subject so entertaining, and so much a cause for speculation—of the most literal kind, I promise you, for I am no stranger to the gaming tables. Mary, from the coffeehouse to the salon, your names are linked on everybody's lips."

Secretly, I was pleased as punch at the duchess's words.

"What have you done with all his letters?" she asked me.

"Bound them with a scarlet ribband in a velvet box, which I keep hidden away in my boudoir. I often take them from their cache and peruse them before I retire for the night, for then I sleep most blissfully."

"Speaking of boudoirs, Fox placed a hundred-guinea bet that the prince has bedded you already."

I frowned. "His Highness has not, I promise you!"

Georgiana clapped her hands with glee. "Well done, *me,* then! I betted the other way!" She kissed me on both cheeks. "If I were a better patroness I should pass my winnings on to you, for I cannot imagine how you afforded that new yellow vis-à-vis, unless it was a gift from"—she winked at me—"*a special someone.*"

"The 'special someone' was me," I confessed. "The same 'special someone' who purchased the bright blue phaeton. And the burgundy landau. Some women buy jewels or bonnets"—I sighed, only half in jest—"and some buy carriages. The truth is, what with all the world thinking I am the prince's mistress, I feel I must appear to play the role. On my salary I can scarcely afford one carriage, let alone three. But you'd be surprised at the number of merchants who fall over themselves to extend credit to the object of such marked royal favor."

"Actually, I'm not," chuckled the duchess. "Shopkeepers no longer surprise me."

"Tell me what to do, Your Grace. Please. The notoriety is new to me. And there are days when I know I am courting it as much as I dread it. I have declined to accept any interviews with His Highness because I am terrified of the éclat such a meeting might engender. It is not merely a scandal that I fear, or to be the object of malicious or speculative gossip—but my heart!" Tears sprang to my eyes and the golden palm trees became a blur. "I find the prince the most amiable, the most charming, the most *desirable* of beings! And how many women are there on this earth who can resist such a man forever? As Apollo petrified Daphne for refusing to yield to his charms, so *I* am petrified of what should befall me if I *do* succumb. Though in the fantastical ruminations of my imagination the liaison would be a lasting one, where would I be if I discover, having acquiesced, that I am merely the dupe of a young man's fancy?"

The duchess took my hand in hers. "From what I hear of his character, he is honest in his affections. But you are right to paint him in the colors of youthful exuberance. Tell me, sweet friend, how long are you prepared to play the game—your interpretation of Daphne flying the chase? Suppose for the nonce that my sources are incorrect and His Highness tires of a fox hunt where the vixen is so evasive that she will not be ensnared, however attractive the lure?"

"You must learn to be more sporting, Your Grace," I teased. "Lures are used in fishing, not for hunting. As for the prince, fatigue would appear to be a stranger to him. I cannot keep him at bay much longer, for—oh, Georgiana, I think I have fallen in love with him!"

Her Grace rose and fetched a deck of cards from a narrow drawer within her escritoire. "Clubs, you withhold your affections; diamonds, you bestow them." She shuffled the deck and fanned the cards in her hands, their pips obscured from my view. "Choose one."

I selected a card and turned it over to look at it. "And what do I do with *this* suit?" It was the king of hearts.

Lord Malden continued to press the prince's cause. A week later, he came to visit me bearing a most extravagant gift. Inside the velvet box—a sumptuous royal purple—lay the prince's portrait in miniature. I required my magnifying glass to read the name of the artist: 'twas the most celebrated Jeremiah Meyer. The likeness shone like the sun, for not only did His Highness's countenance smile upon the viewer, but the portrait was set all the way round with brilliants that caught the morning light, reflecting their effervescent sparkles on every wall of my salon.

"My heavens! This is too—" I had not words to express how overwhelmed I was with His Highness's extravagant gift. "He takes my breath away."

"I am given to understand that there is more," said the viscount. "Lift up the mounting."

I raised the little velvet plinth on which the miniature had lain to discover secreted beneath it a small heart cut out of paper. On one side was written *Je ne change qu'en mourant,* and on the opposite I read its approximate translation, *Unalterable to my Perdita through life.*

I clutched the portrait to my bosom, though fearful of staining it with my hot, happy tears. "Please convey to His Royal Highness that after so many months of doubt and delay, though I never wavered in my devotion to him, it would give me the most felicitous—the most unalloyed— pleasure to see him."

Seventeen

Royal Flush

1780 . . . age twenty-two

I t was the prince's design that I should contrive to be smuggled into his apartments in Buckingham House, disguised in male apparel—my cross-dressing costume from *The Irish Widow,* for example. Through Lord Malden I nixed the notion immediately, for the danger of detection was far too great. Not only that, the indelicacy of such a step made me shrink from the proposal.

My refusal threw His Highness into the most distressing agitation, as evidenced by the letter his customary courier—and courtier—delivered to me the following day.

> I am bereft of all solace, lady, if you do not come to me. My heart aches with the most exquisite pain, which only your tenderest ministrations can relieve. Truly, I believe I may die if I cannot see you. For the sake of England's future, for I may expire of love, I beg of you, do not postpone our meeting yet again.

"I own it wounds my heart to know that I am the cause of such misery," I told the viscount. Yet, he looked quite miserable himself. "Pray, sir, what is it that ails you?" I asked, solicitous of his frail condition.

"I regret that I consented to this entire undertaking," said Lord Malden, after several moments of hesitation.

"I am not sure I take your meaning, your lordship."

"Do not shoot the messenger," he exclaimed, then lapsed into another silence. Finally, he rallied his wits and his spirits sufficiently to explain that he, too, over the course of our acquaintance, had developed a violent passion for me.

I was utterly taken aback, for truth told I had not gleaned the slightest hint from him that he had conceived any attraction for me whatever, so assiduous and diligent had he been with his royal commission.

"Forgive me, Mrs. Robinson. I am the most miserable and unfortunate of mortals." He bowed low and pressed his lips to my kidskin slipper. "I humiliate myself, but I can no longer keep my passion a secret. And yet I understand that a consummation is not to be. It is the acknowledgment that there can be nothing between us that gnaws away at my soul."

What was I to do with such a confession? I both admired Lord Malden and pitied him. And of course he was quite correct that he could not woo me in the name of the prince royal and then attempt to claim the prize for himself. I held out my hand to him.

"Rise, sir. You do me a great honor by flattering me with your attentions, but we both know that nothing beyond the bounds of friendship can come of it. I will promise never to speak of this again . . . and permit you to tell His Highness that I will still agree to meet him—but not at Buckingham House. Perhaps Kew would be a better location for such an"—I dreaded to use the word—"assignation."

The viscount stood, his face as rosy as I had ever seen it. Consulting a pocket watch produced from the fob attached to his yellow brocaded waistcoat, he declared that the time had raced away from him and that he must be going. I felt acutely aware that I was the cause of his consternation and embarrassment.

"I will come to you again, with another proposal . . . regarding the . . . er . . . arrangements," he said, and beat a hasty retreat from my drawing room.

Yet I was still not entirely at peace with my decision. To stiffen my resolve, I thought to return to my chamber, where I kept the prince's correspondence under lock and key, and reread his most tender sentiments and expressions of the sublimest passion. I was halfway down the corridor when I heard something of a ruckus coming from the room.

I tentatively ventured toward the door, somewhat fearful of the bumps and thuds that shook the floorboards within. I listened at the keyhole and could discern no conversation. Perhaps someone was unwell.

"*Hulloo!*" I called.

I rapped upon the door and, receiving no reply, flung it open, only to discover one of the serving wenches—a dirty, squalid girl named Matilda—in the arms of Mr. Robinson, legs akimbo, the nipple of a pendulous breast poised between his teeth.

I shrieked with anger and alarm. "In my very own bed!" I shouted. "How dare you?"

I dashed to the china ewer and doused them with water as one might break apart a pair of rutting dogs. "Out of this house—immediately," I hollered. "The both of you." As Matilda scrambled to rearrange her clothes, I snarled, "And don't be expecting any references."

My bare-bummed husband bent over to hunt for his breeches.

"What am I to do with you?" I lamented. "You mock our marriage everywhere. You don't even have the decency or sense to limit your conquests to strangers in other venues. I know you keep two mistresses—no wonder we never have a farthing. Every penny I make on the stage goes into your pocket, and you shame me in my own boudoir! With a girl so dirty it's a wonder she doesn't carry the plague." Matilda was not the first servant in our employ to become the target of my husband's advances, but perhaps she was the only compliant one, as other girls had complained to me of Mr. Robinson's overtures and I had repeatedly cautioned him to keep his distance from them.

Having located and laced up his trousers, Mr. Robinson made to embrace me, but I flung out my arms to repel him. "Don't even consider a kiss! I'm like as not to catch the clap off you and your scurvy whores." I shook my head in consternation. "What can I do? We are bound to each other for life, before God, no matter how ill you treat me, unless there is some new law under the sun that will rescue me from this farce of a marriage. If I were to invent your low, licentious character in a novel, the fiction would not be half so heinous a creation as the original!"

I fairly kicked him to the curb, and for all I knew he scuttled like a horrid black beetle to his own lodgings.

I rang for Dorcas and she helped me yank the bedclothes from where they lay, tumbled about. "Burn them," I commanded.

She looked at me as though I'd been speaking in tongues. "But, ma'am, you always tell me how these was so costly—"

"I know they were, but I don't care. Burn them. And the candlewicked bedspread as well."

"Are you well, ma'am?"

"No, Dorcas, I am not." I threw myself on the bare mattress, soaking it with my sobs.

"Why are you crying, Mummy? Did someone make you sad?" Maria heaved herself onto the high bed and nestled beside me, shoving her tiny thumb in her mouth. I wrapped my arm around her and drew her to me, her warmth and sweet scent a comfort to my wounded pride.

"Sometimes, my angel, sometimes your papa is not a very nice man."

But I wasn't weeping merely out of the humiliation visited upon me by Mr. Robinson's disgusting conduct with the serving wench. I cried over a pattern I had seen before, and one I knew too well: a pain inflicted on my mother and her children by my own father, Nicholas Darby.

The buds of my husband's neglect and indifference had blossomed into a reeking, cankered bloom. There was no longer a shred of esteem between us, and yet I had done nothing to cause Mr. Robinson's animadversion to me, whilst his own transgressions in this regard would fill a chronicle. His cruel behavior, more than any other element, reconciled my mind to the idea of a separation, and pushed me toward that fateful first encounter with the Prince of Wales.

At length, an evening was fixed for the interview. How I agonized during the long days leading up to it! Among my chief concerns was what to wear to such an event—an assignation with the most comely and noble youth in Europe. I must have changed clothes a half dozen times that day in anticipation of the meeting.

It had been left to Lord Malden to arrange the particulars. At first, His Royal Highness had proposed that I come to the viscount's residence in Dean Street; but the prince's social sphere was too restricted, governed as he was by a rigid tutor; and therefore, slipping off to Mayfair was an impossibility.

At length, it was determined that our initial *rencontre* was to last but a few moments—any longer would have imperiled detection—and would take place at Kew, along the banks of the Thames.

Lord Malden and I dined first at the inn on the narrow spit of land betwixt Brentwood and Kew. Such was my anticipation, so riddled with anxieties, that I was trembling so hard I could scarcely wield my fork.

"Now, once we depart the inn, we must wait for the signal," instructed the viscount.

My heart pounded so fiercely I could scarcely breathe. I admired the prince prodigiously and was grateful for his affection, believing him the most engaging of created beings. By this time I had corresponded with him over the course of many months, and his eloquent letters, the exquisite sensibility that permeated every line, his ardent professions of admiration, had all combined to shake my feeble resolution. The very thought of him buoyed my spirits; I felt as though I walked on air. "Are you sure he will come?" I whispered to Lord Malden.

"He has talked of nothing else for a fortnight," his lordship assured me. "Ah! Look—there is the handkerchief. We must make haste!" Through the dusky gloom, I spied a glimmer of white on the opposite bank. It was our cue. "Give me your hand." Lord Malden held out his own for me to take, and he steadied his arm as he helped me into the little boat that was to take us up to the iron gates of old Kew Palace.

Two men strode silently on the avenue before the gates. The prince was not alone. Accompanying him was his next youngest brother—in a coat so light it fairly begged for our detection. I nearly lost my nerve. What had Prince Frederick been thinking? The rest of us—Lord Malden, the Prince of Wales, and I—were shrouded in somber shades, my own cloak being a deep midnight blue.

The air smelled moist and faintly loamy. The boatman was instructed to wait. Lord Malden guided me onto the shore and made the briefest of introductions because time was of the utmost essence. I curtsied low to His Royal Highness, who then placed his hands on mine and raised me to my feet. Even through our gloves I could feel the heat of our mutual ardor like a bolt of electricity that passed between us. The prince ever so gently slipped down the hood of my cloak that he might look into my eyes. His were the mildest shade of gray, and yet shone with an enthusiasm mingled with eagerness and devotion.

"Oh, celestial creature," he murmured, as he gazed at me. "How you have gratified me this night." He tilted his head and the rising moonlight illumined his pale cheek. "I have so many things to say to you. When may we meet again?"

I was about to ruminate on this exciting query when a

noise of people approaching from the palace startled us. The idea of our being overheard, or of His Royal Highness being seen out at such an unusual hour, terrified our little party.

"We must go," whispered the prince, glancing at his younger brother. Suddenly, he grabbed my hands and clasped them to his bosom, bringing me so close to his royal person that I could feel his heart beat beneath his breast. "Soon—soon! I have waited so long . . . please do not delay for another eternity our next encounter." His eyes conveyed such passion, and his soft lips seemed to wish to yield to mine; but he broke away and departed in haste, leaving me with a great desire to share his company again at the soonest possible moment.

If it had taken months to woo me, in an instant, I had been won. If my mind had before been influenced by esteem, it was now awakened to the most enthusiastic admiration. No longer was I awed by his station; our meeting, though all too brief, now fixed him in my mind as both lover and friend. As I admitted the following day to the Duchess of Devonshire, "The graces of his person, the irresistible sweetness of his smile, the tenderness of his melodious yet manly voice, will be remembered by me till everything else has been forgotten."

"Oh, I love a good love story! When will you see him again?"

"On Thursday evening, again at dusk."

"How thrilling! And in the same location?"

"It seems thus far to be the safest," I told the duchess. "It is a grand and terrifying adventure I embark upon— for once I have given myself completely, there is no turning back."

Her Grace feared that I would be ill prepared for the censure I might receive. "All the world will be envious of you. A word of caution, Mary: you may find yourself more shunned than embraced for your decision."

I was already one foot over the precipice. Below me stretched an abyss.

Our second meeting was as fervent as the first. "When, when can you be mine—all mine?" His Highness entreated me. "Mine—utterly and completely."

I tried to tether myself to the banks of pragmatism, knowing I was headed instead for the dangerous shoals. "You are young," I whispered. "Led on by the impetuosity of passion." I found my nerve and steeled it. "Were I to give myself to you entirely, I should have to quit my husband—and while he is no prince in any sense of the word, our marriage, even such as it is, guarantees me my respectability, something a woman in my profession frequently lacks. Therefore, I must take it where I find it," I added, trying to find the light in such a weighty situation, for my heart was in turmoil.

"Your profession is to me, fair creature, a greater hurdle than your domestic entanglements. You know it is not respectable—"

At this I bristled. "Your Highness, with the greatest deference to your royal opinion, allow me to state that it is the conduct of the actress and not the acting itself that has given rise to the view that those of us who are trained to tread the boards are no better than those who troll the streets and fill the nearby bawdy houses. You realize that I have achieved a great deal of acclaim in the past four years for the versatility of my talent in interpreting the women of Shakespeare as well as those penned by our contemporary dramatists. To be a great actress was all I ever aspired to, and my mother and Mr. Robinson played a hand in dashing those dreams early on."

"But I am not Mr. Robinson." The prince puffed out his broad chest a bit, preening like the young peacock he was. "I am not like any other man on this earth! You must know that it would not be seemly for the heir to the throne of England to take as his lover one of your profession."

We strolled along the banks, daringly arm in arm, His Highness's bulk protecting me from the breezes riffling off the river. How surprised I was to feel as though I could say anything to this exalted being, that I could speak my mind.

"It is rather an exhausting profession, I confess. Learning one role whilst rehearsing another, and performing a third the selfsame evening. Yet it gives me both pleasure and independence. Mr. Robinson contributes precious little to my purse. He has assiduously made it his business to seek no employment, and the only crowns I receive from him derive from his occasional success at the gaming tables. We have a young daughter who must be properly looked after. Were I to quit, then, the career that has brought me joy and fame—and perhaps even more important, an income of my own—I should find myself, and my daughter, entirely at your mercy, Your Highness."

At this the prince stopped and earnestly clasped me to his breast. "My darling Perdita—I will never bring you to ruin! Rather, I will raise you up! As my only, dearest, most beloved, you shall want for nothing if you will only consent to be mine. I—I will offer you proofs of my devotion, you shall see!"

I knew not what he meant. My mind was so torn, for what now would be my greatest desire might also prove my damnation. "Even so—should we become engaged in a public attachment—people will talk, Your Highness. Are you prepared for the calumny that will be on their lips and published in the morning papers? The attempts by all quarters, including your family, to undermine our affections?"

I was older than the prince by a few years. We could not hope to behave like the unseeing ostrich; one of us had to voice the concerns of maturity and practicality. As tempting and alluring as a royal liaison was, I firmly believed that the dangers of such an affair needed to be aired and thoroughly discussed, if for no other reason than to avoid future misunderstandings.

"The abuse may be too great for you to bear, Your Highness. Please dare to imagine the misery I would suffer if, after showing you every proof of confidence, you should change your sentiments toward me."

Yet to every obstacle I broached, the prince assured me of his inviolable affection. And gazing into his noble countenance, I found him to be so sincere, his expression so ardent and earnest, that I finally, and most firmly, believed that the prince meant what he professed. His soul was too ingenuous, his mind too liberal, and his heart too susceptible to deliberately or premeditatedly deceive me.

My own heart and mind teetered on the balance. How I wished to give myself entirely to the prince. I thought of nothing but him, even when I was onstage; at every moment I found myself craving his passionate words, desiring his fond company. Still, it would not be as simple a decision as all that.

It was spring-cleaning time. My rooms were brighter than usual, for the heavy draperies had been taken down, and the mullioned windows scrubbed until each pane shone like a diamond. My maids vented their tempers on the upholstery, beating the drapes and the carpets they dangled from the sills. Woe betide the pedestrian below us!

In my drawing room, amid the clouds of dust motes, homeless after having been drummed from their cozy winter hideaways, sat Mr. Robinson. Absent the merest trace of contrition or compunction, he had paid me a call for the express purpose of encouraging me to open my purse. As much as I wished to box his ears with one of the dustclouts or brooms, I could not refuse him. By law, a wife's earnings were her husband's to spend as he chose.

"Your cruel conduct toward me is pushing me into the arms of another," I told him. "Till now I have not succumbed to any man's advances, but I am falling in love and I fear it will not be long before I have crossed the river that separates the mere idolater from the adulterer." Of course Mr. Robinson's extramarital liaisons numbered in the dozens, but I never sought to gauge myself by his own low character.

Although some might believe that the sauce for the gander will flavor the goose just as well, in truth, nothing could be a falser apprehension; for the wife of even the most rakish of husbands was expected to keep her reputation unsullied. There was, however, an unwritten rule that assumed that if his wife were to give him tit for tat, the husband would passively endure his dishonor, and provide her with the sanction of his protection.

This warping of the social fabric would prove a recurrent theme in my novels; and I could simply look about me for examples of this double standard, as the circles of fashion afforded more than one instance of this obliging acquiescence in matrimonial turpitude. In fact, my dear friend Georgiana, Duchess of Devonshire, who—from her lofty perch atop the very pinnacle of style for years commanded the highest view of societal conduct—lived it herself. Her Grace enjoyed her own extramarital liaisons, whilst the duke availed himself of the charms of Lady Elizabeth Foster, Georgiana's dearest friend.

"I will not stand in your way," Mr. Robinson told me, "if you wish to bestow your affections elsewhere. I may be without scruples, Mary, but I am not without feeling. Should I endeavor to forbid you, or in other ways keep you from—well, shall I leave it at 'enjoying yourself outside the bonds of holy matrimony'—it would be a bit like the pot insulting the kettle for its blackness. You're in for a rough go of it, though, my dear."

"I cannot imagine that I will be mocked any more than I already am for *your* infidelities," I sighed.

"You're really quite a sporting girl, Mary. I don't know of any other woman who would come to her husband, especially one who has been a bit of a rover himself, and give him notice that she plans to do a thing."

"It's precisely because you're a bit of a rover—a *bit*? Egad! You must be jesting. But it's precisely for that reason that I thought you'd understand."

Mr. Robinson planted a friendly kiss on my cheek. "Lord help us, we're more a pair than we think we are." He swatted my bum; that, too, with some degree of affection. "I'll always respect you, wife of mine. And no matter what happens, I'll always take your part. 'For better or worse,' I vowed before God, and by God Himself, I meant it."

I was then about to request an interview with Mr. Sheridan when he informed me that he privately wished to discuss a most pressing matter.

"I can never for the life of me comprehend how you manage to find anything in here," I commented, picking my way through various piles of manuscripts until I found a chair, the seat of which was also hidden by a stack of scripts about to topple onto the floor. The manager's office was capacious enough, but there never seemed to be an inch of available space.

"Terribly sorry about that," apologized Sheridan, gathering the plays into his arms. "Please, do be seated. I would have tidied up for you, but you know one has the best of intentions, and then—*tempus fugit*! Suddenly it's two weeks later."

"Yours is not an easy task," I assented. "And I do not envy you your position. The Theatre is an exhausting enough profession for us actors, who have far less to occupy their days than a man in your position. Even so, after four years of a most grueling—though prodigiously rewarding—schedule, one begins to—"

And here, Mr. Sheridan interrupted me. "I assure you, Mrs. Robinson, as much as the public appreciates your . . . your gifts . . . I value them even more greatly."

"Which is why I wished to speak with you, sir, if you'll allow me—" I laughed because Sheridan had begun to say, "Which is why—" at precisely the same moment I began to speak the words.

"You first," we exclaimed in unison.

"No, you," I said, deferring to my senior.

Sheridan lit a taper to dispel the gloom. The only glimmer in the room came from the glinting metal buttons on his ubiquitous blue coat. Soot covered his windows and no one had bothered to clean them, there always being matters more urgent than scrubbing between the mullions. "You are one of the brightest jewels in the company's crown," the manager began. "It is no secret that the houses are filled to capacity on the nights you're on the bill. And as the gent whose job it is to put bums in seats, you've made me a happy, and solvent, man."

"The pleasure has been all mine, sir. But there comes a time in every actor's life, I imagine, when he considers whatever alternatives may lie before him. . . ."

"It is a hard life," Sheridan agreed, "and often without adequate compensation. But the Theatre is more of a democracy than one might surmise, for the public votes with their feet. And when they flock to a playhouse because a certain favorite is on the boards, a canny manager takes the hint that a rise in salary is in order, so the favorite won't flee the nest and enrich another company. Mrs. Robinson, I should hate to lose you to Covent Garden." And then he leaned forward in his chair and fixed me with his eyes. "Or Buckingham House."

"B-Buckingham House?" I stammered. Had he read my mind?

"Oh, come, come, Mary. One would have to be a blind man not to read what's in the papers. Puffs in one, squibs in another—but all of them giving credence to the rumor that you are the favorite with one far more exalted than John Bull. I could offer twice as many performances with the number of people clamoring for tickets who don't even care how talented you are—they just want to see what His Royal Highness sees! Don't you get it, my girl? It matters little to many of them that you're a fine actress; they want to see you act because you've become a celebrity."

"One takes success where one finds it, I suppose," I replied, not knowing what else to say.

Sheridan rose and opened the doors to a large oaken cupboard, from which he extracted a heavy ledger. Seating himself at his desk once again and opening the worn leather cover, he leafed through several pages of meticulously noted entries, muttering to himself as he perused them. "I am prepared to offer you a considerable increase, Mrs. Robinson. Twenty pounds a week, with an additional two pounds for each role you perform during that week. The more you play, the more I pay," he smiled. "What say you to that?"

It was a significant rise in pay. Perhaps I could have negotiated with him for an even larger salary, but I was of two minds, and neither of them held more sway over my final decision than the other. I did not know how to answer Mr. Sheridan. If I took his proffered hand and shook on the agreement, the bargain was sealed, and I could not turn back without a great deal of discomfort on either side. If I declined and told him I should like to retire from the stage instead, and risk my lot with His Royal Highness, that decision, too, was in my view irrevocable. There were plenty of actresses waiting in the wings, quite literally, to play the roles I had been given these past few seasons, eager and ambitious as ever I was, and who would cost the management less money. In time, they, too, might become favorites with the crowd for one reason or another. "I must . . . Allow me to sleep on it," I told Sheridan.

"And in the meantime you will play?" he asked, eager. Concerned.

"In the meantime I will play," I echoed.

"As a show of good faith, your salary rise will begin the moment you step outside this room." The manager rose and offered me his hand again, on which I bestowed a grateful kiss.

That night, I took the stage as Cleopatra in Dryden's *All for Love*. Waiting backstage for my entrance I mused upon the fact that I had achieved all I had ever wished for. Or had I? Meeting Prince George Augustus Frederick, heir to the throne of England, had changed everything. I consulted my conscience and my heart, and I wryly considered the subtitle of Dryden's tragedy—*The World Well Lost*. I watched my Antony bestride the stage as anxiety fluttered within my breast. Dared I relinquish all for love—or abandon what I loved and what had made me great in exchange for passion? Or would I be leaving behind all I had ever been passionate about, for the sake of love?

In any case, two prominent—and very fine—men waited upon my answer.

Eighteen

The Prince's Mistress

1780 . . . age twenty-two

*L*ord Malden continued to courier the correspondence between the Prince of Wales and myself, though as time went on, his discomfort with such a commission grew more outwardly evident. I sympathized with his predicament; the role of courtier cannot be an easy one, where one has to contain one's own feelings and opinions. By this time, he was squiring me about, and we were often seen together at many public entertainments, giving rise to malicious gossip—taken as gospel, even by those who knew me well—that I was distributing my favors to the viscount as well as to His Royal Highness.

The Duchess of Devonshire counseled me to stop dithering and come to a decision. "Tongues will wag with less velocity once you make your choice, my dear. If it is to be the stage, you release yourself from any future connexion with the prince, and you may gallivant about with Malden till the sky turns green." She lifted one of her spaniels onto her lap and began, absentmindedly, to stroke its muzzle. "But if you choose Georgie-Porgie, it will soon be clear to everyone that your new career, as it were, suffers you to be his and his alone. Tell me, my friend, is it love or money that guides your mind in this affair?"

"I'm a sentimental ninny where His Highness is concerned," I confessed. "But as a mother, with a husband who shuns any form of labor, I must be a pragmatist." I raised my feet and rested them on a brocaded footstool. "Truth told, I am rather fagged by the demands of Drury Lane. There are times when I think I shouldn't miss it much, were I to turn my back on the stage door and walk away from the theatre. When I was a very little girl, my father used to tell me, 'Once you have achieved your dreams, it's time to set new ones.' Perhaps I have done that after all. Perhaps it is time to move on, and the prince's presence in my life has created the spark, as it were, for a brand-new flame."

Georgiana, never one to shy away from gossiping herself, much as I adored her, lowered her eyes and leaned toward me, smiling like a cat after a particularly satisfying bowl of cream. "I must know—is there any *truth* to the rumors about you and Malden?"

I shook my head. "None," I averred. "I wouldn't be surprised if he'd started them himself." I smiled. "He's Malden's chaperonage is intended to distract the hounds from the actual fox."

"*He* rather admires you as well." The duchess chuckled at my metaphor.

"Who?"

"*Fox,* of course. Everyone's favorite Whig. Brilliant man, you know. I'm a partial friend, but mark my words. History will claim him as one of England's finest parliamentarians."

"He always looks so dreadfully rumpled to me. And those bushy eyebrows! I can never look upon him without being put in mind of a beetle."

Her Grace waggled a teasing finger. "Though society may judge a man by the cut of his coat, history has never judged a man by his eyebrows."

That afternoon, Lord Malden arrived, bearing another billet, the envelope thicker than usual. My mind was not arranged for small talk; the duchess's admonition was all I could think about. I pleaded a headache, and thanking his lordship for his troubles, I ushered him to the door myself. Then, seating myself at my escritoire, I opened the packet and gasped so loudly that Dorcas came running.

"Is everything all right, ma'am?" she asked, rapping on the door.

"Yes—yes," I stammered, bursting into sobs.

"It don't sound 'all right.' Shall I bring Maria to you? You always say it calms you to be near her."

"No—thank you, Dorcas. Not just yet. I—I must peruse this."

In my hand I held a document of a most official nature. It was a bond from the prince, most solemn and binding, containing a promise of the sum of twenty thousand pounds to be paid to me at the period of His Royal Highness's coming of age. True, the date would be some three years hence, but here was a protestation of his devotion so generous and sincere that it could never be sneezed at as merely a tempting ploy to bed me. The bond was the genuine article, signed by the prince and sealed with the royal arms. It was expressed in terms so liberal, so voluntary, so marked by true affection, that I scarcely had power to read it and feared I should mar the ink with my weeping. My tears, excited by the most agonizing conflicts, obscured the letters, and nearly blotted out those sentiments that will be impressed upon my mind until I breathe my last.

My emotions were in complete disarray. The indelicate idea of entering into a pecuniary arrangement with His Highness, on whose establishment I would then rely for the enjoyment of all that would render life desirable, both shocked and mortified me. And yet this was the spur that pricked me to render my decision, though it was not as easy a one as people might imagine.

"I have resolved to quit the stage," I told Mr. Sheridan. It was the spring of 1780 and the prince and I had been corresponding and meeting in secret for many weeks now—our passion still unconsummated in the most literal sense. His Royal Highness and I had enjoyed numerous bankside walks at Kew, with many sighs exchanged and whispered words of love amid the animated conversations about our respective childhoods.

"I have been kept so secluded from the world," the prince had lamented. "By parents I would not wish on anyone. My father is always cross—he's the most ill-tempered and remote man on earth—"

"Better remote and present than so remote he leaves you."

"I disagree. I should be happy if *my* father should depart for the Americas, since he seems so fond of them. And my mother is the coldest fish in Christendom. In faith, I cannot recollect ever receiving a maternal embrace from her. Not so much as a tiny hug."

With the back of my hand I caressed his downy cheek. "You poor darling. I would hug you often—and I promise it would not be at all maternal."

The prince laughed and pressed my hand in his. "You don't believe I'm so sheltered and neglected—why, look about you—this re-creation of a farm my father's made of Kew. On the orders of His Majesty, old Farmer George himself, I have received more instruction on sheep shearing than statecraft. I can bake my own bread, but cannot discourse on the merits of a bill. I know far more about planting than about parliamentary procedure, and am more conversant on the needs of His Majesty's cows than of his colonies." He laughed—to me one of the most pleasant and appealing sounds in the world. "Perhaps that's why I became so besotted with you in the guise of a milkmaid."

He broke into a lively country tune, the music puncturing the silence of the night, entrancing my senses. He sang with such exquisite taste that even the rustic ballad sounded to my ears like more than mortal melody. A tear escaped my eye as I lamented the distance that destiny had placed between us. How would my soul have idolized such a *husband*! In my ardent enthusiasm, I had formed the wish that this noble being to whom partial millions were to look up to for protection was *mine alone*!

My rosy memories of stolen nights evanesced under Mr. Sheridan's gaze. "I cannot say that I am not disappointed, Mrs. Robinson. But you know your own mind better than anyone else does. I do not hesitate to tell you I will regret the opportunities I have enjoyed these past four years to spend time in the company of a woman I am fond of and whose gifts I esteem. And the Theatre will be deprived of one of the brightest stars in its lofty firmament."

"As of the first of June," I said, tears welling in my eyes, for I would miss my Drury Lane family most dreadfully. I endeavored to rally my spirits and put a brave face on it all. "Until the thirty-first of May, I have no doubt, Mr. Sheridan, but you will come off well in the bargain when you advertise these next few weeks as Mrs. Robinson's final performances—ever. Words can never express how grateful I am to you for giving me a chance upon the stage, for shepherding my career, and for so many kindnesses as a dear and considerate, compassionate friend."

And then, no longer able to contain my sobs, I gathered up my skirts and fled the room, its aspect blurry through my bedewed eyes.

Sheridan did make the most of my final performances. With a wink to the audience, most of whom had avidly read all the reports of His Highness's especial partiality toward me, and of his lavish gifts, including the jeweled portrait of himself that he had bestowed, my last role was in Lady Craven's comedy *The Miniature Picture,* in the trouser part of Sir Harry Revel. I appeared in the comedic afterpiece that night as well, Garrick's *The Irish Widow.* It seemed fitting that the last lines I should utter on the stage at Drury Lane had been penned by my precious mentor, that most gifted genius, who after a protracted illness, on the twentieth of January in 1779 had shuffled off his mortal coil and joined the Bard of Avon in Elysium. I had written a poetic elegy in memoriam; and now, as I paced the Green Room, waiting for my entrance in the afterpiece, it was all I could do to remember that I was about to play a

228 ❖ AMANDA ELYOT

comedy, so sorrowful was I at leaving the colleagues and
friends with whom I had shared so much. "Oh joy to you
all in full measure, so wishes and prays Widow Brady," I
said to them gallantly, choking back a sob as I quoted the
last lines of my song as the title character.

Yet the effort to conceal the emotion I felt on quitting a profession I enthusiastically loved was of short duration, and I burst into tears the moment I stepped out
on the stage, in full view of the entire audience. My regret
at recollecting that I was treading for the last time the
boards where I had so often received the most gratifying
testimonies of public approbation, where mental exertion
had been emboldened by private worth, that I was flying
from a happy certainty to pursue, perhaps, the phantom
of disappointment, nearly overwhelmed my faculties, and
for some time deprived me of the power of articulation. I
could not speak a single line. Through my bedewed eyes
the faces of the eighteen hundred patrons became one
enormous, colorful blur.

Fortunately, the person on the stage with me had to
begin the scene, which allowed me time to collect myself. I confess that I went mechanically dull through the
business of the rest of the evening, notwithstanding the
cheering expressions and applause of the audience. I was
several times near fainting—it was dreadfully hard to say
farewell.

I wrote to the prince:

> I am yours—unalterably yours. On your urging
> I have quit the profession you found too sordid
> for a *maîtresse en titre* to royalty. My nights are
> now yours as well.

I desire you beyond all measure, desire to see you at the soonest, His Highness replied, and an assignation was fixed for the small but lively inn on the little island in the Thames where Lord Malden and I had supped before my very first meeting with His future Majesty.

We each arrived separately, and masked, His Highness in a borrowed domino that concealed his noble features entirely. The boisterous tavern crowd barely looked up, both accustomed and indifferent to the stream of anonymous beings that ascended the creaking oaken treads for their nocturnal rendezvous.

A single, guttering candle illumined the room, its mean and meager appointments scarcely befitting a lowly holy pilgrim, let alone a prince. "My Perdita—let me look at you," exclaimed His Highness, removing his cloak and clasping me in his arms.

"My Florizel," I murmured, nestling my cheek against his chest. His salmon-colored silken coat was like the caress of a rose petal on my skin. I felt protected. In the amber glow, he appeared even younger, his countenance almost pretty.

He cupped my face in his hands and brought his lips to mine, tasting my tongue with his, eager and ardent. Then, puppyish, he sought to divest me from my garments in such a hurry I feared he might rend them to shreds.

"Oh, my darling, you have much to learn," I laughed, when he appeared utterly stymied by the maze of ties and fasteners.

"Then show me," he urged. "Show me how to undress you."

He was all kisses and fingers. I taught him to unhook my stomacher and unlace my robe and stays, and then untie my petticoats and shift—leaving me in white silk stockings that clung to my thighs through the good offices of a pair of satin garters, and my blue brocaded slippers, to which I had affixed one of his gifts to me: a set of buckles inlaid with brilliants.

"Even in my dreams, you are not this beautiful," murmured the prince, fussing to divest himself of his own attire as quickly as possible.

"Here—allow me," I said, and untangled him from his jacket and waistcoat. "I'm not going anywhere. There's no need to rush."

"Oh—but there is! There is!"

I helped him remove his boots and hose, and watched him perform a rather comical dance about the room, in which he attempted to extricate his legs from his breeches. Finally, he stood before me, in his linen, but for his smooth bare chest. He was indeed well made then; a handsome youth and noble to behold in every way.

I slipped my arm about his waist and drew him closer, and closer still until I could feel him growing firm against my thigh. "I do believe the royal standard is flying, Your Highness," I whispered, and we both broke out into peals of laughter. My Florizel pressed me to his breast and showered me with a thousand adoring kisses. It was the first time in my life that a man had made me feel beautiful— and truly loved. In his arms I felt warm and safe. And, to my astonishment, powerful. The sensation was so heady that I was near to losing my balance from giddiness.

"Teach me about the world, Mary." Our bodies sank as one onto the faded counterpane. "Tell me everything," he murmured into my mouth. "I want to know it all."

Nineteen

Riding High

1780 . . . age twenty-two

As the stage was no longer my world, I became determined to make the world my stage.

Soon, everyone in London knew that I was the prince's mistress and had set myself up in an establishment in Cork Street, Burlington Gardens. The house was neat, but by no means splendid. The accommodations were rather modest, in fact, though the dwelling had acquired some notoriety before I became its tenant, having once been fitted up for the Countess of Derby when she deserted her lord and children for the waiting arms of her lover, the Duke of Dorset.

Here, I entertained the prince and his friends with music and cards in the evenings. His young Highness felt completely at liberty to express himself, free from the scrutiny of his tutors and his parents' disapproval of nearly all of his acquaintances and everything he undertook—or failed to undertake, for in their view he shirked his duties at every possible turn. I knew he was chafing under a very painful bit, so I sought to make the hours we spent together as charmed as a prince royal deserved.

Only a week after my final performance, His Highness invited me to the evening ball at St. James's Palace, to celebrate the king's birthday. Everyone was terribly afraid that the thing might not come off—first it was postponed a day because June 4 fell on a Sunday that year—and of course the Gordon Riots had put the entire city in a state of high alarm.

These dreadfully violent anti-Catholic protests had begun in the face of parliamentary proposals for Catholic emancipation, granting Papists the same civil and political liberties that we Protestants enjoyed.

The royals feared getting caught in the melees, and worse, dreaded the possibility of massacre. For days the streets had been ablaze; angry swarms of Protestants had turned arson and vandal against anyone and anything Papist. There had been a terrible rumor that the mob planned to storm St. James's Palace and upset the king's birthday celebrations; accordingly, many of the nobility suddenly found themselves with something more pressing to do that evening.

I would not have missed the occasion for the world, though I must confess I was not actually permitted to accompany the prince. "I profoundly apologize, my darling," he had told me, kneeling at my feet as if a penitent, "for I'm afraid you must watch the ball from the spectators' box. But at least you will be in attendance. And as certain as my name is George Augustus Frederick, Prince of Wales and Duke of Cornwall, I will show you proof of my affections, that everyone there might know, my Perdita, that my heart is completely and irrevocably yours."

My heart throbbed with a strange mixture of regret and glee—disappointment that we could not publicly be linked at so grand an occasion, and delight that he would find a way around it by singling me out. "What will you do?"

The prince pressed his lips to my fingertips; his smile illumined my salon. "Wait and see!"

Heads turned when, with Lord Malden on my arm, I arrived at St. James's Palace, dressed in the height of fashion, my gown a lavender polonaise shot with gold threads. Though I endeavored to appear dreadfully dignified, it was nigh impossible to mask my delight at setting foot inside St. James's!

Thousands of tapers glinted from enormous crystal chandeliers, rivaling the lavishly jeweled nobility for brilliance. The paneled walls were highly polished. The air was thick with the scents of perfume and pomade.

"I have good news, Mrs. Robinson," he exclaimed. At this, I thought I should dance with the prince after all. "His Royal Highness has instructed me to escort you to the Lord Chamberlain's box, so you will not be insulted by the necessity of taking your place amid the common spectators."

Malden gestured toward an area quite like a grandstand, separated from the dance floor by a low wall paneled in walnut. There were about five rows of seats ascending from the floor, as if the room were some sort of arena.

My disappointed heart sank at his words, but at least my lover had made every effort to honor me.

Still, it stung when the Prince of Wales, looking the very picture of youthful nobility in a sky-blue coat beautifully embroidered with silver, opened the ball with the strikingly lovely Lady Augusta Campbell, daughter of the Duke of Argyll. The envy that I felt was incalculable, made all the more acute by the acknowledgment that no matter how intimate I was with the heir to the throne, my station prohibited me from mingling in this exalted sphere. Seated in the Lord Chamberlain's box, I was but a few feet from the royal family, but the gulf might just as well have been an ocean.

Lady Augusta drew a pair of pink rosebuds from her bouquet. I held my breath. Her intention was clear—the buds were emblematic of him and her; how would the prince handle her flirtation? I all but bit my glove. Her ladyship proffered the gift to His Highness, expecting him, no doubt—as did I—to place them in his bosom. But to the astonishment of the entire glittering assemblage, the prince summoned one of his confidants, the Earl of Chomondeley, and, handing him the rosebuds, whispered something in the young lord's ear. Their dual gaze affixed on me, seated in the Lord Chamberlain's box; and naturally, all eyes followed until they focused on my person. The dancing ceased; lorgnettes were raised, and one could hear even a pin drop in the ballroom.

The earl mounted the stairs and entered my box, offering me the buds with a gallant bow. When his eyes met mine, I could see that he was not pleased to have been asked to perform his commission. His unspoken distaste for me, which clearly expressed the collective opinion of the exalted throng below us, awakened in me a measure of defiance, and I placed the rosebuds in my own bosom, pleased with my victory over my would-be rival.

But my triumph was short-lived.

*　　*　　*

"Half the world would appear to hate me," I lamented to the Duchess of Devonshire as we strolled along Piccadilly. "And most of them are newspaper editors and caricaturists. Yesterday I opened the *Morning Post* to find the most scurrilous cartoon! I snipped it for the portfolio I have begun to keep of every squib and scandalous jibe. In just a few weeks' time, it has grown thicker than my thumb."

We passed a young newsboy hawking a broadsheet. "Perdita Sucking at the Public Teat!" cried the boy vulgarly, his squawky soprano not yet near manhood's deeper tones. His mouth gaped like a fish when I purchased a paper off him.

"Look at this!" I said to Georgiana, pointing at the ugly drawing that covered the better part of a quarter page.

Her Grace scrutinized the caricature in which I was depicted in my new silver and blue carriage emblazoned with my crest, a flowering heart that from a distance resembled a five-pronged coronet. Titled "The new vis-à-vis, or Florizel driving Perdita," the vicious cartoon showed me absconding with the nation's treasury, a fat periwigged nobleman (representing Lord North, the prime minister) supine on the roof of the carriage, bearing a sign marked "royal favor." With His Highness on the box, and Fox as rear postilion, the coach was pulled by a pair of horned goats, a recognizable symbol of the cuckold.

Keenly I felt the malice of my detractors. Georgiana had solicitously informed me that even those whom I numbered among my friends were in truth secret enemies, eager to see me topple from my lofty perch. "So illustrious a lover could not fail to excite the envy of your own sex," the duchess reminded me. It was as plain as fustian that women of all descriptions were desirous of attracting His

Royal Highness's attention, and I had neither the rank nor the power to oppose such alluring adversaries.

"I cannot go anywhere without hearing some vicious slander against me," I said to the duchess, just as an elderly woman shook her walking stick at me. "It seems that every engine of female malice has been set in motion to destroy my repose. There are times when I cannot enjoy a single minute of the happiness I have earned. Every petty calumny is repeated from mouth to mouth, from behind fans and broadsheets, and is so distorted with each repetition that the scandal becomes magnified tenfold." Tales of the most infamous and glaring falsehood were invented and disseminated. I was assailed by pamphlets, by paragraphs, and by caricatures, crushing me with the artillery of libel, while the only being to whom I then looked up to for protection was so situated as to be unable to afford it to me.

The duchess made a show of crumpling the broadsheet with her pretty lavender glove. "I'm terribly sorry. If it's any consolation, tomorrow every Billingsgate fishmonger will be using this caricature to wrap cod filets. They're not much fonder of me," sighed Georgiana. "You have no idea of the scoldings I have received from Mama when she reads all those squibs about my gambling losses. I love her madly, of course, but she's almost as proper as Her Majesty, you know." The duchess frowned. "It's hard to be a mother, I suppose. I hope my own children remain fond of me. I should die of misery if they didn't. Of course, it's not as though *you* approve of my gaming either."

"With all due respect to Your Grace, I don't. The only vice for which I have an unreserved antipathy is gambling. I despise cards and the monsters they make of the players." I laid my hand solicitously on her forearm. "Are you in need of funds? How much have you lost of late?"

The duchess turned her head away from my prying gaze. "Pray don't ask. Canis quizzes me enough in that regard as it is. I fear he's tiring already of paying off my debts." She turned to me. "I wish you could understand the thrill one gets as the stakes mount! One's heart beats so much quicker at the clacking of chips and the clink of coins as the ante is raised from player to player."

"I will sooner be the bride of the Prince of Wales than comprehend that allure," I said glumly.

"Come, come now, Mary. Take cheer in the fact that His Highness honors you whenever he can."

"But even at my own fetes, saving Your Grace, *birthright* takes precedence over what takes place in the boudoir. At the ball he gave in my honor at Weltje's, he danced first with *you*," I reminded her. "I may be his lover, but I'm still a lowly commoner lacking rank and title, and an adulteress, to boot. I know the rules quite well, do not mistake me. Yet the more I feel their restrictions, the more tempted I am to flout them."

"Is that why you took a side box at the Haymarket Theatre?"

There had been a good deal of gossip in the papers about this. The side boxes were considered the purview of ladies and gentlemen of quality and reputation, whereas people of my stamp and character—though I had been the queen of Drury Lane and much admired for it—were expected to be seated up in "the gods" amid the demireps and outright prostitutes.

"I do believe that my circumstances warrant it," I said, referring to the location of my theatre box. I awaited a nod of understanding or a word of approbation from the duchess, but her silence conveyed much.

"You must forgive me if I cut short our interview," said Georgiana, her manner surprisingly brisk. "The Duke of Bedford is having a card party this evening, and I must have my coiffure seen to. It is expected of me to set the fashion."

She turned toward Devonshire House as I endeavored to mask my disappointment in such coolness after several years of affectionate cordiality.

As I stood several yards from her entrance gate, I felt a fissure open between myself and my esteemed patroness, and feared it would widen into an unbridgeable chasm. Here we were, a pair of high-strung contemporaries; but one of us was wellborn where the other was not, and that made all the difference. Though we were the same age, with pious and disapproving mothers, and with husbands who were far from attentive to our needs and sensibilities—mine preferring his doxies and hers preferring his dogs—and though we shared a passion for fashion and literature, it was becoming clear to me that the duchess viewed quite coolly any notions I might have above my station. Despite our common interests, we would never be equals, and it seemed rather pointed—though unsaid—that I would do well to remember it.

But I had a new role to play—that of the acknowledged mistress of the Prince of Wales—and play it I would, all the way up to the gilded hilt.

To the multitudes, I was a curiosity, no longer renowned for being an actress of some note, but famous simply for being famous. Whenever I appeared in public in those days I was overwhelmed by the masses of intrigued onlookers eager to know where I shopped and what I purchased, that they, too, might copy my taste. One morning I placed an order for clocked hosiery; by that afternoon, the figured stockings were all the rage. I was frequently obliged to quit Ranelagh and Vauxhall, owing to the crowd that had gathered around my box, making an enjoyable evening an utter impossibility. And yet I own I thrived on the attention as much as it deterred me from any aspect of privacy when I was out in the world. It was astonishing to realize that the public had been less curious about me when I was the toast of Drury Lane. I had to smile with amusement at the absurdity of it all: that people were more fascinated with someone for being fascinating, rather than for any legitimate skill or talent.

"Mummy, you have as many gowns as the duchess," little Maria observed. "Which one will you wear today?"

"Why don't you choose it, my pet?"

Maria shoved my garments from one side of the massive wardrobe to the other. "Not this one; you were the Amazon yesterday. You looked like the warriors in my picture book."

"You should have seen people gawking at my matching chariot; it was ever so much fun."

"Will you drive the chariot again today?"

"No, not today, sweetheart. Mummy nicked it up a bit dashing through Hyde Park. But I'll warrant you the Duchess of Cramond will order one just like it, for she was green with envy when I whipped past her, sulking in her dull cabriolet, her face as sour as a lemon drop."

"Ooh, I like this one, Mummy!" Maria had chosen my flounced white shepherdess ensemble. A large Leghorn hat and a beribboned crook completed the picture. And this afternoon I would drive through Hyde Park in the conveyance that matched it, a little carriage pulled by four milk-white ponies.

"Well done!" I lifted her into my arms for a kiss. "Oh, my goodness, you're such a big girl now; you're getting too heavy for Mummy to lift." She smelled of apricots, and I buried my face in her soft brown hair. "Well then, since it's Perdita they all talk of, today I shall be Perdita for them."

"What's Perdita?" Maria twined one of my curls about her finger, then popped her finger in her mouth.

"Don't suck your thumb like a stick of sugar candy, my poppet; you'll end up with four fingers and a wrinkly raisin." Maria gave me a disbelieving look and continued to enjoy her own digit. "Perdita is the name of one of the roles Mummy portrayed when she was at the playhouse. And though perhaps it wasn't even Mummy's best role, it's the one for which she'll be most remembered, as I daresay it's become my sobriquet."

"What's a so-brickette?"

"A pet name, darling. And mine, Perdita, means the 'lost girl.' "

Maria seemed to think this was the silliest thing she'd ever heard me utter. Dissolving into silvery giggles, she said, "But *you're* not lost. You're right *here*."

With her sturdy little legs, she climbed into the wardrobe and hid herself amid my numerous gowns and costumes. "Now *I'm* Perdita, too," came a muffled voice. "Come and find me!"

Alas, my estranged husband did not bring me the delight our daughter did. Perhaps he considered that the common knowledge of my infidelity—though my affections could not have been bestowed upon a loftier personage unless it had been the king himself—entitled him to public displays of his own adulterous affairs. I cannot recall when his behavior so scandalized me as the night of October 7, 1780, at Covent Garden, when with my quizzing glass I spied him in one of the upper boxes, in flagrante delicto—for all and sundry to witness—with one of the fancy pieces who trolled the corridors outside the gods.

This was too much for me to bear in silence. Nearly every man and woman of my acquaintance, whether well-born or not, had a lover, a custom that society winked at as long as discretion was observed. Though our liaison was the talk of the town, even the prince and I did not indulge in our amorous conduct in the public eye. Now, before most of London—for those who were not at the theatre that night would surely read of the exploit in one of the several morning papers—Mr. Robinson was making a mockery of our marriage.

I stormed out of my own box and raced up three flights of stairs, lifting my skirts so that I could take the treads two at a time, and reach the uppermost gallery that much sooner. Throwing open the door to my husband's box, I shouted, "You are welcome to shame yourself to your heart's content, but I will not permit you to mortify *me* by your licentious conduct!"

As I thrust myself between Mr. Robinson and his latest conquest—and an ugly little thing she was, too—endeavoring to separate their bodies, he snarled at me for my hypocrisy.

Enraged, I began to beat him about the head and

shoulders with my muff. The commotion caused quite a hubbub in the house below, and all heads turned away from the stage to observe the more interesting spectacle taking place in the balcony.

Subsequent to this contretemps, the derision heaped upon me by the press was sufficient to wrap several barrels of fish. But I was learning to play the game and was determined not to allow Mr. Robinson to win the day in our publicly staged morality wars, getting off more or less scot-free whilst I was vilified and eviscerated daily. I had coin enough to puff myself in the papers, and though had I been Catholic I would have been no candidate for canonization, I was not the debauched demimondaine, as my critics sought to paint me.

Because papers changed editors—and hence, their politics—as often as the well accoutered changed their hose, a broadsheet could be friend one day and foe the next. Printing costs were subsidized by the sale of column space to anyone who could afford it, with no editorial oversight, but even the publishers' items made little distinction between fantasy and fact, opinion and truth. Their job was to sell papers, and the more scandals they printed, the faster they sold. People would have readily believed I drank dragon's blood for breakfast, bathed in claret, and made love hanging by my toes, if the news bore the imprimatur of the *Morning Post*.

But if readers swallowed utter rot, they lapped up pap just as easily. As the curious dogged me wherever I went, it did not seem odd that an item about my charitable works appeared in the brand-new *Morning Herald*, published by an acquaintance of mine, the "fighting parson," Reverend Henry Bate. He had trod the boards himself in his youth, and his wife was an actress whom I had known at Drury Lane.

I had also been very close at the time with another of the company's actresses, Sophia Baddeley. Mrs. Baddeley had been one of Drury Lane's great leading ladies, and an acknowledged beauty, but her trajectory had taken her from fame to—rumor had it—destitution and despair. She had been a highflyer and a mad spender, quitting the theatre for the arms of a titled protector who soon left her for another—a handsome, charming radical who, as irony would have it, had been an acquaintance of my own ne'er-do-well husband! I had heard that Mrs. Baddeley was no longer "going like herself," as we used to say of her during her wild and flagrant days, and thought to pay her a call.

I alighted from my phaeton and instructed my liveried postboys to tether my ponies outside her residence in Spitalfields, a comedown indeed from her former rooms in Clarges Street. There was no servant to admit me; my hostess herself filled that office. I endeavored to mask my dismay at seeing her look so poorly. She was only in her late twenties at the time, not too many years my elder, but she might have been fifty. The birth of her third child had left her looking haggard, and her flesh, once firm, hung loosely about her.

Mrs. Baddeley embraced me as though I was a long-lost friend. "Why, Mrs. Robinson, what brings you here?"

"I heard you were not well," I said quietly. In the room just past the entry, a baby bawled incessantly; the sound of the poor distressed mite was enough to shiver the floorboards. "I came to see if you need anything."

Mrs. Baddeley chuckled darkly. "What do you think?" she replied, gesturing about her. "Many days I have to choose between milk and candles. Either we sit in the dark and make it through another week, or starve in the light." She ushered me into the parlor, and motioned for me to sit, tossing a wooden doll, its painted face faded into little more than a smudge, from one of the chairs. "You're looking very fine, Mary. Happy."

"I *am* happy—and I am in love," I sighed guiltily, remembering my friend's former gaiety. No one had been more of a prominent fixture at parties and routs than Mrs. Baddeley. She'd made history when she was excluded from the then-new Pantheon, as the rules forbade "players" from attending any of the entertainments there. But a public outcry on her behalf from ladies as well as gentlemen who had seen her perform and thought the world of her talents gained her the entry she so desired. Mrs. Baddeley had paved the way for her fellow players in many ways, and I had always admired and esteemed her for it.

"Allow me to help you. Please," I said, and took a purse filled with coins from the pocket beneath my robe.

"I don't want your charity," Mrs. Baddeley replied stiffly.

"Because the purse is *mine,* or because it's charity? I was ever your friend, Sophia, and I mean to remain one. I even named my second child—though she was not long in this world—for you."

Mrs. Baddeley gazed at me in utter astonishment. "Truly?" she asked, her voice scarcely above a whisper.

I nodded. "You were a champion to those of us in the profession who came up behind you." I looked about me and shuddered at how she had come down in the world. An open bottle of claret rested on the table beside her chair, an analgesic, perhaps, for her sorrows. At least it wasn't gin; she hadn't fallen that far into despondency. I thought about Meribah Lorrington. I could not rescue my governess from her mental torments, but I might still be able to relieve some of Mrs. Baddeley's anguish. "Theatre folk are family," I reminded her, "regardless of whether an actor is still on the boards. You are, therefore, as a sister to me, and I would never turn away a sister in need."

"I did not come to you in need, Mary," said Sophia with the utmost dignity. "You sought me out." Then, seeing how her pride had managed to wound my own, for she realized I had meant nothing but good by calling on her, she softened somewhat. "I am a cautionary tale come to life," she said. "His Royal Highness is only eighteen years old; you are the elder, and, by virtue of having lived in the world and seen its degradations through the bars of a debtors' prison, significantly the wiser. My advice to you is to trust no one's honeyed words, choose your friends wisely, and have more than two talents. For once you have fallen from favor, and your looks eventually fade, your children will still need to be fed."

As if on cue, her infant bawled from its cradle. One of her older children went to rock the little berth, but soon called, "Mama, I think you'd better come; she's coughing something dreadful!"

"I—I am so sorry to have to cut short our interview," Mrs. Baddeley said hastily, as I rose from my chair. A russet-colored puppy, looking as sad-eyed and hungry as her children, padded over to me and explored my hem with his wet little nose.

I left Mrs. Baddeley with the purse and a published copy of my poetry, for I knew she was fond of verse, and promised to call upon her soon again. As I mounted my phaeton, I ruminated gloomily on our too-brief encounter. I felt as though I had seen my own ghost: Sophia and I shared more than a passion for spaniels, literature, and lavender drapes—our taste for the high life was strikingly similar as well. Her sad fall from grace would become more than an object lesson to me, for not too many weeks later, in January of 1781, Mrs. Baddeley proved an inadvertent sibyl.

Twenty

Dashed from My Lofty Perch

1781 . . . age twenty-three

Just when I thought I should be able to sustain my impatience for the next twenty months, until that splendid day in which I might behold my adored lover gracefully receiving the acclamations of his future subjects, when he might reach the age of twenty-one and be his own master—when I might enjoy the public protection of that noble being for whom I gave up all—I received a letter from His Highness, delivered not by the viscount but by a young, anonymous page.

We must meet no more!

Suddenly, I could not breathe. It was as though all the life had been sucked from my lungs by a force greater than anything known in nature. Silent tears ran in rivulets down my cheeks, for I was too shocked to sob. The note fell from my hand as I sank into a deep swoon. *We must meet no more!* This was all the letter said. No apologies, no explanations. What had happened? What had changed? Only the night previous, we had enjoyed such ecstasies. His affection then appeared to be as boundless as it was undiminished. Between the most ardent kisses and caresses bestowed on every part of my anatomy, the prince had vowed his eternal constancy and devotion. With whispers and sighs of the most inexpressible delight we touched and loved with the most exquisite pleasure in one another. I could not comprehend this extraordinary volte-face. Had the king forced his heir's hand, quite literally, to pen such a poisonous message?

When I was finally able to rouse myself, still amazed and afflicted beyond the power of utterance, I wrote immediately to His Royal Highness, requiring an explanation. He did not reply. Again I wrote—

> Please, my dearest love, what means this extraordinary cessation of your affections toward me? How can you be so cold, so cruel, as to cut me from your life in such an unfeeling manner? 'Tis unlike you—your nature is such a one as to comprehend the gentlest of sensibilities. Write soonest, my beloved.
> Yours ever—Mary.

And still the prince remained silent, sending me no elucidation of this most heartless mystery. I knew he was at Windsor. And if the mountain was not to come to Mary, she would have to ride out to it!

The most deject and wretched of mortals, my eyes swollen from weeping, their lids as red as if I had lined them with carmine, I set out from London in my small pony phaeton, accompanied only by a nine-year-old boy to serve as my postilion. It was dark by the time we quitted Hyde Park Corner.

At this hour we would not reach Windsor till nearly midnight, as we could not travel more than three miles an hour without endangering the team of ponies. In the dark it was nigh impossible to make out the ruts in the road from a carriage that lacked lanterns.

After a few hours, we stopped at Hounslow for nourishment, though my devastated heart and anxious mind counseled my better nature to avoid any additional delays.

At the posting inn, the innkeeper warned me that for the past ten consecutive nights, every coach that had passed the heath had been attacked and rifled.

"I fear no terror, sir," I told him. "For I am so beyond caring that if I should die tonight, it would be a blessing and a balm to my confounded and most distraught soul."

We thus pushed on, and had not journeyed terribly far upon the heath when a ruffian jumped out of the darkness and made a grab for my ponies' reins. But my carriage was fortunately so light, and the postilion so agile, that the boy was able to spur it on, while the footpad huffed and puffed behind us in the road, endeavoring without success in overtaking us.

Nearly an hour later, we arrived at the next inn, the Magpie, with our hearts pounding in our chests. It had been a lucky escape indeed, for when I removed my cloak to dine, and touched my trembling throat with relief at our flight from danger, I realized that I was wearing in my black stock a brilliant stud of very considerable value, which could only have been possessed by the robber by strangling the wearer.

If my bosom palpitated with joy at my escape from

assassination, it soon regretted I had not faced certain death after all; for upon regaining the road, we passed a carriage just outside of Windsor that bore Mr. Meynell, one of the prince's confidants, and none other than Mrs. Armistead—my former dresser at Drury Lane, who had flown the limited cage of the dressing rooms for the loftier, and more gilded, perch of a fancy woman!

Now I surmised what had occurred. The prince had expressed to me on more than one occasion a desire to know that lady. Suddenly the reason for my curt dismissal was blazingly evident. It was Elizabeth Armistead who had come between us—and His Highness's desire for her that was the instrument of my obliteration from his heart.

I could not bear it! Wracked with sobs, my face wet with salty tears, I urged my postilion to press on. I would see the prince and throw myself at his feet. There was barely a sliver of a moon by the time we gained Windsor. I alit from the phaeton and approached the castle gate on foot. The ground was hard beneath my feet, the lawns spangled with dew.

"I must see His Royal Highness," I told the guards.

"No one is permitted entry to the palace, miss."

"But I must see him!" I lowered my calash that the sentries might see my face, for I was well enough known from all the engravings made during my theatrical career—as well as from all the unfortunate caricatures that had been plastered across the pages of the newspapers. "I am Mary Robinson!"

"I don't care if you're Mary Queen of Scots, miss. We have orders to admit no one in to see His Highness."

"But you have done so! He has been with Mrs. Armistead. I saw her with her—" *with her pimp,* I was about to say. His bosom friend Mr. Meynell, a man I'd oft entertained with the prince in Cork Street, must have been dispatched to act as the prince's go-between with his latest conquest, as Lord Malden had done for me.

I could not cause a scene, for that would have availed me nothing but scorn. There was naught for me to do but flee any further mortification and drive back to London, filled with the despair and degradation of the mocked and defeated.

For half a year after that fateful command performance of *Florizel and Perdita,* I had withheld my favors, doubting the prince's constancy and fearful that his infatuation with me was no more than a young man's fancy. It felt miserable to have been right all along.

Back in Cork Street, I wrote a third letter to the prince.

> If ever you loved me, you must make a clean
> breast of all of the circumstances which com-
> pelled you to break with me in such an abrupt
> and injurious manner.

And then I enumerated the calumnies that had been heaped upon me by my detractors, the thousand taunts and humiliations I had been compelled to endure as a result of our liaison. By now we had been lovers in every way for upwards of six months.

> You are only too sensible of the most obscene
> falsehoods that have been fabricated by my en-
> emies. What little reputation I had has been
> utterly destroyed. It was only the most ardent

and generous inducements that encouraged me
to quit my husband's arms for yours, and well
you know that I kept myself to myself for many
months, battling the war within my soul, for I
never took the stigma of adultery lightly. What
further do I want from you, you may ask. For
now, only this: justice—to be acquitted by you
from the myriad slanders voiced and published
by those who would see me wallow in the stink-
ing gutters of disrepute. Yours ever—Mary.

That much I did receive from His Highness, in response to my passionate plea. Though he had no power to
halt the libels that littered the daily papers, he did admit,
through Malden, that I had been most unjustly maligned
and ill treated.

Yet His Highness unkindly persisted in withdrawing
himself from my society whenever we attended the same
entertainments. And as the days wore on, my situation became every hour more irksome. I was now deeply in debt,
which I despaired of ever having the power to discharge.
I had quitted both my husband and my profession for
the prince, fatally induced to relinquish what would have
provided an honorable and ample resource for myself and
my child.

Though our acquaintance had been strained during
my royal romance, Georgiana's heart was made of such
fine stuff that she was kindly disposed to receive me in my
distress.

Accompanied by Maria, who wished to play with Her
Grace's spaniels, I arrived at Devonshire House in a plain
hooded calash, so my identity might remain concealed

from the public, who were only too delighted to titter about my despair. How the gossips love to see a highflyer plummet back to earth!

Silently we sat while a servant filled our cups with the most deliciously aromatic coffee. I waited until the domestic was dismissed from the room before unburdening myself.

"You cannot imagine how it feels to walk through the streets and hear the sniggering, particularly from those women who only a few weeks ago would have given anything to be in my shoes," I fretted.

"Whatever you do, you cannot let them see your desolation," counseled the duchess. "In fact, you must live as high as ever. Keep your chin up, my dear, and pretend that nothing has gone amiss. It's the only way to silence their wagging tongues, for it provides them with unalloyed glee to see you in disgrace. That's what they want—to see you thrown into the mud—but you can't allow them the satisfaction! Carry on as ever. You cannot go back."

Maria requested a taste of coffee, and I promised I should leave a little in the cup and top it off with cream, for the robust black brew was far too strong for a child of six.

"But I have not your income; how can I afford now to live as gaily as ever? I subsisted on borrowed time," I told Georgiana. "I see that now. Merchants fell over themselves to gain my custom when there was every expectation on all sides that my fame, and the prince's bounty, came in endless supply. Where my mail was filled with invitations until but a few days ago, now I receive nothing but duns." I thought of Mrs. Baddeley's unfortunate plight and the future she had foretold for me. "Those with titles may sin on, financially, Your Grace, but we common folk must pay the piper. And I have seen enough of the grimy walls of a debtors' prison to last a lifetime." After much rumination, I said, "Perhaps I should take up the masks of Thalia and Melpomene again."

The duchess frowned. "I would counsel otherwise," she said gently. "Such a decision would be ill advised."

"But why? Why not assay once again the profession that brought me fame as well as fortune? And I am sorely in need of the latter these days. It has only been a few months since I quit the stage. Surely Mr. Sheridan would welcome me back to Drury Lane."

"I hear things," Georgiana replied cryptically. She handed a biscuit to Maria, who had asked to feed the spaniel; and my daughter, once gratified, scampered off after the puppy.

The duchess leaned toward me confidentially. "Please believe me when I tell you that I do not believe the public will suffer your reappearance on the stage. Their memories are of short duration. They regard you now as a disgraced woman, as . . ." The duchess lowered her eyes in embarrassment. "As a joke."

My jaw fell. I blanched. "It is not possible! Truly you can't mean to say that there is no hope of redemption?"

The duchess shook her head dolefully. "None at present. That is my perspective. But you are welcome to enjoy another vantage, of course."

I thought of the jibe the *Morning Post* had taken at my expense, anonymously publishing a couplet that read:

Now, Lady—where's your honor now? Can no man fit your palate but a prince?

I confess it galled me to think I had so soon become

a pariah where once the selfsame people had seen in me a paragon to be emulated and admired. How I despised the hypocrisy wherein a fallen woman was expected to behave like her betters, when her so-called betters behaved no better than she! For example, the Duchess of Devonshire was up to her pretty elbows in debt—it was common knowledge—the amounts she lost in a hand of cards so astounding as to make one's head spin like a top. Women who gambled prodigiously were thought of as unfeminine and vulgar. And yet, by virtue of her lofty station, the vivacious Georgiana was not only welcomed everywhere but was the most glittering ornament in high society's coronet.

And so, on the advice of the duchess, too proud to let them lord it over me, I assumed a placid countenance when I met the inquiring glances of my triumphant enemies. But inwardly, I was overwhelmed with sorrows and anxieties, with dread for the future, and still smarting from the eviscerating pangs of a broken heart. My distress knew no limits.

And yet, I could not bring myself to despise the prince. In my imagination's fancy, I permitted this self-delusion if only to preserve my sanity. I still considered his mind to be nobly and honorably organized, and refused to believe that a heart such as his—the seat of so many virtues—could possibly become inhuman or unjust. I had been taught from my infancy to accept the premise that elevated stations are surrounded by delusive visions, which glitter but to dazzle, like an unsubstantial meteor, and flatter to betray.

Through Lord Malden, I urged another meeting with His Highness. I was nigh to frantic, for everything was at stake. I could not afford to lose the prince forever. I had yearned for everyone to know my name, had basked in their flattering efforts at imitation, but had not considered well enough the attendant consequences when the whole world knows your business—where you sup, what you eat, where you shop and what you purchase, and whom you choose to love. And when the pangs of disprized love render you the most unhappy of mortals, the public knows, or imagines they do, every sordid detail of your *affaire du coeur* and mocks your pain.

At last, the viscount returned with a message from the prince. "He will meet you at my house in Clarges Street," he told me. "Tomorrow afternoon at three."

How I agonized during those intermittent hours. My heart rose to greet the sun and plummeted back to earth, rising and dipping with agitation. Would he welcome me with open arms, or deal me a final blow?

With great trepidation I drove my vis-à-vis to Clarges Street the following day. I was not kept waiting, but was ushered into Lord Malden's salon, where the prince was waiting for me, alone, occupying his time with a little volume of poetry. I stepped closer and saw that it was mine! That bode well, indeed.

I curtsied to him and lowered my head. Gently raising my chin with his fingers, His Highness gazed down into my eyes. "You look tired, my precious."

My precious! "I have been weeping these past several days," I confessed. "I dared not believe you had the capacity to be so cruel. You are too fine, too compassionate, to treat a lover so . . ." I searched for a word that would not be a direct insult, but would capture the gravity of the situation.

"I never endeavor to be dishonorable," the prince replied, helping me to my feet. He enfolded me in a sympathetic embrace and a cloud of scent, his favorite blend of bay and orange. I closed my eyes and permitted my senses to wallow in the aroma as I rested in his strong arms. "Sometimes it is hard for one to know whom to listen to; so many want one's ear, and believe this privilege entitles them to pour a dram of pestilence inside it."

"I don't take your meaning, Your Highness."

He led me to a divan, and reclining upon it, nestled me against the length of his noble body. "You have many enemies," he explained. "Some of them, concealed as your friends. I fear I am as susceptible to gossip as anyone, and there are times when I do not know what to credit as true."

"If you doubt the slightest thing about me, I beg of you to simply ask me!"

"Would you tell me the truth?" Confounded, I stared at my lover. "For example, have you and Malden been . . . ?" He trailed off, unable to form the words.

"I assure you, Malden is nothing to me but your confidant—and therefore, my acquaintance. I know there are rumors, but there is not, nor has there ever been, anything between us."

"They say you feign to love me because I am the prince royal and such an affair gives you the greatest éclat. It has even been said that it was *you* who set my portrait with brilliants, making it seem a greater gift than I had intended."

"But you know those are nothing but falsehoods!" I said, stunned to the quick. I turned around and pressed my lips to his. His mouth was soft and tasted sweet, of sugared confections. "I relinquished my profession, abandoned my husband—and all for you—after months of painful consideration. I esteem you, adore you—and there is no other on this earth for me."

His tongue danced with mine as we tangled on the narrow divan, our bodies cleaving to each other, despite the voluminous yards of silk and scratchy embroidery between us. We rolled onto the rug in gales of laughter, as passionately entangled as we used to be, all eager hands and hungry lips. The prince was now a master at dispensing of my garments; and, divesting himself of his own, soon we were back on the carpet, enjoying the sweet nectar of our passion and reveling in the delights of love until dusk.

"You are my own dearest angel," the prince assured me, as he escorted me himself to Lord Malden's door. He kissed my little volume of poetry and pocketed it before tasting my lips once again. "My brilliant, my beautiful Perdita."

"Au revoir, my Florizel," I murmured, and kissed him once again before departing. As I rode back to my rooms, I flattered myself that all our differences were adjusted. I replayed the afternoon's events in my head. Who was it who had said that I had bejeweled the prince's portrait myself? I had urged a confession from His Highness, but he refused to name my detractor. That tidbit had not been a defamatory squib in any of the papers, though practically everything else about me had been thoroughly bandied about in the broadsheets. No—the malicious gossip had to have come from an intimate acquaintance of the prince's. Who moved in such exalted circles with the dashing and fashionable young heir to the throne, and might also be a confidante of mine?

I could only come up with one answer: the Duchess of Devonshire. But why would she malign me?

The very next day I took my customary four o'clock drive in Hyde Park, dressed once again in my shepherdess's attire, so all the ton should know that Perdita had triumphed. I waved to the throngs that greeted me as I dashed through the drive. And then I spied, coming up behind me, the prince's blue coach. I slowed down to allow him to pull up beside me. As our horses were neck and neck on the turnpike, I turned to say hello to my love, favoring him with a dazzling smile that afforded the full measure of my adoration—but to my utter mortification, His Royal Highness turned his head to avoid seeing me, and even affected not to know me!

What had I done to deserve this cut direct? My chagrin was prodigious.

Baffled and angry, I requested an interview with the duchess, but she put off our meeting for the first time in our long acquaintance. A few days later, she deigned to see me, but her manner was chilly. "Have you deserted me, too?" I demanded, stifling my tears. What had prompted her turnabout? After all, it was she who had counseled me not to let my detractors witness my disgrace.

"It is ever a danger to aspire to heights beyond one's station," Her Grace replied, this nonanswer telling me all I needed to know. I had lost her, as well, somehow. It had been she, surely, who had spread the tale about my embellishing the prince's miniature, falsely painting me as a self-aggrandizing, ambitious hussy. For some reason that image must have served her better than acknowledging that the prince royal and I had truly loved each other with

a passion that transcended class distinctions. To accept
the truth made rank and title worthless in a world where
Cupid reigns supreme and even kings and princes were
defenseless against the blinkered archer's skill.

The only one who would listen with compassion was
Mrs. Baddeley. After all, she had traveled the same rutted
road as I, and had met with the same disdain from those
whom naught but birthright placed above her.

"What will you do now?" she asked sympathetically.

I told her of my notion to return to the stage, but she
confirmed what the duchess had already said: that the
public would not tolerate it. Would my writing sustain
me, she asked.

"Not without a patron," I replied. "Besides, my creditors call daily; I am inundated with duns. I must have cash
in hand to pay them off, and get my bearings back, to see
my daughter fed and clothed and the landlord paid."

And then I shared the plan that had begun so recently
to unfold within my frantic brain. I still had the prince's
bond for twenty thousand pounds, though that would not
mature until the prince did, when he turned twenty-one
in 1783. But I did have something else in my possession
that was perhaps just as valuable.

"I would never do it otherwise, Sophia, but my hand
has been forced. I may not gain an immediate income
from my writing, but I might do so through *publishing*."

"Convey to His Highness that I intend to hire a printer to
publish our love letters," I instructed Lord Malden. The
viscount had begun to call on me as often as my dunners,
eager to offer his open protection now that the prince
had spurned me entirely. But he had less money than I

did; and besides, although his lordship was ever kind to me, my heart could not hope to recover so quickly. In my view, sex without love was the greatest crime, one practiced as much by the wellborn and the middle classes as by the lowly brothel worker. I have always held that the woman who bestows her person where she can withhold her heart is the most culpable of beings. The venal wanton is not more guilty.

Malden acted once more as a go-between in a series of meetings and negotiations that were canceled and postponed throughout the spring and summer of 1781. And my pecuniary situation was becoming increasingly desperate.

One July afternoon, I was stopped in Albemarle Street by a creditor. He demanded I alight from my carriage, which was immediately "touched"—seized for nonpayment of debts. Some days later it was restored to me, through the offices of a "noble friend," I was informed. It could not possibly have been the prince! I suspected Lord Malden, but if he was as penniless as I, however did he manage it? Perhaps it had not been he after all. "Noble" could have meant the duchess. Had she begun to feel poorly for spreading such gossip about me? I knew her two greatest weaknesses were gossip and gambling. Perhaps she had looked within her heart and comprehended the damage it had done to one she had called her bosom friend.

Finally, on the last day of July, the dithering over my promise to publish the prince's letters ceased. The cause was taken up in earnest when His Majesty himself became involved in the matter.

The king dispatched an aide-de-camp, his treasurer

Colonel Hotham, to meet with me. Hotham visited me in Cork Street, and told me in no uncertain terms that his employer wanted the situation resolved with all due expediency.

"Very well then. It had never been my intention to embarrass the royal family." I knew, though I doubt Hotham did, that the letters contained more than poetic effusions and flighty protestations of the youthful heir's undying love. The prince had known in me his bosom's confidante and had always been quite candid in his correspondence. Several of the epistles included some rather disparaging remarks made against his nearest relations, referring, for example, to the princess royal as a "bandy-legged bitch." The public dissemination of such opinions would cast all of the royals in a decidedly unfavorable and embarrassing light.

"But I sacrificed my independence and my reputation when I agreed to enter the prince's bed," I said frankly, causing the colonel to blush profusely. "I no longer have a means of income. I am perfectly aware that it has long been the custom for a royal to settle an annuity on his mistress after she has served his turn, so to speak. And I am willing to accept such an annuity from His Highness, in consideration of which our correspondence will remain locked in my wardrobe forever."

Hotham took this proposal back to the monarch but met with a resounding "No!" adding that "the king will suffer no lingering embarrassment on the royal escutcheon over this affair. He has reminded me that his son is not of age and therefore is not entitled to provide such an annuity, even assuming I should honor the custom."

I reminded Hotham that I still had in my possession

the prince's bond for twenty thousand pounds. The colonel countered by saying that the instrument had been signed by a minor, and therefore lacked validity. I then insisted that by the bond the prince's intention to see me supported was nonetheless sincere. Therefore, an annuity at this juncture would indicate the good faith expressed by the instrument—which still bore the prince's legitimate seal and signature, regardless of his age at the time he affixed them.

Our negotiations continued throughout the first week in August; Malden acted as my second, as though we were in a duel to the death with the royal family. I reminded Hotham that my prodigious debts needed to be satisfied. He requested me to disclose to him the sum required to discharge them. I estimated this figure to be between four and five thousand pounds, and deployed Malden to provide the colonel with the larger figure.

"And tell the prince that I never would have incurred such debts had it not been for His Highness's repeated assurances that he would provide for me."

Malden did so, returning with the guarantee that the prince's sincerity of intentions had never wavered.

Then the colonel informed me that he had been obliged to undertake a thorough retrospect of my conduct during my affair with the prince.

I was shocked. "And what might you possibly have unearthed that would show me as anything but entirely devoted to His Highness?"

"You will be pleased to hear that your conduct was found to be stainless . . . a bit of an irony under the circumstances."

"I beg of you, Colonel, not to mock me."

"Therefore, having discovered that your relationship with the heir apparent was indeed as advertised, the king has entrusted me to offer you the sum of five thousand pounds for the letters. All of this, Mrs. Robinson, is on the understanding that there is never to be any further discussion of this unpleasant subject."

"But what about an annuity?"

"There will be no annuity, madam. And if you seek to obtain a figure higher than the five thousand pounds His Majesty is prepared to give you in order to relegate this whole sordid business to the dustbin of history, the offer will be rescinded entirely and you will get nothing."

"But that sum will barely be sufficient to discharge Mrs. Robinson's debts," interjected Lord Malden on my behalf. "The king's proposal is extremely circumscribed and inadequate. I am certain that whatever his romantic feelings for Mrs. Robinson are at present, that the prince would never—"

"What the prince may, or may not, have said to you in private conversation is immaterial, your lordship," argued Hotham. "I am the king's emissary, and His Majesty desires Mrs. Robinson to understand that the offer was not intended to give her any expectation, or hope, much less any promise of any further consideration beyond the specific sum on offer."

To have told him of the calumnies rained down upon the royal family in the prince's letters would have then been fruitless. I have never wished to be thought of as a mercenary. I had merely requested the same consideration that every English king and prince and nobleman had bestowed upon their mistresses from time immemorial. We had given them our bodies and our love, sacrificed our virtue—a woman's most prized possession, and one that could never be restored—for their embraces. An annuity was as much a royal custom as noblesse oblige.

"There is one other condition," said Colonel Hotham, his lips curling into what looked to me an attempt not to sneer outright. "The letters must be returned to His Majesty. Every solitary one. And you must attest that you have made no copies, nor has anyone else made a copy of any of the correspondence."

Hot tears filled my eyes. "Whatever do you think I am?" Catching his look, I cautioned him not to reply, for my temper had now been sorely tested. "I have been ill used," I said. "By those who deem themselves my betters, yet whose conduct in this affair has been far more offensive than any behavior they wish to attribute to me. All of this smacks of blackmail. I wish it to be made known that the sum you tender to me is for the restitution of the papers under discussion—and not the price put on my conduct to His Royal Highness during our attachment."

As we were at an impasse, I dismissed the seconds and wrote directly to the prince myself, informing him that

> Your indelicacy in insulting me by such a proposal was totally unaccepted, I confess—my conduct has been *toward you* irreproachable. I hope you will feel every degree of satisfaction in your own mind when you reflect how you have treated me.

Malden took up the cudgels on my behalf once again. He told the prince that I had authorized the release of the letters, but that I had not abandoned all hope of a greater consideration based on the many liberal promises His Highness had made during our affair. After all, he had given me a bond for twenty thousand pounds fixed with the royal seal. What was that, if not a blazing proof of his intentions to see me well settled? But the royals were intractable. Five thousand pounds in exchange for the letters, or nothing at all.

They had worn me down. It was clear I had no more cards to play. Who can win against a king? Hotham called on me for the letters at the end of August. But where is the five thousand pounds? Malden wanted to know. Hotham didn't have it. And yet he had expected me to fulfill my commission!

Infuriated, I wrote to Malden, so that all might know my mind without misinterpretation.

> I have ever acted with the strictest honor and candor towards H.R.H.—neither do I wish to do anything I may hereafter come to repent. I do not know what answer may be thought sufficient; the only one I can, or *ever will be* induced to give is that I am willing to return every letter I have ever received from his R.H. bona fide. Had H.R.H. fulfilled *every* promise he has heretofore made me, I never could or would have made him ampler restitution, as I have valued those letters as dearly as my existence, and nothing but my distressed situation ever should have tempted me to give them up at all.

On September 6, 1781, Colonel Hotham received from me a box of beribboned correspondence. In exchange, I was given a draft for five thousand pounds.

Had the royal family triumphed over me, or was I the one who had finally received vindication? Though my pride remained as wounded as my heart, I took Georgiana's counsel to my bosom. "No matter what disasters may befall you, one must always keep up appearances." That same day I purchased a brand-new carriage in the very latest shade—a mud-brown color called "boue de Paris"—a city where I took the notion to reinvent myself anew, rising like the proverbial phoenix, and recapturing my former glory.

Act Four

***

Passion's Slave

Twenty-one

Leader of the Cyprian Corps

1781 . . . age twenty-three

$\mathscr{I}$ stumbled across a most intriguing discovery during those long months of dreadful and mortifying negotiation: that although the public derided me, they still followed me everywhere and clamored for news about me, devouring every item, both sweet and savory, as though beggars at a banquet. They had crowned me with the cap of celebrity and were unwilling to remove it from my troubled head.

Most delicious of all was that the prince himself had commissioned a full-length portrait of me by the esteemed Gainsborough—after he had severed our connexion! Romantics speculated that it was his father who had made him break with me and that the Gainsborough pastoral, where I pose with a sheepdog at my feet, holding the prince's bejeweled miniature in my hands, was His Highness's way of avowing that, at least in his tender heart, he was indeed unalterable to his Perdita through life.

I must confess I could not comprehend why the prince had made the commission, but when one is nearly *com-*

manded to sit to such an artist as Gainsborough, one does not decline!

I'm told that no one thinks the face resembles me. The body is appropriately slender and slim, and though I'm seated, it's clear enough that I am rather tall, which is indeed accurate. And if there is something amiss about the face—and the artist himself admitted he had great difficulty catching my likeness—the painter portrayed my mood at the time with stunning clarity.

Romney and Reynolds also painted me during those same months—a testament to my popularity, even as the prince's *former* mistress. But it is Gainsborough who most fully depicts the subject who visited his studio—for the young woman, wistful and melancholy, who sits amid the trees looks to me both unhappy and canny. A certain world-weariness has spoiled her rural idyll. Her eyes are narrowed, half in anger, as though vowing revenge for a wrong. The picture in her hands identifies the culprit. Despite all her finery, for she is adorned in the height of fashion, her hair dressed *très comme il faut,* she *has* lost, *is* lost, is truly *Perdita.*

Perhaps the painting was the prince's subtle mea culpa. He would display the Gainsborough portrait so that all might admire it, and come away with his shocking unspoken confession: "Yes, it was I who made her so unhappy." I wondered what Their Royal Majesties would have to say about it.

The other two distinguished artists also captured my mood, though their canvases, being of smaller scope, do not tell the whole story. From their compositions—images from waist to bonnet—I gaze at the viewer, occasionally askance, as if to say, "I do not fully trust you."

But if my countrymen and -women wished still to gaze upon me, they would have to content themselves with viewing the likenesses created by the illustrious triumvirate of English portraitists. I left my daughter in London with Dorcas and took my ducats across the Channel, where I arrived with letters of introduction to the elderly Sir John Lambert, a British banker who resided there. Sir John, who was eminently connected with the highly influential French nobility, then secured me an introduction to the duc de Chartres.

What a man! I do not mean this exclamation to be an encomium. Imagine the reddest face, a nose the size of a squashed and dented chamber pot, garish rings in each of his ears, and yet his enormous wealth and the profligacy with which he spent it attracted any number of females eager to open their orifices to receive him.

La belle Angloise, he called me, and he laid siege to me almost as soon as we met. "You know the word *roué, oui?*" he asked me.

"*Bien sûr.*" I nodded. "Of course."

He pointed to his richly brocaded chest with the pride of a peacock. "It was coined to describe my ancestors. I, too, am quite the roué."

"Yes . . . I can tell, monsieur."

"Please—call me Philippe."

He threw lavish parties in my honor, but I would not yield. I found the man physically repugnant. Nor would I abase myself, at any cost, to become one of his numerous concubines. Everything English had become all the rage in France, from our enormous feathered hats and our loose coiffures to our parliamentary form of government and our freethinking philosophies. But I was not a souvenir!

And yet I was grateful to the duc in one respect, for he arranged an introduction to a woman who had long fascinated me—and it seems the reverse was true as well!

But of course, first I had to pay a *visite* to her dressmaker.

Mademoiselle Bertin was renowned for the confections she created for Marie Antoinette, and I was bound to secure her artistry as well before my audience with the queen. The mademoiselle did not disappoint, designing for me a flounced gown of the most unusual tissue—a fabric with such iridescent radiance that in some light it appeared lavender and in others a delicate seafoam green. The silk mesh tiffany petticoat was festooned with bunches of the most delicate lilacs. A plume of white feathers completed the ensemble. I looked très à la mode indeed.

I was to attend dinner, a *grand couvert* held outdoors at Versailles. I blushed to swallow my national pride, for the palace and grounds were a glittering fairyland to which the likes of the London pleasure gardens could only enviously aspire.

A crimson ribband separated the royals from the other diners, and when I entered the area set aside for the commoners, the duc quitted his place beside the king and took my arm to present me to Her Majesty—who was making a show of eating nothing.

Our eyes met: hers were a fine shade of blue and sparkled with wit and hauteur. I dropped a court curtsy, disappearing into the poufs of my skirts, and rose again to hear the queen say, "I have heard of you—*la belle Angloise* indeed. You are quite the *talent,* I understand. And so I told myself that I must meet you." Her lively eyes conveyed a deeper meaning, as she glanced at Philippe. "We are very much alike, you and I, in that we know how to have good fun, oui? The world is too serious enough as it is." The queen leaned forward and peered at my brooch. I had pinned the prince's miniature to my bodice; as I moved the brilliants caught the light, bathing my face and poitrine with their lustrous sparkle.

"May I?" asked Marie Antoinette, reaching for the ornament.

"Yes—yes, of course." I was so delighted that she found me curious that I could have danced upon my toes.

The queen drew off her long white glove—a gesture she was renowned for, and which, presumably, caused the observer to swoon at the pale beauty of her arms. Though her limbs were lovely, I own I did not swoon.

I unpinned the miniature and handed it to Her Royal Majesty.

"You have very good taste, madame," she giggled. Suddenly we were as two schoolgirls back at Meribah Lorrington's academy. A waiting woman handed a gilded lorgnette to Marie Antoinette and she surveyed me, especially my skin. Nodding at the miniature, she added, "As does His Highness."

Oh heavens—do I correct a queen? I took my chances. "*Had*, Your Majesty. I am afraid I am no longer the object of that young man's fancy." How I hated Elizabeth Armistead!

The queen pouted. Even her moues were pretty. "*Oh . . . tant pis, madame. Vous deviez très désolée.* But perhaps," she added, glancing at the duc de Chartres, "there is another who can bring you consolation." She smiled at me in such a way that no contradiction was possible. "May I borrow this?" asked the queen, referring to the prince's miniature.

I could not refuse her, of course, and endeavored to mask my reluctance at parting with such a treasure.

The queen took the portrait and smiled broadly. Her teeth, like a row of tiny cultured pearls, were perfection. "I shall make certain you receive this tomorrow," said Marie Antoinette. "*N'inquietez-pas, ma chère.* Don't worry. The Queen of France never goes back on her word."

But the future king of England does, I thought.

The following day, the miniature was delivered to me with a prettily decorated bandbox. I untied the blue ribband and lifted the lid to discover one of the little mesh purses that Her Majesty delighted in making for her confidantes with her own royal hands. I cannot remember when I had been so greatly honored. This token, from the kind heart of a truly lovely and most amiable sovereign, was a gift I would forever cherish, along with the approbation of so noble a woman. I felt as though she had asked for my trust and had then rewarded me for bestowing it.

Marie Antoinette had misjudged one thing about me, however. For it was not the duc de Chartres in whose arms I found solace, however temporary. It was Armand-Louis de Gontaut Biron, the amorous—and equally generous—duc de Lauzun, who lavished his attentions on me for two delightful weeks in Paris. The arrangement suited us both at the time, and on parting we promised to remain friends.

This was only my second liaison outside of marriage, and in France, where such arrangements among aristocrats seemed more the rule than the exception, I did not feel sullied by the affair.

The handsome and well-traveled duc was ten years my senior and possessed of a grander sense of the world than many of his exalted ilk, owing to his commission to fight on the American side during our war with the colonies. In fact, he had just returned to the French court to announce General Cornwallis's surrender at Yorktown.

Somehow, Lauzun's successes against the British forces made him all the more alluring, as if I were flirting with danger.

Endeavoring to be gay and to forget the love that I knew in my heart of hearts I never would, I accepted the advances of the duc de Lauzun. I needed to be held, to feel special and treasured, however fleetingly, to hear the tender expressions of affection tickling my ears. And how sweet it was to hear those words in French, the language of love.

Lauzun filled a need and soothed the ache that had settled into my heart.

After a few months in France, I returned home to find the London papers filled with *on-dits,* tidbits of gossip about my continental expeditions, in which it was widely reported that I had become an immediate favorite of the French queen. For once, the rumors were true.

How soon one's fortune can change when the winds of perception alter their course! Just as our family had been shunned in Bristol and later in Tregunter when we had fallen on hard times, yet feted once I was believed to have married well, or had achieved fame, so I was welcomed back to London by the society that had courted my attention when I was in favor with the prince.

Georgiana was quick to host a soiree in my honor, to which the cream of the Devonshire set were invited. With open arms I was welcomed back into a little world where excess was never enough, where gossip and scandal as much as sherry and Champagne were the lubricants of conversation, and where liberal views and sympathies were all the fashion.

How grand it was to see dear old Sheridan again—and how political he had become! He was very thick with "the eyebrow," Mr. Fox, who looked as rumpled as ever. Fox was nothing to look at, to be certain, but his conversation was some of the best to be had anywhere. In his company I was always sure of deriving as much enlightenment as entertainment. Every time I looked at his caterpillar brows, I was put in mind of my former mentor Mrs. Lorrington, and felt even more at home in his presence.

And there was Lord Malden, dressed in richly embroidered pale green satin, from the domino ribband on his wig to his heels. The viscount rushed to greet me, and planted an effusive kiss on my clasped hands.

"My dear Mrs. Robinson, we hear you were the toast of France. You must tell us everything, but not too much— some things I would prefer remained *privé*!" He drew me aside until we were nearly obscured by the draperies in the salon. "When can I see you?" he demanded furtively. "I must see you, Mary. I have been longing for you ever since—" His gaze met mine and his lordship thought better of completing his thought.

I drew in my breath. "Come to me the day after tomorrow," I told Malden.

I had turned a corner. My marriage had long been a sham, and there was no use pretending otherwise. Rekindling my romance with the Prince of Wales was an impossibility. I could stay cooped up at home, stewing in my melancholy over a lost love, or put a gloomy face on the mask I presented to the world, or I could move on.

Amid the circles in which I desired to mingle, there was no dearth of offers.

I had plunged headlong into the abyss of moral scrutiny when I scrupled to enter the prince's bed. With the next lover I took, Lauzun, I found it easier to reconcile my own misgivings.

Mr. Robinson never wanted a marriage free of other liaisons—why should I, who had already started down that path, suddenly embrace a hypocritical virtue, never again to share my body with another man?

I was seeking that which had always eluded me, always slipped through my grasp, as if I were trying to catch a fish with my bare hands. I was looking for love—one that would not abandon me as soon as I had given my heart, my body, and my trust.

But Lord Malden did not prove a terribly original paramour. I was fond of him—a rather temperate affection—and I doubt very much that he loved me. His was an infatuation that I permitted him to indulge because I was terribly lonely at the time. And in retrospect, I suppose I allowed him to pay his addresses to me because in some strange way it felt as though I was maintaining a connexion, however tenuous, to the prince. There were no grand promises made, no lavish tokens exchanged; and though we remained lovers for several weeks, our passion fizzled as many such arrangements do when the bloom fast fades from the rose, leaving the parties to acknowledge that the affair is fueled by expedience and not desire.

And yet, it was a man with the physiognomy of a beetle and the figure of a woodchuck who soon began to captivate me. He was a dreadful gambler as well—often spending days on end at the Cocoa Tree—yet another black

mark against him. But Charles James Fox was brilliant.
Undeniably so. A fiery orator whose passion for the politics of the day had, for me, a certain eroticism. So many of
the Devonshire set feigned an aura of ennui, watching the
world go by as if at a great remove, and as though it was
a dreadful effort to compel oneself to care. But when Fox
fired up a salon with his rhetoric, we listened and were
inspired to change things.

Our affair became public almost immediately, giving
the caricaturists ample fodder for their poisoned pens.
And I perforce contented myself with being known for
being known. The stage was alas behind me, so far as my
appearing on it, for the public still would not have me
there. It was *la vie galante* I led instead, numbered in a
triumvirate of the most famous courtesans of the day—
the odious little Gertrude Mahon, known as "the pocket
Venus" for her diminutive—though perfect—proportions;
and the physical opposite of this "Bird of Paradise," Grace
Dalrymple—"Dally the Tall"—a blue-festooned giraffe
who seemed to make it a point of ensnaring my lovers,
whether I was done with them or no.

Every day I would costume myself for my new role—
that of Mr. Fox's mistress. We respected each other's minds
as much as he revered my body. His brilliance made him
beautiful in my eyes. Fox inculcated me with his staunch
Whig politics and made a convert of me, for my mind has
ever been open to learning.

Throughout my life I never sought to make a conquest;
I was always the prey, though not above flirtation. Flirtation was the coin of the realm and I spent it freely.

Thus, how could my eye not have been drawn to the
striking figure who sat beside me awaiting his sitting in

Sir Joshua Reynolds's studio. I was swathed to the ears in furs, for it was the twenty-eighth of January, 1782, one of those frosty London days when your breath forms warmly foggy words upon the air. I, too, had an appointment to sit for the master portraitist. It would have been impossible for me not to notice at my elbow the dashing coat of the Green Horse Troop, the tan breeches that clung like a lover to the stranger's muscled thighs, the tall black boots shined to such perfection that I might have seen my reflection in them, the impeccable white stock that led my eyes to the sardonic curve of a smile, the laughing eyes, and raffish shako adorned with the feathers of an obliging black swan.

"I know you," said the military hero, his accent most decidedly Lancunian. "Mary Robinson—the Perdita—pupil of Garrick, light of the London stage. I read about your triumphs in America."

Under my bonnet I blushed to the roots of my auburn curls.

"But I have never been in America, sir," I said coyly, the writer in me taking advantage of his dreadful syntax.

"You will forgive me, Mrs. Robinson. I make my point with swords and not with words. What I meant to say was that the American newspapers—"

I turned to my companion with a winning smile. "I know what you meant to say, sir. But you didn't say it. Evidently you are as adept at butchering the King's English as you are at hacking apart his colonial subjects. I know you, too, Banastre Tarleton—'Bloody Tarleton' of the Waxhaws victory, *Butcher* Tarleton, the Americans call you—scourge of the Carolinas. I saw you, you know. Ten days ago. I was sitting in my carriage watching the parade of our returning colonels. It was also the day of the queen's birthday ball, and in truth, I had staked out a rather particular location in the hopes of glimpsing an old amour."

"The Prince of Wales, I take it." Tarleton's eyes flashed like a man unaccustomed to losing—though in point of fact he had made a mess of it at Cowpens, his men suffering such a routing in this South Carolina skirmish that the redcoats forfeited any further hope of a victory in America's southern states.

"Tell me, is it true what dear Horace Walpole says— that you have slain more men and lain with more women than anyone else in His Majesty's army?"

His gloved hand boldly touched my arm. "Frankly, I've never counted."

"I'm glad you're not too perfect," I said, my gaze traveling from his handsome physiognomy to his mangled right hand. Two fingers of his glove were empty. "I don't like my men to be too perfect. It's unnatural."

"Perfection is entirely overrated. I've never been a tremendous admirer of it myself. I am, however, a lifelong admirer of the Theatre—even fancied myself an actor at one time. Don't look so surprised; I'm quite clever at delivering oratory, as long as I'm not expected to write it myself! Ahh—you wish to laugh at me. Well laugh at this, then: back in the seventies, my dear friend Major John Andre and I ran an amateur theatrical troupe in a deserted playhouse on South Street in Philadelphia. And I will have you know that we performed to packed houses—in a city of Quakers, to boot! We even gave them Shakespeare. Our motto was *We act Monday, Wednesday, and Friday*. My own motto, however, and make no mistake about it, is *Swift, Vigilant, and Bold*."

I tilted my chin and gazed at Tarleton. "Do you mean to make a conquest of me, then?"

He made no reply, but said a few moments later, "You were looking at my hand. An unfortunate collision between a rifle ball and my anatomy on the fourteenth of March last year, near Salisbury, in the Carolinas. There was another skirmish a few hours later, in which I was wounded again. With my right arm in a sling, I was compelled to take my stallion's reins with my left—not the best of circumstances, of course. At the end of the day, the surgeon, Dr. Stewart, amputated the fore and middle fingers of my right hand. After that, I was all for retiring from the whole bloody business of soldiering, but General Cornwallis refused my application to return home. 'Damme, Ban Tarleton with one hand is better than anyone else with two!' he declared—and that put an end to the matter."

Even seated, the man managed to swagger.

"Well!" said I. "Your appendage may not be entirely whole, but I vow your ego is certainly healthy!"

Twenty-two

My Heart Dragooned

1782 . . . age twenty-four

The gilded sphere in which we moved encompassed a rather narrow scope. It should have been no surprise to me that all the men I fancied were associates—the prince, Malden, Fox, Tarleton—sharing in common the vices of fornication, gambling, and politics, and not necessarily in that order. They frequented the same clubs and salons, and could be counted on to be found at the same faro tables and coffeehouses. There is not a doubt in my mind that they compared notes about their lovers, particularly when the gentlemen were in their cups.

I continued to despair of funds. But I still retained the prince's bond, considering it a form of security against a rainy day. I wrote to His Highness, but my letters went unanswered.

"You know he'll never cash it," Fox bluntly told me. "For one thing, the youth spends more than you do, and wouldn't have the funds, even if you could call it in. For another, the king would never stand for it."

"But he gave me his word as well as his bond," I insisted. "And I do believe it wasn't airy persiflage intended to bring me to his bed. He was ardent—too green for cynicism—and I believe he always intended to honor the bond."

"It would not sit well with the royal family to have it spread about that the heir apparent was not a man of honor; that's for certain." Fox pressed my hands in his. "Let me see what I can do."

And so he became my advocate, convincing His Royal Highness to agree to pay a five-hundred-pound annuity for myself, the moiety of which was to descend to Maria Elizabeth at my decease, in return for the surrender of the prince's bond, thus settling the balance of my claim. To many persons, the assurance of an independence would have operated as a consolation for the sufferings and difficulties by which it had been procured, but my spirit bent not to that view. I considered my having to grovel for that which was bestowed by custom from time immemorial naught but a degradation.

There were evenings when I entertained both Tarleton and Malden during the time that Malden and I were intimates. And it was abundantly clear, when the conversation turned competitive and tense, that the war hero was desirous of entering his name in the lists as a competitor for my affections. His bravado, though at times I own it could be wearing, made such a marked contrast to Mr. Robinson's congenital indolence that I found the dragoon all the more attractive; for here was a man of undeniable action!

Malden was confident of my fidelity to him, yet I did not feel on romantic terra firma when I'd look upon the lieutenant colonel, who, but of average height, dressed every inch the military hero in a uniform that left one to wonder little how well made he was. Compared with the stout little popinjay Malden, there was no contest for who looked the finer man. Yet the viscount and I had an unspoken understanding between us: he won the right to parade about the Pantheon with a beautiful and celebrated actress on his arm, and I was granted entrée into entertainments I might have otherwise been barred from, had I not been the consort of a titled lord. Such mutually beneficial arrangements were the rule rather than the exception. Wellbred people thought it impolite to speak of love.

But I believe it was love—or something very much like it, something more than common lust—that drove me headlong into the arms of Banastre Tarleton. It was as if every atomy of my being craved his attentions, his voice, his wicked grin, his laughing eyes. I was adrift at sea in a little oarless boat bounding helplessly upon the billowing waves. How could I thus have refused his invitation to accompany him down to Epsom?

There, in a little cottage Ban had let at Barrow Hedges, we enjoyed our first and most delicious assignation. For a solid fortnight I daresay I stepped out of bed only to make the most necessary ablutions. We dined on larks and pheasants, on roasted meats and sugared plums—and on each other.

With the prince, so unlettered in matters of the boudoir, I had taken the lead—an older woman tutoring him in the arts of love; and his puppyish passion for me, his exuberance, and of course his rank and title were, I confess, a powerful aphrodisiac.

But Ban Tarleton! Most decidedly, Ban Tarleton with

one hand was indeed better than any other man with two. His touch engendered within me the most exquisite sensations. The more he filled me, the more I yearned to feel him deep inside me once again. There was no such thing as satiety. I was lost in his arms, utterly, utterly lost, no longer the mistress of my body or my passions.

"You own me completely now," I murmured to him after one of our Olympic tangles amid the sheets. "When you are rough, I crave your tenderness; and when you are tender with me, I yearn for ravishment."

His scent became imprinted on my body, his taste embedded in my lips.

Yet after we returned to London two weeks later, and Tarleton deposited me at my doorstep, I heard not a word from him.

What had happened? I could not fathom the reason for his distant behavior. Not content to wait upon a reply to my many missives, I took myself to the Cocoa Tree, where I caused a stir by sweeping down upon my new paramour, his head bent over a betting book while Lord Malden stood by, sucking on a clay pipe.

"Where have you been these last six days?" I demanded of the war hero. "You promised you would come to me."

"Oh, did I?" he replied laconically. "Are you sure you're not confusing me with another?"

"I don't understand the meaning of your cruelty!"

Tarleton grinned and my knees fairly buckled beneath my skirts. "Congratulate me, Mrs. R., for I've just made a bundle off old Malden here!" To my uncomprehending stare, Tarleton added, "The viscount and I made a wager a while back. So certain of your undying fidelity was he that he bet me I could not seduce you. 'Seduce her? By gad I'll do you one better,' I told him. 'I'll win her and jilt her!' And so I have, and it's a happy day," he exclaimed as Malden sat down to write him a draft for a whopping thousand guineas.

Malden was gobsmacked; *my* consternation and mortification were utter and complete. "Oh—you have both used me ill in your little game," I declared, my Irish temper grabbing my passion's reins. "I am no shuttlecock to be bandied about by either of you for your sport and general mirth." Blinded by enraged tears I vowed to have nothing further to do with either of them, and fled the coffeehouse for the safety of my carriage and the solace of my lonely bed.

A few days later I felt enough myself again to take an airing in Hyde Park, and had no sooner gained the main road when a phaeton overtook me, careening straight into my little chariot and knocking me pell-mell to the pavement in a state of entire insensibility.

Imagine my gleaning through a few squibs in Reverend Bate's *Morning Herald* the following afternoon that it was Tarleton who had rushed to my bedside as soon as he learned of my misfortune! He had kept a vigil all those hours whilst I had lain abed concussed.

"Then it's true what they say in the papers," I murmured to him. My hand felt small and warm inside his, a little sparrow nesting in his palm.

"Are you prepared to forgive me?" His whisper brushed my ear, tickling the tender skin into titillation.

"I may have to." I smiled, despising my own vulnerability. "My need for you is beyond all rational control. You are as good for me—and yet I daresay as ruinous—as morphine."

*   *   *

How to explain that we became inseparable and yet I could not hold him? I was entirely on quicksand with this man, the terrain ever shifting, and always unsure. No sooner had our ménage become public than he purposed to quit it.

"Good news!" Ban announced one chilly January afternoon in 1783.

"Does that mean you will accompany me in Hyde Park today?" I asked him. "If so, I will require the barouche, for I had planned to take my phaeton."

He refolded a letter and placed it in his pocket. "Lord Shelburne has just appointed Cornwallis governor general of India. Cornwallis has asked me to command his cavalry there!"

I felt my stomach plummet. "When must you go? And where will that leave me—once you have departed for distant lands with your mentor?"

Ban kissed me fully on the mouth and my lips melted into his. I became as pliant as putty every time he touched me, and I knew it would be my downfall, even as I desired it. "In your pretty pink satin opera box, entertaining all the beaux and gallants. Come, come! My best girl must maintain all our smart connexions on the home front."

I frowned. "Your best girl?"

"My only girl. How's that, then?" Enfolded in his embrace I was powerless to put up a fight.

It was only luck that quelled my fears, for in mid-February, but a few weeks after Ban unfolded his proposition, Shelburne resigned as prime minister, leaving Lord Cornwallis without a sponsor. How relieved I was to know that Ban would remain in my arms!

We maintained an establishment in Mayfair. Maria was now nine years old, and I had undertaken to school her in the manner in which I had been educated. We corresponded regularly with my mother, still comfortably ensconced at Bristol, keeping her abreast of our activities.

Mr. Robinson was well outside our domestic picture, as ever the prodigious gambler and profligate rake. Yet as my legal husband, he was still legally entitled to come around for a handout when it suited him.

Our smart connexions, as my lover called them, included my former lovers—the prince, Fox, Malden—and almost nightly they could be found at Brooks, Boodles, White's, or Weltje's, their gambling insatiable and incurable. But the news, preliminary though it was, of Ban's imminent departure for India—where his creditors could not touch him—had brought forth a torrent of duns.

In solitude I wept over Ban's innumerable losses. What was it in my stars that fated me to forever be the consort of a gambler? I could not unburden my consternation to my dear friend the duchess, for Georgiana was just as voracious and thought nothing amiss of such a vice. She could not comprehend that wagering made my skin crawl with distaste. She found it as humorous as Ban did that the Prince of Wales had recently lost upwards of eight hundred thousand pounds at cards. Ban himself was then in the hole for thirty thousand, with no possible means of ever repaying his obligations. Debts of honor, he called them. I called them ludicrous.

"A military man on half-pay—how can you possibly behave like this?"

"My love, I gamble no more nor less than your former paramour the duc de Chartres," Ban drawled.

"I was never Chartres's mistress. You mistake him for Lauzun. Nevertheless, that odious Frenchman you refer to has an annual income of six hundred thousand pounds. Were it not for the generous credit extended to us because of our connexions, we could barely subsist. I despise leaving honest tradesmen in the lurch." I reached for Ban's hand and pulled him toward me. Could he not understand how palpable and genuine was my fear of returning to the Fleet? "What will happen when it comes time to pay the piper?"

Ban pointed to the poem I had been reworking for the past three days. "Your feverish little brain, my dear. Publish! Publish! Write faster!" He nuzzled the back of my neck and laughed, his warm breath exciting my delicate flesh.

"Oh—if only my publishing income was commensurate to your gambling debts! I should be the richest writer in England!"

By May, Dame Fortune's folly had turned in his favor and Ban had reduced his debts to "a paltry three thousand pounds"—a sum that still far surpassed our incomes. My every penny supported this heinous habit—a cycle I knew and despised all too well—but I could refuse my lover nothing. When Ban won, we lived very high on the hog indeed; nearly every week I had a spanking new carriage to add to my collection.

The daily papers dubbed me "the Priestess of Taste," for in every way I had become the leader of all things fashionable, slavishly copied by my societal betters as well as my peers, and complimented everywhere for my sense of style, a simple elegance lacking in the fuss and furbelows that had been the rage in genteel Georgian society.

It was I who introduced to England the sashed white muslin shift, dubbed the *chemise de la reine,* after the gowns made popular in Paris by Marie Antoinette. The queen herself had made a present to me of such a frock.

It felt quite grand to be so influential.

But when things went poorly, I drowned in bad news.

Ban still held out hopes for a foreign commission; the prospect of his going to India once again reared its unpleasant head. And I knew that his family back in Liverpool, politically connected Tories whose fortune was acquired through the slave trade in the Caribbean, disapproved of our romance in no uncertain terms. Even worse than their favorite son's turning Whig—in the Tarletons' unclouded view, Ban had chosen a woman who was far beneath him, no matter her celebrity. No doubt, my luster made matters worse for his prim, pragmatic kin. How could the ambitious hero possibly stand for Parliament or follow in his father's footsteps as Liverpool's mayor with such a notorious woman in his bed?

His relations' displeasure, particularly his mother's, was no secret to me. I'd seen her letters. Whilst my lover gambled away the hours with our highborn friends, the management of the household, and of our correspondence, fell to me.

It would have taken a mythological being of adamantine sensibilities to withstand the slings and arrows unleashed by the Tarletons up in Liverpool—and, even more painful, their son's responses, which he desired me to post for him. What tenderhearted soul would not crumble with despair upon reading this note penned to Ban's elder brother:

My dear John,

Only you, and perhaps Mama, can salvage the shreds of what I laughingly call my reputation. I own that three thousand pounds in duns is no sneezing matter, but if you will hear me out, you will agree that you will emerge the better off for the bargain I propose: send me the funds in full, and I will quit London. I will forswear gambling and retire to the country, where I will live quietly and modestly until my India commission comes through. Once that happy position is gained, I will be able to repay your loan—either from the money I earn abroad, *or by marrying well.* I assure you, your admonitions are never far from my thoughts. Absent such a loan, however, I shall be forced to sell my commission, and to play on, endeavoring at the tables to recoup my losses incurred there. My character and fortune are therefore in your hands; with your aid you may rescue me. Without it, I am, truly, ruined.

With fondest devotion, Ban

My soul was wounded to the quick, my heart in tatters. He was willing to abandon me in exchange for three thousand pounds! I had been bedding a Judas. It was enough to bring my health to the very brink; I took to my bed, physically unwell and too weak to face the world.

Imagine my surprise when I awoke from a fitful slumber one afternoon to see two familiar faces peering at me with the utmost solicitousness—the rosy, cherubic cheeks of the Prince of Wales, and Fox's bristling brows. I remained fond of them; time had healed many of the wounds inflicted on my being by the prince, and we were now amicably reconciled in the bosom of friendship. After he had cast me off for the charms of Mrs. Armistead, I found solace in the news that she alone could not hold him—as had I. In the months just after our liaison was ended, His Highness had turned dissipate, seeking, but not finding, satisfaction in the arms of many other women whose names were often linked in the same breath with scandal. An incestuous lot we were, for it was Mrs. A. who had taken up with the slovenly Fox after my affair with the parliamentarian fizzled like fireworks set alight and sent aloft on a damp and dreary evening.

"We'd heard you'd fallen monstrous ill," said the prince, peering at my pale complexion.

"We're much concerned for your welfare, my dear," Fox murmured.

"Then don't let Ban linger with you at the tables," I said. "If you love me, send him home to me, rather than carousing night after night until he sees no alternative but to forswear me forever. As a lieutenant colonel of the King's Dragoons, he is on a half-pay of one hundred seventy-three pounds a year! Not counting tradesmen's debts, he has monstrous obligations to two of London's most prominent faro bankers: a three-hundred-twenty-pound promissory note coming due to Drummond on the ninth of June, and he owes a fortune to Weltje as well. Close to seven hundred, I think. Jane Tarleton thinks me the root of Ban's troubles—that it is *I* who leads him into vice and degradation! If the Tarletons only knew I was fighting on the same side as they! I know Ban can make something of himself again—here, and not in far-flung regions abroad—and I will do everything within the scope of my talent to help him, if only he can be persuaded to abjure the gaming hells!"

I rang for my maid, who adjusted the bolster and propped me up against the pillows. "If I lose Ban, I lose my life," I said, without any trace of exaggeration. "Truly, I cannot live without him; my constitution cannot survive a permanent separation."

"Egad, my dear Perdita, you cannot expect us to be the man's nursemaid!" exclaimed the prince.

"But perhaps we can see to it that Ban does not drag you into the poorhouse with him," soothed Fox.

The very thought of seeing the inside of a debtors' prison once again chilled me to the marrow. It formed the chief subject of my nightmares, the reason I often slept so fitfully, even after the most satisfying lovemaking I had ever enjoyed.

Our wellborn friends were incapable of seeing Ban's deepest vice as anything greater than mere folly. Certain they would win me over, a few days later Fox proposed that the seven hundred pounds in gambling stakes they won at Brooks be used to buy me a new equipage. The exterior of the shiny brown carriage was ornamented with colorful mosaics, while the silk upholstery, elegantly trimmed with pink and silver lace, was the color of fresh straw. Caricaturists had a romp depicting me driving my lover in the shiny vis-à-vis, captioned as "The Fools of Passion" or "Love's Last Stake."

But those who joked at my expense that I was dashing hither and yon in my new carriage begotten through winnings at the faro tables were penning fictions. I was too ill to take the air for very long.

Lord Cornwallis, no ally of mine, either, wrote to Ban's father, Thomas, in Liverpool that on his word of honor, their wayward son would decamp for the Continent—France or Germany, if Jane Tarleton had her way—and reform himself, if the family should agree to cover Ban's debts.

But the Tarletons' position was that Ban's family and friends had already helped him enough, and it was impossible for them to do any more for him; Thomas Tarleton's edict was that Ban would just have to live on his pay. No alternative was acceptable.

The matter continued with no satisfactory resolution in sight. Careless as always with his papers, Ban left a letter lying atop a stack of duns. Dated June 29, 1783, his mother had written:

> Your obligations must be met in full before you embark for the Continent. I know you believe your debts of honor—those incurred through wagering—are to be paid first or your character will be ruined forever, but as your mother, I would counsel you to first settle all of your outstanding balances owed to the trade—the sums due and owing for lodging, expenses for clothing and other habiliments, food, &c. In any event, your father and I remain adamant that all of your fiduciary responsibilities must be completely discharged before you quit England. It is of little use to style yourself as Lt. Col. Tarleton abroad, if the smart military ca-

chet you wish to maximize is lessened by your reputation as a debtor.

Speaking as your mother, I think it would be in your best interests to raise the thousand and distribute it equally amongst *all of* your creditors. However, Lord Cornwallis has impressed upon me the importance of seeing to it that your debts of honor are settled in full. This, with heavy heart will I do, so long as I bear no responsibility for the *remainder* of your debts. It is my understanding that these debts of honor you have amassed currently amount to approximately £1000. Although your father and I are well situated, this is a vast sum of money to acquire at once. I require six months' notice to call in my money from interest for the 1000.

I must also add before I conclude this letter that it will give me real pleasure and satisfaction to hear that your connexion with Mrs. Robinson is at an end; without that necessary step, I refuse to secure the means of releasing you from your financial obligations and all my endeavors to save you from impending destruction will be ineffectual.

Your loving mother,
Jane Tarleton

Enraged, I confronted my lover. My knees wobbly with fear, my heart overflowing with trepidation, I said, "Do you not know how it makes me feel to read that your pecuniary salvation is predicated upon your severing our relations? Imagining you in India has filled my every atom with dread, depicting you on the Continent barely less terrifying. But to think that you would sell me for the means to pay your debts—for thirty tainted pieces of silver—!" I flung myself into his arms. "If you do not abandon me, she will not raise the funds you require to discharge your obligations."

Ban nestled me in his embrace and covered me with a thousand kisses, one for each pound he owed to Weltje and Drummond. "I cannot leave you," he swore. "You are as much a part of me as—" He glanced at his own hand, but unfortunately it was the mangled one.

"That is just what I fear," I sobbed. "And it wounds me to the core to know that your mother, who has never even met me, imagines me a gorgon, a Circe, who has ensnared her son and enticed him into depravity and degradation. If she only knew it was *domesticity* that I have yearned for by your side!"

From dusk to dawn Ban vowed never to desert me; he would flout his family and find other channels through which to satisfy his creditors.

True to his word, he somehow convinced Cornwallis to sign the seven-hundred-pound bond to Weltje. I suppose his lordship feared that Weltje, as a long-standing confidant of the Prince of Wales, would destroy Tarleton's reputation with His Royal Highness if my lover were to welch on his debt.

"Let me gratify my mother in one respect," Ban begged me. "I will decamp to the Continent—but you must come with me. She need never know." He must love me, I reasoned, for he had not replied to a single one of his mother's letters in which she urged him to abjure me.

"I fear I am too unwell to leave the country," I told

Ban. "Such a distance might undo me." Did he divine the reason I was afraid to travel? I was terrified to confess it, fearful I might lose him if he learned he was to be a father. And yet Mother, though healthy, had lost Papa by refusing to accompany him to North America.

"But I will see you tonight at the opera, yes?" I asked Ban anxiously.

Ban drew a small leather-bound book from his pocket and opened it, flipping the pages for a few moments. "The twenty-third of July—Handel's *Julius Caesar*. Yes, I have it written down," he assured me. With a swift embrace and a passionate kiss that left me pining for more, he added, "A conqueror never forgets."

1783 . . . age twenty-five

I felt so dreadfully hollow after Ban departed from my apartments that morning. And yet I was not empty—I had been filled by him so completely that in one way he remained. I carried a part of him within me now at every moment. I had not begun to show the physical signs of our domestic contentment, but I felt the emotions surge and change within me hourly as though I were a tempest-tossed sea turned inside out. Weak tea and dry salted biscuits, even ginger root, did little to quell my daily bouts of nausea.

I had to keep Ban beside me—and if not so in the most literal sense, then at least in London, at least in Albion! Absent his debts of honor, he would not need to flee. If I could raise the money . . .

I dressed in haste, donning a walking frock of hand-painted China silk, and left my auburn curls unpowdered, ringlets flirtatiously peeking from beneath the respectability of a muffin-shaped white bonnet. It was but a brief walk from my flat in Berkeley Square to Clarges Street, where I instructed the servant to inform Mr. Fox that Mrs. Robinson was waiting to see him.

"My darling Mary!" He greeted me effusively, pressing my hands in his. "What means such an early visit?"

"We must keep Ban in England," I said, coming straight to the point. "I daresay you and his betting cronies will miss him as much as I—and I hold you accountable in part for the necessity of his departure."

Fox looked surprised. "I? I hold no man against his will."

"Not literally, perhaps. But you never send him home when his losses have amassed to such a state as—"

"Egad, my good girl, I am not the man's wet nurse!"

"Nevertheless, he admires you in every way, from your politics to your wagering. Lend me the money and we'll both get what we want."

"You do know we've managed to get him on full pay again, don't you?" I regarded Fox quizzically. "With Drummond's note a veritable sword of Damocles over Ban's head, his connexions got him gazetted as a lieutenant colonel of the new American Dragoons! Rather ironic, don't you think?"

This was welcome news indeed, but I explained that Ban had far more duns than Drummond's.

Fox inquired as to the sum Ban owed in gambling debts, his bushy brows furling at the amount. "I can manage three hundred today." He wrung his hands together as if to wash them. "And I can send you an additional five hundred pounds tomorrow—if you can wait that long. My poor girl. You look so despondent. No hard feelings between us, of course. It's the way of the world. But I hate to think that being in love can bring you so much pain. 'Tisn't how it's supposed to be at all."

"That's because in our circle love is not expected to be part of the equation. Except in poetry. One is permitted to be as effusively in love as possible, if it's in verse. And even then the hyperbole is so extreme that no one believes a word of it anyway, unless they're either daft or deluded. But we live in an age of effusion, at least in our strata of society."

With three hundred pounds in my reticule and the promise of the balance on the morrow, I searched for Ban to bring him the good news. But he was not at Boodles, nor at White's nor at Weltje's. No one at the Cocoa Tree had seen him either, and I left word for him at every venue.

That night the duc de Lauzun joined me in my opera box. But by curtain, Ban had failed to appear. "Perhaps *you* are the reason for his absence, my dear duc. Not because you and I have been lovers, but because you and Ban were enemies on the battlefield. He will not discuss with me your encounter, but as he is not present to prevent my hearing it, I beg of you to tell me the story."

The opera was about to commence, but typical of the fashion, the better part of the audience was more interested in making and renewing acquaintances, arranging rendezvous, or quizzing the rest of the assemblage in search of the next adventure.

"Not two years ago—1781—the thirteenth of October," whispered the duc. "Ban and his men were foraging in the woods at dawn, when they received news that the enemy—that would be my hussars—was advancing on them in great force. We swept down upon them before they knew what had hit them, as you say." The violinists raised their bows and the conductor lowered his baton for the downbeat. "Roaring like the devil in the van of his green-clad English dragoons, Ban was charging toward us when his black stallion reared! He fired his pistol—right at me—aimed straight for my head." The duc poked at his temple with a bejeweled finger. I trembled in fear, even though I knew Ban had survived the onslaught. In my mind's eye I could see the carnage, smell it, knew the bitter copper-tinged taste of blood on my tongue. "Just at that moment one of the French uhlans drove his lance into another dragoon's horse. The wounded beast careened against Tarleton's stallion, toppling both horse and rider—and you know the rest."

"Though he'd been soldiering with a mangled hand for months, the injuries he sustained in that disastrous fall ruined his fighting career," I murmured. "Perhaps I should thank you for it, or Ban and I never should have found each other." I raised my quizzing glass and anxiously glanced about the theatre. Perhaps he had first paid a visit to another box. All through the opera, I fidgeted with my fan, my gloves, and my glass. Ban never did arrive.

It was nearly midnight when the performance ended. Riddled with consternation, I sent my footman to each of Ban's favorite haunts, scouring the clubs in search of my lover. When Giles returned to Berkeley Square he was in such a state that even his shoe buckles seemed to tremble.

"What—what is it, man!" I exclaimed.

"Colonel Tarleton's left—gone—fled—gone—for Dover, ma'am."

"Dover!" I didn't know whether to swoon or make a dash for it. Had he heeded his mother's directives after all? What to do? What to do? Do I stay? Follow? I could not bear to imagine Ban fleeing from me into the night, forswearing our rendezvous and abjuring me forever.

Certain I could not live without him, my decision to give chase was sealed. I would catch up with his carriage and convince him to reverse his course. If he'd already crossed the Channel I'd be lost, for I could not simply follow him. I'd have to return to London, arrange for a passport to France, and then secure a booking on one of the packet boats bound for Dover. I had not a minute to lose!

"How are the horses?" I demanded of Giles.

"They'll never make it to Dover, ma'am. You'd have to change them at a posting inn at least once on the journey."

"Too difficult to arrange to have mine brought back here."

"Might I suggest you hire a post chaise, ma'am?"

"Do it then—and quickly!" I rang for Dorcas and instructed her to watch over Maria, for I was quitting my establishment immediately and did not know when I might return. I did not even take the time to change into a suite of traveling clothes; the gold tissue faille gown I had worn to the opera would have to serve, though it was tremendously décolleté and would not ward off an evening chill, even in July. Within the half hour, Giles had secured the post chaise. It was two o'clock in the morning when the coachman cracked his whip and, otherwise unaccompanied, I departed Berkeley Square for Dover.

The coach lurched and rumbled on the open road, its clattering wheels keeping time with my heartbeat. The motion engendered such sharp and lingering pains in my belly that I thought to rap on the box and demand that the driver stop at the nearest inn, so I might rest. The air inside the carriage was stale and rank, the odors of sweat, of hair pomade, and a half dozen different perfumes lingering in the tatty velvet upholstery.

"I think I spy a coach up ahead," the coachman yelled, just as I was prepared to tell him to quit the highway.

"We must overtake them!" I shouted as I let down the glass. I leaned my head and torso out as far as the opening would permit, craning my neck to catch a glimpse of the fleeing conveyance up ahead. Though reason would dictate that Ban was well away from London by now, emotion declared it had to be his barouche.

The night air cooled my perspiring breast. I strained to keep my eyes on the other carriage as the horses kicked up the dust with their hooves and the wind churned up the chalk ruts lining the roads, caking my nostrils and lungs with the fine powder and making unruly tangles of my coiffure. I was damp all over.

But in time I grew too exhausted to play the panting puppy, and withdrew my head and my exposed poitrine back into the post chaise. The chills, or something very like them, had indeed overtaken me, for I could not seem to stop my limbs from trembling. The pains below my abdomen increased and I rattled to and fro within the confines of the carriage like the contents of an egg being shaken by an ill-tempered child.

As we bounced and clattered at breakneck speed one of the wheels rolled into a rut and we jounced along in a sort of rolling limp as the coachman tried to right us. We lurched again and I was tossed about, frantically groping for a leathern strap to grasp. I cannot say whether I then fell asleep or lapsed into a state of insensibility, but at some point I was conscious that my limbs had seized up,

306 ❖ AMANDA ELYOT

erupting into uncontrollable spasms. Then all went black before my eyes.

When next I opened them, I was lying on my back staring at the underbelly of a timbered roof, the odd piece of hay poking out from the thatch like an unruly strand of flaxen hair. A chambermaid was lighting a rush candle.

"Am I dead?" I whispered.

"No, miss. But you was carried inside by the coachman and the innkeeper, Mr. Alsop. Dead frozenlike you were."

I had been cold; I remembered. "Why can't I move my legs?" I muttered.

"Dunno, miss. There was a midwife here yesternight, and she thought it best to send for the doctor."

I glanced about the room. Beside me on a stool rested a basin of water. The rag draped upon it was splotched with blood. Mine?

It was sticky between my heavy legs that would not move. I reached for the rag to mop my brow and discovered that my fingers, clawlike, would not unbend to clasp its edge.

Panic seized my breast. I had surely lost Ban, for he was undoubtedly in Calais by now. And why did my extremities disobey my commands?

"How long have I lain here?" I asked the girl.

"Nearly a day, miss. You was insensible for several hours."

"Why wasn't the doctor sent for immediately?"

"Well, first, no one knew who you was, miss. And then Mr. Alsop, he come up here and says he's seen the caricatures of you in all the papers comporting yourself like a hussy and you deserved whatever was coming to you, 'specially after the midwife could do nothing more. It was Mrs. Alsop that nearly beat him about the head for daftness. She said that even the lowest of humans deserves succor when they're ill. It was Mrs. Alsop sent one of our postilions to fetch Dr. Thistleton. But the doctor's wife told Mrs. Alsop he's delivering Mrs. Pickford's baby out in Faversham, and hasn't come back yet."

Daylight had waned by the time the doctor arrived at my bedside. Holding aloft his lantern he peeled back the thin sheeting that served as bedclothes to discover my skirts caked with blood.

"Were you . . . with child, ma'am?" he asked, his expression alarmingly grave.

I nodded. "Enough to be sensible of my state, yet not so far along that the world might know it by my silhouette." It was an effort to speak. My words sounded funny to me as they bubbled forth from my lips.

"I regret to say that your condition has . . . changed," said the doctor. "You have lost the child."

I had not been conscious when the midwife had attended my bedside, and knew not what, if anything, she had done. "Can I bear another?"

The medic shook his head. "That I cannot say." And as he manipulated my legs his doubt grew more pronounced. "And, alas, I cannot tell what caused this trauma to your limbs." He could not unclench my fingers either, without engendering the most excruciating pain. "I understand your coach met with an accident on the road not far from here, and you were carried from the wreckage to this room. It may be an unfortunate coincidence that you were overtaken by a strange and mysterious illness nearly at the very moment that your conveyance toppled; or it may be that you are suffering from injuries you sustained in the mishap with the carriage, or—I regret to propose—as a result of poor midwifery. In any event, madam, I am most certain that you are no longer with child. As for the palsy to your limbs, I cannot unequivocally state the cause. I would prescribe sea bathing, which will alleviate some of the pains in your joints. It is very likely that from now on, you will require assistance wherever you go—even to walk from your bed to the commode."

Convulsive sobs overtook me; hot tears bathed my cheeks. The doctor gazed at my face, as if to draw it. I wondered what he saw there, and asked for a glass that I might look for myself, but there was none in the room.

"How old are you, madam, if I may ask?" I could see that the doctor was calculating in his head how many years of pain and disfigurement remained to me. That alone was enough for me to wish myself dead.

"Only twenty-five, sir. Do you know who I am?" I breathed. Dr. Thistleton shook his head. "Have you never been to the theatre?" I received another nod in the negative. "I am Mrs. Robinson," I said. "They call me 'the Perdita.' "

The doctor's countenance grew even more solemn. Finally, after a ponderous silence, he said, "Mrs. Robinson, you are, I fear, lost indeed . . . it is my considered, though humble, medical opinion that, if you harbor any designs to do so in future . . . you will never be able to take the stage again."

I was conveyed to London the following day, my legs and fingers still palsied. Being carried as though I were a piece of furniture engendered in my bosom the utmost mortification; but ambulating on my own was an embarrassment even more painful. Every step I assayed was a Herculean effort. One leg would not seem to follow the other; I must have looked a bandy-legged crone.

Nine-year-old Maria was beside herself with agitation. "If I had gone with you, Mummy, I should have kept a lookout for Colonel Tarleton's coach and then you would not have taken sick."

She smelled like honeysuckle, fresh and sweet. Biting back my tears, I stroked her hair and said, "You may have to be my legs now. And even my hands sometimes, for every word I write from now on will be born of pain."

As my curious daughter helpfully endeavored to uncurl my fingers, I winced in agony. "They are hard, Mummy, like wax tapers. But mayhap if we warm them up, they will melt and be like new again." She wrapped my ungainly hands in her own tiny ones as if to trap a pair of monstrous fireflies and blew upon them like she was cooling a spoonful of soup.

"Would you fetch your mama a glass, my sweetheart?" I had not yet garnered the courage to look upon my reflection, but had to conquer my fears eventually. Why not now, when it was just the two of us in my boudoir?

"I don't know if you can hold it," said Maria, offering me a silver-backed hand mirror.

My clenched fingers closed about its handle and I beheld my countenance for the first time since the fateful accident. What I saw terrified me beyond words. For my features seemed to have settled into a frown. I had been a famous beauty. Would I ever recover my looks?

And insult was heaped upon injury when I read in the *Morning Herald* on July 31, 1783, that:

> Mary Robinson is dangerously ill
> at her house in Berkeley Square.
> The environs of her sex, those
> distaff members of her social
> sphere, attribute her indisposi-
> tion to the declining influence
> of her charms.

They hinted, too, that the cause of my affliction was venereal, concurring that my indisposition was due to my love of gaiety and an abundance of midnight revels.

What vipers! And their supposition for my "indisposi-tion" most patently untrue. Not only that, my night flight had been entirely for naught; as Dame Irony would have it, Ban had *not* taken the road to Dover that night, but had gone instead to Southampton.

In late September I fled London in utter mortification. A few weeks of vapor baths in Brighton, according to the instructions of my own doctor, the eminent Sir John El-liott, availed little. I was horribly lonely and the autumn air at the burgeoning seaside resort was damp and chilly, so I returned to the delights of London, endeavoring to make the most of them even in my compromised state.

When I returned to the opera, I knew all eyes would be upon me.

There was no way to make an unobtrusive entrance. My infirmities rendered nothing unobtrusive from now on. So, rather than seek to hide the obvious from the public's prying eyes, in true Perdita fashion, I chose to make the most of my calamity and transform it into a performance. I would hold my head high. No one would see me wince in pain or shed a pitiable tear when two of my manservants made a great show of donning long white purpose-built sleeves that they withdrew from their pockets, and lifted me onto their crossed arms. Resting atop this human sedan chair, I was conveyed to my seat in the box. The process would be repeated when the performance was over and it was time to take me to my carriage.

Yet the general titters were audible. Even the mirrored walls of my box seemed to mock me. I heard the whispers behind fans and gloves, and caught the inquiring glances with raised eyebrows that lowered as soon as the gaze met mine.

Lord Pembroke thought himself discreet when he murmured to a companion, "Her face is still pretty, but I say—don't you think her illness has given her mouth something of a scowl? Rather disadvantageous to go about like that all the time, eh wot? She is quite *defaite*. Utterly unmade, don't you think—barely dragging herself about?" As the companion stole a glance at me and nodded in the affirmative, Pembroke added, "Well, she may possibly come about again, but she must not go anymore to an opera on the day of miscarriage."

Everyone knew that I had all but dashed from my opera box onto the open road on that fateful night in July! I dared not question how. Surely there was a spy amid my domestics, or else the country doctor flapped his tongue about, thinking perhaps to make a name for himself.

All throughout the evening, people gasped and ogled at me, but I had expected as much. Tongues wagged and clucked in amazement or disapproval—and the following day the press reported every detail.

With my extremities crabbed and crippled, Maria had become my trusted aide and amanuensis, bringing me the morning papers and journals, and transcribing my poetry when my fingers failed to guide a quill. My young daughter did not comprehend society's fascination with scandal. She saw the caricatures and knew they were meant to wound, though she couldn't have understood the sexual innuendo in them—such as the one that showed me as a whirligig signpost over an inn, the spike impaling me between my spread legs, whilst Tarleton, saber in hand, had decapitated the white plumes of the Prince of Wales. Despite my debilitation, and the fact that His Highness and I had not been lovers for years, the vicious caricatures of us as a couple, and of me as a scheming wanton, continued to fill the newspapers and print shops.

"Why do people mock others, Mummy?"

"Newspapers do it to make money," I sighed. "As for the rest, I think they believe it makes them feel superior to abase others."

"Well, I think it's cruel. Oh—may I iron the newspapers for you?"

I stroked her soft brown hair, remembering how blond and fine it had been when she was born. "Only if Dorcas supervises. You're too young to handle an iron on your own."

Maria climbed onto the chaise and nestled beside me. "Do you blame Colonel Tarleton for your sickness?"

"No, I do not." I rested my lips on the crown of her head. "When I think about him, I can only remember the rosy times. His kindnesses . . . his gentle solicitousness . . . his laughter . . . his bravery."

"Hmph," said Maria, and I do not know whether the child was surprised by my answer or thought her mother a deluded fool.

*   *   *

In early December, Dame Fortune smiled upon me, when one morning I heard a familiar "Halloo!" outside my windows. My heart leapt with joy. I heaved off the eiderdown, and if I could have bounded out of bed and descended the risers two at a time, I would have done so. As it was, I made it as far as the window, though it took several *halloos* before I could get to the sash.

There on the cobbles below stood Tarleton in full uniform, his green dragoon's coat a refreshing splash of color against the gray morn.

"Ban!" My hair was in disarray beneath my nightcap; my face bare of powder and paint. Could he tell that I was grinning from ear to ear, deliriously happy to behold him once again? My features, at least, had recovered considerably. Still, I wished to be more beautiful for him.

"Don't move! I'll come up to you!" he shouted.

If he'd only known how difficult it would have been for me to dash down to greet him.

In a trice, he appeared at the door, striding into my boudoir and lifting me off my feet. In the time he took to drink me in, he had not noticed anything different. I feared what might happen when he discovered the truth. My clenched fingers gripped his strong back as he laid me tenderly on the bed. "Oh, how I've missed you," I moaned. A tear escaped my eye and Ban kissed it away.

"I couldn't do it; I had to come home," he said, his voice husky as he unbuttoned his breeches and entered me, all preliminaries dispensed with. If he noticed how changed I had become since his departure in July, he did not permit any disappointment to interrupt his ardor. How wonderful it felt to have him crave my body as ever, rather than shy away from its deficiencies!

"You *are* home," I murmured, reveling in the joy of having him inside me once again, in my arms and in my heart. "Please don't ever leave me again, Ban. I couldn't bear it."

"Nor could I. No matter what my mother says—egad, I'm twenty-nine years old, not her suckling babe! I wanted you to join me in France, if you recall."

"I could not," I replied. "Later I will tell you why. Let me enjoy you now with no other thoughts than our mutual happiness."

How I trembled to describe the dreadful journey I had endured on the open road that fateful night! I feared for certain he would bolt when I disclosed to him the nature of my subsequent infirmity, adding that my physician, Dr. Elliott, had admitted that the condition was likely irreversible. A brave, bold soldier would surely be repulsed by the news that his lover, once the toast of London, was now a cripple.

But I was happily mistaken. "You remember I once told you perfection was overrated," said Ban. "After all, what call has an eight-fingered colonel to complain that his lover's figure is imperfect? I blame myself!" he exclaimed, throwing himself to the carpet. Thus prostrated and genuflecting worshipfully before me, he declared his love unswerving. "You need never look to another for anything."

Bold words from a bold man. Within the day he had moved into my Berkeley Square establishment. My dearest wish had been granted. Or had it? That night, he betook himself to Weltje's and reunited with his wagering confederates. With a clearer head, I read between the lines. Ban had sought the shelter of my embrace—and my roof—

because the precarious state of his finances would not permit him to lease rooms of his own. Once again I would struggle and scrimp to afford his habits, for a gentleman did not sully his hands with employment. But would I have been happier if an outbreak of war had ripped him from my arms? Most certainly not; and Ban knew it. He had betted on my too-devoted heart to deny him nothing. And damn the magnificent hero if he wasn't right.

1784 . . . age twenty-six

In March of 1784, Fox was embroiled in a rough reelection contest for MP of Westminster, and we did everything we could to support him. His East India Bill, calling for a separation of powers in India whereby trade would be controlled by the East India Company and the governance of the region by a committee of seven men (who turned out to be his cronies), had passed in the House of Commons the previous December. But the bill failed in the House of Lords after King George had unleashed his flaming sword, vowing that any member who voted for it would henceforth be considered a foe of the crown.

"Come—you must help me on the hustings," Georgiana demanded. "We Whig ladies are to mount the election platform and court votes in every way we can."

"I have heard of buying rounds of beer at the alehouses—"

"We'll leave that to the men. I've got another idea brewing," she said. "Who wouldn't vote for our dear Mr. Fox in exchange for a kiss from a beautiful lady—especially an aristocratic one?"

"I doubt very much they would want one from me in my present condition. If they see me coming toward them with pursed lips, it might tempt them to vote for the opposition."

"Bah! You are still a beauty, even if you must remain seated," exclaimed the duchess. "You are 'the *Perdita*.' They once clamored to see you on the stage. They dreamed about holding you in their unworthy arms. What man would not willingly exchange his vote to kiss the same lips that were kissed by the Prince of Wales?"

I didn't quite see it Georgiana's way, but I agreed to help Fox if my lips were left out of it. "I'll write his campaign songs—will that suit? Besides, Ban needs me, too, now. He's standing for Parliament in Liverpool. I've promised to draft his stump speeches. Oh, Your Grace, I'm so frightfully proud of the man."

I also became frightfully jealous when I journeyed with Ban to his birthplace and he ripped a leaf from Georgiana's program, kissing all the pretty market girls—who of course had no vote! "I doubt their swains will plump for you now," I fumed, "and they're the ones who count."

But it was impossible to remain angry with my lover when he took the hustings in full dress uniform, gallant and noble, and, appealing to the common man, held aloft his mangled hand, exclaiming, "For King and Country!"

It made a theatrical spectacle, but it was not enough to win the day. In fact, Ban came in third in a field of as many candidates. He demanded a recount, but the second tally left him short as well. With the top two vote-getters winning seats, my poor Ban was left out in the cold, and we limped back, rather literally, to London, where at the very least we could celebrate Fox's victory. He'd barely squeaked by, but that was good enough for the Prince of Wales to host a lavish celebration in his honor at Carlton House. Six hundred guests, Ban and I among them, wore the Whig colors of buff and blue; and the prince opened the first dance with the Duchess of Devonshire, whose kisses no doubt garnered as many votes for Fox and his fellow Whig candidates as the number of vicious cartoons they prompted from the daily press.

Ban had lost more than the Liverpool election; he had lost a fortune, much of which was mine, during the costly campaign. Although he regained a considerable amount of money by beating the prince at several games of tennis—those two could not seem to do a single thing without placing a bet upon it—the sum was not nearly enough to cover our debts.

In despair I wrote to the prince.

> If ever you cared for me, I beg of you to see your way to relieving my financial distress. I am your devoted supporter, as is Ban.

I appealed to him not only as his former lover, but as his political ally. And from Brighton I received a kind, though brief, reply.

> My dear Perdita, though my own purse is some-what strained, I will see what I am able to do for you within my means.
> George

Signing the note with his Christian name was a good omen. But it could not prevent the sheriff of Middlesex from placing an execution on all my possessions. Once more the spectre of the Fleet hovered before me. If someone—anyone—were to post a bond of two hundred and fifty pounds, my property would be released to me, but not a soul stepped forward. I was in anguish.

In torment I watched as my cherished belongings were auctioned off, one by one, including Gainsborough's full-length portrait of me as Perdita, which now hung in my turquoise salon. All I was able to save was the diamond-studded portrait of the Prince of Wales, the same miniature I clasped in the Gainsborough and which Marie Antoinette had much admired. That most prized gift from His Royal Highness would have to be pried from my cold dead hands.

There was only one thing to be done: flee. My former lover, the duc de Lauzun, offered refuge at one of his châteaux, and thus we evaded our creditors and bolted for the Continent.

In the autumn of 1784, accompanied by Maria and my mother, Ban and I boarded the Brighton-Dieppe packet boat and began our new life together in Paris. We holed up in the small but sumptuously appointed L'Hôtel de Russie. On October eighth, we returned from a walk along the Seine to discover Ban's elder brother John, waiting for him. John's broad face could not mask his surprise at seeing me.

I suggested to Mother that she and Maria might wish to rest in the adjacent room.

"I thought you wrote to Mama that this connexion was closed," John said, after my relatives had quitted the salon. His voice was quiet but firm. I guessed that the family had set him up to fetch his prodigal brother and bring him home. "Were not those your exact words, in point of fact?" John Tarleton tilted his head and raised his eyes, the better to recall Ban's letter. " 'Mrs. Robinson is too proud to follow me, and she has long been too generous; always I should have said to become a drain on her lover and thus increase the poverty of any man—I most solemnly assure you she has not been the occasion of my bankruptcy—play alone, which I abjure, has . . .' "

"When did you write that?" I asked Ban, but received no reply. I had no idea he had absolved me before his family for his pecuniary misfortunes. I blinked back grateful tears.

"Mary has been terribly unwell," Ban told his brother. "You can see for yourself how compromised is her condition. It is not expected she will last the winter." My stomach started at such a remark. Did my lover know something I did not? But then I caught his gaze and in his eyes I read the cleverly worded chapter John would take home and recite to their mother. Jane Tarleton would glean from it that our liaison was on its last legs, as God was planning to call me home within the season. My agenda was nothing of the sort, however. I had Ban back and would do everything in my power to keep him in my arms.

"Our parents have been quite clear that I am to manage on my own from now on," Ban said evenly. "I appreciate your concern, John, but it affects no sway in my decisions. We are set to depart by week's end for Villefranche, where it is hoped that the temperate climate and the soothing waters will alleviate Mrs. Robinson's suffering to whatever extent it is possible. If her health improves, it is our expectation to journey from there to the warm springs of Aix-la-Chapelle, on the advice of her physician."

John Tarleton left Paris, his embassy unfulfilled. Ban and I enjoyed the delights of the glittering city and the hospitality of our friends, spending the winter of 1784–85 safe and cozy in Lauzun's country château.

"I could do this every night," I murmured, nestled in Ban's warm embrace after a particularly enjoyable evening of lovemaking.

"We do," Ban grinned, stretching like a cat on the duc's thick Aubusson rug. The amber glow from the imposing marble fireplace illuminated his strong jawline and the sculpted planes of his torso.

I buried my crabbed fingers into the dark matted curls on his chest, savoring the now-soft, now-prickly sensation of his hair against my hand.

"More," I whispered, kissing Ban's chest a dozen times, then nuzzling his neck, journeying upward until my lips met his. "No matter how often you satisfy me, you always leave me craving more," I breathed into his mouth.

"Well then, my angel must be satisfied," sighed Ban, breaking into a smile even as he feigned hardship.

We began to pleasure each other anew, the licking flames mimicking the flicking of our tongues on each other's warm and fragrant flesh.

We did not travel to Villefranche until the spring. There, the balmy climate did much to improve the pains in my joints, and for the first time in months I began to feel almost myself again. Ban was ever solicitous, carrying me tenderly to and fro, from my carriage to the coastline, where the moist mists of the sea breezes caressed my skin almost as lovingly as Ban did.

We journeyed then to northern Germany, where the mud baths and hot mineral springs of Aix-la-Chapelle rejuvenated me even further, though it seemed I was the only resident taking the celebrated baths for something other than syphilis. We set up housekeeping in an ivy-covered cottage just outside the thirteenth-century Marching Gate, where I penned my poetry beside a trellised rose garden as I savored the sunshine's gentle rays.

Mother tended to keep to herself, her devotional reading occupying the better part of her days.

Maria was growing taller and more slender, a dark-haired sapling with a studious demeanor that belied her youth. From her sixth year I had undertaken to educate her, stuffing her young head with the same kind of knowledge—of the sciences, astronomy, philosophy, and mathematics—that had been branded as a "masculine education" when I myself had been mentored by Meribah Lorrington. So much did I feel I owed to that unfortunate woman's tutelage that I deemed it my crusade to pass on Mrs. Lorrington's curriculum to my own daughter. While Maria excelled in her studies in our idyllic cottage retreat, she had developed a weakness for printen, the local confection that resembled a cross between gingerbread and masonry. If I did not despise gambling, I'd level a wager that the stuff had been used for roofing in Charlemagne's day. And with the state of dentistry as ancient as the Roman ruins that could still be found about the spa city, I despaired of Maria's losing all her teeth to a sheet of printen. My eleven-year-old also deplored the odor of the hot springs. "Why would anyone bathe in rotten eggs?" she repeatedly questioned. Because of the stench, she refused to join me, and would not believe the benefits of such a foul-smelling place could in any way be healthful. Too much the cynic for her tender years, Maria was convinced it was all a clever joke, a ruse concocted by generations of town elders to bilk the tourists and increase the municipal coffers.

When we were not availing ourselves of the spa city's social whirl, which was nearly as lively as London's, it was a cozy domesticity we four enjoyed, although I doubt Ban and Maria would have been natural allies had I not been the link between them. What they shared in common was their love for me and their desire to ease my nearly constant pain. I never complained of it, but they could read it in my face, and in the amount of time it took me to complete a line of poetry on the page once it had been forged in my imagination.

In our little cottage Ban himself drew my baths, sprinkling them with fragrant rose petals harvested from our garden.

To cheer me, the two of them had taken to standing below the window of the bathroom, serenading me as I soaked. Ban had purchased an old viol from a luthier in the village, and though he was an abysmal musician, his baritone was clear and pleasant, and Maria's sweet soprano harmonized charmingly.

As I languished in the tub one morning, contemplating the damp gray walls, the scratchy low moan of the viol wafted through the tiny window, accompanying a song that went like this:

> *Oh, Mary is my flower*
> *Asleep in her fairy bower;*
> *No one can overpow'r my senses*

Like my Mary.
You crumble my defenses—
And shatter my pretenses
Be my amanuensis.
If you write my story you'll cover with glory
The battlefield triumphs of Ban
Much better than I can . . .

By this point I was convulsed with laughter. I had not felt better in weeks. "Thank heavens you have no poetic aspirations!" I exclaimed. "*Maria* had a better talent for scansion and rhyme at age four!" My daughter, in fact, with her studiously observant eye, had the makings of a true writer.

"The lyric was Maria's idea—you know. She thought it would give us both a project." Ban slipped a fragrant bloom through the narrow opening of the window. It fell limply to the floor, fracturing the tender connection twixt blossom and stem.

"Sort of a riposte, if you will, to Clinton's scurrilous assaults of me in the London press," he added.

I smiled in spite of myself. The man could be maddening. "Oh, is that what Maria says? I had no idea my eleven-year-old daughter was reading Sir Henry Clinton's *Narrative.*" The seventh edition of Clinton's military memoirs had been discussed at length in the English papers. Fox saw to it that Ban and I were kept abreast of developments back home by sending us clippings of import. Sir Henry Clinton's published correspondence with Ban's mentor, General Cornwallis, revealed the blunders made by the British army in the Carolinas during the campaigns of 1780–81, and in particular eviscerated

Ban for his ignominious showing during "the unfortunate day at Cowpens"—a defeat that presaged our loss of the American colonies.

"O, be my ghost, for I love you the most," Ban sang. I could hear Maria giggling beside him.

Though we were both Whigs, my lover and I did not often see eye to eye politically. For example, the Tarletons' fortune had derived, and continued to thrive, from the slave trade in the Caribbean. I had long held that no being should be disgraced or degraded by another because of the color of his skin. What good did our Enlightenment do to exalt the merits of humanism if we treated our darker brethren as less than human?

Yet Ban had also won many days on the battlefield and had sacrificed part of his body in the service of our country. He was legitimately a military hero . . . moreover, he was *my* hero. Though we often scrabbled like a pair of cats, and he could wound me like no other on earth, he was also capable of exquisite tenderness and night after night had led me over the brink of sublimest ecstasy; and I could deny him nothing. If my skills with a pen could extract clarity from the fog of war and rub away the sooty accusations that besmirched Ban's name in the public eye, I would gladly lend my cramped hands to the cause.

Eyes shut, I clasped a rose petal and traced my cheekbones and chin with its velvet softness, imagining Ban's fingertips there, lightly skimming my skin until it tingled. My thoughts turned inward. Mayhap Ban overestimated the worth of my pen. "You know, my love, the songs and campaign speeches I wrote for you when you stood for Parliament did not avail . . ."

Suddenly he was kneeling beside me, gently smoothing

a strand of hair off my forehead. "I don't blame you for my showing," he murmured, kissing my eyelids. "Your words roused the rabble. I just couldn't afford enough pints of ale!" Though my eyes remained closed, I could almost see his devilish grin. Ban reached into the warm water. His fingers painted a wet trail down my throat and between my breasts.

"You're quite a persuasive client," I teased, as his hand glided over my abdomen, heading for points netherward. My body ached for his. If he had asked me to write his memoirs in Greek, adoring him as I did, I would have willingly complied.

Twenty-five

A Woman Made of Words

1786 . . . age twenty-eight

I had not felt so alive in months! There did not seem to be world enough and time in which to transcribe the outpourings of my soul as the brisk winds of 1785 ushered in the frosts of 1786. Even as I was hard at work on Ban's memoirs, verse after verse sprang forth from my pen, each drop of ink a seedling of creation. And the *London Chronicle* rewarded me by publishing them. From the ashes of Perdita rose a phoenix poetess.

As my lover's ghostly amanuensis, I had my marching orders. Ban was keen on exculpating himself—yet remained unwilling to offend his mentor by implicating Cornwallis in any cockups in the Carolinas, particularly since Cornwallis was a Tory, whilst Ban of course was a Fox-supporting Whig, and nearly persona non grata for it. My lover retained every expectation that Cornwallis would still be posted to India, and hoped a commission would still be on offer from him, regardless of their divergent political alliances. Ban also relied upon Cornwallis's approval to reprint their letters to each other in his memoirs.

My mother returned to Bristol in late autumn for an extended holiday. It had devolved upon Maria to look after our daily correspondence, and she seemed to take delight in being such an active and responsible participant in our daily affairs. She welcomed each packet of letters with glee as though it were a holiday gift, knowing how eager we were for news of our affairs and of the world beyond the medieval walls of Aix-la-Chapelle.

"News from Grandmama!" she announced one December afternoon. Maria had seen to it that the courier enjoyed a trencher of food and a glass of beer and that the man's horse was fed and watered. "And Mr. Sheridan has sent a letter as well. Oh, may I read them to you?" she asked gaily. Inheriting my theatrical talent she had taken to dramatizing our letters from abroad, imbuing each with the voice and mannerisms of the sender, and providing no end of entertainment, even when the news was less than we'd hoped for. She was quite the wicked mimic.

"Where shall I begin?" Maria queried, and when I opted to hear Sheridan's note first, she broke open the seal with her thumbnail and unfolded the paper. Even from a few feet away, I could see that it was rather brief.

"Well?"

Maria adjusted herself in the chair and tilted her head back, gazing down her nose at the letter, with a sidelong glance in my direction. " 'My dearest Mary,' " she read, adopting a subtle Irish brogue. " 'I have taken the occasion to peruse the comic opera you sent to me. Many of the elements are quite charming, of course; your wit is ever evident, and the story holds a sufficient amount of interest. However, I regret to say that I must decline to offer you a production at this time.' What a devil!" exclaimed my child. "He has the temerity to address you as 'my dear,' and then he turns down your opera!" In silence she perused the entirety of the letter once more. "No, I have not missed a word. He praises your efforts and then with no explanation refuses to produce it. I do not understand such disloyalty, Mummy."

Neither did I apprehend it, and turned my head to hide a falling tear. I was quite proud of the comic opera and was certain it would fare well at Drury Lane, having banked in more ways than one that my colleague of so many years, and friend for many more, would add it to the repertoire. I sat abed, stewing. Was it verily the opus that had been rejected, or was it Mrs. Robinson? Had the opera been penned by any other, or submitted under a pseudonym, would Mr. Sheridan—after seeing fit to enumerate its merits—have accepted it for production?

I felt the injury keenly, that a professional acquaintance of such long standing could be ruptured so cavalierly—and personally, I felt betrayed. It would pain me to look Sheridan in the eye when next we met, and given the circle in which we moved, such a *rencontre* was inevitable.

"Well, then," I sighed, "the news from my mother will be a welcome tonic, now."

Maria opened the letter and began to read. " 'Dearest Mary, it is with heavy heart that I write these words . . .' " My daughter raised her eyes from the page. "Perhaps it is better if I do not read this aloud."

"No—pray continue; whether I hear the words from your lips or read them silently, 'twill not alter the message."

"As you wish, Mama." Maria squirmed uncomfortably on the settee. " 'Though it took your father some time to find his bearings, he always had the call for adventure. And as you know, he finally found his sea legs in the Russian navy, where he rose to the rank of captain. Although I knew in my heart I should never see him more after he departed for the east, I console myself in memories of the happy hours we spent together after he returned to the life we had lovingly cherished in our youth. I regret that you and he never reconciled, for now the hour is too late. Your father departed this world for a better on the fifth of December last. Though I mourn him as a proper widow, it is my last remaining hope where Nicholas Darby is concerned that his children remember him fondly and as a man who wished for nothing but the best for his family. I trust you and Maria are well and hale. You may give my compliments to Ban. Your loving mother.' "

I reached for the letter, which Maria neatly folded and brought to me. I could not tamp down my tears as I reread her words. Nicholas Darby had been my first hero—true, he had turned out to be a flawed idol, even a false one, but he was still my father. And I grieved for his demise and for the loss of the relationship he might have enjoyed with his grown daughter and growing grandchild.

"May I do anything for you?" Maria asked, tenderly placing her arms about my shoulders. I held her close and she stroked my hair, twining her fingers amid the curls until my scalp tickled and she forced a chuckle from my lips. "I wish I could cheer you, Mummy."

My heart commanded my brain to engage my imagination and honor my father the way a writer best can—with ink and quill. Maria fetched my writing desk and set it upon my lap. Inside it lay everything I needed to complete an elegy.

Just as I had done upon the death of my mentor, dear David Garrick, my pen paid homage where my tongue could not. Line after line I scratched until my hands grew too cramped and I called upon Maria to transcribe the remainder of my tribute.

A chapter of my life had closed.

The first man to abandon me—yet alas, not the last—had gone to God.

His narrative completed, Ban departed soon after to return to England to have the memoir published. The India prospect was back on the table as well, it seemed. As he left me once again, I felt like a little skiff adrift on the bounding sea, rising and falling precipitously with every wave.

Banastre Tarleton could make my senses swell and sink like no other man I had ever known. There were times I despised myself for feeling so helpless in his thrall. Maria, too, though she put up with Ban for my sake, deplored his ability to be so solicitous in one moment and to treat me so cavalierly in the next.

"Perhaps it is no defense, but you have no idea," I told her, "what a paragon Ban is compared to your ne'er-do-well of a father."

I remained at Aix-la-Chapelle, taking the cures and scribbling away as the seasons waxed and waned. If my poems had not been published regularly in the London papers, one might have imagined that the world had all but forgotten Perdita. Perhaps some of them had. . . .

"Mummy, it appears that you are dead!" exclaimed Maria one summer day in 1787.

"What the devil do you mean by that?"

With her nose in a newspaper, my daughter proceeded to read me my obituary. It seemed that I had died a few days earlier, in Paris, and that I was the *natural* daughter of Nicholas Darby, facts that most assuredly bore correction, along with much of the rest of the article—although the author did mention my liaisons with both Lord Malden and Ban Tarleton, and had fairly accurately described my theatrical career, with a nod to my charitable efforts, among them my connexion with the unfortunate Mrs. Baddeley.

"Should we not tell them you are very much alive?" Maria suggested.

"A capital idea, my darling."

"Shall I write the letter?" She fetched quill and ink and seated herself at our dining table.

"Please." I was not amused. Hobbling about the room as I dictated the angry note to the editor, I said, "Don't forget to put the date and place—twentieth July, Aix-la-Chapelle, Germany—at the top."

"I'm not a ninny, Mum. I've been writing your letters for over a year, you know."

"I know, my pet. I'm not upset with you—just upset. It makes one rather ill to discover that one is dead." Perhaps I should have found more humor in the situation, but there were grave consequences, so to speak, to consider. If I were really deceased, the prince's annuity payments would be vastly reduced, leaving us to muddle through on the two hundred and fifty pounds annually payable to Maria upon my demise. That was no laughing matter. 'Twas vile enough that I was ridiculed in the press for soaking up the taxpayer's hard-won and painfully relinquished money by my annuity, despite the fact that in the intervening years His Royal High-ness had enjoyed the favors of several mistresses, each of whom had been similarly compensated with nary a second thought.

I cleared my throat. " 'Dear Sir'; no—just 'Sir' will be sufficient. Sir—With astonishment I read in the *Morning Post* of the fourteenth instant, a long account of my *death*, and a variety of circumstances, respecting my *life*, equally void of the smallest foundation.' What have we got so far?" Maria read the sentence back to me. "Lovely. Let us continue. 'I have the satisfaction of informing you, that so far from being *dead*, I am in the most perfect state of health; except for a trifling lameness, of which, by the use of the baths at this place, I have every reason to hope, I shall recover in a month or six weeks.' "

I had elected to shave the truth a bit, too vain to admit that my condition was a little more than "trifling," though the therapeutic waters of Aix-la-Chapelle had improved it.

After clearing my throat, I dictated, " 'I propose pass-ing my winter in London, having been near two years on the Continent.' " Maria's quill continued to scratch out my words as I drew up a footstool. " 'Lest it should be received and understood in the world that your account of my life is genuine, I beg leave to contradict two very ma-terial circumstances respecting my family connexion. In the first place, my father, Captain Nicholas Darby, whose *legitimate* daughter I had the happiness of being . . .' "

And here my words trailed off into the air, for I had indeed adored him when I was but a girl, before he left us for distant lands—and the allure of a mistress. But had he not been instrumental in terrifying my mother into marrying me off at such a young age, rather than permit me to pursue my theatrical dreams? Had Mother not been so hasty, perhaps my life would not have taken so many unpleasant turns. No Mr. Robinson, and hence, no debtors' prison. I glanced at my lovely daughter, her fringe flopping over one eye, her tongue peeking from her lips as she earnestly formed every letter. Yet I would not have a different child for all the world.

Maria looked up and tilted her head quizzically. "Mummy? What comes next?"

"Where were we?" I replied absentmindely.

My thoughts refocused on the task at hand. " 'Captain Nicholas Darby, whose legitimate daughter I had the happiness of being . . .' Whatever possessed them to think I was his natural child?" I muttered. Suddenly the Inuit boy appeared in my mind's eye. Because Papa likely *did* have at least *one* natural issue, I suppose. "Yes, 'Captain Nicholas Darby, et cetera—died six months since, on board his own ship, of seventy-four guns, in the Russian service, having previously distinguished himself in His Majesty's Royal Navy as the commander of an ordnance vessel during the siege of Gibraltar in 1783.' "

I went on to correct the editor's misapprehension regarding my maternal side of the family, and clarified that in November 1757 I had been born in Bristol, and there educated by Hannah More. Before concluding the letter with the usual obloquies, I asked Maria to write, " 'As a man of feeling I request you to contradict the report with candor, and all possible expedition. I have brothers in Italy, who will experience the greatest anxiety should such a detail reach their ears.' "

The *Morning Post* never printed the retraction, but

they did publish my letter in its entirety. Nonetheless, it felt good to be "alive" again!

Ban's memoir had been published in the spring of 1787, but at sixteen shillings a copy it was not likely to earn its hero a proper income. So Ban had done what he did best in peacetime: he became a professional gambler, opening a faro hall in Daubigney's tavern. He had left me in a fit of temper, reminding me that I had no legal claim to his affections, and returned without me to London.

Now that I was no longer required to act as my lover's amanuensis, I devoted the entirety of my talents to worshipping at the shrine of Erato—penning nothing but poetry, including a series of sonnets that were published in *The World*. My verses and stanzas, written under a plethora of pseudonyms—that they be judged on their merits alone and not on their author's name—now graced the pages of several periodicals. Though it delighted me to see so many of my efforts in print, it would have brought greater pleasure if it had been disclosed to the readers that they were enjoying the work of the woman they all knew as the scandalous Perdita.

Ban and I were quarrelling more often than we made love, which, given that we were at the time residing in different countries, was not terribly astonishing. His fancies had begun to wander, and I could not countenance his straying passions. It was a small world we inhabited, where everyone knew each other's business—or pretended to—and gossiped about it prodigiously. By September Ban was once more standing for Parliament, campaigning in Liverpool, and undoubtedly kissing everyone with a cleavage.

Wounded, heartsick, and embarrassed, from our vine-covered cottage in Aix-la-Chapelle, I could only exact revenge and remonstration through the point of my pen.

On October 31, 1787, *The World* published my lengthy four-stanza opus, "Lines to Him Who Will Understand Them," a few of which I include below:

> *THOU art no more my bosom's FRIEND;*
> *Here must the sweet delusion end,*
> *That charm'd my senses many a year,*
> *Thro' smiling summers, winters drear.—*
>
> *Yes; I shall view thee in each FLOW'R,*
> *That changes with the transient hour:*
> *Thy wand'ring Fancy I shall find*
> *Borne on the wings of every WIND:*
> *Thy wild impetuous passions trace*
> *O'er the white wave's tempestuous space:*
> *In every changing season prove*
> *An emblem of thy wav'ring LOVE.*

Such were my pangs of disprized love. And everyone who read them guessed correctly as to whom I made my dedication. Each time a published poem referenced my feelings for Ban, however obliquely, our affair ended up being chronicled in the press. I was winning sympathy with my pen.

And when once again Ban Tarleton tasted defeat, on my tongue the bitterness of his failed election bid was sweet.

Yet I missed him dreadfully; living with him could be purgatory, but life without him was an eternal hell. Besides, I longed for my native soil, for my old friends, and desired to be closer to my publishers.

So in January of 1788, Maria and I returned to London, taking up residence at forty-two Clarges Street. Mother joined us from Bristol. Ban settled into a flat down the block from us at number thirty. And suddenly, his family changed their song. My soul rejoiced to discover that after so many years the Tarletons had finally come to accept our love and regard us as a couple, despite the extralegal nature of our liaison.

We were ruled by our passions, Ban and I. Our love-making had always attained a fever pitch—a mutual need that neither of us ever seemed able to slake—and when we fell out, woe betide whoever might be underfoot. He sought revenge in the arms of other women, or in the faro hells. I sharpened my quill.

Yet, my obsessive love and my physical need for him trumped all else, including my political philosophies. So I could not compel myself to remain on the sidelines when in 1790 he once again stood for office. This time I accompanied him to Liverpool, wrote his campaign speeches, and coached him on their delivery. Standing on the hustings like the war hero he was, Ban played that card to win, holding aloft his mangled hand and delivering our version of Henry V's St. Crispin's Day speech, rallying his supporters to action.

Although Ban's character was brought into question by his two opponents, who raised the issues of his appetite for gambling and his open cohabitation with a notorious—and married—woman, this time the voters would not be swayed by free food and beer. The most vocal Tarletonites claimed that the other candidates were endeavoring to prevent a free election, stealing votes from Ban by force, if necessary. A riot erupted; there was mayhem in the streets. The atmosphere, so highly charged, was as frightening as it was exhilarating.

"The incumbents wish to drum me out of town!" Ban declared. "Will you let these cowards banish a man who risked life and relinquished limb in the service of his king and country?"

The answer they returned was a resounding *no*, and when all the votes were counted, Ban finally made his family proud and attained his dream: a seat in the House of Commons as the MP from Liverpool.

We returned home high as summer clouds, and enjoyed days and nights of celebration and roistering. Ban's grand success spurred me to apply myself even more assiduously to my writing.

A few years earlier, when we were still living in France, I'd become enamored of a florid and prodigiously popular style of poetry promulgated by Robert Merry, who wrote under the pen name Della Crusca. His acolytes—fellow poets, among whom I soon became one of the most worshipful—called themselves Della Cruscans. In 1790 Merry and I began a sort of cat and mouse game in *The World*, carrying on a poetical correspondence; one day his poem would be printed, and the next day readers would find my response, and so on. Speed of composition was therefore necessary, and in this realm I excelled. The deft fluidity had its artistic merits as well as its pragmatic ones, for spontaneity—deemed the natural enemy of artifice, in the form of belabored study—had become the rage.

I usually wrote under the names of Laura or Laura Maria. Sometimes I adopted a male identity. Mr. Bell, the

editor, delighted in the game, for it compelled his readers to buy the papers every day in order to catch the next
sally or riposte. And the poems were reprinted in regional
magazines, further increasing my income. Once again, I
had fine clothing and carriages.

Plump with self-esteem from my pseudonymous successes, I felt impelled to drop the veil of anonymity and
submit a poem under my own name. Imagine my astonishment when I received a letter of rejection from Mr.
Bell!

> Dear Mrs. Robinson,
> Perhaps you intended it as a jest to send me
> a poem in the Della Cruscan style, identify-
> ing yourself as the author of the stanzas I have
> published above the names of Laura and Laura
> Maria, but I must inform you that I happen to be
> well acquainted with the author of those poems,
> and know the writer's true name. I did find the
> poem you wrote to be vastly pretty, and applaud
> your efforts, but I fear they fall too far from the
> standard established by the author previously
> mentioned for me to ink the presses. I do, how-
> ever, wish you poetical success in future.

What gall! And what a fiction, on his part, to claim to
know the real "Laura"!

Through my footman I summoned Mr. Bell to Clarges
Street. "I demand to know the identities of Laura Maria
and Laura," I said, ushering him to a chair covered in
green striped silk. My parlor was littered with fragments
of unfinished manuscripts.

"Begging your pardon, Mrs. Robinson, but it is an editor's prerogative to maintain all confidentiality when one trusts him with their pseudonym."

I offered Mr. Bell a cup of tea and politely asked him if prevarication was also under the purview of editorial prerogative.

"I'm afraid I do not take your meaning," said Mr. Bell, looking as if he were solving a riddle for which he knew the answer but could not for all the world recall it. "But I will have the tea, ta. Milk and sugar too, please."

"I'll be but a moment," I said, excusing myself. He watched me limp out of the room.

My maid returned with me, bearing the tea tray. Beside the creamer rested a sheaf of papers. Mr. Bell looked as though he feared to touch them.

"Mrs. Robinson, if you intend to convince me to publish any more of your poems by serving me an excellent Darjeeling, I will have to decline both. People might not think it, but we editors do have our scruples, you know."

I smiled, knowing I'd not only caught him out, but that I'd ensnared him. "But, Mr. Bell, you have already published these poems. I invite you to peruse the papers by your elbow."

The editor nervously took the pages from the tray and placed them in his lap.

"As you can see from thumbing through them, you are looking at fair copies of the last several efforts printed by The *Morning Post* as attributed to either Laura or Laura Maria."

Mr. Bell gazed up at mc, his mouth flapping open and shut like a fish out of water. "M-Mrs. Robinson. I had n-no idea."

"Of course you didn't," I said quietly. "But you didn't have to lie about it so brazenly. And I expect you to make amends for insulting me and wasting my valuable time."

I took a stack of papers from a mahogany sideboard. "This is my latest collection of poetry. *Ainsi Va le Monde*— 'So Goes the World,' I call it. You will find the style of some of the pieces quite different from the flowery Della Cruscan poems. The rhyme schemes and meter are modern and daring, and several of the poems have something of a philosophical bent. In all, the collection is to be taken quite seriously. And you will publish it for me, as the work of Mary Robinson."

Mr. Bell glanced at a few of the poems. "These— these are quite excellent, madam," he admitted, somewhat astonished.

His surprised reaction irked me. "Then your penance will not be a painful one," I said, as a smile stole across my lips. "Now, if you'll forgive me, I must curtail this interview. I have an unfinished sonnet that awaits my attention, and you must return to the business of running a newspaper."

I rang for the maid, who escorted the editor to the door.

But Mr. Bell's lies taught me a valuable lesson that perhaps I had been unwilling to con: that Mrs. Robinson's character was weighed and found wanting, and that the name alone of a notorious lightskirt would be judged before something penned by her was given the slightest credence.

It would seem that nowadays I could only gain artistic success if I pretended to be someone other than myself. Not so awfully different from my days at Drury Lane, in some respects. But I fought the petty-mindedness and won out eventually.

Later that year, the very same Mr. Bell published the sixteen-page collection of my poems titled *Ainsi Va le Monde,* which ran through several editions and was then translated into French. The following February, the *Monthly Review* lauded the anthology, and my writing in general. I was in heaven.

And Ban, now on full pay and promoted to the rank of colonel, owing to his new prominence, took his seat in the House of Commons, immediately taking up the cudgels against the abolitionists. His most formidable opponent was the Tory from Yorkshire, William Wilberforce. Wilberforce resembled a misshapen troll, but his heart was in the right place, as far as I was concerned.

On December 10, the Yorkshireman introduced a bill that would abolish the slave trade and found himself going toe-to-toe with my lover, trading heated barbs across the aisle. Maria and I witnessed the fireworks from the gallery, as Ban had asked me to script his speech.

"How could you do it?" my daughter whispered, shielding her face with her fan that her words might not be overheard. Yet there was no disguising her disgust. "You— who dressed as a Quaker on your wedding day and have always despised the institution of slavery—how could you put words in Ban's mouth that might very well postpone or prevent abolition?"

There were tears in my eyes as Ban thundered, "The common sense of the Empire will strangle this modern attempt at mistaken philanthropy!"

"Because I love him," I murmured to Maria. And— what I could not confess to my young daughter—because every fiber of my being was in thrall to him. I was a sexual creature and no other man had ever brought me to such heights of ecstasy; Banastre Tarleton was the drug my body could never get its fill of. Too well I knew his capacity for cruelty, but I could not help myself. There are mortals from whom we can bear even severity, which from others would be wholly insupportable. And Ban was, for me, such a one. I might have been the speaker in Shakespeare's Sonnet 57 who says, "So true a fool is love that in your will, though you do any thing, he thinks no ill." Since when have Passion and Reason danced hand in hand along the strand?

That is why I agreed, despite morals to the contrary, and against all reason, to write Ban's anti-abolitionist speeches. And, though I despised my own culpability in the sordid business, when one uses a quill to flagellate oneself, the sensation inflicted by a feather is, alas, but a tickle.

Ban rose to his feet again and leveled his arm at the center of the room, pointing with his three-fingered hand at Prime Minister Pitt. "As a member of the Opposition, as well as the voice of the people of the port city of Liverpool, whose economy and commerce are shackled to the slave trade and for whom abolition would prove disastrous, I cannot bring myself to think this is a convenient time, the country in an eligible situation, or the minister serious in his inclination to make an experiment which presents a certain prospect of no probability of advantage. An abolition would instantly annihilate a trade which annually employs upwards of fifty-five hundred sailors, upwards of one hundred sixty ships, and whose exports amount to eight hundred thousand pounds sterling."

Curling his mangled hand into a fist, he shook it at Pitt,

adding, "And the same experiment would undoubtedly bring the West India trade to decay, whose exports and imports amount to *six million* pounds sterling, and which gives employment of one hundred sixty thousand tons of additional shipping, and sailors in proportion; all objects of too great magnitude to be hazarded on an unnecessary speculation, which, in all probability, would prove ruinous to the commercial consequence, the national honor, and the political glory of Great Britain!"

I bit back my disagreement, and from the gallery added my voice to the chorus crying "Hear, hear!" in resounding approval of his oration. Maria made a point of sitting on her hands.

I confess I was proud of her.

Utterly devoted to each other, though officially domiciled a few doors apart, Ban and I lived elegantly and stylishly then, "making adultery respectable," as even our detractors were compelled to admit.

Mr. Bell agreed to publish by subscription another volume of my poetry, which I had stitched together at the prompting of my dear friends, Sir Joshua Reynolds and the philosopher Edmund Burke. Reynolds even offered to paint my portrait for the frontispiece, a three-quarter view of my face, fittingly called a "lost profile," a style that was very popular for authors' printed images, for its serious literary overtones. Like Ariadne, I look back contemplatively at that which I have lost.

The first edition was printed on May 12, 1791, handsomely bound in mahogany-colored leather tooled in gold. I had secured a whopping six hundred subscribers in sixteen weeks, a veritable catalogue of the titled and influential; the list, printed within the volume, was headed by none other than my former royal paramour, His Highness, the Prince of Wales. The names of several other royals followed George's, and of course dear Georgiana, the Duchess of Devonshire, was there, along with Fox, Sheridan, Reynolds, the poets Peter Pindar and Robert Merry, and many, many members of the ton. But what brought both smiles and tears to my face was the inclusion on the list of twenty-one of Ban's friends and relatives in Liverpool—proof positive that Jane Tarleton was no longer ashamed to have my name linked with hers.

The critics were quite kind, seeing in my verses the seeds of a new literary movement, which they dubbed Romanticism. I was charting new territory, among the first to plumb the deepest recesses of my own experience and mine the ore I found there. Unlike those of my fellow scribblers, my stanzas were both autobiographical and intensely personal. It was an age when Nature was considered one of the rare permissible outlets for emotion, and in my poetical lines I employed Her many attributes as the theme for my personal turmoil and travail. She was as much a character as the humans I invoked.

That summer, Maria and I ventured to Bath, whilst Ban remained in London, spending most of his time entering his name in the betting books at Brooks's—when he was not chasing the charms of another woman. He had left me once again, taking a suite of rooms not far from his favorite haunts in St. James's. No sooner had his mother accepted our ménage, after so many years of insults, than my lover made a mockery of our victory. His betrayal stung like a whipping.

"I thought you despaired to be without him, Mummy,"

Maria confoundedly observed, as arm in arm we strolled past fashionable pedestrians in the North Parade. My daughter was keen on my enjoying a daily constitutional despite my disabilities.

"I despair more to imagine him in another's arms," I replied softly. "He has begun to stray toward some low caprice, I fear."

"Don't cry," my daughter softly said, drawing me closer beside her. "Ten of him is not worth one of you." And finally she bravely spoke the words that I realized she'd long feared to voice. "I do not much care for Colonel Tarleton."

My face was bathed in tears. "If only I could feel the same way, my sweet."

"He is naught but bluff and bluster, with no substance underneath," she added soothingly, thinking, I suppose, that she was cheering me. We ceased our promenade whilst she searched her pockets for a handkerchief.

"Then is there another man I've known whom you would prefer to see my paramour?"

Maria shook her head without giving the matter a second thought. "Not a one, Mum. Every man-jack of them has used you ill."

"Wherever do you learn such language?" I chuckled ruefully. But I knew the answer; she'd been living with a soldier for years. There was a part of my soul that acknowledged, of course, that Maria's words were not ill reasoned. By now she was sixteen years of age; I'd not been much older when I'd given birth to her. Perhaps she realized—if only by the unfamiliar physical sensations a girl experiences at such an age—that I knew *precisely* what it was about Ban Tarleton that made me take him back time after time. I permitted myself to swallow his false-hoods because he made my body feel so exquisite when I was nestled in his embrace. There seemed to be no magic sufficiently strong to rescue me from the power he had over my senses.

But the change of scene and the waters of Bath had availed little. On our return to London, my thoughts were so given over to Ban's desertion that I was utterly exhausted, physically, emotionally, and mentally. I had no appetite for anything, whether it be food or gaiety.

At Maria's suggestion, I took up writing prose. Drafting a novel would distract me from my anguish, though I reminded my daughter that it was not considered a respectable occupation for a woman. "We may compose poetry and publish it to our heart's content—but novel writing is considered too vulgar."

"What rubbish," Maria exclaimed. "No doubt it is an ugly rule invented by envious male novelists to secure all the thunder for themselves. And besides," she added with a chuckle, "you are no stranger to the taint of vulgarity."

So all through the autumn months I scratched away with my quill, and when my fingers ached too much from rheumatic complaints, I dictated the narrative to Maria.

My maiden voyage, *Vancenza, or The Dangers of Credulity,* was published on the second of February, 1792. As with my poetry, I tapped the wellspring of experience, this time exploring the plight of a royal mistress.

The public, eager for such a roman à clef from Mrs. Robinson's pen, scrambled to obtain a copy, and the entire edition sold out in a single day! So avid remained the readers to glean any secrets about the sexual proclivities of the Prince of Wales, however fictionally veiled, that four subsequent editions of *Vancenza* were snapped up just as rapidly. And Maria entered my study brandishing the daily papers as if they were medieval pennants, eager to read me the notices.

"Mummy, I have the *Monthly Review* for March," she announced one day, and began to quote it before I could even make the request. " '*Vancenza*, it is true, is not written in the simple style, but it is written, and in our opinion well written, in the style of elegance peculiar to Mrs. R. The richness of fancy and of language, which the fair author had so successfully displayed in her poetical productions, she has transferred to prose narration, and has produced a tale, which, we venture to predict, will be much read and admired.' " Dropping the journal into my lap, she threw her hands about my neck as she used to do when she was a tiny slip of a girl. "Bravissima! Well done, Mum. You're a novelist!"

I demurred. "I was a pupil of Hannah More, you know, though in my youth she was more the educator and dramatist than the popular evangelical she has become of late. Therefore, I'm afraid I must decline the title of novelist, my darling. The species of composition known by that denomination too often conveys a lesson I do not wish to inculcate."

Maria looked at me, utterly appalled. "So you *do* believe just as the moralists do—that the content of popular novels corrupts the mind? Then inculcate your *own* lesson," she insisted. "In any event, you're obviously terribly good at it."

I should have been floating on a silver cloud to see my maiden efforts at narrative fiction so well received by both proles and peers. But the praise was merely a temporary balm. It did not bring Ban back to my achingly lonely arms; he remained enamored of his gaudy new mistress.

On the fourteenth of February, I penned "To My Dear Valentine," in which I prophesied that my devoted heart would haunt Ban from the grave, for so ill was I with rheumatic ailments that I verily believed an earthy entombment was on the horizon.

Meanwhile, I listened with admiration to every report of Ban's performances in Parliament; he had been winning plaudits for his oratory, and though I was no longer penning his speeches, my bosom swelled with pride for his sake.

I could not live without him, and my course grew ever clearer. I would have to woo him back with the point of my pen.

Twenty-six

Courting Trouble

1792 . . . age thirty-four

While Ban's name led the rest in Brooks's Betting Book, I wrote a poem titled "*The Adieu to Fancy*: Inscribed to the Same." It captured the power of Ban's magnetism, and how—aided by my imagination's fancy and fantasies of the life we might share—he had bewitched me from the start, but my fondest hopes had proven mere delusions.

I sent Ban the poem, but received no reply. In sorrowful desperation, I left Clarges Street and let rooms at thirteen St. James's Place, within shouting distance of Brooks's, but it did not bring him closer.

On July 23, 1792, I wrote a confidential letter to my old friend Sheridan, complaining of poor health and a broken heart after the severing of an irreproachable ten-year connexion, averring that my only recourse seemed to be to quit London, where the imprints of Ban's voice and image were everywhere etched. For all the stones the public hurled at me, aiming to shatter my reputation, it is worth mentioning that for the entire time I was Ban's lover, I never once considered tasting the charms of another man. Though flawed, he was my sine qua non; if he were an illness, I was irrevocably afflicted.

The following day, my widowed mother, Maria, and I boarded a boat for Calais. Our ultimate destination was Leghorn, a port city on Italy's Adriatic coast. I was eager to see my brother George, who had become a merchant there. Our elder brother John had died in 1789. I had not seen George in years; but the situation in France made overland travel exceedingly perilous. Times had changed since last I'd lived there. The Bastille had been stormed, the monarchy reduced to the merest cipher, and anyone with a pedigree was imperiled. Vicious demagogues were in control, not only of the Frenchmen's new form of government but of their sanity as well. Whilst my philosophies had been sympathetic to the plight of the common man, what the common man did with the *liberté* he ripped from the jeweled hands of the *ancien régime,* turned my stomach with its vileness.

From a deck chair, to the rolling accompaniment of the swelling waves between Dover and Calais, I wrote a poem called "Bounding Billow," which I dedicated to Ban. The sea spray misting my cheeks commingled with my tears.

I hoped to kindle some compassion in his breast with the stanzas:

> *I have lov'd thee,—dearly lov'd thee,*
> *Through an age of worldly woe;*
> *How ungrateful I have prov'd thee*
> *Let my mournful exile show!*
> *Ten long years of anxious sorrow,*
> *Hour by hour I counted o'er;*
> *Looking forward, till to-morrow,*
> *Every day I lov'd thee more!*

Fare thee well, ungrateful rover!
Welcome Gallia's hostile shore:
Now the breezes waft me over;
Now we part—TO MEET NO MORE.

Calais was crowded with English expatriates living
cheek by jowl, whiling away their days with insipid entertainments until it was safe to journey farther. We let
a comfortable suite of rooms, installing ourselves until
such time as travel to Italy might be safe. Our little distaff
ménage brought me heart's ease. My daughter had grown
into a lovely young woman, tall and self-possessed; and I
had missed my mother's gentle spirit, particularly during
the difficult times with Ban.

Yet somehow Mother seemed to bring the devil with
her, as she had done so many years earlier. She gave me
to wonder whether she had remained in contact with Mr.
Robinson all this time, even when I had not—for soon
after our arrival he appeared at Calais, calling on us with
his elder brother William, now a commodore lately returned from the East Indies. My husband's hair had grown
thin, his complexion even paler than I had remembered it.
Years of disporting himself in low pursuits had taken their
toll upon his face and figure.

His brother bore little family resemblance; he was of
stouter stuff, excepting that the upturn of his mouth, as
if to indicate a state of perpetual affability, was a trait he
shared with Tom and their father, though I had learned
long ago from the latter two that there was no substance
behind the mask.

My mother poured the tea as we all sat down like a
civilized family, which in itself was a recipe for risibility.

"My brother has a proposal," said Mr. Robinson flatly, his tone an indication that he had some prior knowledge of its purport.

The commodore's boots were dirty. "Indeed, I do, ladies," he said, picking at a bit of fluff on the facing of his lapel. He fixed his eyes on Maria. "Your daughter is a lovely young girl of seventeen—and ripe for marriage, if I do say so."

"You don't say," muttered Maria. Oh, how she reminded me of myself when, so many years earlier, I had sat in a drawing room, nubile and naïve, enduring the unexpected attentions of a naval man. She looked at me for a cue and I pursed my lips and lowered my eyes to convey that she should hear her uncle out. I shuddered to discover that I had reacted just as Mother had done in front of Captain Fredericks.

Commodore Robinson puffed out his chest. "I am wealthy—I make no bones about it. I've earned my way in the world and am proud to boast of it. I can make Maria Elizabeth a fine husband; the match has everything to recommend it. She will want for nothing—quite a change, I expect, from the way she has been brought up."

What an oaf! For one thing, despite our previous descents into penury—due to the conduct of his own brother—we had lived very high from time to time. I had been pressured into a loveless match by one-third of the people who were at present sipping my tea in my drawing room. And I had vowed before Heaven that I would never consign my child to a likewise fate.

"There is of course a condition; there are always conditions," said the commodore. I did not care for his smirk and could see that Maria wished to wipe it from his face with the tea towel. He glanced from me to his younger brother. "Should Maria accept my exceedingly generous offer—and, I daresay, I doubt there will be many more to follow of an even remotely similar magnitude—she must renounce the pair of you. Yes, even you, Tom, for your character does your daughter no credit; and if she wishes to rise in the world—which she must perforce do at my side"—Commodore Robinson grinned, quite pleased with himself—"her own reputation must be stainless. You of course, madam," he added, leveling his gaze directly at my bosom, "are less of a credit to your sex than was Jezebel."

Such gall! I was but one breath from booting Commodore Robinson and my disgusting husband out of the room. My mother looked distinctly embarrassed. Had she known in advance of the commodore's intentions? I loved her with all my heart, but experience had been a strict teacher.

It was time to allow Maria to speak for herself. Knowing my daughter, I awaited her words with more pride than trepidation.

"Sir," Maria began, placing her tea saucer on the table and rising majestically from the divan, "I would not countenance your proposal if you were Adam and I Eve, and we should be assured of never falling from Paradise."

Mr. Robinson's brother looked like he had been stung by a hornet. His complexion changed color from rose to red to violet, but it did not deter Maria from stating her piece.

"Though no man or woman can claim themselves perfect in God's eyes, my parents nonetheless brought me into this world and together they sustained me in my first years upon this earth. For that reason alone, I would not conscience your terms and renounce them forever for the sake of a few new bonnets and shiny carriages. You may know your brother well, Commodore, but you do not know my mother at all. Mrs. Robinson is the woman who gave me her own milk until I was well past my second year, shunning the services of a wet nurse after all but my earliest days. She devoted herself to me entirely after my father destroyed her reputation by abandoning us for the lure of gambling hells, gadding about with a cadre of rakish confederates, and consorting openly with any number of fancy women. She has looked after me for all of my seventeen years, and for nearly half that time I have known the need to care for her in her infirmities. Commodore Robinson, if my mother will permit me to escort you from our apartments, I will be happy to do so immediately. You insult the both of us with your degrading proposal." Maria stood before the naval man, her hands politely folded in front of her waist. "As there is nothing more to say, I bid you good day, sir."

Had I been able to rise from my chair unassisted, I would have done so and applauded my daughter. My mother, ever the appeaser, ushered the gentlemen—who were not even deserving of such a nomination—to the door, apologizing all the way for the failure of their errand.

"You knew of it, then, Mother," I said testily when she returned to the drawing room. My angry eyes were little more than slits.

She gave a self-conscious assent. "Of the intention, yes, but not the terms." Sinking to the sofa beside me, she burst into tears. "Oh, no, my darling—not the terms."

"Nonetheless you would have willingly sacrificed my

daughter to another Robinson, knowing what you have known for years about Tom's unscrupulous behavior—and his tendency to avoid the truth whenever possible?"

"Forgive me, Mary. I only wanted to see Maria well settled. All I have ever wanted for my girls is the best. Answer me this: What do you expect to become of her as the years wear on? Is she to be your nursemaid forever, turning her back on all prospects of another life?"

"I think that decision must be hers," I replied evenly. "I do not hold her against her will, nor make her feel she must look after her invalid mother forever in preference to her own desires. Maria has never spoken to me of marriage, except to mention that it is furthest from her thoughts at present."

There were no more discussions on the subject.

But there was deliriously wonderful news on two fronts. For starters, one day in August, Ban arrived.

"My darling!" He swept into the foyer and scooped me into his arms, carrying me straight to the boudoir, forgoing all preliminaries such as conversation.

I didn't care. There would be plenty of time later for words. My need for him was unquenchable, my skin on fire from his touch, for the excited attentions of his fingers and tongue. "I've even uttered prayers in the hope that you would return to me," I confessed, between passionate kisses and embraces.

"I'm a firm believer that God helps those who help themselves," Ban murmured, nibbling my earlobe, fully aware how insatiable I would become whenever his tongue teased me there.

I wriggled against him, feeling the heat rise once more within me. "Whatever do you mean by that?"

"Only that whilst the power of prayer may have had some small effect, it is the power of your pen that wooed me back. Once I read 'Bounding Billow,' in the August issue of *The Oracle,* I could not bear the thought of spending another moment without you."

Our lips met in a melting kiss.

"And your gaudy mistress?" I asked.

"Gone forever," Ban replied. "After I read your poem I severed the connexion and rode posthaste for the Channel."

My arrow had hit the intended target. All reason fled, so willing was I to embrace him once more, happily forgiving his past transgressions and his errant heart.

"Does that mean, then, that this time you have returned to me forever?" I could almost feel my nerves aquiver as I voiced the question for which I dearly wished to hear an assent.

"I'm afraid, my love, this reunion must be brief."

At this news my stomach churned like an angry sea. "And why is that?" I whispered.

"I have plans to depart for Paris."

"Paris!" I exclaimed. "It's hardly safe there nowadays." I had heard from those who knew firsthand that the situation there was becoming worse by the day. "No one who calls an aristo their friend is considered out of harm's way."

"Even Robespierre himself daren't harm a British MP," Ban assured me. "It would provoke an international incident the Legislative Assembly can ill afford, particularly when they wish to court the sympathies of other nations. I have some business to see to, and besides, I miss my friends. For all we know, their days are numbered."

I shuddered at his words.

"But I've made my reputation by besting an angry rabble," Ban assured me as I clung to him, and there was no dissuading him from his purpose.

"Come back to me, safe and whole," I begged Ban. "I cannot bear to lose you again."

My only consolation at parting from him so soon was the other bit of good news Ban brought me. Sheridan had decided to produce my opera. I would have been ecstatic at this, for it meant money as well as prestige and a chance to return to the Theatre—my first love—but my fears for Ban's safety formed my mind's chief occupation.

My lover was adamant that I return to London at once, as the gates of Paris offered no guarantees that the bloody mob violence would remain contained behind them.

On the second of September, 1792, my mother, Maria, and I sailed for home. As fortune had it, we'd fled in the nick of time, for only a few hours after we departed the *arrêt* arrived, by which every British subject throughout France was restrained; and the following day was recorded as the most violent since the bloody revolution began. The tumult of discontent perverted the cause of universal liberty. Indiscriminate vengeance swept before it. Twelve hundred French souls loyal to their king and queen were slaughtered like spring lambs.

I despaired for Ban's life when I read the newspaper accounts of the atrocities perpetrated in Paris on September third—how the breasts and auburn-coiffed head of the Princesse de Lamballe, lady-in-waiting to Marie Antoinette, were paraded on pikes through the street. The hapless young noblewoman had been hacked to pieces by a rabble daring to denominate themselves members of the human race.

Understandably, my elation was boundless when on September twenty-ninth, Ban returned—in one piece, though full of the most alarming reports. "I read about Lamballe," I said, quivering with anger. "How ghastly!"

"I was there," exclaimed Ban. "Dining with the duc d'Orleans. There we are, two dozen of us, enjoying an evening of Monsieur's finest brandy, when we hear the shouts in the streets below. People are singing 'La Marseillaise'— dreadfully off-key—and a pair of drummers leads the procession as though it were a festival. And lo, we look out the duc's windows to see the princesse's head, and what was alleged to be her poitrine and limbs, borne aloft by the mob. The duc gazes upon the carnage, and as is his wont, ever so calmly says to his guests—Mary, may I die unloved if this be untrue—'*Ah, c'est la Lamballe. Je la connais à ses cheveux!*'"

"What a vulgar comment. How could he jest at a time like that? To say, 'I'd know that hair anywhere,'" I muttered.

"I believe they call it sangfroid," Ban replied tersely. "It may be the only way a man like Philippe can handle the significance of the changes in the Parisian air. Though he's among the few aristocrats to sympathize with the rabble, I wouldn't bet it will save his neck from the madmen's bloodthirstiness." He took my hands in his and drew me close. "Let us thank God and King George and the patriotism of John Bull that the English are a saner breed than their brethren across the Channel."

I swam in his embrace as we made love, glorious sensations that brought me, body and soul, more relief from my painful infirmities in a single hour than any spa bathing could have accomplished in a lifetime. And as dusk settled outside my window, Ban helped me dress. Tenderly lifting me into his arms, he carried me down to the street, gently placing me in his landau, and we clattered off for the Haymarket theatre. Throughout the evening, my smile never dimmed. I was satiated and ecstatic. The only man I ever truly loved with every fiber of my being was proudly and most publicly proclaiming me the woman he considered his wife. That night I placed a golden ring upon Ban's finger, a symbol of the marriage forged in our hearts, if not in the church.

Yet God did not see fit to grant me too many months of happiness, for in August 1793, my mother departed from this world after a brief illness. Maria and I nursed her as best we could after the doctor bled her and advised us to keep her comfortable.

She grew frailer and frailer with each passing day, and by the end of a week she resembled a tiny sparrow with large searching blue eyes. One evening she refused the soup I had brought for her supper.

"You mustn't," I said softly, as she pushed the spoon away. "You need your nourishment."

"Not where I'm going," she replied, her voice small and faint. Mother reached for my hand and asked for her devotional. I placed the little prayer book in her hands, and suddenly recognized it as one of the gifts Mr. Robinson had brought her when he was trying to woo me.

"I'm sorry, Mary," Mother said, clutching the book. "I never wished you any ill. I always wanted the best for you." She beckoned for me to come closer. I bent down and she kissed my forehead as if she were bestowing a benediction. "You have suffered much," Mother whispered. "But God has given you beauty, immense talent, and a loving heart.

Use them well. And make sure Maria Elizabeth knows how much I love you both."

She closed her eyes and let the prayer book rest atop her chest, which soon ceased its rhythmic rise and fall, her death in itself a metric stanza.

She did not open her eyes again.

I had become an orphan.

Disconsolate by her passing, I took to my own bed. Though Mother and I had been occasionally at logger-heads, she was most tenderly loved and sincerely lamented. A special bond was forged between us from the first hour of Father's failure and estrangement from his family, a bond no son, however close, could understand.

I knew not how I might thrive without her. I was in no condition to face the world, sure I should never be cheer-ful again.

By the fall of 1793, Ban, Maria, and I were ensconced at Old Windsor.

We had decided to find a quieter place to reside, where the country air and a patch of green to admire would be more healthful and relaxing than London's hurly-burly, yet would enable us to return to town within the day.

Charming Englefield Cottage filled the bill to perfec-tion. The grounds abutted the edge of Great Windsor Park. Not only had Englefield Green become a fashionable summer venue for the gentry, but I was now the prince's neighbor, the Great Park the only separation between my former royal lover's abode and my own. When all was said and done, I suppose I have never entirely been able to re-linquish a sense of proximity to that noble man who had so affected my destiny.

Though I supplied the funds to purchase the cottage, the deed was put in Maria's name, that she would always have a home should any disaster befall me, and upon my eventual demise.

France had declared war on England, and to my relief, Ban, who had badly sprained his knee that September, had not been well enough to run off and join the fray. One day I slipped from my crutches, injuring my legs and hip. What a doddering pair of cripples we made, and neither of us yet forty.

Though I was quite the success as a poetess, there were days so painful that only laudanum and Ban's love got me from dawn to sunset. His passion—and of course my daughter's devotion—were the only sure things in my life, as every week I was inculcated with an object lesson in the nature of fame. My poems were being printed in India, sold at a guinea apiece. And "Lines to Him Who Will Understand Them" had been set to music and was now a popular tune in London drawing rooms and throughout the world. As Britain's finest mistress of lyrical poetry, I was hailed as "the English Sappho."

But one success was no guarantee of another. My old friend Sheridan, as well as the manager of the Royal Haymarket, rejected my opera *Kate of Aberdeen,* an opus for which I'd had high hopes.

Nonetheless, I was carving a niche for myself in the pantheon of lady authors, writing, as with much of my poetry, from my own experiences, whilst my sister scribblers, such as Mrs. Burney, composed fantastical gothic novels that combined the sort of rollicking adventures one might read in Sterne or Smollet with the morality tales of Hannah More.

On Valentine's Day, 1794, my second novel, *The Widow, or a Picture of Modern Times,* was published. By March, the entire first edition of three thousand copies had sold out—and the fashionable women of London were up in arms at the effrontery I had displayed by holding the mirror up to nature, depicting them in their follies and vices as the shallow, grasping, and voracious creatures they too often were. When one character assails another for daring to equate her recognized literary talent with that of rank, I was writing from the depths of my own experiences, exploring a theme that would become one of my touchstones: satirizing a society that places birth above genius.

I collapsed from a fever whilst I scrambled to prepare a second edition, but from my sickbed my maternal bosom swelled with pride at Maria's twin debuts.

My daughter's first novel, *The Shrine of Bertha,* was published on March 22. Those who read it would recognize strains of my voice in Maria's prose style, and her narrative structure was derivative of my own, but it was to be expected from a maiden effort. The critics were not as kind as I would have wished, but as her doting mother I rejoiced to see that readers were enjoying it.

Maria was making a social splash as well as a literary one. I had never expected her to walk in my footsteps in any way, though it's a mother's fondest hope that her child will emulate the good conduct and eschew the bad. I was proud of my daughter's achievements with the pen, and nearly as pleased with her fashion sense. It was Maria Elizabeth who had set the craze among young women to wear turbans instead of broad-brimmed hats, and to sport the tasseled red Greek caps as well.

364 ❦ AMANDA ELYOT

One evening she appeared before me in a lovely gentleman's suit of red velvet, showing to perfection the curve of her slender hips and white-stockinged calves.

"Mummy, how do I look?" she asked, beaming happily.

"And where might you be off to in such attire?"

"A masquerade at Brandenburg House." She paused to regard my reaction. "Why are you crying, Mum?"

"Because . . . because you remind me so much of myself when I was your age." I wiped away a falling tear with my fingertip. How many times had I scandalized the ton by visiting the pleasure gardens in my cross-dressing costumes from Drury Lane?

"You'll stun them all," I told Maria; and I meant it as a compliment.

The following morning I read the newspaper accounts of the masquerade at Brandenburg House. Maria was singled out as being among the prettiest young ladies in attendance that evening. I smiled to know that she glittered in the company of many of my old and dear friends—Lord and Lady Melbourne, Fox, Sheridan, Georgiana, and of course the Prince of Wales.

But after the giddy news of March, the rest of 1794 descended downhill with the speed of a runaway stallion. Ban and I quarreled miserably that summer; I was once again supporting his gambling habit from my literary earnings, and his vices claimed every penny faster than I could make them. He was beginning by now to run to fat, nearly gray at forty. He rarely rode anymore, and had all but given up his other beloved sporting pastimes of cricket, tennis, and boxing. I had suffered the same laggardly behavior from my husband; why should I continue to conscience it in a lover?

Unable to face another week of his stumbling home after a long night of cards and drink, in mid-August I packed up and moved back to our cottage in Old Windsor—with Maria, of course. But no sooner did I place one toe over the threshold than I began to miss Ban dreadfully. I poured my longing into a series of forty-four sonnets titled *Sappho and Phaon,* writing as if I were Sappho, betrayed and abandoned by her male lover. I was no longer writing in the florid mode of the Della Cruscans. That literary fashion was now passé, re-placed in the public's esteem and taste with a consider-ably less baroque poetic style.

The sestet from the eighteenth sonnet in the Sappho cycle expresses the anguish I bore in my heartsick soul:

> *Why art thou chang'd? dear source of all my woes!*
> *Though dark my bosom's tint, through ev'ry vein*
> *A ruby tide of purest lustre flows,*
> *Warm'd by thy love, or chill'd by thy disdain;*
> *And yet no bliss this sensate Being knows;*
> *Ah! why is rapture so allied to pain?*

The *annus horribilis* continued. Ban returned to Old Windsor, but then we had another spat, more ferocious than the previous one, and he took off for London again.

Maria endeavored to cheer me, filling every room with fragrant blossoms until the air hung with a heady perfume. She encouraged me to get out of bed and walk about as much as possible, but I found safety in the confines of my four-poster oaken bed and the worn-out eiderdown in which I cocooned myself no matter the season, for the cottage was always drafty.

"What can I do to dull the pain, Mama?" my daughter asked.

"Bring me laudanum, my sweet. Use Dr. Sydenham's formula this time."

"You must forgive me for not recalling it." I could see that she was stalling for time.

"Strain into a pint of canary wine two ounces of opium, an ounce of saffron, and a dram of cinnamon and cloves."

"Perhaps we'll try that recipe tomorrow. I think you've had enough for today; it makes you too morose."

"The laudanum is not to blame; it is the critics. The best they could say about the volume of *Poems* published in January was"—and here I mimicked a snooty reviewer—" 'Many of Mrs. Robinson's poems relate to incidents in her own connexions and are *proudly plaintive.*' They deride me for writing for money. As if earning a living by my pen is something vulgar and low. Why is it considered ladylike to scribble away in the privacy of one's home, but not to put forward the same efforts for the public eye? They have been so unkind of late that I would sooner open a vein and bleed before them than ever pen another line."

I glanced at the sheaves of paper scattered upon nearly every surface of the room. There was not even a chair where one could sit, or a table where one might enjoy a cup of tea. The cabriole legs of my pretty French bedstead swam in a sea of discarded manuscript pages. "I might as well toss my works in progress on the fire as well. Fuel is dear and we haven't got any money."

Maria plumped my bolster and smoothed the counterpane before settling down on the bed beside me as she had when she was a chubby toddler. "You do not mean that. You are brilliant and courageous; and they are petty and envious, and have not the talent to write anything more comprehensive than a two-hundred-word snipe at their betters." Kissing my throbbing temples, my daughter added, "They were not so complimentary to me, you know, and you don't hear me threatening to burn my manuscripts."

"In any event, for all my endeavors, we've barely got a pot to piss in, regardless of Ban's gambling vices. My mental labors have failed through the dishonest conduct of my publishers. My works have sold handsomely, but the profits have been theirs. Maria, how can we subsist on five hundred pounds a year"—I sighed, ignoring her encouragement—"when it costs two hundred just to maintain my carriage?" I stared at my nearly useless legs, amorphous logs beneath the quilt. "Once upon a time my coaches were a luxury," I said. "Now, just one of them is a necessity."

My sonnets from Sappho to Phaon worked their magic and brought Ban's heart back to me.

Women are most relenting victims when they subdue a rebellious lover, I mused. If one such man should ever reappear to plead, our anger instantly subsides and his penitence only served to attach us more strongly than ever!

Our broken hearts were healed, but Ban's gambling seemed a disease for which there was no cure. The dignity of office made no difference in his conduct, for he was as laddish as ever he'd been before he was made an MP. When he was happy, he stayed at the card tables for hours on end; and when things took a downturn for him, he entered his name in the betting books with just as much frequency. The wagering sprees had increasingly involved copious drinking as well—shades of my ill-starred life with Tom Robinson—and I grew ever more disgusted, particularly when the corrupting influences included close friends who were well acquainted with my opinions on the subject. Among these confederates of Ban's was Richard Brinsley Sheridan, who had been steadily moving away from his demanding mistress, the Theatre, preferring to embrace the world of politics instead. Ban and Sheridan were fast buddies, and their shared affinity for gaming and drink made them closer than ever.

Rather graphic images of my inebriated lover staggering through the streets of London were immortalized in verse by both Samuel Taylor Coleridge and Robert Southey when the *Morning Post* printed "The Devil's Thoughts." I was livid—not at my fellow poets, but that our dirty linen should be so exposed.

There I was, so protective of our characters for propriety's sake; and yet in retrospect, I suppose it was a bit silly of me, for our reputations were already in the gutter, those horses long gone from the barn!

Twenty-seven

Nobody

1794 . . . my thirty-seventh year

Back in 1792 I had submitted to Sheridan a rather biting satire that I had titled *Nobody*. It held the mirror up to the faces of the nobility, hideously disfigured with greed by the vice of gambling. Finally, in 1794, with Sheridan concentrating on politics and John Philip Kemble now managing Drury Lane, Kemble decided to produce the play and a cast was selected. The performers were less excited about it than I, however, even though their roles were plums; for despite the rigid separation of class between the actresses and the women they would be mocking, many of us who had attained fame in our profession did socialize with the likes of the liberal-minded Duchess of Devonshire and other female gamesters from the cluster of upper-class Whigs. Putting it bluntly, the actors feared reprisals from the ton, were they to play my satire. In fact, I mocked myself from my high-flying Perdita days as much as I skewered the ladies of the ton.

My former rival at Drury Lane, Elizabeth Farren—who had been set down to assay Lady Languid, the principal part—quite abruptly withdrew her participation, not comfortable in a comedy that lampooned Georgiana, who was a close friend. Things began to look rather dicey for us until we found a willing replacement. Dear Dorothy Jordan, however, a woman who feared nothing, dived into the role I had written for her, that of a saucy maid—the type of part in which Dora had achieved her fame upon the stage.

Dora had earned an equal measure of notoriety as the mistress of King George's third son, the Duke of Clarence. Needless to say, she and I understood each other well.

The premiere of *Nobody* was scheduled for November 29, 1794—the same night as the opening of the gambling ladies' faro season. No sooner had the play been announced than Dora Jordan and I each received anonymous letters, threatening "*Nobody* shall be damned." The original counterparts of my fictional creations had heard about the plot and vowed to "finish the comedy"—in other words, to put an end to it.

As the play shone a torch on the voraciousness of the upper-crust gamblers, it also derided the hypocrisy of those titled ladies who enjoyed clandestine adulterous liaisons while openly condemning other women who engaged in extramarital affairs. Once again, I was writing from experience.

How could Mrs. Jordan and I be receiving threats that the satire would be "finished" before it had even premiered? During the rehearsal process, had Sheridan discussed *Nobody*'s plot among his cronies in the Devonshire set? Had the Farren flapped her envious tongue to our tony acquaintances?

"Chin up, Mum," Maria counseled. "It's not so very

different from the squibs the papers used to run. I expect all the hubbub will bring even more people flocking to the theatre to see what the fuss is all about. I've learned a lot, being your daughter. Never underestimate the public's curiosity—particularly when they smell debacle."

"That's not terribly reassuring, my sweet." Though I was eager to see my two-act comedy performed, I was begrudgingly compelled to acknowledge that the climate of the times had shifted. The revolution in France blew fetid winds across the Channel, and the English aristocracy was fearful of anything that might feed the public any republican, or even bourgeois, sensibilities. "Consider the argument of the play—the plot," I said to my daughter. My heroine, if one could call her that, was an aristocratic gamester up to her bonnet in gambling debts (as was Georgiana). She is taken under the wing of a virtuous and philanthropically minded middle-class banker from the City who rehabilitates her from her vice.

"Well, then, perhaps the boxes will be empty—but the stalls and balconies where John Bull sits will be filled to the gills," said Maria.

Apart from a return to my flat to dress and make my toilette for the premiere, I spent the entire day at Drury Lane, making sure all was ready for *Nobody*'s debut. All was well enough with the theatrical elements, but on the other side of the stage, a very different sort of production was being set in motion. Following the usual method of reserving the choicest seats, members of the upper crust sent their servants to the theatre on the afternoon of the first performance to secure the premium places until that evening, when their betters arrived to claim them. But the ton had "done up" the play, paying their lackeys to do more than temporarily warm the best seats with their unworthy bums. As soon as the curtain rose on the debut, there was a cacophony from the gods—the cheap seats in the highest galleries where sat the retainers fortunate enough to have employers who permitted them to attend the theatre.

Kemble had remodeled Drury Lane's interior, enlarging the auditorium until it was nearly cavernous, with a seating capacity of more than three and a half thousand, nearly double the size it was when I had played the house. Actors were now required to have lungs of sterner stuff if they wished to be heard in the gallery, which now seemed miles from the stage.

The ruckus was astounding—louder and more vociferous than anything I had ever seen at Drury Lane. It was customary for an audience to indicate their displeasure with a play or particular performance by issuing no end of catcalls and insults, but rarely had the detractors been so relentless as to disrupt the piece beyond all hearing. That night, not a soul could discern a single word uttered by Mrs. Jordan or any of the other brave thespians who had consented to perform my comedy, for the servants seated in the uppermost galleries drowned out the dialogue with their deafening invective.

The usually imperturbable Mrs. Jordan became so flustered—and affrighted that the vulgar crowd might do her some physical harm—that she fluffed her lines.

From my side box near the stage, I gazed up at the gods and clearly recognized the liveries worn by my vociferous critics. I was intended to do so. Their employers, the most fashionable women of London—and particularly those who knew their fictional counterparts were on the stage—were triumphantly identifying themselves as my conspiring detractors.

I was in tears when Ban tenderly carried me out to my carriage, and I promptly canceled the post-performance dinner I had planned to host, wishing to see no one but my lover and Maria.

By the second performance of *Nobody,* the novelty had worn off—such was society's reaction at the time to the latest thing—and the play was given a lukewarm approbation. After that night I sat down to rework it, but at the piece's third performance, the script, though revised, was not well received and Sheridan withdrew it from the theatre's repertoire.

Maria refused to allow me to wallow in grief or self-pity, though the funds I had counted on from the receipts of a long and sold-out run would now never materialize. This pecuniary hiccup compelled us to quit our apartments in St. James's Place and take up residence instead in the less fashionable Burlington Street. Well, at least we were still in Mayfair, never far from the royal residences and the town houses of the nobility.

I took up my pen again and began work on another novel. Though my body had betrayed me, as long as my mind was clear as water I would persevere with ink and quill.

Times were certainly changing. By 1795, some of the more prominent Whigs had begun to sport republican fashions, cropping their hair short and forgoing the use of powder. Though Ban retained the old style, Fox and the Duke of Bedford—the latter always a renegade—were in the vanguard of the new style. Disaffection with the monarchy was in the wind. In October, the king barely escaped assassination when a deranged woman fired a pistol right into his carriage. And that spring, the Prince of Wales had finally buckled to the pressure to marry, wedding the odious (and odiferous) Caroline of Brunswick. His Highness was now vastly heavier and more floridly complected than he had been in his youth, no longer dashing or attractive. Wags whispered in the privacy of their homes that he should now be dubbed the Prince of Whales. I surprised myself with the discovery that I felt not even the slightest twinge of jealousy or regret to see my former royal lover nuptialized.

On January 4, 1796, *Angelina,* the novel I had begun to write just after the *Nobody* debacle, was published by Hookham & Carpenter. The entire first edition of the three-volume, 1,030-page novel sold out almost the moment it saw the light of day, and I immediately began the preparations for a second edition.

Mary Wollstonecraft, a woman whose philosophical essays I admired tremendously, wrote a highly complimentary critique in the *Analytical Review.* She evinced a thorough understanding and approbation of everything I had strived to express about the plight of women and the unappreciated genius of the artist by his social superiors.

Although other critics thought I had created too broad a canvas, with an ensemble of characters too vast for readers to cheer for any specific heroine, the public purse trumped the tepid reviews and *Angelina* joined the ranks of my other novels as what Maria creatively referred to as a "best seller."

And, not unexpectedly, the more guineas I earned, the faster did Ban head for the faro tables.

"I'm glad you enjoy writing so much, Mum," Maria commented tersely.

I did—in several disciplines—scribbling poetry, prose, and plays with prolific abandon, though on occasion, unscrupulous publishers and producers would endeavor to unjustly enrich themselves from my efforts.

In 1795 I had penned a blank verse tragedy, *The Sicilian Lover*. A theatre producer held on to the manuscript for several months, doing nothing with it, much to my consternation. I would have been more than happy to take it elsewhere if he was going to let it lie about collecting dust. It was mere chance that, after such foot-dragging on the part of the producer, I had the opportunity to peruse a script written by a minor dramatist of the day, which, lo and behold, contained a pivotal scene that included one of *The Sicilian Lover*'s most striking plot points! Not only that, this work of drivel was scheduled for imminent production.

I called for my carriage and headed for Henrietta Street to confront Mr. Ballantine, the man who had promised to produce *The Sicilian Lover*.

His office was immaculate, even pristine. Not a thing was out of place. His case of leather-bound books looked spanking new, as though their spines had never once been bent. One could have supped off his gleaming desk, which was devoid of all but blotter, ink, and quill stand.

In my experience of producers and publishers, this distinctly Spartan and scrupulously clean workplace was emblematic of a distinct lack of industry.

Mr. Ballantine, alone at his desk, was cleaning his spectacles with his breath when I arrived. I was relieved that he had not seen me drag myself up the stairs.

"I am Mrs. Robinson," I reminded him, as he rose from his chair. "And I should like to speak about *The Sicilian Lover*. To put it succinctly, I wish to see the tragedy in rehearsal by month's end."

"These things take time, madam," said Mr. Ballantine, nervously adjusting his eyeglasses, which were now as spotless as the rest of the room.

The producer tried to forestall me, claiming that he planned indeed to put my play before the public.

"But when?" I inquired, my tone firm, though in fact I felt both neglected and betrayed by this laggard. "You have not done a bloody thing with it for well over a year and I harbor no regrets about reclaiming my manuscript."

I took back my tragedy that very day and brought it to Hookham & Carpenter, demanding immediate publication, in an effort to preclude the piracy of my idea. Hookham consented with alacrity, knowing they could bolster sales of *The Sicilian Lover* by capitalizing on the tremendous popularity of *Angelina*.

Ban, too, had a sobering experience that year. His elder brother, John, a staunch Tory, chose to run against him for Liverpool MP. The contest caused a dreadful rift in the Tarleton family. Ban decided to crop his hair and was decried as the scapegoat of the Whig party, and worse—a Jacobin—for how else could he have walked the bloody streets of Paris unmolested during the city's darkest and most dangerous days? Ban's younger brother, Clayton, and their father refused to vote. John, oddly enough, ended up voting for Ban rather than for himself; and when the tallies showed him in third place, John withdrew from the contest. Though Ban emerged the victor, the ugly experience resulted in the permanent alienation from the bosom of his family. As her final act of charity toward him, Jane Tarleton bequeathed Ban five thousand pounds in her will to square his gambling debts.

"You'll always have me, my darling," I assured him, then chuckled. "Somehow, no matter what you say or do to me, I remain your lodestar."

"What should you say, Mary, if I proposed to remain at home this evening?"

My heart had stopped at the word "proposed." It took a moment or two for me to realize what Ban was really saying. "You are not heading off to Brooks's, then?"

Ban shook his head. "I will never again enter my name in the betting book." I questioned how he could keep his word and so abruptly change his conduct. He held his mangled hand before my face. "One day I had five fingers; the next, three. For the rest of my life, with no alternative possible, I have had to make do with the trio."

And then I wondered, if he could now be so resolute, so adamant, why could he not have come to the same decision earlier? It would have spared us so much anguish.

"I am sorry," Ban said, kneeling at my feet and placing his head in my lap like a penitent. "Today I turn over a new leaf. I promise you." He buried his head in my skirts and I felt his hot breath suffuse the silks until my skin grew warm and tantalized beneath them.

"Will you do me a favor?" he murmured, and whatever he might ask of me, I knew I could not refuse. "I should like to publish a second edition of my *Campaigns* and would be ever grateful for your assistance. More than you know, you have shown me how to be a better man. In your womanly tenderness, most assuredly, so, but also as an author. You, my dearest love, and your literary tri-

umphs over social adversity and charges of moral turpitude are beacons that light my way."

So in the summer of 1795, while my novels became a
success on the Continent, making history for an English
author, we revised Ban's memoirs—though once again the
Battle of Cowpens was omitted. The second edition was
well received, praised for its literary merit as well as for its
content, and Ban could not have been more pleased.

Later in the year Hookham & Carpenter published
my Sappho and Phaon sonnets in volume form, followed
by *Hubert de Sevrac,* my first attempt at gothic romance.
The latter, though not deemed a critical sensation, was
nonetheless a popular one, exploring my philosophy that
a poor mind can be just as fine as a rich one and a peasant is no less of a person because of his birthright. The
novel was soon translated into both German and French.
So well regarded were my literary efforts on the Continent
that a German publisher bought a manuscript that had
been rejected by every one of their English colleagues!

In February of 1796, the poet Robert Merry, also
known by his pen name Della Crusca, wrote to ask if I
would allow him to present two of his dear friends, who
he thought might provide my mind with some necessary
stimulation, since Ban and I had increasingly little to say
to one another. As several of my antislavery poems were
being published in the popular papers and periodicals, my
lover still argued on the floor of the House of Commons
in favor of his family's economic interests and that of other
Liverpudlians in the traffic of human souls.

Naturally, I responded to Mr. Merry in the affirmative, and one day later that month, he paid a call on me
in London.

Robert Merry, just three years my senior, looked old to me, making me feel rather antiquated myself. His once-dark curls were now grayish, and cut short, in the Titus-style ringlets so favored by his fellow Jacobins.

"Pray do not rise," he exclaimed with a wink in my direction, knowing full well that crossing the room to greet him and our two guests was nigh impossible for me. "Allow me, Mrs. Robinson, to introduce my dear friend and radical sympathizer, William Godwin—the man who claimed he would rescue the Archbishop of Canterbury from a burning house before he would save his mother from the flames, on the grounds that His Grace had done more for the world to continue to deserve living in it."

"I don't quite know how one replies to such an introduction!" laughed Godwin, bending over my hand and bringing his lips to my fingers. He had tremendous élan as well as striking good looks, with a head like a handsome Roman orator, his skin pale nearly to the point of translucence. His eyes were the deep brown color of treacle, yet were lit from within by a tremendous intensity.

"And of course, his . . ."

"You may refer to me as his lover, Mr. Merry," said my third guest.

"We were introduced only last month," interjected Mr. Godwin.

Mr. Merry colored in embarrassment at his friend's frankness. "And Miss Mary Wollstonecraft—author, of course, of—"

"*A Vindication of the Rights of Women.* Yes, I know." I smiled, immensely gratified to make her acquaintance. "In fact, I have one of the first editions. I hope you won't think me terribly gauche if I ask you to autograph it. I am a tremendous admirer of yours, Miss Wollstonecraft."

How lovely to spend the day with a roomful of contemporaries, all of us between the ages of thirty-six and forty-one—to stretch the elastic muscles of the mind by indulging in good conversation.

"Dare I ask if you are penning another such provocative opus?" I asked Miss Wollstonecraft.

"I have indeed been hard at work, though I have not your gift of speed," said Miss Wollstonecraft. "I am elbow-deep in *The Wrongs of Women*. No doubt you will have written three novels, a tragedy, a comic opera, and a volume of poetry before I have reached my last page. You are quite the prolific one."

Did she mean it as a compliment or a jibe? I could not tell.

"William is composing a tragedy at present," Miss Wollstonecraft added.

"Well, at present, I am enjoying Miss Robinson's clove biscuits," teased Mr. Godwin, grinning at Maria.

"You know quite well what I meant. For a philosopher, you can be dreadfully literal, you know." She favored Mr. Godwin with the sparkling gaze of one newly in love. She had known the philosopher but a few weeks, and the spark between them could have ignited a bonfire.

Merry raised his eyebrows and glanced at me, as if to say, "A lovers' quarrel, eh?" I endeavored to laugh at his comical expression.

"A tragedy, Mr. Godwin? Rather unusual territory for a philosopher and political scientist, nonetheless," said I. "I do hope you are enjoying your exploration of the genre."

"I fear nothing," said Godwin boldly. "If I am to fail, at least I have made the endeavor. But the drama affords me yet another bully pulpit, if you will, from which to inculcate the public with my credos. You see, I believe our virtues and our vices may be traced to the incidents that make the history of our lives, and if these incidents could be divested of every improper tendency, vice would be extirpated from the world. I appreciate a story told in five acts; I find it cleansing to know that vice will be punished in the last one and that virtue will triumph."

Mr. Godwin helped himself to another biscuit. He gazed at me so oddly, as if I and not Miss Wollstonecraft were the object of his ardor. I felt rather flattered, actually, and stole a glance at his lover, hoping she had not caught Mr. Godwin's flirtatious look.

"I confess, Mrs. Robinson, being a helpless admirer of women who can boast of brains in addition to their obvious physical charms, I should like to call upon you from time to time, as you have far more experience with the genre than I, from both sides of the pit and the pen. If a humble suppliant may avail himself of your wisdom and experience . . ."

He'd made me laugh, longer and louder, and with more genuine feeling, than I had done in years. "You do me far too much honor, sir. I don't deserve such encomiums. But I should be delighted to discuss the dramatist's technique with you whenever you feel the urge to call upon me. It is not as if I am off every day gallivanting about the countryside."

Being familiar with some of Mr. Godwin's work, I was thrilled by the afternoon's opportunity to learn more of his mind; now the prospect of spending more hours together, that I might come to know the man's soul as well, was almost too heady an honor to contemplate.

"Perhaps Mrs. Robinson would crave the time to devote to her own writing, William," said Miss Wollstonecraft, her tone as supple, yet firm, as a rapier. "After all, whilst a writer may race through a first draft, it often requires much patience and many painstaking hours to revise it, to add shade and nuance, to ensure that every character has been given his due, and every storyline a logical arc that, though it may venture onto a tangent, always arrives at a satisfying conclusion. Mrs. Robinson is so prolific that I feel certain her precious time might be devoured by too many social engagements."

With her golden brown hair and open countenance, I found her quite lovely to look at. From her frankness, it was plain to see that she was also extraordinarily fearless as well as brilliant. As such, it was difficult to dislike her, though I sensed that she might be less fond of cultivating my friendship as was her intriguing lover.

"Are you saying that you find my writing rushed?" I inquired, suppressing the edge in my voice. I had never forgotten my training at David Garrick's heels. "For I would be gratified to hear your opinions, that I might apply them—the better to strengthen my efforts. Perhaps you are right, Miss Wollstonecraft; mayhap I should devote more time than I already do to polishing each sentence until it shines like a newly minted sovereign. Recently, I have also accepted the responsibility of editing the poetry page of the *Morning Post*. Alas, the Almighty has yet to increase the number of hours in a day, and as it is I burn my candles down to stubs, but I will toil all through the night, if need be, to increase my income. It pains me to confess this to such a new acquaintance, but as we are both authors, I admit that it has been my unhappy history that all too often I find myself caught up short when it comes to funds. And my only expectation of further subsistence is to take up the pen again that I may profit by it. You must indeed be fortunate to write at leisure without fear of never seeing more of the world beyond the stony walls of a debtors' prison."

Her lover broke the mounting tension. "There's a bit of a competition between Mary and me to see who can sell more pamphlets," Godwin told me, brandishing another biscuit and glancing ardently at Miss Wollstonecraft. "You heard what Prime Minister Pitt said of my *Poetical Justice* when it was published back in ninety-three? He said that there was no need to censor it because, at over a guinea a copy, so few people could afford it anyway."

"But when the corresponding societies began reading it to the illiterate 'unwashed masses,' William's philosophy caught fire like dry reeds. He's too modest to mention that over four thousand copies have sold," added Miss Wollstonecraft.

"We're tremendous admirers of your novels, Mrs. Robinson," said Godwin. "*I* have dabbled with some modest success—"

"I have read *Things as They Are, or the Adventures of Caleb Williams*," I told him.

"You have?" Godwin tried not to appear gleeful, but his color deepened, emphasizing the planes in his cheekbones.

I nodded. "Indeed, and I found it extremely entertaining. You managed to strike a delicate balance between the popular gothic novel and your own political themes."

Miss Wollstonecraft shifted in her chair, clearly put off by this society of mutual admiration formed twixt her lover and myself on our very first encounter. She appeared confident when it came to matters of the intellect, but in the realm of the heart, to me it was evident that she was not in the least sure-footed. Yet another opportunity for empathy, if she'd only known.

"We 'lady scribblers,' as they are wont to call us, must be very brave," Miss Wollstonecraft averred. "For the press will skewer us and serve us up for dinner, in order to undermine the public position we adopt in our writings. No doubt you, too, have experienced it, Mrs. Robinson: every salacious, scandalous, sordid detail of our private lives is exposed and used against us. Never mind that four years ago *A Vindication of the Rights of Women* revolutionized the way our sex viewed their place in society, and of course continues to do so. No—hoping to trumpet to the world that my treatise is nothing but a load of freshly minted horse manure, all the press cares to print is that Mary Wollstonecraft is mentally unstable, having twice tried to take her own life over the demise of an unhappy love affair."

I nodded my head. "Man is a despot by nature; he can bear no equal. To our sex's benefit as well as to our detriment, the pen is the great equalizer. And I have come to discover, the older I become, that men fear it more than the point of a sword."

With my numerous recent literary successes, I should have been wallowing in money, but alas, the reverse was true—I received a note from my bankers, informing me that I was twelve hundred pounds in debt. And I was still supporting Ban, even though he no longer squandered my resources in the faro hells.

After an especially fine dinner of capon with roasted almonds, I confronted my lover with the alarming letter from Coutts. As he sipped a bowl of brandy from the last of the bottles he'd managed to sneak out of France, I had to face the music.

"I have bought no luxuries for myself of late," I told Ban. "No matter how much I earn, I never seem to have enough. Can you honestly recall the last time you made a purchase from your own funds?" He could not. The more he continued to savor his cordial, stretching his limbs before the fire like a contented cat, the greater grew my ire. "How can a man call himself a gentleman when he so unchivalrously permits a woman—his wife in every way, save the sacrament—to support him?"

Ban looked at me, his expression hard and glittering in the candlelight. Then he kicked away the footstool and wordlessly retired to our bedchamber, opening the armoire.

He began to pack his bags.

"Where are you headed?" I asked him.

"To Liverpool. My mother is dying."

I knew about Jane Tarleton's will. "She has left you a generous bequest to settle your debts of honor, several of which remain undischarged. Is it not honorable to tender your lover of nearly fifteen years some reimbursement or compensation for her financial sacrifices on your behalf?"

Ban demurred.

I despaired of sounding like a fishwife.

"I never asked you to support me, Mary."

"Nor did you even once reject my assistance. My purse

was always open to you, as was my heart. I do truly believe you should make amends from your inheritance."

"Are you mad, woman?" Ban thundered, the old warhorse emerging from the now stocky, graying parliamentarian. "You cannot wrap me like a skein of silk about your fingers; *no one* can manipulate Banastre Tarleton—not even you!"

"Are you saying that you refuse to offer me the merest shilling in restitution?"

"I thought you gave of your own free will, Mary. I never obliged you to pay my bills. Tell me true, did I ever compel you to spend a single penny on my behalf? You cannot answer that, can you? You cannot say you gave me aught for any other reason than your love for me. And now that my mother is at death's door, you have the temerity to insinuate that all this time your seeming munificence has been a loan?"

"You are cruel indeed, with a heart of adamant, and the conscience of an adder!" I shouted. "I ask you to review the situation from my eyes; to acknowledge that much of it is of your own making. Have you no decency, sir? Would you see me utterly penniless, and idly stand by? How could you be so ungrateful?"

"Mary, I have reached the end of my wits with you," exclaimed Ban. "Fifteen years of my life, and all you can demand of me is my mother's money."

"That is not *all*—good heavens, how you twist my words! I demand only that you behave with honor, conduct to which I know you are no stranger."

Ban shook his head. So, he refused to help me. "I cannot endure this anymore," he said crisply.

How could a man be so tender at times and yet so cruel

at others? He was indeed a bloody butcher, as the American colonists had tagged him. For he had sliced my heart and guts to ribbons and then stamped brutally upon the steaming entrails.

"I should have done this long ago," Ban declared, and donned his hat. "Our connexion is at an end, Mary. I can assure you, no matter how plaintive your poetry, I will not return. This time, Mrs. Robinson, I mean it."

He left the room, slamming the door with ferocity. I took a generous draught of laudanum and crawled under the counterpane, my face wet with tears. The boudoir echoed with my hysterical, heaving sobs. My throat soon burned from wailing.

It was April 1796, and I had loved Ban and no other man on earth since the spring of 1782. Now I had lost him forever.

Who was *nobody* now?

Act Five

In Polish'd Form of
Well-Refined Pen

Twenty-eight

Mightier Than the Sword

1796 . . . age thirty-eight

When next I woke, Maria suggested that a change of scene might be welcome. Wearily, I agreed, and we set out for Bath, always one of my favorite places for rest and recuperation. But I fell ill along the journey, and made it to town more dead than alive. As I lay delirious with fever, Ban haunted my every thought; my mind could fix on nothing else but the events of the decade and a half I had devoted to him. And now he was lost to me forever—all the more reason to despair. What a curse is memory to those who have outlived the sustaining power of hope! Why are we destined to retrace the paths of pleasure, in imagination, while our weary footsteps tread on the thorns of disappointment?

"Mark you, I seek no pity," I sniffled to Maria.

"Fear not; you shan't receive any from me."

For many moments, I gazed at her in silence. My daughter. The only person in my life who had never betrayed me. My rock. My shoal. My anchor. She was indeed strikingly attractive in a way that was entirely devoid of artifice: tall and willowy with soft brown hair, cut short now, in the modern fashion; and a pair of gray eyes that conveyed volumes of intellect and astuteness behind them. Her countenance was always open and agreeable, belying her capacity to be quite judgmental when it suited her. *She's old for her tender years,* I thought, realizing she would turn twenty-two in October. "You're a grown woman now, Maria. You can choose your own path. Perhaps we should begin looking out for a husband for you."

"Why should we look when I do not wish to locate one?" my daughter replied, her manner calm but direct. "My life is here with you. That is the path I choose. I see neither shame nor harm in being your happy acolyte, and find such a decision immensely preferable to any other. I have more dignity and autonomy as your daughter than ever I would have as any man's wife." Her pointed look demanded no further contradiction.

Maria sought to raise my spirits by suggesting slyly that I skewer Ban in print. "If we were Papists and I a priest, I should exorcise you from your demon."

At least she'd made me smile. "But we're not, and you're not."

"You have always given Ban far greater due than I ever thought he deserved. And now I'm old enough to know what I'm talking about."

And so from my sickbed, playing and replaying in my mind the tumultuous events of our relationship, I wrote a novel titled *The False Friend*—after which Maria determined it was high time I made some new ones. Of Treville, the antihero of *The False Friend,* I wrote that he was "a coxcomb by education; a deceiver by practice, a flatterer by profession; and a profligate by nature." Ban's avatar was a libertine of the most dangerous species—"A dissembling sycophant, a being who hovered round the wealthy and the highborn to poison domestic happiness. . . ." Had I been a painter instead, my portrait would have been too realistic for the fashion of the times.

Perhaps it was because I had vented my spleen on the page, but suddenly one morning I awoke to feel more alive and vital than I had in years, as though a ponderous weight had been lifted from my chest. I had wallowed in my grief and loneliness long enough. No longer would I replay my recollections of Ban's betrayal, his outbursts of temper, and his lies. I realized that although I still missed the pleasures we had shared over so many seasons, I had begun to consign our connexion to the rose-colored hues of fading memories.

In that instant, as the sunlight streamed through the casement, I knew I should have no trouble living without him for the remainder of my days. No trouble at all! The moment the spell which claims the senses is broken, the phantom of love takes flight, leaving no substitute but regret and indignation. The room no longer felt musty or gloomy; the Wedgwood-blue walls now seemed a cloudless open sky, offering endless possibilities for happiness and redemption.

I wanted to write a different sort of story. There was something that I, Mary Robinson, needed to tell the world: that I was not the flighty, shallow whore they accounted me, but a woman of parts, of sense as well as sensibility—with a fine mind, a devoted heart, and a profound soul.

My heroine would be a girl educated with a "mascu-

line mind"—meaning that she was taught the same subjects, and in the same way, as a boy of the day would have
been. And such a woman as I wished to draw is feared
and despised, deemed "unnatural" by her own sex as well.
Though there would be several adventures that were entirely fictitious, because of the heroine's upbringing, and
the savage and cynical world in which she lived, in many
ways *Walsingham* would be my own story.

The seeds of this concept had been planted in my
fertile brain for some time now, but it took Mary Wollstonecraft to water them. As my friendship with this esteemed woman and Mr. Godwin had blossomed, so my
imagination ached to explore a marriage of the new (and
prodigiously radical) pro-female philosophy with that of
traditional storytelling.

Kneeling at the skirts of Meribah Lorrington, I had
been inculcated with the concept that the mind has no
sex. Hannah More in her early days as a pedant taught us
the same lesson, as did my mother during her too-brief
experience in the schoolroom. These women had molded
their pupils' minds into mellow instruments capable of
performing in more than the simple key of C major.

It has been my observation all through life that, even
among the greatest thinkers of the day, the Age of Enlightenment was reserved for the male of our species.
Imagine my astonishment on reading that the visionary
philosopher Jean-Jacques Rousseau firmly held that wom-
en's minds should remain uncultivated—that we "might
be most agreeable and companionable to men." What
utter rot—to have an empty brain, and little choice but
to remain subservient and silly creatures. And for years I
felt that I was wandering alone in the wilderness until I

met Mary Wollstonecraft and keenly saw in her a kindred spirit.

I felt perfectly poised to create my unusual heroine, drawing upon my own education—and that which I had given to Maria—as well as by my experiences in the several trouser roles I had assayed as an actress.

The breeches roles were among my favorites in my Drury Lane days; they conferred upon their wearer a certain freedom. And the concept that, whether inside or out, "a man is not the sum of the parts of his suit" was something I now wished to convey in prose. Though a character is literally a female, beneath her skin resides a mind and a soul that should not immediately invoke a certain prejudice against (or for) her by the outside world. Perhaps that is why I delighted in shaking up society when I'd kept my theatrical costumes on, and wore my breeches in public at the pleasure gardens.

My rambling narrative was a salmagundi of literary genres, a stew comprised of one part gothic novel, one part sentimental romance, one part metaphysical discourse, one part burlesque, and one part satire.

Remaining true to my literary roots, I drew many of the characters in *Walsingham* from my life, penning portraits of my young self, my mother, and Mr. Robinson's father.

The novel poured out of me, as if it was a raging river uncontainable by the dam of my imagination. I wrote until my fingers grew too stiff to handle the pen, and then I would continue to dictate the story to Maria. The next day she would read aloud my new pages, whilst, with closed eyes, William Godwin and I would listen to her voice coloring my words with its soft and subtle tones.

What a reaction I received when she got to the chapter in which the eponymous hero excoriates the literary critics:

" 'Let some of our modern dispensers of unlettered wrath, before they condemn a trembling author to shame, and sometimes to despair, ask their own sapient heads if they could produce such books as their malice would consign to oblivion. Is there no punishment due to the being who wantonly destroys another's hopes, and takes from talents, industry, and truth, the means of obtaining an honorable subsistence?'

"Well, Mum, you've certainly done it this time!" my daughter announced. "I shouldn't wonder if the reviewers were to prove to you just how unchastened they are by your invective. You are brave indeed if you do not beware them after this."

I widened my eyes, playing the innocent. "Remember, my darling, that in fiction there is always a distinction to be made between the opinions of the author and of the novel's narrator."

My two artistic careers fed upon each other: I brought the experiences of my theatrical background to my writing, taking my stage techniques to the page. In *Walsingham* I played many of the parts—all of them aspects of my own soul: the wronged and jilted woman who sacrifices herself for the object of her affections and has her bounteousness of spirit and liberalities of friendship taken advantage of; and the melancholy "child of nature" who discerns the falsity of his social betters and is made to suffer for preferring blunt truth to hypocrisy.

I believed profoundly that in the momentous times in which we dwelt the most powerful of the human race were men of *letters,* not men of *title*—those who could guide the pen and influence the country by the genuine language of truth and philanthropy. If only they would permit us women to join them—united, what mountains we should be able to move!

All through the summer of 1797, living almost exclusively at Englefield Cottage, my hours were chiefly devoted to writing *Walsingham,* though I confess my body was in astounding pain. Rheumatic complaints confined me to home twixt bed and couch; I lay in one or reclined upon the other, penning the pages as quickly as my cramped hands would permit. I sold my carriage, for I no longer had any need of it—travel anywhere was far too arduous for me; and besides, I could scarce afford the upkeep any longer. Although my physician had informed me that by exercise only could my existence be prolonged, the narrowness of my financial circumstances obliged me to forgo the only means by which it could be obtained.

In October, *Walsingham* went to auction. Longman outbid Hookham & Carpenter for the manuscript of the four volume novel, paying one hundred and fifty pounds, a price that the press deemed almost unequaled for a work of the same species. How grand it felt, not only to receive such validation for my efforts but to extricate myself from debt! The novel that might just as well have been my confessional was published on December 7, 1797. The initial print run of a thousand copies was gone in a twinkling.

Another stroke of good fortune occurred: The *Morning Post* scooped the *Oracle* and began serializing *Walsingham,* swelling my popularity among the readers to such an extent that reprints of previous novels were demanded. My candles guttered well into the wee hours of the morning as I struggled to prepare so many new editions for the press, poring over each line, rewriting here and there to correct typographical errors or rephrase an inelegant sentence. Sometimes I'd even revise the content to keep the story current. The solitary activity, though it occupied my every hour, did not replace my craving for the society of others, particularly my witty philosopher friends, where our open exchange of ideas made me feel so keenly alive.

Miss Wollstonecraft and Mr. Godwin welcomed me into their circle of friends, which included other female writers, such as Amelia Opie and Elizabeth Inchbald. I was the only one, however, who had mingled among the nobility, and even when I was feeling low, Godwin would remark that I invariably added a dash of glamour to their salon. Though the room was filled with brilliant and incisive thinkers, I had inhabited a different world from them, and had at the outset of my career jettisoned all hope of being considered respectable gentry—though respect as an artist was everything I craved. No, I could never be deemed a lady because I blew my own trumpet; it did not satisfy me to raise my ink blotter before my person as if to shield my modesty and hide from public scrutiny.

Mr. Godwin and Miss Wollstonecraft had visited me frequently throughout 1796 and into the following year, though our acquaintance was rather abruptly cut short soon after Godwin broke his self-imposed vow of eternal bachelorhood and married Mary in March of 1797. Though I sensed she had initiated the termination of our visits out of jealousy that perhaps I held some sort of fascination for William—who did in fact regard me fondly, and once confessed I was the most beautiful woman he had ever seen—I nonetheless felt a renewed admiration for her. She had managed to effect what was thought to be impossible. And it soothed my heart like a balm to believe that love indeed possesses the power to change a person's long-held credos.

But not too many months later—on September 10, 1797—Mary Wollstonecraft died of childbed fever. The world had lost one of its brightest and most promising luminaries—and modern women found themselves bereft of their finest champion. She and I were never two flowers on one stem; yet I'd felt anointed by her to carry on the legacy she had left behind, to wave the banner proclaiming the rights of women in front of everybody's eyes until they could not help but read it.

In January 1798, four months after Mary's death, William Godwin resumed our visits. He always found me scribbling with such a zealous intensity that my quill points snapped from puncturing the paper, leaving amorphous blots of ink in their wake.

I was ill again, and my ailments transcended the daily discomfort I had endured since my carriage accident so many years before. Fighting melancholia and a nervous fever, I told William that the root of my present distresses was "an excess of sensibility"—that which has haunted me since my earliest recollections. I had been so foolish as to think myself well past the point of nostalgia. There were days—and nights were worse—when my sentimental longing for Ban was so great that I could not shake my melancholy. Sadness metamorphosed into physical pain, and only laudanum could bring me ease.

Glancing at my writing desk one day, William solicitously asked, "Is this how you fight it?"

"Maria's suggestion," I murmured. "I am in the painful—yet liberating—process of editing Ban Tarleton's name and all references to him from my verses and rearranging the revised poems for republication."

That April, I announced the opening of a subscription list to finance the publication of my *Poetical Works*. My eyes flooded with tears when it was signed by many of the ladies of the ton, including my old friend the Duchess of Devonshire.

Yet my elation was short-lived. Maria, my gazetteer, had taken it upon herself to peruse the morning papers for puffs and squibs, or even something approaching a genuine news story, that featured one of my old friends.

"Well then, it seems Ban Tarleton is finally about to receive another commission!" she announced one September morning. "In Portugal! And there is another item about him . . . 'Colonel Banastre Tarleton betook himself to Houghton, the seat of the Earl of Chomondeley, in Norfolk, where a grand shooting party was on the bill of fare. He bagged a brace of pheasants, three hares, which were promptly jugged by the cook, and the young mistress of the house, Susan Priscilla Bertie, the natural daughter of the late Duke of Ancaster, with whom the colonel served in His Majesty's Army during the war with the colonies in the 1770s. Now that our cavalry hero has broken free from his lengthy entanglements with a certain prominent lady scribbler and once-notorious actress and courtesan, he is at liberty to pay court to Miss Bertie—tho' this fresh English rose is easily less than half the colonel's age.'" Maria ducked. "Mummy, please don't throw your inkwell! We cannot afford new wall coverings!"

On December 13, 1798, the *Oracle* announced that

Ban's nuptials to the dewy Miss Bertie were to take place four days hence. The young lady brought to her husband a sizeable dowry—an amount speculated to be anywhere from twelve to thirty thousand pounds. Maria embraced me, blotting my tears with her handkerchief. "I choose to think of it this way, my dearest Mum: now some other unfortunate woman will become responsible for his debts!"

Twenty-nine

Brandishing the Banner of Women's Rights

1799 . . . age forty-one

In 1799, as Colonel and Mrs. Tarleton prepared to sail for Portugal, I put pen to paper once again in an effort to assuage the myriad sensations of loss, regret, and betrayal that continued to plague my mind. *The False Friend* had been rushed into publication to coincide with the hubbub over Ban's wedding; and the public eagerly snapped up the copies. By the end of May, the entire first edition had sold out and the second edition went on sale. At the same time, French and German translations—*Le Faux Ami* and *Der Falsche Freund*—were published in their respective countries.

In their review of *The False Friend* on February 18, 1799, the *Morning Post* took great delight in revealing an element of the plot, which they correctly construed as the author's gleeful attempt at a swift and terrible revenge. If she could not wreak it upon the original, the avatar would be made to suffer. *"Mrs. Robinson makes the hero of her new novel perish on his voyage to Lisbon."*

My friends cheered; Ban's condemned me in their letters to the editors and in notes of admonishment delivered to my doorstep by the Royal Mail, but I never imagined they would do otherwise. And the *Oracle*'s critic tartly wrote, "*Bravery in the Field* is not always accompanied by *Fidelity in the Closet.*"

On March 5, 1799, when the Tarletons finally sailed aboard the *Hyena* (I was too morose to appreciate the mirthful irony of the vessel's name), I penned another Sappho stanza, filled with despairing invective. Perhaps it was best to acknowledge that I could never entirely purge Ban from my soul. And wherever he sailed, and whoever traveled beside him, he would always carry a piece of my heart. Mayhap I was destined never to be whole again.

With Maria's encouragement, I began a new novel. Still livid with Ban, I had intended, at first, to tarnish the rosy reputation of the former Miss Bertie, by reminding those who had not read her marriage announcements that she was the natural daughter of Bertie, the Duke of Ancaster, and Rebecca Krudener, his mistress whilst he was garrisoned in Philadelphia during the war with the colonies.

I was the one who came up short, however, when I could not uncover a single word of scandal or reproach regarding Susan Priscilla Bertie. Her birthright had not been of her own choosing, and she had been a stainless young lady. Suddenly, I felt sorry for her, and while my title remained unchanged, my plot evolved into something else entirely. *The Natural Daughter* metamorphosed into a slim, fictionalized autobiography. My avatar was Martha Morley, an actress and authoress, a much-maligned woman who at one point exclaims, "Of all the occupations which industry can pursue, those of literary toil are most fatiguing. That which seems to the vacant eye a mere playful amusement, is in reality an Herculean labor; and to compose a tolerable work is so difficult a task that the fastidiously severe should make the trial before they presume to condemn the humblest effort of imagination." As Maria succinctly put it, I had returned to my literary leitmotif.

Of course, I created a publisher as well, a character named Mr. Index, who counsels Mrs. Morley to "write with a lancet, not a pen. Cut your subject keenly." It is the knowledgeable Mr. Index who informs the budding authoress on how to create a certain success, counseling her to fictionalize a real-life scandal, give it a provocative title—and the readers will undoubtedly devour it.

As delicious as I found it to preempt the critics' lashing by striking first, I came to the determination that fiction alone did not offer a broad enough canvas. It no longer satisfied what I saw as my duty: to carry on where dear Miss Wollstonecraft had left off.

But the year 1799 had brought with it a backlash against those of us who had dared to speak out on the inequalities to which our sex had been permanently subjected. We were equated with Jacobins and other rebels who threatened to destroy the comfortable status quo, upsetting the apple cart of humanity as we knew it. The previous November, under the pen name of Anne Francis Randall, I had published *A Letter to the Women of England on the Injustice of Mental Subordination,* the treatise that took up Wollstonecraft's philosophical banner.

I had assumed the pseudonym because I did not desire that the pamphlet be connected to the scandalous image of the Perdita, but rather to be judged on its own merit. It was the same reason I had once written poetry under so many pen names. And the *Letter*'s composition became a lesson in itself.

For several weeks in 1798, I dictated the tract to Maria, as much to remind her of our second-class state and show her how we might claim strength rather than weakness for ourselves, as I had need of her healthy fingers. I opened the *Letter* with a provocative question:

"Supposing that destiny, or interest, or chance, or what you will, has united a man, confessedly of a weak understanding and corporeal debility, to a woman strong in all the powers of intellect, and capable of bearing the fatigues of busy life: is it not degrading to humanity that such a woman should be the passive, the obedient slave, of such a husband? Is it not repugnant to all the laws of nature, that her feelings, actions, and opinions, should be controlled, perverted, and debased by such a help-mate?"

"Not a help-mate at all, in my opinion," muttered Maria, as her quill scratched away, committing my words to perpetuity.

"Precisely, my darling. But we are both aware that English common law as we know it condemns every woman living under its jurisdiction to this purgatory."

"Because the laws are made by men!" exclaimed Maria, angrily averring the obvious.

I winced in pain. "And in my lifetime, particularly as there is not much left of it, I fear, we shall never witness a change in that regard. Rather impossible, when a woman cannot even vote, even if she owns property in her own name! I see this *Letter to the Women of England* as more of a call to thought than a call to arms; and when enough of our sex have been armed with knowledge, even if it is merely the acknowledgment that we are not treated like rational creatures, then—oh, then—we shall begin to see some changes in the world."

"If enough people believe themselves oppressed, they will rise up against the tyrants and revolt in mass, 'tis true. But what if there is a women's revolution? And it turns bloody and violent?" Maria asked, momentarily advocating for the Devil. "Will you not then arrive at the same conclusions you did of the revolution in France?"

As my daughter spoke, I began to ruminate on the concept of women taking up arms in some just cause. An idea was forming, and I had to give it voice. "Write this, Maria: 'The barbarity of custom's law in this *enlightened* country has long been exercised to the prejudice of women; and even the laws of honor have been perverted to oppress her. If a man receive an insult he is justified in seeking retribution. He may chastise, challenge, and even destroy his adversary. Such a proceeding in *man* is termed honorable; his character is exonerated from the stigma which calumny attached to it . . . but were a *woman* to attempt such an expedient, however strong her sense of injury, however important the preservation of character, she would be deemed a murderess. Thus custom says—to a woman—you must be free from error; you must possess an unsullied fame; yet, if a slanderer, or a libertine, even by the most unpardonable falsehoods, deprive you of either reputation or repose, you have no remedy. *He* is received in the most fastidious societies, while you sink beneath the uniting efforts of calumny, ridicule, and malevolence. Indeed, we have scarcely seen a single instance where a professed libertine has been either shunned by women, or reprobated by men, for having acted unfeelingly or dishonorably toward what is denominated the *defenseless* sex.

If *woman* be the weaker creature, her frailty should be the more readily forgiven.' "

I was suddenly flooded with a wave of recognition that the French call déjà vu. The sentiments I had just dictated tasted familiar on my tongue; and through the hazy scrim of memories long buried, I recollected that in nearly the same words, they are also those expressed by none other than Nicholas Rowe's Jane Shore in a speech I first performed when I was but a green girl with dreams of Drury Lane. The same sense of outrage at our inferior state that was so close to my heart at age fifteen had traveled in my bosom across the decades, and now was as much my own credo at the age of forty.

I watched Maria write; her tongue peeked out from between her lips when she was deep in concentration. Suddenly I saw the little girl whose lot it had been to be the child of a woman like the one I was writing of—condemned to suffer the slings and arrows lobbed by a hypocritical society. "No wonder you have not courted the company of men, Maria."

"I should be happy to live quite retired all my life," she replied. "I saw enough of the world as a girl, and have in the past few years partaken of sufficient entertainments to inform my decision more than adequately." She had no taste for adventure, as had I in my youth; but at least she had sense, which perhaps would serve her better.

I continued to expound upon my theme. "This dichotomy—that the *weaker* sex is expected to have stronger constitutions when it comes to avoiding the vices and temptations of the world, whilst the purportedly stronger sex is given license to indulge in the enticements that frail woman must at all costs avoid, maddens me to such a degree that I can actually feel the bile bubbling within my spleen. 'Has vice then a sex?' " I posited. "Ah—another 'eureka' moment! Please dip your pen again, my sweet."

My entire career, both on the stage and on paper, has been influenced by the greatest writer in the English language. Just as I had tapped the wellspring of experience, having played his Viola and his Rosalind, I imbued the trouser roles I wrote in my novels with echoes of Shakespeare's own cross-dressing heroines; and the Semitic music of his Shylock seeped into the recesses of my brain. Now, like a specter, his cadences haunted me. " 'Let me ask this rational question,' " I dictated. " 'Is not woman a human being, gifted with all the feelings that inhabit the bosom of man? Has not woman affections, susceptibility, fortitude, and an acute sense of injuries received? Does she not shrink at the touch of persecution? Does not her bosom melt with sympathy, throb with pity, glow with resentment, ache with sensibility, and burn with indignation?' "

Through the secretarial skills of my lovely and sensible daughter, of whom I was so proud, I channeled my own philosophies. Were it not for the acquaintance of Miss Wollstonecraft and Mr. Godwin, I don't think I should have had the courage to air them in such a public forum.

Longman & Rees reprinted the *Letter* in November 1799, with my true name attached to it, avowing that I had been the original author of the work, and defending my previous employment of the pseudonym of Anne Francis Randall.

Toward the end of the year, the shipping news reported the Tarletons' return to England, on—of all ironies—a ship called *Walsingham*. Gossip held it that Ban's young wife had metamorphosed from a dewy English rose into an imperious termagant. "He got what he deserved," sighed Maria. "You were always far too good for him, Mummy, no matter how much you loved him."

Evidently the former Miss Bertie was a bad-luck charm all around, for I was given to understand that Ban was now unhappy in their union, and the novel I'd begun with her illegitimacy in mind fared little better.

The Natural Daughter was not beloved by the critics, nor did the book garner me the sales I had hoped for, so as 1800 dawned, I decided to take a respite from novel writing. I had poured my soul into that manuscript; both my psyche and my sensibilities were too wounded to begin another story. Instead, I flung my energies into my editorial duties for the *Morning Post,* and through those channels I broadened my circle of acquaintances to include other poets whose trajectories were just beginning to blaze a trail in the literary firmament. Among these burgeoning luminaries was the twenty-seven-year-old Samuel Taylor Coleridge.

He was living in Keswick at the time; as I was rarely at my flat in Chapel Street, I no longer spent much time in London unless it was to see to my editorial responsibilities or attend the occasional play or opera. I invited Coleridge to visit me at Englefield Cottage, where I spent more than the moiety of my days in such discomfort that I rarely left my bed. The writer of the magnificently wrought *Lyrical Ballads* did not disappoint in person. He stood before my bedside, his face pale, almost womanly for its lack of angles, his lips soft and full as a female's. Auburn locks the color of my own when I was his age tumbled past his collar.

"I thought not to come down to Windsor today after all," were his first words. "Between melancholia and tooth-ache, and my omnipresent neuralgic complaints, I was certain I would not be a welcome visitor for an invalid."

"If pain is your boon companion, then you have met a kindred spirit in me. Many years ago—when I was younger than you are now—I suffered an accident from which I have never fully recovered. There are times when only lau-danum will carry me through the nights." I smiled. "And days. I worship at the shrine of Dr. Sydenham."

Coleridge nodded gravely. "We are two cherries on one stem, then," he said. "Laudanum gives me repose, not sleep; but you, I believe, know how divine that repose is, what a spot of enchantment, a green spot of fountain and flowers and trees in their very heart of a waste of sands! I began to avail myself of laudanum at first to alleviate the mortal pain that visited me daily. In time, I found I could not do without the sleep of the external senses—the pleasures it afforded my imagination, the flights of fancy and of phantasmagoria to which I was transported, and I admit to you that I am now a much devoted member of the class of men that denominates themselves as opium-eaters. In this life, if one is to be miserable in one way or another, one may as well do so under the self-induced de-lirium of the sainted poppy, particularly when one enjoys such a relatively solitary and retired existence."

"Truly then, Mr. Coleridge, do you find it makes the world brighter and sharper? For though I have ingested the juice of the poppy for several years . . . I believe a ref-erence first seeped into a stanza in 1791 . . . laudanum has not yet had that effect upon my imagination."

"Not sharper, no . . . unless you consider that through

the filmy gauze one can see even more clearly. Or so I believe. And if your view of the scenery about you has remained somewhat earthbound, perhaps you have not ingested enough of it at once! Or you have diluted it sufficiently to reduce your quantity of pain without parting the curtain onto the fantastical world beyond. Dr. Sydenham's formula is, to my view, quite a conservative dosage."

Coleridge drew a thick packet from the pocket of his coat. "Mrs. Robinson, allow me to broaden your knowledge of opium's exquisite wonders." He asked if we possessed a wine decanter, and Maria was immediately charged with the task of filling it with warm, unsweetened negus.

Coleridge drew up a chair as we awaited Maria's return with the wine. "I must confess, this journey of the senses on which I am about to guide you is but small recompense for the gifts you have given me. In fact, I may be so bold as to aver, Mrs. Robinson, that you have already had a most profound impact on my poetry."

I blushed at such a generous compliment. "But I fear my contribution has been merely editorial—to ensure that your efforts are introduced to the public eye."

Coleridge shook his head. "It is one of your own poems to which I refer."

I regarded him quizzically. "One of mine?"

" 'The Haunted Beach,' " said Coleridge. "The rhyme scheme was so unusual; the meter took one on a journey with its rhythm. Wordsworth, too, I must tell you, admits its influence on his verses as well. We are of a mind when I say what an impact it had when first we read it."

The poet closed his eyes and began to recite my words, murmuring them softly, making them tumble over each other like water burbles over stones.

Then while the smoothly slanting sand
The tall cliff wrapp'd in shade,
The Fisherman beheld a band
Of Spectres, gliding hand in hand—
Where the green billows play'd . . .

He could not see through shuttered lids, but my eyes were dimmed with tears.

Maria entered the room, set the decanter of negus on the table, and frowned when she saw the rivulets that had begun to bathe my cheeks.

I indicated to her that nothing was amiss. It was praise that had made me weep.

"I have experimented with as many as eight thousand drops of opium a day, but I daresay you should begin with a far lesser quantity. My druggist is a god," said the poet, opening the packet. He lifted a teaspoon from my breakfast tray and measured out a number of spoonfuls of the dusky brown compound, pouring the earthy opiate into the decanter, now filled well past the bowl with the ruby-colored negus. "There are approximately one hundred grains of opium to a teaspoon," he said sagely, dropping spoonful after spoonful into the watered-down wine Maria had prepared. "I think one thousand grains each is a good beginning. It's rather a generous dose, but I am keen for you to ascend with me to the same heights I dare to experience."

"A thousand grams of opium apiece?" I exclaimed. "My old friend, Mrs. Baddeley, tried to kill herself with three hundred drops of laudanum—an elephantine amount. My physician recommends that I take no more than nineteen drops!"

"Nineteen drops are but a mild stimulant, three hundred a generous sedative. But in the amounts I have oft-times consumed it, we are speaking of a powerful narcotic, and it is these properties that I wish you to explore with me."

With no small degree of trepidation, I placed my trust in Coleridge's vast familiarity with the drug. Throughout the day, we drank the opium. Within the first hour, I found that I could not stop smiling. Every sense was heightened. I could taste my hearing. The most mundane and trivial thing became a new discovery, an epiphany as curious as it was exhilarating.

"I love everyone!" I exclaimed, pressing my lips to the poet's hand. "O, celestial drug, how I might come to worship thee!"

As Time's winged chariot sped upon its diurnal course, and I ingested more of Coleridge's ambrosial gift, my thoughts spiraled downward from euphoric to solemn, and yet even then I comprehended the clarity of which the poet spoke. The only exercise remaining was to write a poem whilst under the influence of so much opium, to discover whether the destination was as fantastical as was the journey.

"Promise me you will return," I said to Coleridge, "that we might continue this experiment. Your genius keeps me keen to write, even on my worst days, and I should like to try another magic carpet ride in the comfort of your companionship."

Coleridge assented. He became a bosom friend; and the brilliant poet and I shared a few more flights of opiate fantasy over the following months. But I found that I could not tolerate such quantities for very long, and soon grew content simply to drink enough to medicate my pain. If I did not soar to the same heights my young colleague achieved, so be it. I could live with the acknowledgment that no matter how much opium I ingested, and no matter how many poems I wrote under its mighty spell, I would never be another Coleridge. His voice was that of a new generation of writers; I was a relic of its glorious past.

Perhaps it had become time to set that past, and my place within it, in its proper perspective. We had just entered a brand-new century; what better time to look back on an eighteenth-century life than from the invisible field of the infant nineteenth?

I felt assured that my former conduct, judged harshly for so many years, had been redeemed in part through *The False Friend* and *The Natural Daughter*—which had been confessionals—and through my *Letter to the Women of England*. Even so, I knew I would be forever remembered as the Perdita, the lost girl, the cast-off mistress of the Prince of Wales. How could I account for, and justify, our connexion in a way that the world might comprehend what really happened, and what manner of woman I truly am?

With that concern in mind, in March I began to write these memoirs. Paper being dear, we were too poor to buy the vast quantity necessary to complete them, thus I began to compose these pages on the empty leaves—the versos—of correspondence I had saved from old friends. When a publisher peruses these lines, were he to lift the paper to the light, he would read the letters to me from a number of sources who are rather high in the instep— among them the Duchess of Devonshire and the Duke of Clarence.

On April 5, as I sat propped up by bolsters in my bed,

reading the *Morning Post*'s report that I was penning my memoirs, and had gotten so far as the chapters relating to my liaison with Florizel (who else but I would have provided that puff), an officer of the law brutally announced his arrival by knocking on my cottage door with such force that the china rattled in the cabinet. Maria had no choice but to admit him.

"Mrs. Robinson?" The newspaper slipped from my crabbed fingers and fluttered to the chilly floor. With the counterpane pulled up to my chin, I fearfully nodded in the affirmative.

"You are under arrest in the king's name, for the crime of undischarged debts."

Had I been struck by a bolt of lightning I should not have been paler and more petrified.

"I?" Suddenly, I was jolted back to the nightmares of years previous; my fifteen months in the Fleet with Mr. Robinson, the time when my carriage had been "touched" in 1781, and three years later, when my possessions were auctioned off by the sheriff of Middlesex.

Maria and I had been quite fastidious with our accounts. And in any event, everyone from the Prince of Wales to the nobility to half the gentry lived on credit.

"How much does my mother owe?" Maria challenged the man. She was nearly his height, and did not seem to fear him in the slightest.

"Sixty-three pounds," replied the officer of the law.

"Sixty-three pounds? Is that all? But she is owed two hundred and fifty. By none other than the Prince of Wales, who is once again remiss in the timeliness of his payments. Do you not know whom you address, sir?" Maria's eyes sparked like flint. "My mother is a celebrated authoress."

"Then she should have no trouble discharging her obligations."

My deepest fears had been realized. They now stood before my eyes, armed and nearly six feet tall. "I should die in debtors' prison! These days I cannot even get out of bed and walk to the sitting room. To reach the commode is a Herculean labor."

"Well, you have my sincerest apologies, madam, but I'll have to bring you to the sheriff nonetheless." The officer shifted from foot to foot, uneasy at arresting an apparent invalid.

The indignity of being borne out of my home in chains, no better than a convict, surpasses the ability of my quill. I would not be carried in a chair; I refused. Thus I walked, slowly and mournfully, as if attending my own funeral. My ankles had grown thick and puffy, filled with fluid, the doctor told me, which rendered ambulation all the more painful.

My direst nightmares, those that for years had deprived me of the balm of sleep, now manifested themselves in the reality of captivity.

The sheriff was kind to me, and embarrassed at the position demanded by the exigencies of his office. "I would you had been compelled simply to remain within your cottage until your debts are discharged," he said, as he slid the bar and turned the iron key in the heavy lock. The sound chilled me, reverberating through my limbs.

"Sir, I cannot concur more. There are times when for lack of mobility I am confined to my home indefinitely. And," I added, glancing at my hands and legs, so affect by rheumatoid complaints, "my own body is prison enough."

"If it's any consolation to you, Mrs. Robinson, and if I may be so bold to say so, your face is still lovely as ever it was." He allowed that he had seen me on the stage, yet had never read any of my writing. "I'm not much for the poetical works," he admitted, "but my wife is a novel fancier. I'm certain she's read one or two of your books."

I tried to make myself comfortable on the straw pallet that was to serve as my bed until such time as I could scrape up sixty-three pounds and secure my release. I needed a chamber pot, and was mortified that I should be impelled to relieve myself absent one iota of privacy.

Maria had accompanied me to the little jail in Old Windsor, but I insisted she return to Englefield Cottage. Why should she suffer my deprivations as well?

Her argument was the same as mine had been more than a quarter century earlier when I had voluntarily joined my husband in the Fleet: that family must stick together.

But I wouldn't hear of it and sent Maria home. Not only would she be more comfortable there than in a cell no larger than my wardrobe room, but from the cottage she could coordinate our campaign for my release.

She visited me daily, bringing me roast meats, cheese and bread, bottles of wine, and sheets of composition paper.

I could have walked, or rather hobbled, away from the debt; I was still married to Tom Robinson, which would make my financial obligations my husband's legal responsibility. But I would not take that road, though it might have been easier than suffering an incarceration in my constrained condition. We had no household together, and the debts were my own. Though the law was on my side, my conscience would not permit me to seek him out and involve him in this fresh misery.

From the dank and airless cell within the sheriff's quarters, I penned a letter to the Prince of Wales. "If you could see my state, you would but pity me," I wrote, entreating him to pay me a visit and release me from my degradation.

His Royal Highness's reply: "There is no money at Carlton House." And of course he never called on me.

The sheriff granted me but one month's time to garner the amount of my obligation, during which I would remain in his custody. If I failed, I would be sent down to a spunging house in London within the King's Bench.

I poured out my despair in letters to Coleridge and to Godwin, and just before my period of leniency had lapsed, I learned that my friends had taken up a collection and paid the sixty-three pounds, thereby discharging my debt. Tears of gratitude and joy bedewed my cheeks. I knew that even if the prince should tender his long-awaited annuity payment, I should never be able to repay their kindness.

We had a little celebration upon my release, and my friends thought it meet to gratify my self-esteem by informing me that according to the press, "Banastre Tarleton has not made one good speech in Parliament since his desertion of the Muses." Everyone knew whose name they invoked.

In early autumn, Coleridge wrote to announce the birth of his son Derwent, and in the infant's honor, I penned an ode, complimenting his father as well in its allusions to Coleridge's own poetic vocabulary.

Coleridge responded, thanking me for the unique and most appreciated baby gift, and enclosed a copy of his latest manuscript for my perusal. His letter said:

> From your "Haunted Beach" I have rowed out into the pounding surf. I have been visited by dreams such as man has never seen nor known. My imagination has been oared into the ether by a prophet of sorts—a radical poet most assuredly—taken on a journey filled with color and wonder, bolstered by billows of cloud and sea. Perhaps more credit is due to the euphoric effects of my romance with opium, without which I cannot survive from the rosy hours of dawn to dusky twilight and beyond, but if you are indulgent enough to critique it, I should be ever in your debt.

I snipped the string and began to read:

> *In Xanadu did Kubla Khan*
> *A stately pleasure-dome decree:*
> *Where Alph, the sacred river, ran*
> *Through caverns measureless to man*
> *Down to a sunless sea.*
>
> *So twice five miles of fertile ground*
> *With walls and towers were girdled round:*
> *And there were gardens bright with sinuous rills,*
> *Where blossomed many an incense-bearing tree;*
> *And here were forests ancient as the hills,*
> *Enfolding sunny spots of greenery . . .*

From the poem's first lines, I knew that I was looking at a work of genius. Everything about it was new and indeed radical. The language, the rhyme scheme, scansion, and rhythm took the reader on an undulating journey through a world of fantasy and phantasm. Critique it? I adored it! And the only way I could think of to thank Coleridge for the sublime pleasure of this poem was to pen a response of sorts, a counter-poem in this new, revolutionary style.

But I knew, even as Maria posted it, that my poetical effort was to Coleridge's technique as pap is to Cognac.

As I write now, the year 1800 is nigh upon closing. The November winds whistle through the trees outside my window; Maria has laid the fire to keep us warm. Englefield Cottage is a cozy oasis, though I am bedridden—and despite my inability to perambulate, I cannot stop writing.

Publication of my poems brings in but a few guineas, so an English translation (from the German) of Dr. Hager's *Picture of Palermo* will not wait for my condition to improve. I remain hard at work on my series of essays titled *Society and Manners in the Metropolis of England* for the popular *Monthly Magazine*. There is the arrangement of my *Poetical Works* to complete and Longman & Rees will publish my collection of *Lyrical Tales* by Christmas.

I hope I live to see it. My extremities are swollen with water and the doctor fears to lance them again. In September, my coachman, mistaking my person for a bale of hay, heaved me so high when he carried me indoors one day that I was clocked in the head when my pate met the ceiling! Thank goodness it was only timber and lathe or I should have been dead from the injury; but ever since,

I have suffered the most frightful headaches. My scalp is blistered, which does nothing for my vanity—and I have so little beauty to protect nowadays that I jealously guard what I can.

The worst of it is that some days the pain is so great that I cannot concentrate, and my editors have accused me of indolence. If only they realized how prolific and quick I have been with my quill this last decade—perhaps even too quick—and this is in the face of a progressively crippling illness, they would know that something must be terribly amiss with Mrs. Robinson to have forgone a deadline. To the last, they lack all respect for the artist, except as an alchemist who turns words into gold for their coffers.

I have been fighting melancholia, spectrally haunted by the characters that starred in the grand production of my life.

Forgive me while I lay aside my pen and allow my fingers to reach into the desk drawer. Their memory of a distinct pattern of raised tracery locates the framed miniature of a familiar face and brings the portrait into view. Nicholas Darby, my father—of black Irish stock, though American born, embodying the best and worst of his ancestors' character. The painting almost springs to life in my palm. His half smile makes me blink back tears. But are they of sorrow or of joy?

I have begun to pen an elegy in verse for my late father, "All Alone," a bittersweet reconciliation with the ghost of the first man who betrayed me.

My portable writing desk contains a rogues' gallery—a repository of portraits of the seducers who shaped my destiny. As I made myself, so they remade me, and from this clay emerged—I am pleased to admit—a rather extraordinary creature, a *rara avis* even among other outrageous birds of plumage: recognized, if not admired; admired, if not loved; loved, if not tenderly cherished; tenderly cherished, if not ultimately abandoned.

I laugh to consider that I suffered so many reversals of fate and fame before my fortieth year that one might call me a female Job. But each time I found myself on the downswing of Dame Fortune's wheel, I gripped it with all my might and through my wits and wiles managed to ride it back up toward the stars. I have lived during an age of great inventions. *My* greatest invention, refined every few years into something more worthy of a permanent legacy to society, has been myself.

Verily, my life has been the stuff of gothic novels—born during a tempest, my crusted eyelids first lighting upon a cheerless room in the shadow of a Bristol churchyard, where the ponderous tones of the organ were my earliest lullabies. No wonder that as a child I derived odd comfort from the mournful and the melancholy, seeking solace in my casemented chamber whilst the wind whipped and whistled around the dark pinnacles of the St. Augustine monastery's minster tower! Even my mother had to agree that I was destined for high drama. In fact, it would not be a falsehood to say that every event of my life has borne the hallmarks of too acute a sensibility.

We have a superstition in the Theatre that the first role a performer assays comes to define him in his private life. For my most *famous* role as well as my "lost" reputation, the public dubbed me "the Perdita," but in truth I was closer to poor Jane Shore, the cast-off mistress of an English monarch. It was as Jane Shore that I first attracted the attention of Mr. Hussey, my tutor at Oxford House; and it was the role in which I auditioned for Mr. Thomas Hull and for my dear mentor David Garrick, my affinity for the character arising from the unhappy circumstances of my childhood and my father's abandonment of my mother. Jane Shore's plea to right the wrongs perpetrated by the laws of man against womankind subconsciously became my own. How could I ever have prognosticated that in some respects my own trajectory would so closely mirror Mistress Shore's?

It was Mr. Garrick who would always remind me that "an actor's name is writ in water." True enough indeed, for anyone's memories of my performances at Drury Lane have long ago drifted away and become commingled with the sea. But as a writer, I should like to think that my words are writ in stuff far less elusive. I should like to think that, even if only in my epitaph, my words are writ in stone.

Afterword

By late December 1800, Mary Robinson was suffering from dropsy, a swelling of the soft tissues of the body due to the accumulation of excess water. The condition was nearly suffocating her. "Poor heart, what will become of thee?" she murmured to Maria. "Should I recover, I wish to commence a lengthy work on which I shall bestow great pains as well as time." She acknowledged that Miss Wollstonecraft—and her critics—were often correct, adding, "Most of my writings have been composed in too much haste."

On Christmas Eve, Mary asked her daughter, "How near is Christmas Day?"

"Tomorrow, Mother," replied Maria.

"Yet I shall never see it."

Even at the very last, Mary Robinson somehow stage-managed her life. Toward midnight, she cried out in pain, "O God! Just and merciful God, help me support this agony!"

On Christmas evening, she sank into a stupor; her final words, summoning Maria, were a whispered "My darling Mary." She lapsed into a coma and breathed her last at noon on December 26.

A few days prior to her decease, Mary Robinson collected and arranged her poetical works and her memoirs and bound her daughter by a solemn abjuration to see them published. Of the memoirs, Mary told Maria, "I should have continued it up to the present time, but perhaps it is well that I have been prevented. Promise me that you will print it."

Shortly after her death, two persons received a lock of the author's auburn hair: Banastre Tarleton and the Prince of Wales. It was said of the latter that he bore Mary's hair in his own coffin.

The Sun published an obituary, and Mary was buried as she had requested, with little fanfare in Old Windsor. Only two mourners walked behind her coffin—William Godwin and the poet Peter Pindar. Maria Elizabeth was not present, as it was not the fashion of the day for women to attend funerals, no matter how close their relation to the deceased. The Reverend—and romantic poet—Samuel Taylor Coleridge delivered the benediction.

Her gravestone bears an uncharacteristically pedestrian legend for a woman who enjoyed such celebrity during her rich and colorful life. The actress-courtesan-poetess-novelist-feminist's epitaph says merely:

MRS.
MARY ROBINSON
AUTHOR OF POEMS,
AND OTHER LITERARY WORKS,
DIED THE 26TH OF DECEMBER, 1800,
AT ENGLEFIELD COTTAGE,
IN SURREY,
AGED 43 YEARS.

Maria Elizabeth Robinson remained at Englefield and completed her mother's memoirs. She never married, instead residing there for many years with Elizabeth Weale, a female companion she referred to as "my most excellent Bessie," and who came to stay at Englefield Cottage during Mary's last few months. Maria left her entire estate to Miss Weale upon her own demise in 1818.

During the 1790s, Mr. Robinson dropped out of Mary's life entirely. The remainder of his life is a mystery.

Poor dear Mrs. Robinson . . . That that Woman had but been married to a noble Being, what a noble Being she herself would have been. Latterly she felt this with a poignant anguish.

O'er her pil'd grave the gale of evening sighs;
And flowers will grow upon its grassy Slope.
I wipe the dimming Water from mine eyes—
Ev'n in the cold Grave dwells the Cherub Hope!

—Samuel Taylor Coleridge, 1801

*M*uch of what you have read in *All for Love* is based on factual information and on actual occurrences in Mary Robinson's life, her love affairs, and her brilliant careers as an actress, writer, and feminist. The poetry excerpts are hers, as are the sentences she dictates to Maria from her *Letter to the Women of England.* The text of most of the letters she exchanged with the Prince of Wales, and Tarleton's letters to and from his relations, are my own prose and are the gist of that correspondence, based on what modern biographers have written about the subject.

With regard to the strange and mysterious illness Mary suffered subsequent to the late-night carriage ride toward Dover in pursuit of the fleeing Ban Tarleton, medical men at the time arrived at no diagnosis—only the theories and suppositions expressed by the fictional country doctor in my scene at the wayside inn. According to Maria, after a fever that persisted for six months, "the disorder terminated in a violent rheumatism, which progressively deprived her of the use of her limbs." That would likely have been the medical determination at the time, and the way the friends who knew Mary well described her condition. It is quite possible that Mary might have been afflicted with acute rheumatic fever, which was very prevalent in her day, and which would have, over time, manifested itself in the infirmities from which her contemporaries claimed she endured.

Modern doctors have speculated that Mary suffered from Guillain-Barré Syndrome, a rare disease that affects the nerves, the onset of which may have coincided with her carriage accident. For more information on GBS, readers can visit www.jsmarcussen.com/gbs/uk/overview.htm, a Web site that explains the disease in laymen's terms. There is still no cure for GBS, so even if the syndrome had been discovered and diagnosed in Mary's day, she would not have been able to recover from it.

Mary Robinson really did have a bone to pick with both literary critics and her publishers, and she channeled her frustration into her novels by putting that dissatisfaction into the mouths of her characters. She truly did complain that "my mental labors have failed through the dishonest conduct of my publishers." Though her works are read today primarily in the context of women's studies courses, if at all, she was in fact breaking new ground by incorporating her own life experiences into her poetry and prose.

The friendships I depict in the novel are also based on fact. Mary was mentored by David Garrick, the greatest actor of the age, and performed under Richard Brinsley Sheridan's auspices at Drury Lane. Georgiana, Duchess of Devonshire, did become her first literary patron, though I took some literary license regarding the impact of this event. In fact, Mr. Robinson's release from the Fleet was not entirely predicated on the financial success of the volume of Mary's poetry, publication of which the duchess had sponsored; but the book sales most assuredly made a major contribution to it.

In my novel, Mrs. Robinson's lovers are the actual personages she was linked with; she did befriend Godwin and Wollstonecraft; and she did indeed discuss poetry—and probably the effects of opium—with that great lotus eater himself, Samuel Taylor Coleridge, whose early efforts she helped usher into print, as the poetry editor of the *Morning Post*. Both Coleridge and Wordsworth acknowledged the influence on their own work of Mary Robinson's poetry, particularly her poem "The Haunted Beach," which employed a new and different meter that inspired Coleridge's "Kubla Khan" and other poems of his and of William Wordsworth.

Late in life, Mary Robinson began to write her own memoirs, but died before completing them. When she could not afford paper, she really did scribble her own life story on the versos of correspondence she had saved— letters that had been written to her over the years by other famous or illustrious people. That semiautobiography, which leaves out the juiciest bits regarding Mary's numerous passionate affairs, abruptly ends just as her liaison with the Prince of Wales is about to pick up speed; and the manuscript was finished by someone else, most probably her daughter. It was published during the first decade of the nineteenth century, and I used it as a springboard from which to find Mary's voice and immerse myself in her life from her own point of view, and not that of a modern biographer. Most of the events in the book did actually take place. In my efforts to relate some of them in my novel, and remain true to Mary's own version of them, however, I realized how much Mary must have fictionalized her own autobiography for effect. After all, by the time she began to write her life story, she'd become famous for a style of novel that cheerfully included wildly improbable, and rather gothic, elements.

One such anecdote is Mary's agonized night flight to Windsor (her first of two fateful nocturnal journeys in the book) after the Prince of Wales has unceremoniously ended their affair. It's all rather melodramatic, with the mad dash from London in a pony phaeton, a young child as her only postilion, the thwarting of a highwayman on Hounslow Heath (now near Heathrow Airport), and the stop to catch her breath where she realizes that she's been wearing a costly jewel the entire time and what a lucky escape they had made!

Well . . . as *All for Love* is a fictionalization of Mary's point of view, I let the event stand more or less as she had originally depicted it. Yet I am certain that some of my readers, upon coming to those passages, promptly dropped the book in their laps, wondering how, or why, it could have happened the way I described it. Here's what a reader well versed in the era might have thought:

Wait! We're reading about a woman who collects carriages—so why, of all coaches, would she take a lightweight phaeton, which was not equipped to carry lanterns, and which was pulled by a team of ponies, not nearly as sturdy as larger horses, on a night flight where time was of the essence? And why, even at three miles an hour, which would have to have been the appropriate speed of travel to ensure the safety of both human and horse, would she have stopped *twice* during a journey of less than six hours—to dine, she says—when she's in such a hurry?

But there you have it.

More than two hundred years later, from the safety of our history books, and our knowledge of horses and carriages, and research into eighteenth-century travel times, it might not make much sense. Perhaps it didn't even happen the way Mary and I described it. Perhaps it couldn't have happened that way. But Mary Robinson, given her background as one of the most-talked-about celebrities of the day, and herself the author of what today we call "spin," was keener than just about anyone of her era never to let the truth stand in the way of a good story!

So, why did I write a novel about Mary Robinson—why did I choose to "play" her in print? As a redheaded actress-turned-author who still enjoys a career on the stage as well as on the page, and who has counted twentieth-century "celebrities" among her acquaintances, I found Mary's allure, and her life story, irresistible. I identified with her ambition early on for a career in the Theatre, with the tension she faced from parents who did not support that choice. I related to Mary's struggles to be taken seriously in certain circles and with her rage to be recognized for her talents. And I sympathized with her seemingly constant struggle to make ends meet, no matter how much she economized and how prolifically she wrote. Periwigs, panniers, and patches have given way to blue jeans and T-shirts, but from century to century, some things never change.

—Amanda Elyot

Acknowledgments

Many thanks to my editor, Claire Zion, whose always incisive comments are precise enough to fully illuminate my way through the labyrinthine revision process, yet broad enough to allow my imagination free rein; to my agent, Irene Goodman, who never pulls her punches while always believing in my talent; to Michèle LaRue, who offered late-night copyediting reassurance; to my amazing husband for always being so understanding, patient, and kind; and to the members of RWA's beau monde, whose wealth of knowledge and lightning-quick response time to any question posted to the loop never cease to amaze me.

About the Author

Photo by Ron Rinaldi

Amanda Elyot has written several works of historical fiction, and is a pen name of Leslie Carroll, a multipublished author of contemporary women's fiction. An Ivy League graduate and professional actress, she currently resides in New York City. Visit www.tlt.com/authors/lesliecarroll.htm to meet the author online.

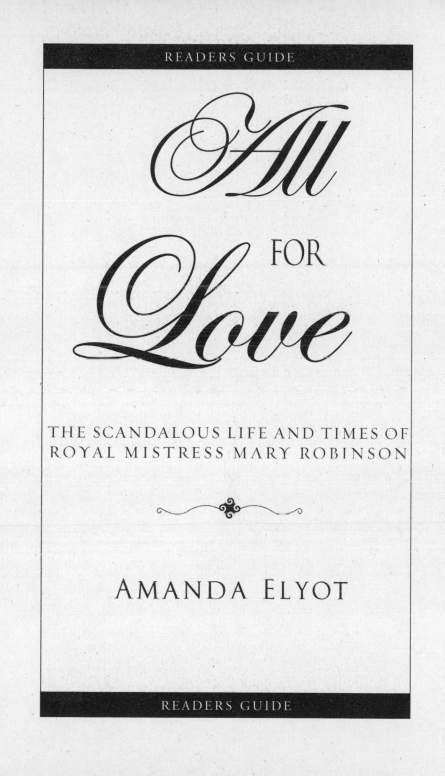

All

FOR

Love

THE SCANDALOUS LIFE AND TIMES OF
ROYAL MISTRESS MARY ROBINSON

AMANDA ELYOT

QUESTIONS FOR DISCUSSION

1. When she was only seven years old, Mary Darby's father abandoned his family. How much of her life do you think was shaped by this event?

2. Mary's parents, particularly her father, were very much against her ambitions for a theatrical career. Do you agree with their decision? How much of what Mary experienced do you think was due to the fact that she became a celebrated actress, and how much was due to other factors? If you think the latter plays a part, what other factors do you think shaped her destiny?

3. Mary's mother was keen to see her enter a respectable marriage, regardless of Mary's own desires, marrying her off when she was in her mid-teens, young even for the Georgian era. Given the period in which these women lived, and the maturity level of a relatively sheltered fifteen-year-old girl, was Mrs. Darby right? Was Mary right? What would you have done if you had walked in either of their shoes?

4. In order to become the prince's mistress, Mary gave up a lucrative career and a financial independence that was very rare for a woman of her day. Do you think she was justified in insisting on an annuity after he ended the relationship?

5. Mary lived at a time and in a society where a member of the gentry and lower classes could not get a divorce. Clearly she endured countless humiliations from her wayward husband, but was bound to him for life. Do you blame her or applaud her for seeking—and finding—love and happiness in the arms of other men? What would you have done if you were in the same situation?

6. Smart women, foolish choices. Or not. Why do you think Mary remained with Tarleton for the better part of fifteen years? What did each of them get from the relationship? Have you ever been there yourself?

7. In a letter written to William Godwin toward the end of her life, Mary referred to Maria as "my *second-self*." Maria stuck by her mother for all the days of her life. What do you think of this decision? Why do you think Maria never married? Contrast that to why Jane Austen never married.

8. In the last year of her life, Mary was jailed for debt. By law, a husband was financially responsible for his wife, including paying her debts, whether they resided

together or not; yet Mary, who was ill and in pain at the time, chose imprisonment rather than involving Mr. Robinson (whom she hadn't seen in years) in her predicament. What do you think of this decision, given Mary's complicated relationship with her husband and debts?

9. Mary is considered one of the first "celebrities." She was the subject of extensive gossip among all strata of society. Her every action was noted and written about in the papers, and she had no compunction about getting good press by "puffing" herself. Women wanted to emulate Mary's fashion sense, yet at the same time she was considered vulgar—not just because of her many (and much-publicized) love affairs, but because self promotion of any kind was thought to be unfeminine and immodest. If Mary lived today, with whom do you think she'd be sharing the tabloid headlines? What differences might she find between her own society and ours? What similarities might she find?

10. Mary was considered a literary pioneer for using her own life experiences in her writing. As a poetess she experimented with scansion and meter, and Coleridge and Wordsworth openly acknowledged her influence on their own work. In her novels, Mary's uncanny skill in holding a mirror up to the foibles of contemporary society presages the sly wit of Austen and Thackeray, two authors whose names and novels live on and remain widely read. Mary Robinson was immensely pro-

lific, writing in more genres (poetry, novels, comedies, tragedies, satires, operas, philosophical essays, and journalism) than any other female writer of her time—and yet relatively little of her vast body of work is available today. It isn't regularly studied in high schools and universities. Discuss why this might be the case. Now that you know about her life, are you interested in reading Mary's novels and poetry?

11. In Mary's 1799 novel *The Natural Daughter,* the publisher Mr. Index counsels the heroine, a budding author, on how to write a surefire bestseller: fictionalize a real-life scandal, give it a provocative title, and the readers will devour it. Has much has changed since then?

12. Had you heard of Mary Robinson before you read this novel? Now that you know something about her, what do you think her legacy is?